What Readers Are Saying about

KAREN KINGSBURY'S

Books

"My friend Shelley and I call your books 'peanut butter books' because when we start reading we just can't stop, and our families know it's peanut butter and jelly for dinner that night!" —**Cathy S.**

"Everyone should have the opportunity to read or listen to a book by Karen Kingsbury. It should be in the Bill of Rights." —**Rachel S.**

"Karen Kingsbury's books are filled with the unshakable, remarkable, miraculous fact that God's grace is greater than our suffering. There are no words for Ms. Kingsbury's writing." —**Wendie K.**

"Because I loaned these books to my mother, she BECAME a Christian! Thank you for a richer life here and in heaven!" —**Jennifer E.**

"When I read my first Karen Kingsbury book, I couldn't stop. . . . I read thirteen more in one summer!" —**Jamie B.**

"I have never read anything so uplifting and entertaining. I'm shocked as I read each new release because it's always better than the last one." —**Bonnie S.**

"*Let Me Hold You Longer* is breathtaking! My friend read this story to me— the first night we both left our new babies overnight. And by the end, the two of us were bawling. She bought me my own copy for Mother's Day, and I read it to everyone . . . and each person cries as I read the words. I now buy it for every baby shower I go to. I think every parent should own or read this book. I read it as often as I can." —**Shannon**

"My husband is equally hooked on your books. It is a family affair for us now! Can't wait for the next one." —**Angie**

"I told my husband I want to pack up our home and three kids and move to Indiana and become a Baxter. . . . Your stories have touched my heart."
—**Christy P.**

"Every time our school buys your next new book, everybody goes crazy trying to read it first!"
—**Roxanne**

"Recently I made an effort to find GOOD Christian writers, and I've hit the jackpot with Karen Kingsbury!"
—**Linda**

"When Karen Kingsbury calls her books Life-Changing Fiction, she's merely telling the unvarnished truth. I'm still sorting through the changes in my life that have come from reading just a few of her books!"
—**Robert M.**

"I must admit that I wish I was a much slower reader . . . or you were a much faster writer. Either way, I can't seem to get enough of Karen Kingsbury's books!"
—**Jillian B.**

"I was offered $50 one time in the airport for the fourth book in the Redemption series. The lady's husband just couldn't understand why I wasn't interested in selling it. Through the sharing of Karen's books with many of my friends, many have decided that contemporary Christian fiction is the next best thing to the Bible. Thank you so much, Karen. It is truly a God thing that you write the way you do."
—**Sue Ellen H.**

"Karen Kingsbury's books have made me see things in ways that I had never thought about before. I have to force myself to put them down and come up for air!"
—**Tabitha H.**

"Karen, how did you get inside my head and heart to portray your characters so accurately? I identify with so many of the Baxter family in every one of the Redemption series! Due to all the tears I have shed in reading your books, I have enhanced the sales of tissues big-time. So in a word, between us we are helping the economy."
—**Maxine B.**

Karen KINGSBURY

SUNSET

TYNDALE HOUSE PUBLISHERS, INC.
Carol Stream, Illinois

Visit Tyndale's exciting Web site at www.tyndale.com

Visit Karen Kingsbury's Web site and learn more about her Life-Changing Fiction at www.KarenKingsbury.com

TYNDALE and Tyndale's quill logo are registered trademarks of Tyndale House Publishers, Inc.

BAXTER FAMILY DRAMA is a trademark of Tyndale House Publishers, Inc.

Sunset

Designed by Jennifer Ghionzoli

Edited by Lorie Popp

Published in association with the literary agency of Alive Communications, Inc., 7680 Goddard Street, Suite 200, Colorado Springs, CO 80920.

Library of Congress Cataloging-in-Publication Data

Kingsbury, Karen.
  Sunset / Karen Kingsbury.
    p. cm.
    ISBN-13: 978-0-8423-8758-3 (sc : alk. paper)
    ISBN-10: 0-8423-8758-7 (sc : alk. paper)
    I. Title.
    PS3561.I4873S87 2008
    813'.54—dc22   2008022512

Printed in the United States of America

14 13 12 11 10 09 08
 7   6   5   4   3   2   1

To Donald, my prince charming

Can it be that we are celebrating our twentieth anniversary? I still see you as you were then, on that sunny July morning in front of our friends and family—love in your eyes and hope in your smile. You have marked these two decades with a sort of faith I never could've found on my own. From the early weeks of our marriage you believed God could do the impossible, and now . . . well, here we are. Impossible things have happened, and I thank God every day that among them he led Prince Charming to me. The years have flown by lightning fast—the births of our three babies, the moves from California to Arizona and finally to Washington, the adoption of our three Haitian sons, and the journey of seeing our oldest graduate this year. You and I hear songs now and then about the speed of life, and we look at each other with tears in our eyes. Yes, life really is a mist that appears for a little while. Only a little while. But today, when the vapors still shine brightly, while the voices of our children still fill our home, let's hang on to every minute. That way, when the sunset of our years is upon us, we will have a million hours of memories to sort through, a million reasons to smile again. I love you, Donald. . . . You are my best friend, the one I lean on, the one whose stalwart faith is still the rock of our home. Yesterday I was that girl in my early twenties with a heart full of dreams, and God knew exactly the man who would take my hand and lead me toward them. Thank you for never wavering. I love you always and forever.

To Kelsey, my precious daughter

You are nineteen now, a young woman, and my heart soars with joy when I see all that you are, all you've become. We prayed that through the teenage years you would stay true to who you are, to your great faith in our Lord and Savior, and to the promise to keep yourself pure for God and for the young man He has waiting for you somewhere. Here, as you enter adulthood, we celebrate that God has answered our prayers, that you remain that one-in-a-million girl. Whether God leads you into a season of dancing or singing or acting, whether He takes you to a local stage or one far off, I know that these coming years will find you shining brightly for Him. And I know that our home will be a little less bright without you here. I am grateful you're not rushing off just yet! The days of you and Tyler filling our house with song are too few as it is. But wherever God leads, know that you take a piece of home with you, and we will be cheering you on, believing that you will be that bright light for Christ you've always been. I love you, sweetheart. I couldn't be more proud.

To Tyler, my lasting song

What a transition you've made, my precious oldest son. You've gone from the young middle school boy with stars in his eyes to a dedicated young man who now stands taller than his daddy. God has allowed you the lead role in a number of plays, and each time I've seen you grow not only in your ability to act and sing but in your faith as well. When I look at you today, I can see the man you're becoming, one who is kind and loving, loyal and true. But one who is also strong in his convictions and purpose—much like your dad. You're sixteen now, and I see you noticing the girls around you, sorting through their character traits and trying to understand the way females think and act. It'll be a lifelong course, honey, but I'm so glad you're sharing your thoughts with me along the way. "I'm not sure about her," you'll say. "She doesn't believe like I do." I smile to myself, once more seeing your father in you. God knows all these things, Ty. . . . Stay close to Him, and He'll lead you to the right girl when the time is right. Until then, keep shining for Him. However your dreams unfold, I'll be in the front row to watch it happen. Hold on to Jesus, Ty. I love you.

To Sean, my happy sunshine

Just yesterday you showed me a perfect score on your science test, and you and I shared a smile. Of all our kids, your A's mean the most because you work the hardest for them. But here's what makes your dad and me so very grateful: you try harder with every passing semester. You want to succeed, because you believe what we've always told you—to whom much has been given, much will be expected. And, Sean, we have been given so much. I know that among the great plans God has for your life, He has many, many more years of education. You are a very smart and gifted young teenager, and it warms my heart that the same intense effort you give on the soccer field and basketball floor you also give in the classroom. Wherever God leads you in the years to come, we'll be cheering from the sidelines, Sean. I pray that God will use your great joy and positive spirit to always make a difference in the lives around you. You're a precious gift, Son. Keep smiling and keep seeking God's best for your life. Make sure the bar's set high—not only at track practice. I love you, honey.

To Josh, my tenderhearted perfectionist

Every so often when you're out there conquering the athletic world around you, I pray that you'll never lose the kindness that was innately yours as a young child. And then something happens like what happened recently. There we were at one of Kelsey and Tyler's plays, and it came time for the raffle drawing. The number was announced, and you held the winning ticket.

But instead of rushing up for your prize, you handed it discreetly to Brooke, our friends' young daughter. She gave you a quick smile and raced to the stage waving the ticket, fully thrilled to take the prize basket. Here's the best part—you wouldn't have told us. If Brooke's mom hadn't mentioned it, we never would've known. And so I smile when I see you win race after race, game after game, because I know that not only are you still the kind boy you were when you first came home to us, but you have learned to be kind with humility. How great a privilege it is to call you our son, Josh. I love you always.

To EJ, my chosen one

How wonderful this past season has been with you, EJ. It's as if you are finally coming into your own, entertaining us with jokes and silly songs and opening up to us about your thoughts and dreams. We have always treasured your sweet nature and deep loyalty to our family, but watching you now, your dad and I are brimming with excitement over the direction your life is taking. We had a family meeting the other night, one of those talk sessions you kids sometimes tease us about. The subject was a reminder that sitting around the dinner table each night are the very best friends you'll ever have—your sister and brothers. You're a wonderful brother, EJ! Every day, every season, just give 100 percent, okay? Because God has great plans for you, and we want to be the first to congratulate you as you discover those plans. Thanks for your giving heart, EJ. I love you so.

To Austin, my miracle boy

Yesterday you did something that reminded me again of your special heart. You came through the door, a smile stretched across your face, your hands behind your back. You walked up to me, your eyes sparkling; then you held out a bouquet of dandelions. "Here, Mom. I picked these for you!" Your joy was untainted, the gift beautiful in your sight. And it was indeed! You had used one dandelion stem tied around the others so the other yellow buds stayed together. I held them to my nose and took a long sniff, and then I hugged you tight and said, "They're the most beautiful flowers ever!" You grinned, thrilled with yourself for having done such a fine job and for making me so happy. With that you ran off to the kitchen, ready for a snack and a time of homework. I looked at the dandelions in my hands, and I blinked back tears. Then I set them down beside my keyboard and grabbed my phone, and before they could wilt even a little I took a picture of them. And in my heart I hoped that no one would ever tell you that dandelions are weeds. Thank you for your great love, Austin. . . . You are so special to us. I know that eleven years ago when you faced emergency heart surgery at just three weeks old, God spared you for a reason. Keep being that strong soldier for God, buddy. I love you always.

And to God Almighty, the Author of life,

who has—for now—blessed me with these.

ACKNOWLEDGMENTS

I can hardly believe I've come to the end of a fourteen-book journey with the Baxter family and Tyndale House Publishers. I can only say that I have the utmost respect for the wonderfully talented and loving people I've worked with at Tyndale and that each of you will always remain my friend. Thank you for an incredible experience with the Baxters. I am convinced that somehow the Baxter family will remain in our hearts and minds, and there will be more stories about them in the future.

Also thanks to my amazing agent, Rick Christian, president of Alive Communications. Rick, you've always believed only the best for me. When we talk about the highest possible goals, you see them as doable, reachable. You are a brilliant manager of my career, and I thank God for you. But even with all you do for my ministry of writing, I am doubly grateful for your prayers. The fact that you and Debbie pray for me and my family keeps me confident every morning that God will continue to breathe life into the stories in my heart. Thank you for being a friend, a godly example, and so much more than a brilliant agent.

A special thank-you to my husband, who puts up with me on deadline and doesn't mind driving through Taco Bell after a basketball game if I've been editing all day. This wild ride wouldn't be possible without you, Donald. Your love keeps me writing; your prayers keep me believing that God has a plan in this ministry of fiction. And thanks for the hours you put in working with the guest-book entries on my Web site. I look forward to that time every day when you read through them, sharing them with me and releasing them to the public, praying for the prayer requests. Thank you, honey, and thanks to all my kids, who pull together, bringing me iced green tea and understanding about my sometimes crazy schedule. I love that you know you're still first, before any deadline.

Thank you also to my mom, Anne Kingsbury, and to my sisters, Tricia, Sue, and Lynne. Mom, you are amazing as my assistant—working day and night sorting through the mail from my reader friends. I appreciate you more than you'll ever know.

Tricia, you are the best executive assistant I could ever hope to have. I treasure your loyalty and honesty, the way you include me on every decision and exciting Web site change. My site has been a different place since you stepped in, and along the way the readers have numerous ways to grow in their faith, so much more than a story with this Life-Changing Fiction. Please know that I pray for God's blessings on you always for your dedication to helping me in this season of writing. And aren't we having such a good time too? God works all things to the good!

Sue, I believe you should've been a counselor! From your home far from mine, you get batches of reader letters every day, and you diligently answer them using God's wisdom and His Word. When readers get a response from "Karen's sister Susan," I hope they know how carefully you've prayed for them and for the response you give. Thank you for truly loving what you do, Sue. You're gifted with people, and I'm blessed to have you aboard.

Thanks also to my forever friends and family, the ones who rushed to our side this past year as we lost my dad. Your love has been a tangible source of comfort, pulling us through and making us know how very blessed we are to have you in our lives.

And the greatest thanks to God. The gift is Yours. I pray I might use it for years to come in a way that will bring You honor and glory.

FOREVER IN FICTION

A SPECIAL THANKS to Julie Nordlund, who won Forever in Fiction at the Life Christian School auction. Julie chose to honor her daughter Sarah Nordlund, fourteen, by naming her Forever in Fiction. Sarah has type 1 diabetes but still wants to be like all her friends. She is five foot two with dark blonde hair, the oldest of two girls. Sarah likes snowboarding, water-skiing, competitive figure skating, and working as a camp counselor. Her favorite food is pizza.

Sarah's character in *Sunset* is that of a young teenager looking to find a crowd where she fits in. I chose Sarah's character to impact Katy Hart Matthews as God uses her to affirm Katy's decisions and to restore meaning to her life.

Julie, I pray that Sarah is honored by your gift and by her placement in *Sunset* and that you will always see a bit of Sarah when you read her name in the pages of this novel, where she will be Forever in Fiction.

Also, thanks to John and Marilyn Smits, who won Forever in Fiction at the Central Wisconsin Christian School harvest auction. The Smits chose to honor Marilyn's deceased father, Andrew Westra, ninety-six, by naming him Forever in Fiction.

Andrew was a tall, handsome farmer who was married to his childhood sweetheart, Effie, for seventy-six years. She preceded him in death by just four months. Andrew worked the same farm for forty years and passed on his love of farming to several of his grandchildren. He knew the Bible well and shared his love of God with the people he and Effie visited—the sick and lonely, the elderly and hurting in their community.

Andrew loved music, and his grandchildren remember Andrew and Effie sitting in the front seat of their car, passing the time on a road trip by singing together. They were spry and healthy, active in the lives of their family until the very end. Andrew loved family, and his best vacations were spent visiting his sister, Harriet, and sharing time with his and Effie's six children, twenty-one grandchildren, fifty-four great-grandchildren, and one great-great-grandson.

Near the end of Effie's life, Andrew asked his beloved if she was afraid to die. She held his hand and said, "No, Pa," and then in a shaky voice she started the two of them in singing the old hymn "Have Thine Own Way, Lord!"

I chose to make Andrew Westra's character Landon Blake's grandfather—a man who helped shape Landon and who left behind a legacy that would mark Landon's life forever.

John and Marilyn, I pray that Andrew's memory is honored by your gift and by his placement in *Sunset* and that you will always see a bit of Andrew when you read his name in the pages of this novel, where he will be Forever in Fiction.

Finally, a special thanks to Joan Polson, who won Forever in Fiction at the Agape Pregnancy Center auction. Joan chose to honor her deceased mother, June Johnson, sixty-nine, by naming her Forever in Fiction. Before her death in 1989, June was an attractive woman with gray hair and blue eyes, a woman known for her feisty energy and her great love for her family. June had two children and six granddaughters, each of whom she was very close to. June was a former schoolteacher whose favorite times were spent at the family vacation house on Lake LBJ outside Austin, Texas. But June also loved singing at church and telling stories of her days as a little girl, growing up with her father who was a pastor.

June's character in *Sunset* is the new pianist for CKT, a woman who agrees to volunteer with the theater group because of her love for her granddaughters—something June certainly would've done.

Joan, I pray that your mother's memory is honored by your gift and by her placement in *Sunset* and that you will always see a bit of your mom when you read her name in the pages of this novel, where she will be Forever in Fiction.

For those of you who are not familiar with Forever in Fiction, it is my way of involving you, the readers, in my stories while raising money for charities. To date this item has raised more than $100,000 at charity auctions across the country. If you are interested in having a Forever in Fiction package donated to your auction, contact my assistant, Tricia Kingsbury, at Kingsburydesk@aol.com. Please write *Forever in Fiction* in the subject line. Please note that I am able to donate only a limited number of these each year. For that reason I have set a fairly high minimum bid on this package. That way the maximum funds are raised for charities.

CHAPTER ONE

JOHN BAXTER HAD DREADED this day with everything in him, but the knock at the door told him the time had come. It was the last Tuesday in January—Christmas far behind them and long past time to take this step. He'd made the decision months ago, and now he needed to follow through with it.

"Coming . . ." He walked from the kitchen to the front door and opened it.

"John." Verne Pick nodded. He was a friend from church whose kids were involved with CKT, and he had a reputation for being one of the best, most thorough Realtors in Bloomington. His expression told John that he knew this was going to be a rough day. "You ready?"

John steeled himself. "I am." He opened the heavy wooden door and welcomed the man inside. "Let's move to the kitchen table."

He had brewed a pot of coffee and poured cups for both of them. They made small talk, and after a few minutes, Verne pulled a folder from his briefcase. "We have a standard questionnaire we need to deal with first."

John blinked, and a memory came over him. When Elizabeth died, it had taken every bit of his strength to walk through the planning of her service. But he remembered this one detail: the young woman from the funeral home who helped him with the process had presented every question couched in concern, as if she wanted to apologize for each step of the ordeal. That's exactly how Verne was now, his brow raised as he waited for a response.

John motioned to the two closest chairs. "Let's get the questions out of the way."

"Okay." Verne opened the folder and took out the document on top. He drew a long breath. "I guess we better talk about the fire first. It's bound to come up."

"Right. Just a minute." John went to the next room and found a folder on the desk. He brought it back and set it on the table in front of his friend. "The garage has been completely redone, and all the repair work was signed off on. Everything's in the folder."

"Good." Verne lifted his chin and sniffed a few times. "No smell of smoke?"

"Not at all."

"The place is really something." Verne's smile was tentative. "Should have it sold by summer, I'm guessing."

"Yes." A bittersweet sense of pride welled in John's chest. "It's a great house. Held up well through the years, even with the fire."

Verne settled in over the paperwork. "I've got some of this filled out already. Let's do the basics first." He lifted his gaze, pen poised over the top sheet. "Number of bedrooms?"

John pictured them the way they'd looked twenty years ago. He and Elizabeth in the large room at one side of the house upstairs. Brooke and Kari across from each other at the south end of the hall, Luke in the next bedroom on the left, and Ashley and Erin sharing a room at the north end. He pushed away the memory. "Five." He took a quick sip of coffee. "Five bedrooms."

The interview wore on, each question stirring another set of memories and reasons why he couldn't believe he was selling the place. When they reached the end of the document, Verne bit his lower lip. "The tour comes next. I need to measure each room, get an official square footage."

"The tour?" John looked toward the stove, and he could almost see Elizabeth standing near the kettle. *"John'll give you the tour,"* she would say when company came over. *"He's so proud of the place—I like to let him do it."*

"Sure." John gave his friend a smile. "Let's start in the living room."

They worked their way from one part of the house to the next, and as they went, Verne pulled out his measuring tape and captured the length of the walls.

John remained quiet. He wasn't seeing his friend taking matter-of-fact measurements of the house he so loved. He was seeing Elizabeth rocking their babies, Ashley learning to walk, Brooke bringing in a bird with a broken wing, and Kari screaming because she thought it might attack her. He could hear the piano, filling the house with hour after hour of not-quite-perfect songs during the years when the kids took lessons, and he could see the grandkids gathered around their tree each Christmas.

Whatever the square footage of the house, it couldn't possibly measure what these walls had seen or the memories housed here.

They finished the final room, and Verne closed the folder. "Well, that's about it. Just one more thing and I can get back to the office and list it." He walked toward the front of the house. "I'll get what I need from the car."

John followed him into the entryway, and when he was alone, he slumped against the doorframe. For a heartbeat, he felt like he was no longer attached to his body. What was he doing, selling the house? Certainly one of his kids should've wanted it, right? He had six of them in the area, after all. But John had already asked each of them.

Brooke and Peter liked the house they lived in because it was easy for Hayley and comfortable. "We have our own memories here," Brooke had told him. "The Baxter place would be much too big for us."

Kari had felt the same way about having her own memories. Ryan had designed the log house they lived in, and it had a sort of rugged lodge feel both Kari and Ryan loved.

Ashley had been a possibility at first. She had told him a number of times that she would love to raise the boys here, where she'd grown up. But she wasn't painting enough to bring in regular money, and the mortgage on the house would be far beyond what Landon could afford, especially with their growing boys.

Once John had even considered calling Dayne, because it would've been nothing for him to loan Ashley and Landon the money—maybe at a lower rate or for a longer period of time. But Ashley had begged him not to. "I don't want Dayne to think of us like that, using him for his money."

John could've argued with her, but there was no point, really. Ashley was right; the situation would have been awkward.

As for his other kids, Luke and Reagan needed to be close to Indianapolis for Luke's job, and things were still very shaky between them. They'd found a nearby church, and John was encouraging them to get counseling at a local center. There was no way they'd be interested in moving again.

Last there were Erin and Sam. At first, when Erin called to announce that they were moving back to Indiana, John thought he had his answer, a way to keep the house in the family. But Sam worked long days, and Erin was busy with the kids. Upkeep on a house with acreage was more than they were willing to take on even for the sake of nostalgia. So they were out.

John wandered into the front room and peered through the window at Verne. Way down at the end of the driveway, his friend had taken a large For Sale sign from the back of his car. John's heart swelled with frustration and futility as he watched Verne position the sign not far from the road. The Baxter house . . . for sale. John gritted his teeth and looked away. This was where he'd wanted to live out the rest of his days, so maybe he was wrong. Maybe this was all a mistake. He looked out the window again and narrowed his eyes.

No, there was no mistake in what he was doing. Living in this house into his twilight years meant sharing it with Elizabeth, and since she wasn't here, the house could go. It had to. He and Elaine Denning were moving ahead with their plans to marry, and they needed a new place to begin their life together and—

The echo of a mallet against a stake resonated deep within him. It was barely loud enough to hear, but John knew the sound. He took a few steps closer to the window as Verne hammered the sign into the ground.

Why, God? Isn't there some way to save the place?

In response there was only the sound of another blow, another strike of the mallet.

John winced as Verne finished the job. Yes, his years in the Baxter house were over. The time had come to move on, and with God's help, that's what John would do. He gripped the windowsill and breathed in deeply the familiar smell of his home. He would survive letting go of this place because he had no other choice.

Even if it all but killed him to say good-bye.

Ashley Baxter Blake flung open the bathroom window, braced herself against the sink, and stared at the mirror. Her hands trembled and her heart raced as she glanced at the clock on the bathroom counter—9:31 a.m. *Okay, here goes. . . .* She marked the second hand and stared at the mirror again. The next minute was bound to drag, and Ashley couldn't make it go faster by watching the clock.

How could she have lied to herself for so long? She leaned closer, studying her look. Her makeup didn't cover the dark circles under her eyes. She was dizzy and weary, drained from another morning of dry heaves, and no amount of fresh air staved off the nausea.

Through Christmas she had given herself a dozen reasons why she might be late—busyness and excitement during the holidays, running after Cole and Devin almost constantly, and the heartache of missing baby Sarah. It could take a year after losing a baby before her body found its normal routine of cycles. That's what her doctor had told her. A year. It hadn't been nearly that.

But she'd had just one period in the last four months, and finally Ashley had done what she thought about doing weeks ago. She bought a test, and now in less than a minute she'd know the truth. Not that she needed the test at this point. She touched her fingers gently to her abdomen. It wasn't exactly bulging, but it was slightly rounded and firm, the way she'd always felt when she was in her first few months of pregnancy.

The difference was that other times she had been ecstatic about maybe being pregnant, ready to rush to the drugstore for a test the moment she suspected she was a day or so late. Even in the weeks after losing Sarah, she and Landon had wanted nothing more than to try for another child. But somewhere along the journey of letting go of her daughter, Ashley had realized something deep within her.

She couldn't lose another baby.

By God's grace and with Landon by her side she'd survived losing Sarah, but another child? Ashley wasn't sure she'd survive. The sound of her too-fast heartbeat echoed against her temples, and she blinked at her image in the mirror. Standing here on the verge of having her answer, there was only one way to describe the way Ashley felt. She was terrified.

Her strange and new fears were impacting every area of her life—even her relationship with Landon. By now she should've told him about her suspicions, but she'd kept the possibility to herself. Every time she considered telling him, she stopped herself. If she told Landon, then she'd need to visit a doctor and go through the same steps as last time—the tests and ultimately the ultrasound. And that meant she had to be ready to handle the news that something could be wrong again. News she couldn't face. Not yet anyway.

Besides, if she told Landon too soon, he'd get his hopes up and then if . . . if something was wrong, they'd both be crushed. Almost as if by saying something, she would instantly open the two of them to all the grim possibilities. Whereas by keeping her concerns to herself, she could avoid giving Landon a false sense of hope, avoid the doctor appointments and most of all the dreaded ultrasound.

Ashley squinted at the test window. Was it her imagination or was a line forming down the center? The line that would confirm she was carrying another child? She closed her eyes and breathed in sharp through her nose. *I can't do it again, God. I can't lose another baby. Please walk me through this.*

Losing Sarah was the most wrenching pain she'd ever been through. Yes, she and Landon had found the miracle in Sarah's brief life, and they would treasure forever the few hours they shared with her. But since then, she couldn't walk past Sarah's nursery without aching from the loss, couldn't drive in the direction of the cemetery without seeing her painting, the one of her mother holding Sarah in a field of flowers in heaven.

She leaned hard against the bathroom countertop, her arms shaking. The doctor had said a repeat diagnosis of anencephaly wasn't likely, but it was possible.

Landon must've known she was worried about having future children, because he'd brought up the subject only once since Christmas. "Do you think about it, Ash . . . having another baby?"

"At first. But lately I try not to." Her voice had been kind, gentle. But fear put a sudden grip on her throat. "I couldn't do it again. Go through what we went through with Sarah."

Landon touched her cheek, her forehead. "My grandpa always told me God never gives us more than we can handle."

"I know." Ashley smiled, and in that instant she could see Sarah in her arms, feel that warm little body against her chest.

She swallowed, trying to find the words. But they both dropped the subject.

Since then she'd talked briefly with Landon about her fears of having more children. But the truth was, somewhere along the days of pain and grief Ashley had formed a mind-set: better not to have more children than to face the possibility of losing another baby.

The thing was, in her life God had sometimes given her things that He must've known she'd survive, and she had indeed come through on the other side. God had always brought her closer to Himself through the process. But she was weary of the heartache, tired of the path of pain God sometimes led her down. If she was pregnant now, she would fight the fear of loss every morning, every hour between now and the birth of her baby. So maybe she hadn't been crazy to deny the evidence of her body for this long. She simply wasn't ready to face the sorrow that might be around the next corner.

More than a minute had passed, so whatever was in the test window would be visible by now. Ashley picked up the stick and looked at the two straight lines, both dark and pronounced, and the answer was instantly in front of her. No doubt whatsoever—she was pregnant. Fear tap-danced across the moment, but it was joined by an unexpected partner: the flicker of hope and joy. She was pregnant, and for now, no matter what might lie ahead, a brand-new life was growing inside her. The news was terrifying and thrilling at the same time.

Now it was merely a matter of finding the courage to tell Landon.

CHAPTER TWO

SOMETIMES LUKE BAXTER felt like he was walking under-water, lost in a world all his own as he went through the day-to-day motions of existence. Guilt put him there, but Reagan played her part too. She admitted as much, but otherwise she said very little. They needed counseling, of course, needed to dig through the muck and mire and sift to the surface whatever lay buried beneath. No matter what came to light in the process.

But first they had to agree to make an appointment with a counselor.

Luke let up on the gas. He'd be home in five minutes, and he still wasn't sure how the conversation with Reagan would start or where exactly it would go. His father had offered to take the kids for the weekend, so he'd dropped them off with their overnight bags and a promise to call often.

"Let God give you the right words." His father had walked him to the door and hugged him before he left. "Be honest. You and Reagan have a lot to talk about."

Luke turned onto Adams Boulevard and headed west. Maybe

they didn't have that much to say, after all. Since Christmas they'd been together more often, shared more nights with the kids than before. Gone were his frequent trips to New York City, and she had stopped visiting with her firefighter friend. But they were no longer the young couple so in love, no longer the two people who couldn't exist without each other.

Luke sighed. It was the first Friday in February, and for two months he and Reagan had lived more like roommates than married people. He tightened his hold on the steering wheel. This weekend had come at Reagan's request. "We need to get to the truth," she'd told him. "I can't live like this anymore."

A pit formed in Luke's stomach. Maybe his dad was right. If their time together this weekend went well, they could at least agree on counseling, and by doing so they would be taking a first step. One that could lead them back to the flames of love.

Or maybe not.

Luke pulled into their driveway, killed the engine, and slumped forward against the wheel. He stared at the front door of his house, at the dimly lit windows and the shadows that fell across much of the siding. In this lighting, the place looked cold and ominous, like something from a horror film. He felt sick to his stomach. Exactly how honest were they going to be with each other? Was he supposed to tell Reagan the details of his theater nights in Manhattan? Would she want to know what happened between him and Randi Wells late one night on a Mexican beach?

He drew a slow breath, straightened, and opened his car door. No wonder Reagan had been quiet and distant for the past few months. She was probably torn between waiting for him to be honest and dreading the truth. Because the truth was going to hurt, no way around it.

Luke pulled himself from the car and trudged up the front steps. Week-old, dirty snow was a foot high on either side of the dry, frozen walkway. Once he was inside, the atmosphere warmed considerably. The smell of fresh-brewed coffee mingled with something sweet and home-baked, and he heard the crackling of a fire in the next room. He felt himself relax a little. "Reagan?"

"In here."

Luke followed her voice into the living room. She had pulled two chairs close to the fireplace, and she sat in one, her feet pulled up beneath her and a thick blanket tucked around her legs. She held an oversize mug close to her face. "Hi." The nervous anticipation in her expression must've matched his own. For a moment, he saw the fresh-faced college girl she'd been, full of dreams and purpose and virtue.

A sudden nervousness came over him, and his heart pounded. He tried to find an easy smile. "Hi."

She looked away. "I thought we could talk by the fire."

Luke hesitated, his heartbeat twice its normal speed. Was he really supposed to tell her everything? "I'll get some coffee." As he headed for the kitchen, he felt again like he was walking across the bottom of the ocean. How did two people start a conversation like this? Where would it take them, if the things they learned today were too great to move past?

He poured himself a cup and made his way back to the living room, to the chair beside her. As he sat down, he wondered if she too could hear the thud of his heart.

"How were the kids?" Reagan glanced at him over the top of her coffee cup. Their chairs faced the fire, but they angled slightly toward each other.

"Fine." Luke's palms were sweaty, but he kept them cupped around his drink. "I went over everything with my dad. Malin's ear drops, Tommy's latest tricks."

Luke allowed the briefest smile. Tommy's antics were constantly keeping the rest of the Baxter family on their toes. These days the boy was finding every possible chance to slip into the garage, climb into the driver's seat of whatever car was available, and search for ways to work the steering wheel or the gearshifts. Luke's dad sometimes left his keys in the car if it was in the garage. Luke shuddered.

He could only imagine what might happen if Tommy found keys in the ignition.

"That boy needs more structure." Reagan sighed. She stared at the flames dancing behind the wrought iron screen. Then she turned to Luke. "But I guess he's not the reason we're here."

"No." After leaving his dad's house, Luke had prayed for guidance. Just like his dad asked him to do. And now, without giving the idea a second thought, he set his mug down on the floor beside him and reached out to Reagan. The only sound in the room was the crackle of the fire. "Pray with me, Reagan. Please."

She looked almost surprised, and somehow her reaction cut Luke deeply. Had that much time passed since he'd asked her to pray? Maybe that was part of the reason they were in this position.

Reagan shifted her cup to one hand and held out the other, lacing her fingers between his. "You say it."

A memory flashed in Luke's mind, a time when he and Reagan were both at Indiana University and once in a while they would meet at a favorite bench between the buildings where they had their separate classes. More often than not, Reagan would take his hand and impulsively ask if she could pray for the two of them. Back then, prayer came as easily as breathing for both of them. Luke wished he could figure out exactly when that changed or how they could return to that place.

He took a quick breath. "God, we come to this place not sure of what's next. So lead us, please." He thought about the details he might have to share in the coming hour. "Whatever is said today, give us the right words to bridge the gap between us, the strength to see tomorrow on the other side of today, and the grace to love each other no matter what."

They released the hold they had on each other's fingers, and they both fixed their eyes on the fire. For nearly a minute, neither said anything.

Then Luke shifted in his chair and faced Reagan. "Honesty, right? That's what this day is about?"

"Yes." Reagan's eyes were dark, layered with a sorrow and bitterness that had taken years to build. "How should we do this?"

"Well—" Luke swallowed—"I can go first, I guess. I mean, what do you want to know?"

"I'm not sure." Reagan lifted her mug and took a sip. "I guess start at the beginning. How things got this way."

Luke tried to think of an entry point that would make his wanderings seem less a violation of his promise of faithfulness. But there was none. He settled into his chair and drifted back to the days when they first moved to their house near Indianapolis.

Maybe it was the pressure of the new job, knowing that Dayne was counting on him, or dealing with the struggles Reagan was having at home with their kids every day. Whatever it was, Luke had started taking trips to New York. "I didn't have to go. I could've gotten the details about the meetings later, in an e-mail or a conversation." He kept his tone even. "The trips were helpful, but they weren't necessary. That's the first thing."

Reagan kept looking straight ahead, as if she was preparing herself.

Luke sorted through the next pieces of the story. None of it would get any easier. "The girl at the office, she wasn't anyone special. Just a new hire who gave me extra attention. I wanted to think she saw something in me, but . . . probably it was all about Dayne being my brother."

He held his breath for a few seconds. He was like a man in the middle of Times Square, bombarded on every side by noise and chaos and options, not sure which way to turn. But as he exhaled, the next part of the story came in a rush. "I started pulling together theater nights. Anyone in the office could go."

Reagan's look changed and fell just short of accusatory, but still she didn't speak.

Luke blinked. "She . . . she always came along." He explained that sometimes the excursions included other lawyers from the firm, and sometimes they didn't.

He was midstream talking about how he'd let himself believe that no harm could come from hanging out with a woman on the road, someone who was kind and complimentary and seemed to enjoy his company, when Reagan turned and interrupted him. "Did you kiss her?"

He pictured the young paralegal, how close he'd come two different times. "No." He ran his tongue along his lower lip and felt his heart ricochet hard against the walls of his chest. "Almost . . . a couple times, but no. There was nothing physical between us."

Her look grew more intense, as if she were seeing beyond the details of Luke's story to the part he wasn't saying, the part about how he'd sat next to the woman in the theater, their arms touching, and how he'd thought about her long after he'd returned to his hotel room. But if she was thinking that, she didn't say so. "I guess the real story is Randi Wells."

"Yes." Luke suddenly felt like someone was standing on his shoulders. He crossed his arms and tried not to look as defeated as he felt. How had he allowed such a crazy thing to happen? And why hadn't he thought about how his actions would harm his marriage?

Reagan was still waiting, still watching him. She took another drink of her coffee. "You know what makes me mad?"

Luke could only imagine the list.

"That you would let everyone think it was Dayne in that picture." Her voice was quiet, controlled. But it held both anger and bewilderment. "I mean, how low is that?"

Luke hadn't wanted to defend himself, but he couldn't resist. "You have to know something." He rubbed the back of his neck and exhaled hard, his frustration showing. "I didn't go to Mexico looking for a fling with an actress." But even as he said the words, he recalled his reaction when he saw Randi the day Dayne drove him from the airport to the film location. He released the memory and reached for the coffee mug beside his chair. *Honesty. I have to be honest.* He swallowed. "What I mean is . . . I didn't go looking for an affair, but I didn't have the right attitude either. That's the truth."

Reagan stared into the flames. "Go on."

Luke wasn't sure either of them was ready, but they had no choice. His actions had brought them here, and it was too late to do anything but come clean. The story moved ahead like a car with engine trouble, in jerky fits and starts. He told Reagan how he'd been on the beach that night, sitting around a campfire, and how Dayne had been called away to one of the editing rooms. Left alone together, Randi asked Luke to take a walk.

At that point in the story, Reagan flashed him a look, her way of marking the fact that the walk was the first of his compromises.

There was no point justifying why he'd agreed to the walk or thought it was okay to stroll into the dark of night on a remote foreign beach alongside a single, beautiful woman. Luke didn't even try. Instead he stuck to the facts. He and Randi walked a distance, and when they stopped to talk, her phone rang. The news was about her mother, and it wasn't good.

"She started crying, and I . . . I went to her. Maybe I was thinking I could comfort her—" he looked down—"or maybe I wanted something more. I'm not sure."

Reagan's expression told him that she knew the answer even if he did not. She didn't blink, didn't turn away as she waited for the rest.

This was the part Luke could've done without. Wasn't it enough that the tabloids captured the kiss for all the world to see? Did he really need to go into details about what happened as the hug between him and Randi became something terribly more?

Luke clasped his hands and sighed. "Again, it wasn't like I planned it. We were hugging, and the next thing I knew we were kissing."

"How long?" Reagan's question came sharp and quick, her eyes wide, her emotions a mix of cool anger and indifference. "How long did you kiss?"

"I don't know." Irritation crept into Luke's tone. "Awhile, okay? We kissed for a while. We didn't see or hear the photographers; I can tell you that."

Reagan didn't ask what else happened. She didn't have to. The look on her face asked it without any words whatsoever.

Luke rushed ahead. "There was nothing more. We kissed, and then at some point I pulled away and told her I needed to go. We . . . we held hands back to the bonfire, and when we were almost within sight of the others, we split up. I went to my room, and she went toward the fire pit. So no one would think we'd been together all that time."

"But there was more." For the first time, the hint of hurt crept into Reagan's voice. "That night, right? And after that?"

She was right, and Luke hated this part just as much. Things between him and Reagan might be different today if only he'd come to his senses as soon as he reached his hotel room. He rubbed his temples with his thumb and forefinger and summoned the strength to tell Reagan the rest of the story.

Hours after the kiss, Randi had knocked on his door, and when he opened it, she was in his arms before he could stop himself. Again they kissed, and this time Randi told him she was attracted to him, drawn to him.

"She told me she knew I was married, and she was willing to wait until I figured things out."

"Nice," Reagan muttered.

The guilt was a physical presence, eating through him like a disease. Luke ached all over, the way he'd felt freshman year of college when he got the flu. "For a while after that we would text each other. We talked on the phone. Eventually she asked if I was willing to leave you."

Reagan raised her eyebrows.

"I told her the truth." Luke felt like the world's worst creep. "I said I was attracted to her, but I couldn't imagine leaving you."

Reagan nodded. "Considerate."

Luke hated her sarcasm, but he deserved it. "Nothing I did was considerate. I just thought you should know." He raked his fingers through his hair. "Even caught up in the moment, I couldn't picture life without you."

For a moment, she didn't say anything. Her eyes softened the tiniest bit. "I'm glad." She looked away. "Really."

He wasn't sure what to make of the subtle shift in her attitude, so he didn't acknowledge it. His story was almost finished. He could hear the defeat in his voice as he continued. When the pictures hit the tabloids, he and Randi talked about the damage done, and she begged him to stay quiet. Dayne would take the fall, which Dayne could do a lot easier than Luke. No one would ever know the difference.

"Only neither of us could live like that." Luke didn't intend to sound self-righteous. What he'd done was wrong; there was no denying the fact. "Eventually I called Dayne." He pursed his lips and exhaled. "And here we are."

Reagan hugged her knees to her chest, and for a long time she stared into the fire, as if she were absorbing every painful blow, every detail finding its place in her heart, where she could later sort through the fragments. Then, without warning, she turned to him. "I guess it's my turn."

Her turn? Luke's heart skipped a beat. In all the time he'd spent thinking about this moment of truth, planning for it and dreading it, he hadn't once thought about what she might share with him. He was the bad guy in the story, right? She was the victim.

But now she folded her hands. "It started out as a friendship."

The room tilted, and Luke felt his heart slam out a few double beats. What was this, her firefighter buddy? Was that the friendship she was talking about? She would only have more to tell him about her own recent past if . . . if . . .

Reagan looked at him for a few seconds. Just long enough so the guilt on her face was vividly apparent. "I didn't mean for anything to happen." Her opening statement sounded strangely like his.

Luke felt his muscles tense up. "The firefighter?"

"Yes." Reagan's eyes were lifeless, lost in what could only be a distant moment Luke knew nothing about. "After the incident with Tommy, he came by the house to check on me, to make sure things were okay."

"I remember that." Luke reminded himself to exhale.

Then, like a floodgate, the story spilled from Reagan. The fire-fighter started coming by the house for an hour each afternoon when Tommy and Malin were down for a nap. At first he and Reagan sat in the family room and talked, but at the end of the week, when Reagan walked him to the door, the two shared a hug that led to a kiss.

"The next day when he came over, it was like we both knew. We tried to act like nothing had happened, but it was there for both of us."

Luke stared at the floor. How could he be hearing this? All this time he'd been afraid to have this talk because it meant coming clean with his recent behavior. Not for a minute did he think Reagan was hiding something.

She was still talking, explaining herself. It took all his concentration to process what she was saying.

"We talked for a few minutes, and then the kissing started again. Until it was too much and . . . I told him to leave." Reagan lowered her feet to the floor. "I'm sorry." The pain in her eyes was raw and unresolved. "You weren't expecting this."

Luke studied his wife. Her admission was screaming at him, replaying again and again at the center of his mind and shouting at him that this was only the beginning. Because her tone told him there was more. "And . . . ?"

"I didn't want him to stay." She looked at him, pleading with him. "But I didn't want him to go, either."

A sound that was part cry, part groan came from Luke, and he was suddenly on his feet. "Are you serious?" He took three steps toward the doorway, then spun around. "Am I supposed to sit here and listen to this?"

Reagan's expression hardened. "What, Luke? You mean the way *I* had to?"

Luke glanced around the room as if there might be an escape, a way out of the truth. But there was none. Half a minute passed, and finally his shoulders fell forward, the fight inside him morphing into defeat and desperation. He could leave, but there would be no turning back. Not with the mangled pieces of what remained of their marriage. He positioned himself against the nearest wall so he wouldn't fall to his knees.

The question hung in the air between them until he had no choice but to ask it. "Are you saying . . . you slept with him?" His words were incredulous and strained, barely loud enough to reach her.

When Reagan's words came, they were aimed more at herself than him. "I let it go too far. I won't deny that." She gave a slow shake of her head. "But I didn't sleep with him. I sent him away before . . . before things—"

"Stop." Luke held up his hand. He couldn't bear to hear another word, not one more detail. Warring emotions ripped through his heart and soul—shock and betrayal, sorrow and regret. But furious anger quickly took the lead. Wisdom shouted at him not to ask the question, but he wasn't listening. "You know what I can't believe?"

Tears appeared in her eyes, but she didn't answer him.

Luke didn't stop himself. "I can't believe you didn't learn from the first time . . . when the guy on your couch was me." As soon as his words were out, he regretted them.

Reagan jerked back as if she'd been slapped; then she froze, her expression unlike any he'd ever seen before.

My son, reach out to her; tell her you're sorry. . . .

Luke dismissed the quiet whisper in his soul. His anger doubled, and he stayed anchored against the wall. *This is her fault too. Why should I make the first move?* He could feel the Holy Spirit urging him forward, pushing him to erase the distance between them. Suddenly he was a teenager again, furious with his sister Ashley because of the choices she'd made, and he could hear his mother's voice echo clearly through the halls of yesterday. *"Luke, you have to forgive the people you love. . . .. Relationships take a lifetime to build. Pride destroys them in a moment."*

He clenched his fists. *No, this is different. It's too late, too far gone for forgiveness. For either of us.*

Reagan stood and stared at him. "Can you hear yourself?" She took a few steps backward, her tone wounded and incredulous. "Never mind. This isn't going anywhere." She studied him a moment longer before turning and running toward their bedroom.

As she left, Luke thought of a hundred things he should have said or done. He could feel God telling him to follow her, to apologize and return to the place where reconciliation seemed possible. But the only words that came to mind were the ones Reagan had just said. Their relationship wasn't going anywhere.

Luke exhaled hard, and he realized he'd been holding his breath. A flashback shot through his mind—he and Reagan getting married, their families surrounding them. How far had they fallen since then?

All this time, he'd thought of Reagan as the victim, when really . . . really . . . He couldn't complete the thought. What did it matter, anyway? They'd broken their vows and lied and cheated. They couldn't talk about it without the conversation ending at an impasse. There was no point chasing Reagan and trying to make amends, because she was right about their marriage.

No matter how it had started out, this wasn't going to be a season of healing.

It was going to be a season of saying good-bye.

CHAPTER THREE

IT WAS SNOWING OUTSIDE, and a joyful chaos filled the packed Bloomington Community Theater as Katy Hart Matthews hurried down the center aisle and took her place at the front of the room with the other judges. The auditions today were for *Joseph and the Amazing Technicolor Dreamcoat*, and the buzz in the room belied the citywide expectations. Katy and her husband, Dayne, now owned the building, and January had been full of delays while contractors made basic improvements. But now it was open for use, and after the kids of Bloomington had fought so hard to keep their theater group, people figured this might be the best Christian Kids Theater production yet.

Katy was four months pregnant and no longer feeling sick the way she had before. She wasn't showing, but her waist had disappeared, and she felt more breathless than usual as she took the middle seat at the narrow table.

"A hundred and fifty kids and counting." She leaned in close to Dayne. "The show's going to be incredible."

Dayne squeezed her hand. "I keep thinking . . ." He looked

around the room at the kids of all ages and sizes, each wearing an audition number. "Where would these kids be if you hadn't come back?"

The love in his eyes reached straight to the depths of her heart. Katy smiled at him. "If you hadn't bought the theater, you mean." She gave him a quick kiss. Already they'd started plans for the diner and coffee shop that would eventually stand on either side of the theater. "We're here now. That's all that matters."

Dayne looked at his watch. "It's time." He handed Katy the first ten audition forms. "Better get going."

Katy took the forms, stood, and faced the crowd of parents and kids. Usually at this point on audition day, the room would quiet down and Katy would give the familiar speech, explaining the process so the new families would know the protocol. Kids would be called up in groups of ten, no one could come or go during those auditions, there'd be a five-minute break before the next set, and so on.

But today, as she opened her mouth to begin, the Flanigans, Picks, Shaffers, and Farleys stood and smiled at her. Then they began to clap. Before Katy could understand what was happening, other families rose and joined in the applause until finally everyone in the building was clapping and howling and hooting.

A rush of emotion came over Katy, and she looked back at Dayne. He put his hand on the small of her back, supporting her, sharing in this clear show of appreciation.

Next to them on either side, the rest of the creative team joined in the applause. Besides Dayne, who was her codirector and chief sets builder, there was her sister-in-law Ashley, who would oversee set designs and cheer for her son Cole, who was auditioning for the first time, and Tim Reed, one of her favorite former CKT kids, now a college student, sitting in the first row with a handful of the volunteers who would teach CKT classes that session.

Katy shifted her gaze and there, also on her feet, was the new twenty-eight-year-old dance instructor who had moved to

Bloomington from New York City and volunteered her services as choreographer. The young woman's sisters had long been involved with CKT. And a few feet away was their new pianist, June Johnson, applauding and grinning.

Katy smiled at the gray-haired woman, a former teacher whose granddaughters had been involved in CKT the year before it closed. She was a brilliantly talented soprano, full of the sort of spunk that would make her quickly loved by the theater kids. But what Katy appreciated most about the woman's decision to be part of the show was the fact that she'd done so as a way of spending more time with her grandkids. The same reason so many parents and grandparents got involved in CKT.

Before the kids began arriving this afternoon, June had pulled Katy aside. "I always thought my favorite days were the ones I spent with my granddaughters at our lake house." She looked around the theater, her eyes sparkling. "But I have a feeling this will be even better."

Katy could only agree.

She focused on the cheering crowd of parents and children, and she did the only thing she could do in that moment. She pointed straight up to heaven, to the One who had given all of them this second chance. Then she held up her hands, asking them to quiet down and return to their seats.

Dayne's presence beside her was enough to help her find her voice despite her emotions. She looked from one family to the next, seeing a mix of so many happy memories in this very space and feeling the awareness of so many more yet to be experienced. "You are my friends . . . my family." Katy massaged her throat, struggling to keep her composure. "Since God has given us another chance here, it seems only right that we should start today by thanking Him."

A hush fell over the room as people bowed their heads.

"Dear Lord, we thank You." As the words came, Katy felt herself growing stronger. Her shaky voice became clear, her prayer directed straight to the Creator. "You've given us our building and our theater group. Most of all You've given us hope. For that, we are so grateful, and we pray that this production will bring You great joy. The way we know it will bring us great joy. In Jesus' name, amen."

Another round of applause filled the room, and then Katy started in with her introduction. The first audition of the afternoon was Ashley's son. Cole had just finished a season of basketball and still planned to play baseball, whether he won a part in the play or not. But Joseph was his favorite story from the Bible, and he wanted to audition.

Though Ashley was on the creative team and acting as a judge today, she wouldn't be able to cast a vote for her son. Katy glanced at her as Cole took the stage. In this moment she was merely a nervous parent, same as the others in the theater.

Cole tucked his hands in his back pockets and grinned at the judges. "Hi. My name is Cole Blake, and I'm nine years old. I'll be singing 'Take Me Out to the Ball Game.'" His smile faded, and he looked straight at Ashley. "Because my grandma used to sing it to me."

Ashley gave him a reassuring smile and a slight nod.

From where Cole was standing, Katy guessed he couldn't possibly see the tears welling in his mother's eyes. Ashley's mom had died several years ago, but the pain was still there. Maybe even more lately, from what Ashley had said. After all, this was the year her father was going to remarry. Maybe because of that or because she was still grieving the loss of her infant daughter, Ashley seemed quieter than usual.

Her husband, Landon, was in the audience with their younger son, and Katy caught a glimpse of him giving Cole a thumbs-up.

Katy turned her attention to the boy. June had his sheet music, her fingers poised at the piano, and Cole gave her a look that said he too was ready.

As Cole began, Katy realized she'd never heard him sing. When he and Landon had stopped in at the theater with Ashley during some of CKT's long evenings of painting sets, Cole was always full of enthusiasm, ready with a story about a ball game or an anecdote from school. But he had never had a reason to sing.

As the song began to grow, Katy was pleasantly surprised. Cole had a clear voice, right on key. Better still, he had a way of connecting with the judges and the audience, making eye contact and showing a confidence that was rare in a child his age.

Katy had a feeling that his grandmother had given him more than a love for the old tune she used to sing to him so many years ago. She'd probably given him a love for singing too. Katy glanced once more at Ashley. She was glowing with approval for her son, but there was no mistaking the tears on her cheeks.

When the song ended, Katy had a certain feeling that Cole would be part of the *Joseph* cast. She checked the callback box at the bottom of the form, the one intended for any performer who she thought should come back the next day for a second, more involved audition.

The others in the first group made their way to the front one at a time, and the afternoon took on a sense of familiarity that warmed Katy. She and Dayne exchanged a grin when the third child announced she'd be singing "Part of Your World" from *The Little Mermaid*. On a typical audition day, they were bound to hear the song seven or eight times, something Katy had shared with Dayne before they were married. Now it gave them a reason to smile—at least with their eyes.

The Flanigan kids were in the second group of ten, and both Bailey and Connor sang beautifully. No question they'd be part of the callbacks tomorrow.

At the break after their group finished, Bailey hurried over to the table, and after a quick hello to Dayne, she turned to Katy. "I met this girl. She's new. Anyway, she's in the next group, and she's really nice. Her name's Sarah. I think she really needs this. I'll tell you more later." She gave Katy a hug. As she pulled away, she whispered, "Just thought you should know."

Katy watched Bailey return to her seat. She loved that about the Flanigans and so many of the CKT kids. They truly cared about their peers. Bailey seemed unconcerned about the obvious competition between herself and the new girl and only wanted Katy to know that beyond this new girl's ability to sing, there might be a greater reason to cast her.

Halfway through the next set of ten kids, a petite girl with dark blonde hair took the stage. She smiled at the judges, and in her eyes Katy saw confidence and determination. "I'm Sarah Nordlund. I'm fourteen, and I'll be singing 'Home' from *Beauty and the Beast*."

The song was a tough one, an unforgiving ballad that would reveal exactly how trained Sarah was as a singer. Katy uttered a silent prayer that she could pull off the number since Bailey seemed to believe it mattered deeply for the girl to be cast in the show.

The music began, and partway into the first line, Sarah froze, her words forgotten. She hung her head. "Sorry. I already know the drill—no second chances." Then she turned and started walking off the stage.

No second chances? Katy wanted to pull the girl into her arms and soothe away her doubts. "Wait!"

Sarah stopped and looked up. "Yes?"

"CKT is all about second chances." Katy smiled and hoped it might calm Sarah's anxious heart. "Do you know the song?"

"Yes." Sarah shrugged. "I just blanked out."

"Okay, then." Katy nodded to June at the piano. "Let's try it again."

Sarah returned to center stage, appearing a little less confident than before. But when the music began, this time she remembered every word. The song grew and built, and Sarah hit the high notes with a clear voice that was right on key.

After every audition, the kids in the room always applauded. Sometimes when the student auditioning was someone the CKT kids knew well—like Bailey or Connor—there would be an especially loud applause. But when Sarah finished her song, the room erupted into the loudest cheering since the auditions began.

"Thank you, Sarah." Katy marked the callback box on the girl's form.

Sarah's expression shouted her gratitude. Katy had a feeling she was going to like Sarah Nordlund and that this was the first of many future auditions for her.

The creative team focused on the next girl taking the stage. Later, when auditions were over, Katy would find out what Bailey knew of Sarah Nordlund.

As it turned out, she didn't have to wait that long. During the break, while Dayne and the others at the table were in the lobby getting water, Sarah came up to Katy. "Am I allowed to talk to you for a sec?"

"Sure." Katy adjusted her chair so she could see her better.

"Okay, well . . . thanks for that. For letting me have a second chance."

Katy melted. "Honey, of course. Everyone forgets the words once in a while. We want everyone to succeed."

Sarah squirmed a little. "I'm . . . I'm an ice skater. Competitive figure skating." She shook her head. "No second chances there."

"Oh. I see." She smiled. "Well, I'm glad it worked out for you."

"Something else." Sarah seemed nervous. "I'm a type 1 diabetic." She wrinkled her nose. "I hate it, you know? 'Cause I just wanna be like other kids." A sparkle came to her eyes. "So, thanks. What you did . . . it meant a lot."

As Sarah hurried off toward the others, Katy was overcome by a flood of emotions. Sarah might've needed CKT, but on this day—when Katy had walked away from a life of making movies and being on the big screen—she was the one who needed Sarah. Without knowing it, the girl had given confirmation that this was where Katy belonged. Where she would always belong.

The afternoon became the evening as one group of ten after

another filed to the front and took their turns auditioning. There were the usual surprises, where a student who had been earning occasional ensemble roles used this audition to break through to another level, and there were the disappointments, students who clearly hadn't prepared and would receive a lesser role or no role because of that.

Fourteen girls sang "Part of Your World," and twelve boys sang "The Bare Necessities" from *The Jungle Book*. Only two kids came in full costume, including a twelve-year-old boy, Sander, who wore a homemade Phantom of the Opera mask.

After mumbling through two lines of "The Music of the Night" from the Broadway play, Katy kindly interrupted him. "Sander, I need you to take off your mask."

The boy slowly removed the white plaster piece that covered half his face. "But—" he lowered the mask—"it helps me sing in character."

"I'm sorry. We can't understand your song." Katy hoped she sounded as compassionate as she felt. Sander was a good boy from a nice family that had long supported CKT. "With acting, it's important to find your character in here." She put her hand over her heart. "Okay?"

"Yes." The boy sighed and set the mask down. "Here goes."

When his song began again, Katy had a better idea why the boy wanted a mask over his mouth for his audition. The notes were too high and too low, and the words never quite on beat. His voice cracked three times.

Katy glanced down at his form and saw that as a second choice the boy was interested in working with the tech team in sound and lighting. Relief flooded her. As Sander left the stage, Katy marked the tech box on his audition form.

Dayne looked over her shoulder. "Lighting and sound?" he whispered.

"Definitely." Katy met his eyes. "Thankfully."

They were midway through the final ten kids when an older-looking girl took the stage. She was dressed in tight jeans and a tighter sweater. As she faced the judges, a section of her long dark hair hung over her eye. She jutted her chin, her jaw set. "My name's Miranda Miles. I'm sixteen, and I'm singing 'Stay' by Sugarland."

Katy resisted the urge to cringe. On the audition packet and on the CKT Web site, kids were advised to sing something from a musical. Karaoke CDs were allowed, and half the kids chose that as their accompaniment over working with the pianist. The song Miranda had chosen wasn't only in the wrong genre; it was also a song about an affair. Not exactly wholesome.

Poor girl, Katy thought. Everything about Miranda shouted rebellion and defiance, something Katy rarely saw at auditions. CKT required too much time and volunteer work for a parent to force a kid to participate. Katy sat back in her chair, curious. *If she's here for a reason, please show me, God.*

Miranda's performance was average. She didn't project the way she should, but her notes were on key. The fact that her hair swished across her face covering one eye seemed proof that she wanted to hide—not only from the judges but from the world. Ordinarily, if a student auditioned the way Miranda did, Katy would have to make the tough decision and pass. After all, half the kids who took the stage wouldn't get parts.

But Katy was drawn to Miranda like no other student who'd appeared before them today. When the girl was done, Katy leaned slightly toward Dayne. "I feel like we have to see her tomorrow."

Dayne hesitated. "Then mark the callback box."

Patrick and Lydia Moynihan—a brother and sister who had been with CKT for years—rounded out the group, and Katy was struck by the way their already good voices had matured in the past few months. Both were taking voice lessons, and their songs sent chills down her arms. They were brilliant.

When Patrick finished his song, Dayne whispered, "God alone gives a kid a voice like that."

"Exactly." Katy felt a warmth come over her, one that stayed as she dismissed the families and explained that they should check the CKT Web site for a list of kids who would be called back for tomorrow's longer audition. As the kids began milling about and as the building took on the noise and excitement from earlier, the warmth grew and filled her soul.

Katy looked around, taking in the moment and everything about it—the mix of voices, the musty smell of the old theater, the creak of the wooden floor as people headed for the doors, and the presence of Dayne a few feet away chatting with his sister Ashley. Dayne was finished with his movie and grateful to be at the start of a two-year break from Hollywood. His name was fading from the tabloids, and around town people were less starstruck by his presence. Exactly the way they'd prayed things might go.

She understood the warmth inside her, because it was God's very presence, His Spirit, reassuring her that He was having His way in her life. This place was where she belonged. And this was her calling, to give kids with faith and a desire to serve God a place where they could grow and develop and showcase the gifts He'd given them. Here kids like Sarah, Sander, and Miranda could work alongside kids like Bailey, Connor, and the Moynihan siblings and grow together the way God wanted His children to grow.

The amazing thing about CKT was this—on the whole, the group was very talented. More talented than most theater groups Katy had ever worked with. Even so, an agent could walk through the door waving movie contracts and suggesting that the families move their kids to LA, and for the most part the CKT parents would tell the guy no. They weren't interested because no amount of money or fame or promises from directors and agents could replace the experience these kids would get right here with Bloomington's CKT.

It was a lesson Katy had learned the hard way.

CHAPTER FOUR

BAILEY FLANIGAN COULD hardly wait to get out of the theater. When she and Connor and their mom were finally belted into their Suburban and headed home, she released a sigh that had been pent up since her audition.

"I hate when that happens." She groaned and let her head fall back against the seat. "I work so hard for the perfect audition, and then I don't bring everything to the stage."

"What are you talking about? You were great. You'll get a callback for sure." Connor was sitting next to her, since the front passenger seat was taken up with their mother's computer bag in case she had time to write her latest magazine article during the auditions. But like always, the bag never left the vehicle. The auditions were way too entertaining.

"Thanks." Bailey let some of her frustration fall away. "Still . . . I didn't sing it like I can."

"You were both fantastic." Their mom glanced in the rearview mirror and smiled. "Did you mark on your sheets your first choices if you get called back?"

Their mother already knew what roles they wanted, but kids who auditioned weren't obligated to write a specific character preference on their forms.

Bailey sighed again. "I wrote narrator."

"I put down Joseph but that I'd take anything." He flashed Bailey a concerned look. "You put you'd take any part, right?"

"Of course. I've played my share of townspeople and ensemble roles. If that happens this time, I'll survive. I was just hoping . . ."

"It's your last year." Connor gave her a weak smile.

"Right." Bailey looped her arm through Connor's and rested her head on his shoulder. She'd turned eighteen over Christmas break—three years older than him—and until a couple years ago she'd had the height advantage as well. But now he was nearly six feet tall with their dad's build. Bailey loved that she could lean on Connor at a time like this. Not only that, but he seemed to always know what she was thinking and how she was feeling. He could practically finish her sentences. Wherever the coming years took them, he would always be her closest friend.

"Should I give you the pep talk again?" Mom's tone held the usual audition-day compassion.

"Maybe you should." Bailey squeezed Connor's arm. "Right?"

"Yeah, Mom. Good idea."

"Okay." She settled back in her seat. "God had all this figured out long before today arrived." She sounded patient and concerned. "When the parts are handed out—if there are parts to be handed out to the kids in this family—they'll be the parts God intended for you. Each part or lack thereof comes with its own life lessons. Things you couldn't learn any other way." She went on, talking about the judges and how they were a loving, faithful group who would be fair above all.

Bailey didn't mean to, but she tuned out. Just the sound of her mother's voice was enough to bring her comfort and peace. But it didn't change the fact that she hadn't turned in her best audition, and there was a reason. She'd been distracted by Tim Reed. Until

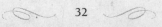

this past Christmas, CKT had seemed a thing of the past. Tim was attending Indiana University, studying music, and he'd been dating a girl from his church. But things with the girl didn't work out, and today Tim was there, back in Bailey's life again. His face had lit up when he saw her, and he hugged her. "Can you believe it? CKT and Katy and this old building, even you and me. Here. Just like things should be."

Except Tim was a teacher now, and that meant he had to keep a certain distance from the students, even students as old as Bailey. Not that he'd ever really shown much interest. Still, his presence today was enough to confuse her. Especially when her last letter from Cody Coleman was sitting on her bedside table.

Cody, her friend. The one who was writing less often now, even though Bailey still wrote every few weeks. Cody had explained the reason in his last letter. She tried to remember the crucial few lines. Something about her being innocent and pure and deserving a guy who was the same and how he would never want their letter-writing to stand in the way of whatever God had for her future. Same sort of stuff he'd told her before he left for the army last summer.

From the front seat, her mother continued the familiar talk. "So here's how the weekend will go: we will pray for the judges, for the decisions they have to make—"

Connor cut in. "And we'll pray that some parts go to new kids or kids who really need to be involved in CKT."

"Exactly." A calm marked their mother's words. "Being a lead takes more time and effort, and it brings less time with friends during rehearsals."

"True." Bailey sat up straighter. "I always forget that part."

"Being in the ensemble means getting closer with a whole group of kids." Connor leaned against his door and grinned at Bailey. "But no matter what, we'll stay up until one in the morning or whenever they post the callback list on the Web site."

"If we're called back, we'll ask God to help us do our best." Bailey smiled in the rearview mirror at her mom. "Right?"

"Right. Because callbacks should be treated as a one-day performance, when you should bring your very best before the judges."
Their mom's voice grew more serious. "The Bible tells us God
knows the plans He has for us. Plans to give us hope and a future.
He alone knows how this weekend fits into those plans."

"Jeremiah 29:11." The verse was written across Bailey's heart and
soul and bedroom wall. It was a wonderful reminder that God was
in control of their lives, no matter how things seemed. She glanced
at Connor. He had his cell phone out and was texting someone.
They were crossing a busy intersection, and Bailey was about to say
something about Sarah Nordlund, who she'd met this afternoon,
when she saw a cement truck run the red light and come barreling
straight for them, straight for Connor's door.

"No!" she screamed just as the truck swerved around them, missing them by maybe a few feet and narrowly avoiding two other cars
before clearing the intersection. Bailey couldn't breathe, couldn't
feel her heartbeat. "Mom!" She gripped the back of her mother's
seat, and her heart lurched into double time. "Did you see that?"

Her mom's eyes were wide, her face pale. "Not until he was
almost through the intersection."

"He almost slammed into the side of us." Bailey looked at
Connor. The lines on his forehead showed his concern, but none
of them had seen it like she had. "If he'd hit us . . ." She couldn't
complete the thought. Not out loud anyway.

The truck would've barreled right into them, and Connor
would've been killed instantly. Almost for sure. Probably Bailey and
her mom too. The adrenaline racing through her veins let up, and
she felt suddenly exhausted. She slumped against the backseat.

Connor patted her knee. "It's okay. It didn't happen."

But it could've. Bailey closed her eyes, trying to imagine the outcome, how everything about their lives would've changed forever
in a single instant. The way it changed for people all over the
country on days like this when the cement truck didn't swerve
in time.

"Jesus, thank You. . . . We feel You with us," their mom whispered.

"I guess that puts CKT auditions into perspective." Connor's voice held a new sense of understanding.

Bailey opened her eyes and stared at her brother, her best friend. What if in that little space of time he had been killed? Sure, he'd be in heaven, and there would be peace in that. But how could she live without him? Bailey slid closer to him and rested her head on his shoulder once more. He was right. The moment certainly brought perspective.

They were quiet the rest of the way home, but the incident took Bailey back to her thoughts about Cody. He was in Iraq, and he faced dangers every day. She pictured him, her father's former star football player dressed in fatigues and carrying a machine gun, dodging conflicts and wary of roadside bombs. Every time she thought of him she only wanted him home, back in their downstairs guest room.

But what was *he* thinking? Had Cody forgotten the connection they'd made in the weeks before he left? how their friendship had seemed like so much more? Bailey looked straight ahead. He hadn't kissed her, except on the cheek, but even then the feelings that summer day didn't seem to be hers alone. Either way, she wanted him out of Iraq and home safe.

As soon as they pulled into the driveway, their dad flipped on the front porch lights, and he and the younger boys rushed out of the house and began jumping around and waving, acting goofy, the way they always did. Their mom parked in the garage, and the whole family met on the lit outdoor basketball court that stretched across the driveway in front of the other garage doors.

"So . . . ," their dad began. He'd been at a basketball practice with BJ, Shawn, and Justin. Ricky had tagged along because, as he'd put it last night at dinner, "Basketball is addicting."

"Are you the narrator?" BJ had a ball tucked under his arm. He dribbled it between his legs. "Do you know?"

"Not yet." Bailey frowned in her dad's direction. "It wasn't my best."

"Really?" Her dad held out his arms.

Bailey gave him a hug. "We almost died on the way home."

Her dad stiffened and pulled back, searching first her face and then her mom's.

"It's true." Mom still didn't look quite back to normal. She swallowed and came up along the other side of Dad.

"Was Bailey driving?" Justin gave her a teasing look, and the other boys giggled.

"Hey—" Connor shook his head—"it isn't a joke, guys."

"I was driving through the busy intersection, the one a few blocks from the theater." Mom sounded shaky.

"A cement truck ran the red light." Bailey looked at her dad. "He was heading right for Connor's door, and at the last minute he swerved."

"He ran the light?" Dad's expression held the same shock she'd felt, as if he could see the near accident in his mind.

The boys gathered in close so they could hear, their giggles replaced by looks of concern.

Mom nodded. "I saw him pass behind us. I mean, a couple feet behind us."

"He almost hit two other cars." Connor crossed his arms. "It was pretty crazy."

For a moment, the family stayed close together in the damp cold, as if all of them were trying to process what almost happened. What could've happened.

Their dad put his arms around the shoulders of his two girls. "I guess that means your good news beats mine. Because God chose to bring you home safely to us."

Their mother raised her eyebrows at him. "What good news?"

He winked and nodded toward the house. "Let's go inside. We can talk about it there."

Suddenly Bailey remembered the silly way the boys were acting.

Way too excited for a simple after-audition greeting. It was that time of year, the off-season for the NFL, when management from one or another team still knocked on their dad's door, hoping they could get him to take a coaching position.

Her stomach flip-flopped as their group headed through the garage and into the house. What if he'd taken a job on the other side of the country? CKT was finally back, and Bailey had no intention of leaving. She wanted to study theater at Indiana University and maybe travel with her CKT friends to New York for an audition every now and then. Also, if her family left, what home would Cody have to come back to?

When they were inside, Bailey watched the younger four boys exchange looks that said they were about to burst from keeping the secret. Dad directed them to the brown suede sofas that rounded out the family room. Bailey and Connor swapped a look that confirmed one thing: Connor was worried about the news too.

As they all took their seats, Mom beside Dad, she studied him. "Jim? Tell me."

He put his arm around her and grinned. "I got a call from the Colts. The only team that hasn't called before."

The Indianapolis Colts were only an hour from Bloomington. Bailey felt her fears ease, but even so she wasn't sure. She liked her dad coaching at the high school, liked the idea that he'd be there for her brothers as they grew older.

The younger boys were squirming, giving each other virtual high fives across the room and barely able to contain their joy.

"They offered me an assistant position. Meetings would start the middle of March."

Their mother smiled, but she looked dizzy, and Bailey understood. It was a lot to handle. All eyes were on her, waiting for her reaction. She laughed, then stood and threw her arms around Dad's neck. "That's wonderful. I can't believe it!"

Like every time something big happened in their lives, Bailey was sure there'd be more conversations between her parents later when the kids weren't around. "So, you said yes?" Bailey was on her feet now too and slowly moving toward her dad.

"I told them I'd talk to my family and let them know on Monday."

Ricky let out a shout of victory and flung his fist high in the air. "Say yes! Of course!"

"Yeah!" Shawn danced around his brothers, his smile exposing a mouthful of braces. "Dad's gonna coach in the NFL again!"

"That's great." Connor was quieter than the others, and Bailey thought she knew why. Just a few months earlier, Connor had transitioned from CKT to football, playing for his dad. Now with CKT back in full swing and their dad probably taking a job with the Colts, Connor would most likely be finished with football.

"Your mother and I have a lot to talk about. I wanted you kids to know so you could think about things over the weekend. If any of you has doubts about this, talk to me." Dad paused, making eye contact with each of them. "Everyone has a right to an opinion, so I want to know."

Their mom had a Crock-Pot chicken and rice dinner going on the kitchen counter, so they set about the meal, and when they were seated around the dining room table, the conversation went in three main directions—basketball, football, and the auditions.

Shawn and BJ kept things interesting by entertaining them with random facts, the way they often did. There were days when the craziness at their dinner table frustrated Bailey, testing her patience when she had something to talk to their parents about. But tonight their banter was a welcome distraction.

Anything so her mind would steer clear of Tim or Cody.

Her parents were talking in low tones about the position with the Colts and Connor was saying that he thought the Picks turned in their best auditions yet when Shawn jabbed his finger into the air. "Did you know," he said to no one in particular, "a cheetah can run seventy miles per hour for seven hundred yards without stopping?" He had been fascinated with animal facts from the day he came home from Haiti six years ago, so no one at the table was truly surprised.

"That right?" Dad stroked his chin twice and then turned back to his conversation.

"This is better." BJ pulled a book from beneath his chair. It was *Uncle John's Bathroom Reader*, a gift he'd gotten from Shawn this past Christmas. "Take a guess how many calories are in the world's largest burrito." BJ held up his hand and shook his head. "Wait . . . don't guess. You'll never guess!"

Ricky didn't wait. "Four hundred thousand."

"Not four hundred thousand." Justin rolled his eyes.

"It could be." Shawn giggled. "That's how much Justin eats in a day."

"That's how much you eat in an hour." Justin volleyed back. He wasn't serious, but he liked having the last word. Even though he wasn't the oldest of their adopted siblings, he often acted like it. "I'll bet it's four hundred million."

BJ tossed his hands in the air and let them fall back to his lap. "Now you ruined it. I said not to guess!"

"Okay, okay." Justin laughed and elbowed BJ, who was sitting next to him. "Go ahead. It's four hundred thousand, right?"

Bailey felt a little sorry for BJ. He was the least excited about school or reading or studying, and at least now he was enthusiastic about something. Their parents weren't really listening, so she gave Justin a mild warning look. "Let him tell us."

"I am." Justin laughed, the way he always did when he didn't want to get in trouble. He meant well, but he could sometimes take his teasing a little too far.

BJ seemed to appreciate Bailey's support. He sat a little taller in his chair. "Eighteen million calories! Can you believe it? There were two thousand tortillas and a thousand pounds of sour cream and lettuce. Eighteen million calories!"

"That would be enough food for . . . ." Connor looked up, doing the math in his head.

"Eleven years!" BJ held up the book. "Says so right here."

The trivia took them through the meal and into the dishes and cleanup that followed. They watched a nature video about polar bears that night, and Shawn kept a running dialogue, reaffirming or commenting on half the facts provided by the show's host. Again, Bailey welcomed the distraction.

The younger boys went to bed around ten, and Bailey finished talking to her mom about seeing Tim at auditions and how that felt compared with how this spring might've played out without the theater company.

After an hour, Connor took a chance and checked the CKT Web site. "It's up!" He hovered over the keyboard.

Bailey peeked over his shoulder. "Well? Are we there?"

"Yes." Connor pointed to the screen. "We're on it! We both go from ten to two tomorrow!"

Bailey felt relief, and immediately she was consumed by one thought: how true the Scripture from earlier really was. God knew the plans He had for her—to give her hope and a future. For some people that future might mean an early exit, an early arrival to heaven. The way she and her mom and brother might've wound up if the cement truck hadn't swerved. But it did swerve, and all because God's plans for her life were still centered here . . . in the life He'd given her to live.

Bailey and Connor surveyed the list and talked for another half hour. When Bailey turned in for the night, she thanked God for letting her live through the day. Her eyes fell on the framed Scripture on her wall and she smiled.

She thought about Sarah Nordlund, battling diabetes and struggling to be like other kids. And then, for the first time in a long while, her thoughts turned to a different Sarah. Sarah Jo Stryker, the CKT girl with a brilliant future, the one whose life had been snuffed out by a drunk driver two years ago.

Yes, Bailey would sing and act and dance tomorrow with everything she had to give. She would perform leaving nothing behind, and she would do it in a way that would bring honor and glory to God. It would be the least she could do to thank God for the gift of living another day.

As she fell asleep, just one more request rose from around the edges of her heart. That somewhere in Iraq, God would grant Cody the same gift.

CHAPTER FIVE

ASHLEY WASN'T SURE IF her exhaustion was more from the drain of auditions that weekend or because of her pregnancy or maybe because she was tired of keeping the news a secret. By late Sunday afternoon as she helped Kari chop carrots and broccoli in the kitchen of the Baxter house, Ashley knew her weariness was showing.

"You feeling okay?" Kari's question held only mild concern. A few feet away Annie was sleeping in her windup swing, and from the next room came the laughter and conversation between their dad and Elaine and between Kari's older two, Jessie and RJ, and Ashley's boys, Cole and Devin.

The sound soothed Ashley's soul. She smiled. "Just a little tired."

"The auditions?" Kari used a paper towel to transfer a pile of broccoli into the skillet.

"I guess." Ashley hated the half-truth. Nearly a week had passed since her pregnancy test, but every time she thought about telling Landon, she would convince herself that maybe it was wrong. Maybe she was still recovering from Sarah's birth, and that would explain why her entire system was out of balance. She certainly hadn't gained any weight, and though she felt nauseous now and then, the sickness wasn't bad enough to be pregnancy related. At least not most of the time. Her fears were strange, really. How had she gone from wanting a baby to take the place of the one they'd lost to being terrified of losing another one? She was angry at herself for being afraid, and in most moments she told herself if she could find the faith to overcome her anxiety, she would immediately tell Landon about the possible pregnancy. Even with her fears, she wanted to talk to him about the test she'd taken, but there hadn't been a single moment when the time felt right. No wonder she felt exhausted.

The front door opened, and they heard the voices of Brooke and Peter and their girls. Luke and Reagan were not expected tonight, so once Katy and Dayne arrived, everyone who was coming for dinner would be here. They were having roasted chicken and vegetables with a cheese and potato casserole Elaine had brought.

"So—" Kari took a head of cauliflower from the fridge to the sink—"I'll bet the kids were thrilled to be back at the theater."

"Like nothing I've ever seen before." Ashley uttered a light laugh. "Katy and Dayne looked so happy. And the Flanigan kids and all the rest." She cupped her hands around a mound of sliced carrots and transferred them to the pan. "I think the reality that Katy and Dayne and the theater are here for good is still hitting everyone."

"How's the pregnancy?"

Ashley's breath caught in her throat, but then just as quickly she realized that Kari was talking about Katy's pregnancy. "She, uh . . ." Ashley exhaled, composing herself so Kari couldn't hear anything different in her voice. "She said she's doing well. Not feeling sick and just a little more winded than usual."

"July's right around the corner."

"Yes." Ashley blinked. For the first time since she'd taken the pregnancy test, it dawned on her that she and Katy might have babies within weeks of each other. The way she and Kari had babies within weeks of each other last summer. An icy panic released itself into her veins. One more reason events seemed to be playing out the way they had last time when—

"How'd Cole's audition go?"

Ashley dismissed her previous thoughts. "Great." She set her knife down and leaned against the counter. "I was so proud of him. He sang the song Mom used to sing to him."

"'Take Me Out to the Ball Game'?" Kari angled her head, her eyes tender. "That's so sweet."

"Don't say anything." Ashley lowered her voice. "He wants to tell everyone tonight. He got cast as one of the kids of Simeon, Joseph's brother."

Kari's eyes lit up. "That's fantastic. We'll have to get everyone there for opening night."

Brooke entered the kitchen carrying a bag of dinner rolls. "Okay." She set them down and smiled at her sisters. "Put me to work."

"Too late." Kari laughed. "The pan won't hold much more."

Hayley tagged behind Brooke, wearing a pink coat, her blonde hair framing her sparkling blue eyes. "Hi, Aunt Kari, Aunt Ashley!"

"Hi, princess." Kari grinned at her.

Ashley moved to her niece's side. "How's school?"

"Very good." She looked at Brooke. "Right, Mom?"

"Better than ever." Brooke was washing her hands at the sink, but she blew her younger daughter a kiss.

Hayley scampered back toward the family room, where the joyous sound of the cousins had risen to another level.

When Hayley was out of earshot, Brooke's tone softened. "Did you ever think that girl would be *reading*? She's not at grade level, but she read the first page of *The Cat in the Hat* on the way here." She glanced over her shoulder toward the room where Peter and the other men were tending to the kids. "Peter had tears on his cheeks by the time she was finished."

The story should've eased Ashley's anxiety, splashed warm rays of peace over everything she was feeling. Clearly God was faithful.

What else could possibly be the testimony of their precious little Hayley? But instead Ashley shivered, and her fears tripled. Hayley's progress was miraculous, but the same God who had allowed Hayley to live had also allowed baby Sarah to die. If Ashley was pregnant, there were no guarantees. Nothing to make her feel even a little confident about the future.

Landon poked his head into the kitchen. "The kids want to watch Jessie's Hannah Montana DVD." He smiled at Ashley, but he must've noticed that something wasn't right. He gave her a look that showed his instant concern. "Do we have time?"

"Definitely." Kari didn't seem to notice the exchange between Ashley and Landon. She moved to Annie's swing and reset the timer. "We won't eat for thirty minutes at least."

"Okay." His gaze lingered on Ashley. "You girls need anything?"

Ashley shook her head and tried to use her eyes to tell him she'd explain later. "Thanks for watching the kids."

"Are you kidding?" Landon chuckled. "The guys are gonna play Texas hold 'em. Every child out there is crazy about Hannah Montana." He left, and after a minute, the sound of the TV came from the family room and the noise of the children tapered off.

Brooke found a bowl under the far counter and used it for the dinner rolls. "I needed this tonight. Being with you two." There was a depth in her voice that hadn't been there before. She moved closer to Ashley so they were facing each other. "Tough week at work."

Ashley wasn't sure she could handle a story about sick kids. She absently began chopping another carrot, looking back at Brooke so her sister wouldn't think she was rude.

"What happened?" Kari was finished with the cauliflower. She placed the pieces in the pan and added a little water.

"You might've seen it in the paper. Ethan Teeple passed away." Her eyes grew damp. "Fought as hard as any four-year-old I've ever seen, but the cancer was too much for him."

A rush of nausea came at Ashley. "I . . . I didn't know."

"Peter and I will attend his funeral tomorrow."

"That's so sad." Kari rested the pan on the counter.

Brooke nodded slowly, and a sad smile hung on the corners of her lips. "He wanted to marry his nurse when he got older."

Silence settled between them for a few moments.

Brooke drew a slow breath. "But there was good news too. At Sarah's Door."

Ashley's heart skipped a beat. With the auditions and the exhaustion she was feeling, she hadn't heard news about their new crisis pregnancy center in more than a week. "Tell us."

"Two teenagers and a college girl made decisions this week not to abort. Three in one week!"

Somehow hearing the report made Ashley feel stronger than she'd felt all weekend. Even now good was coming from Sarah's death. So how could she allow herself to be so afraid of the future?

The sisters marveled over the difference the center had made so far, and Brooke reminded them that their first client's baby was due in April. They talked about Luke's absence tonight and agreed to keep praying for his marriage. Ashley enjoyed thinking about something other than babies. She promised she'd spend time with Luke, find out how things were really going and whether the Baxters were doing enough to help.

"Hey, there's something else we need to talk about." Kari added a splash of olive oil to the vegetables, set them on the stove, and turned on the gas flame beneath. "What about a wedding shower for Elaine?"

It took Ashley a beat, but she liked the idea. "With people from church, you mean?"

"No." Kari covered the vegetables and faced her sisters. "Maybe just us girls at my house. Dress up a little, make her feel special."

"And welcome." Brooke's eyes shone. "I like it."

Ashley gave her sisters a thoughtful smile. "That'd be nice. Elaine's wonderful." She was no longer dreading her father's June wedding, but no matter how much she liked Elaine, it was still bittersweet seeing him marry someone new. A shower would help all of them have their hearts in the right place.

They had barely finished talking about the idea when Elaine breezed into the kitchen and glanced at her casserole. "Looks good." She used the pot holders sitting beside the stove and removed the glass dish from the oven.

"Here." Brooke rushed to spread a towel out on the counter.

As Elaine set the dish down, she smiled at Brooke and then at the others. "Smells wonderful in here."

"Tell that to the boys." Ashley laughed. "Cole wanted pizza and ice cream."

Kari put her hands on her hips and grinned. "Mom would've told him there's a time and a place for pizza, and it's not Sunday din—" She seemed to realize who was in the room and cast a regretful look at Elaine. "I didn't mean . . ."

"Don't apologize." Elaine's smile was warm and genuine. "Your mother was my friend." She pulled Kari into a hug. As she drew back she kept her hands on Kari's shoulders. "I want you to talk about her. It would be strange not to."

The three sisters seemed to release a collective sigh of relief. Ashley watched Elaine, the easy way she had about her and how she moved from Kari to Brooke, putting her hand on Brooke's arm and asking how the girls were. When she reached Ashley, Elaine's smile faded a little. "You feeling all right?"

Kari laughed. "I asked her the same thing."

"A long weekend, I guess." Ashley felt her heart relax a bit more. Elaine truly cared; she'd proven that time and again. She brought wisdom, maturity, and deep faith to their gatherings. No matter how sad it was that her father was in the position to remarry, Ashley didn't need to be convinced that he had found a wonderful woman to spend the rest of his life with. Already Elaine felt like part of the family, enough so that it would've been strange to have a Sunday dinner without her.

Not until they were seated around the table did the subject of the Baxter house come up. Cole was thoughtfully chewing a piece of chicken when he held his fork in the air. "Hey, what's that sign out front, Papa?"

"Put your fork down, Cole." Landon was sitting beside him. "Be a gentleman, remember?"

"Oh, right." Cole winced and set his fork down. "Sorry."

Seated on the other side of him, Maddie giggled and gave him a teasing look. "Cole? A gentleman?"

"Maybe not now, but someday I will be." Cole jerked his chin up. "Right, Dad?"

A smile played in Landon's eyes. "That's our prayer, buddy."

Ashley sat on the other side of Landon, and she put her arm around his shoulders. "All the Blake boys are gentlemen. I can vouch for that."

Devin was in his high chair, and he banged his fists on the tray, as if he understood and wanted to add his agreement.

Ashley surveyed the table, Hayley on the other side of Maddie, then Peter and Brooke, Katy and Dayne, Kari and Ryan and their kids, and her dad and Elaine near the head of the table. There was nothing better than the full conversation of a dinner at the Baxter house. But for now all eyes were on Dad.

"Well, Papa? What about the sign?"

Ashley and Landon had talked about this a week ago, how it was time to tell Cole that the house was on the market. But her dad's Realtor had said it could take months to sell the place. Ashley had been too consumed with the pregnancy test to think about telling Cole just yet.

Her dad seemed slightly bewildered, as if he figured everyone already knew about the sign. "Well . . . that's a For Sale sign. It means I'm trying to sell the house."

Cole's mouth hung open. "You're selling it? With all the birds and frogs and our new bridge across the creek out back and the best pond in the world?"

Ashley's heart broke for Cole. Landon tried to put his arm around their son's shoulders.

But Cole leaped to his feet and walked around the table until he was face-to-face with his grandpa. "Don't you have enough money for it?"

"You can't sell it, Papa." Maddie shook her head, her eyes wide. "This place has the best hide-and-seek ever." She got up and joined Cole.

"And I like Aunt Ashley's painting room upstairs." Jessie smiled in Ashley's direction. The girl was fascinated with coloring and drawing, and Kari had already said she could see a lot of Ashley in Jessie.

The looks on the faces of the other adults at the table said no one was sure who to feel worse for, their kids or their father.

Deep sorrow colored their dad's expression. "You know that Grandma Elaine and I are getting married in a few months, right?"

"Right. So?" Cole was undeterred, as if that bit of news held no relevance whatsoever in the matter of selling the house.

He glanced at Elaine, and the sympathy in her eyes was clear to everyone at the table. Then he turned back to Cole. "Grandma Elaine and I are going to get our own house. Somewhere closer to the university and the hospital."

"But you have lots of room for her here." Cole gave Elaine a sheepish grin, probably worried that he'd overstepped his bounds somehow. "Right? There's room here, right?"

Peter cleared his throat. "That's enough, guys. Why don't you take your seats."

"It's time for a change." Ryan leaned his forearms on the table, his tone marked by the same sadness they were all feeling. "Sometimes that happens."

Maddie sat down, but Cole hesitated. "You must be so sad, Papa. Because we have a katrillion memories here. And Devin never even got to look for tadpoles in the creek or anything."

"I am sad." Ashley's dad put his hand over Cole's. "But we'll be sure to buy a house with a new creek. So that'll give us more to explore." He turned and gazed deep into Elaine's eyes. "Uncle Ryan's right. It was time for a change."

When Cole finally sat down, he looked at Landon. "Does that mean strangers are gonna buy it? And take over?"

"New people, yes."

Around the table, conversations broke out. Overall the feeling was one of sadness and an overriding inevitability. Katy talked about how her parents had sold their family home in Chicago when their health deteriorated and how difficult that time was for all of them.

At the same time, Landon continued the quiet dialogue with Cole.

"What if me and Maddie and Jessie put all our allowance and birthday money together?" Cole kept his voice to an urgent whisper. "Then could we buy it?"

"No." Landon shot a sad smile at Cole. "It wouldn't be enough. Now shh. Aunt Katy's talking."

Ashley stayed quiet while the children talked about the egg hunts and campouts and endless games of tag they'd played on the Baxter property. The noises around her blurred, and Ashley wasn't picturing the young cousins playing on the acreage outside. Rather she was picturing Brooke and Kari and Erin hunting for fireflies near the trees that bordered their property, Luke shooting baskets out front on a summer night, and herself seated behind an easel trying to capture the fading sunset as it sprayed oranges and blues across the fields adjacent to the house. She was seeing her mother tending to her rose garden out back and her dad coming home from the hospital and sitting in the porch swing next to her when the gardening was done.

Devin pounded on his high chair tray. "More cawwots, peas. . . . More cawwots!"

Ashley turned to her younger son. "Okay, baby . . . just a minute." She put three carrot slices on his tray and cut them in fourths, glad for the reason to turn her back to the others. Not because she had nothing to add to the conversation about the house and all it had meant to them over the years and why it would be sad to bid it good-bye.

But because she didn't want Cole to see her tears.

CHAPTER SIX

DINNER WAS OVER and the guys were finishing up the dishes, talking about the Super Bowl and whether the Patriots would be back.

"Don't rule out the Colts." Landon grinned. "They're always in the top few teams, and now with Jim Flanigan on the sidelines, next year could be their best ever."

"You got that right." Ryan raised his eyebrows. "They'll be strong for a while."

"Which reminds me." Peter was scooping leftover salad from the bowl and placing it in a Ziploc bag. "We need to get to some home games next season. With Erin and Sam moving here, we could make up a pretty decent tailgate party."

"Jim tells me he can get us seats, so maybe if we plan early . . ."

Landon was drying a pan, ready to agree about heading to Indianapolis for a few games when he realized he hadn't seen Ashley in a while. Devin had been fussy after dinner, and Ashley had taken him from his high chair, cleaned him up, and swung him onto her hip. She'd muttered something about Devin being tired and that she was going to take him upstairs to walk him until he fell asleep. But her smile had stopped short of her eyes.

Now Landon dried his hands and moved toward the doorway. "Save me the counters. I'm gonna check on Ash."

Everyone could see that Ashley hadn't been the same since the conversation about the Baxter house, but Landon had a feeling there was something else going on. She hadn't been herself lately, more distracted and nowhere near as connected to him and the boys. He was at the stairs when his phone vibrated in his back pocket.

He was on call at the fire station, so he pulled it out and checked the caller ID. It was his mom. She and his dad had moved to Wisconsin a few months ago to be closer to her aging parents. Landon and Ashley and the boys were planning to visit at the end of summer for a reunion on his mom's side of the family. Usually Landon didn't talk to his mother more than once in a weekend, so he had a feeling the news wouldn't be good. He opened the phone and held it to his ear. "Hey, Mom."

"Landon . . ." Her voice cracked, and for a few seconds she didn't say anything. "I'm sorry. It's your grandpa. He isn't doing well."

"What?" Landon moved down the hallway where it was quieter. "I thought you took him out for ice cream the other day."

"We did." She sniffed. "He had a heart attack after church. He's in intensive care." There was another pause and the sound of her muffled crying. "Pray for us."

"Do you want me to come?" Landon had flown out months earlier when his grandma died after a long illness. Ashley had still been physically recovering from Sarah's birth, so she and the boys stayed home. But she was sorry she'd missed that time with him, and if Landon had to leave tonight, he knew Ashley would give him her blessing. "I can be there by morning."

"No. He's unconscious." She uttered a ragged breath. "Just pray."

"I will. I'm sorry, Mom. I'll look into a flight." The call ended, and Landon turned toward the wall. He raised his arm and rested his forehead in the crook of his elbow. *Be with my mom and give her*

peace, God, and be with Grandpa Westra. If it's time to bring him home,
please . . . let it happen peacefully the way it did with Grandma.

No audible response moved across his soul, but Landon felt a
peace deep within. Peace and sorrow in equal parts. The relationship Cole shared with John Baxter was much like the one Landon
had shared with Grandpa Andrew Westra.

Landon wasn't ready to see Ashley or the others just yet. He
needed to process the news. He stepped outside through the back
door and was met by a blast of cold air as he walked around the
covered porch to the swing out front. The old chains creaked as
he sat down and set the swing in soft, subtle motion. He sighed,
and his breath formed a white cloud that hung in the air a moment
before fading.

Landon gripped the swing chains and gazed at the starry sky. The
full moon reflected against the snow made the night far brighter
than usual. Old Grandpa Westra. The man was something else,
one of a kind. The legacy he would leave behind was one Landon
hoped to leave decades down the road. He pictured his grandparents Andrew and Effie. Until Effie's death, it was impossible to
see the two of them apart. In Effie's final years, she couldn't see as
well as before, and his grandpa's hearing was going. And so, to the
end, they completed each other, and no wonder. They'd begun
dating when they were teenagers and were married seventy-six
years before Effie died.

Seventy-six years.

A breeze blew across the snowy ground, and Landon wished
he had his coat. If his grandpa didn't pull through, then his death
would come just months after losing his beloved wife.

Grandpa Westra had always been there, a rock of a man. Back
when he was a boy, Landon enjoyed climbing on his lap and hearing stories about the old days. He remembered his grandparents
driving their homemade cheese to the dairy, setting off for another
afternoon of visiting the sick and shut-in from their community
and church, and singing together as they drove. Somehow Landon's

memories of his grandparents always included singing. As if all of life was one beautiful song for two people with such strong love for the Lord and each other.

"We have it so good, don't we, Pa?" his grandma would say.

And the response was always the same. "Yes, we do. Yes, we sure do."

But not until his grandma died did Landon truly understand the deep faith and love of family that made up Andrew and Effie Westra's marriage and life, the rich heritage they had passed on to their six children, twenty-one grandchildren, fifty-four great-grandchildren, and one great-great-grandson.

Stories told at Effie's funeral would stay with Landon forever. How in her final weeks, Andrew asked her, "Are you afraid to die?"

Effie merely shook her head and even in her weakened state began to sing "Have Thine Own Way, Lord!"

The story that stayed with Landon most was how his grand-parents spent their final day together. The end in sight, Andrew asked one of the family members who'd come by that day if he could carry Effie up to their room so they could sleep in the same bed one last time.

Landon remembered the way his grandfather had looked dressed in a suit at his wife's funeral. His eyes were distant, as if he were see-ing it all happen again, every wonderful one of the seventy-six years they spent together. Anyone watching Andrew Westra that day could see that his heart was broken. Small wonder he'd suffered a heart attack—the toll of living without his dear Effie was that great.

Another sigh filtered across Landon's lips and hung in the air. He stared at the moon, the subtle definition that made up the distant surface. The loss of people like Andrew and Effie couldn't really be measured. People who stood for faith and family, hard work and helping others. But with God's help, he and Ashley could live their lives in a way that would've made his grandparents proud.

There was a sound of a door opening, and Landon turned toward it.

Ashley stepped out through the front entry. "I thought you might be here." She was wearing her coat and carrying his.

"Come here." He slid to one side of the swing and watched her, the gentle way she had about her. He couldn't remember a time when he hadn't been crazy about her, and tonight was no exception.

As she reached him, their eyes held. "Devin's asleep." She handed him his coat. "Ryan said you were looking for me."

"I got a phone call." He patted the empty spot on the swing. "Sit with me. Please."

She settled in beside him. "The station?"

"No." He pursed his lips, his sorrow as strong as it had been when the phone call came in. "My mom. Grandpa Westra had a heart attack. He's in ICU. It doesn't look good."

Ashley's expression fell. "I'm sorry." She folded her arms across her chest and looked out at the moonlit snow. "He couldn't live without her."

"No." He and Ashley had shared many precious visits with his grandparents. She knew the details of their love and marriage. Now Ashley clearly felt the sadness as sharply as Landon did.

"Should we go?"

"Not tonight." Landon thought for a moment. "Eventually. I told my mom I'd look into flights." He hesitated. "He's unconscious right now, so he wouldn't know we were there. And my parents are surrounded by family." He narrowed his eyes, imagining the Westra gang supporting each other, gathering at a few houses and talking about all Andrew meant to them. All he would leave behind if this was his time to go. He drew a deep breath. "Mom just wanted me to know."

"Losing your grandpa . . . it'll be like the end of an era." Ashley slid a little closer to him and rested her head on his shoulder.

For a minute or so, they were quiet. Landon took Ashley's hand and slowly eased his fingers between hers. He never tired of the sensation of her skin against his. He set the swing in motion again, and at the far edge of the property, two deer sprang through the snow and disappeared into the woods that lined the creek.

"Beautiful." Ashley sat up straight again. "I always loved that about living here, being so close to town but seeing wildlife right outside our windows." Her tone was even sadder than before. "I can't believe he's really going to sell it."

Landon had thought of every possible way to make the house their own, but there was none. "I'd buy it for you if I could." He softly kissed her temple. "You know that."

"Of course." With her free hand she pulled her coat more tightly around her. She turned to him, and her expression filled with something that was maybe a mix of fear and guilt. "Landon—" she swallowed, and her voice fell a notch—"I came out here for a reason."

A flash of concern brought his attention into clear focus. Usually when Ashley used that tone, the situation was serious.

She stood and leaned against the porch railing. "I should've told you a long time ago, and I'm sorry I waited." She lifted her hands and let them fall to her sides. "I just . . . I was too afraid to bring it up."

Landon brought the swing to a stop. Whatever she was talking about sounded ominous, and he fought the sudden panic building inside him. Things were fine with the two of them. They'd come through so much together and with every ordeal they'd become stronger. Even after losing Sarah. So what could make Ashley so afraid that she had kept some news from him? Her health or something wrong with one of the boys? "I don't . . . Where's this going?"

She came to him and took his hands in hers. Her eyes were wild with a desperate fear Landon had never seen in her before. "I'm pregnant." She didn't give him a chance to respond. "Three months or more, but I didn't take the test until last week and . . ."

Awe and disbelief and confusion spread through him. And frustration because she should've told him when she first suspected.

But all of that paled compared to his concern for her. He stood and circled his arms around her waist, searching her eyes. "You were afraid to tell me *that*?"

"No. I mean, yes . . ." Tears filled her eyes. Emotion seemed to overcome her, and she choked on her explanation. "I was afraid if I told you, then . . . then it would be real." Her tears spilled onto her cheeks. "I'm afraid for me and for you. For the baby." She pressed her forehead against his chest and clung to him. "I'm scared to death because it can't . . ." Her voice became quiet, gut-wrenching sobs. "It can't . . ."

"Shh. Sweetie, it's okay." Landon sheltered her, one hand cradling the back of her head, the other holding her steady against him. He was about to reassure her that of course what had happened to Sarah wouldn't happen again. But there were no guarantees.

Ashley trembled in his arms, but gradually she began to calm down.

Landon thought about the road ahead of them, and as he did, the reality of what she'd just told him finally hit. "You're serious?" he whispered close to her face, but he couldn't contain his joy. "You're pregnant?"

She sniffed and drew back. "I can't go through it again. It took everything I had."

"God knows that." He ran his thumb gently across her cheek. "A baby isn't a reason to cry. We have to believe the best."

Ashley lifted her chin, something she'd done in the face of trials as long as he'd known her. She closed her eyes for a moment, and another breeze blew over them, drying the tears on her cheeks. When she opened her eyes she looked slightly stronger than before. "My first appointment is this week."

Landon's mind raced. Were they really about to take this ride again? Allowing their hearts to soar with possibilities and then taking the tests and waiting for the results? He steadied himself. "They'll do an ultrasound?"

"It'll be too soon to see anything but the heartbeat." She took a few quick breaths, still finding her composure. "We'll find out more sometime in April. Whether . . . whether . . ."

Landon understood. His heart hurt for his wife, for the fear she'd been handling by herself. "If this baby's healthy or not."

Ashley blinked. "Yes." She held his gaze a little longer; then she closed the slight distance between them once more.

They stayed that way awhile, clinging to each other.

Ashley broke the silence first. She straightened, and the fear in her expression was replaced completely with a deep remorse. "I'm sorry. I should've told you."

Landon brushed the side of his face against hers. "We could've talked about it." He loved everything about her, even this—the impetuous, independent Ashley who sometimes had to find her own way back to the place where once more she could trust him. "I hate that you've been dealing with it by yourself."

"I know. Forgive me."

He looked deep into her eyes, to the frightened corners of her heart. Of course he forgave her. But rather than tell her, slowly he brought his lips to hers. The kiss grew and became something more, Landon's way of telling her his feelings. His way of assuring her that together they would survive whatever lay ahead and that they'd grow stronger as a result. They would love God and each other and pave the way for their kids.

The way his grandparents had done.

He drew back, breathless from the kiss and the cold air and the mix of feelings pressing at the seams of his heart. "Have you heard the old hymn 'Have Thine Own Way, Lord'?" His voice was quiet, and the sound of it blended with the breeze. "It was kind of my grandparents' life theme."

A hint of a smile colored her eyes. "It was one of Irvel's favorites."

Irvel. The sweet Alzheimer's patient who had made such an impact on Ashley during the days when she worked at Sunset Hills Adult Care Home.

Landon looked out at the moonlit landscape and then at Ashley again. "Sing it with me?"

Ashley's smile turned shy, but as he began to sing, she joined in. The song started slow, hesitant, and somewhat awkward. But after a few words, their voices found the right rhythm, and the song surrounded them with hope and truth and a commitment to stand in the face of whatever was coming—trial or triumph.

"'Have Thine own way, Lord! Have Thine own way! Thou art the potter; I am the clay. Mold me and make me after Thy will, while I am waiting, yielded and still.'"

As the song ended, Landon felt something change in Ashley's attitude, a change from deep inside. Because this was life, really. Clinging to each other, eyes set on Jesus, certain of the eventual outcome even if that was the only certainty at all. In this next stretch of their journey, he and Ashley would do better to let go of their own desires and fears and simply trust God. He really was the potter. His way—whatever it was—would be best.

They hugged again for a long time, then linked hands and walked inside. Landon considered Grandpa Westra. If he didn't survive the heart attack, Landon would feel the loss greatly. But the things his grandpa had taught him would never die, because they would live on in Landon and later in Cole and Devin and whatever other children the Lord might bless them with. In that way Andrew Westra would remain a part of them always whenever they needed to remember what was important.

The way they had needed to remember it tonight.

CHAPTER SEVEN

LUKE PARKED HIS CAR adjacent to the city park and looked over his shoulder at his children, Tommy and Malin, buckled into their car seats. Two-year-old Malin was asleep, sucking on her pacifier, and Tommy, at four, was straining at his belt.

"Look, Daddy." He pointed to the swings. "Even a Tyrannosaurus rex could hide in that park. It has a million trees!" He held his hands up in a clawing position and let out a roar. "Today I'm the T. rex."

The sound made Malin jump, and as she did, the pacifier fell from her mouth and bounced onto the floor mat. Her face slowly morphed into a twist of angry frustration—the way it often did before a breakdown—and she began to cry in protest.

"Here we go," Luke muttered. He killed the engine and noticed a long peanut butter smear from his elbow halfway to his wrist, proof that he'd forgotten to wash Malin's hands before setting her in the car. He sighed. Until the trouble with Reagan, he'd never spent significant time alone with the kids, never really understood what Reagan was up against taking care of them every day and often without his help.

This weekend Reagan was in New York visiting her mother, trying to decide the next step in their marriage. At the rate it was deteriorating, he could only imagine what might come next. When he and Reagan talked, the conversation was brief and terse, functional dialogue about the kids or the day's schedule. Luke wasn't sure what Reagan was trying to figure out by spending a weekend away. Anyone could see where they were headed because only one solution loomed on the horizon. A painful, devastating divorce.

Luke climbed out of the car, hurried around to the other side, and opened the back passenger door. He found Malin's pacifier on the floor and dusted it off. After unbuckling his daughter, he clipped her pacifier to the corner of her jacket and lifted her into his arms. Next he clicked Tommy's seat belt, and the boy scrambled down onto the sidewalk. The stroller was in the back of the car, and with one hand Luke pulled it out and snapped it open. He situated Malin and set her pacifier back in her mouth. They could break her of the habit later when their family wasn't falling apart.

Tommy watched as Luke locked the car. "Why isn't Mommy here?" He'd asked three times since breakfast. Never mind that the child wasn't in kindergarten yet; he understood what was happening around him. The tension at home had been unbearable.

"Well, kiddo—" a heaviness gripped Luke's heart—"she's visiting Grandma in New York. Remember?"

"By herself?" Tommy slipped his hand in Luke's as they walked between the trees toward the playground. "How come by herself?"

Luke stopped to zip Malin's coat. It was the second Saturday in March, and a week of warmer temperatures had melted most of the snow. But even with the puffy clouds and sunny sky, it was still cold enough that they wore their winter coats.

Tommy cocked his head. "Daddy, I said how come by herself?"

They started walking again. "'Cause Mommy needed time alone to talk to Grandma." Luke's tone was patient. The nightmare between him and Reagan wasn't the kids' fault.

"Alone isn't as fun as together." Tommy kept close to Luke's

side. The confident T. rex he'd been in the car was more of a timid brontosaurus now that the conversation had turned to his parents. "Right?"

"Not always." Luke chose his words carefully. No matter what their feelings for each other were, neither of them wanted to force the kids to choose sides. "Sometimes people need to be alone so they can talk to God and think things through."

Tommy set his jaw. "I don't like alone."

They reached the playground, and once more Luke could see a change in Tommy. Before the troubles at home, Tommy would've run off with barely a good-bye, in a hurry to join the two other kids already racing up and down the slide. But today he circled his arm around Luke's leg and leaned in closer. "I think I'll wait."

"For what?" Luke pulled out the top of Malin's stroller so the sun wouldn't be directly on her face.

"Aunt Ashley." Tommy walked over and plucked Malin's pacifier from her mouth. "No more poppy, Mali." He wagged his finger at her. "You're a big girl now."

"Mine!" Malin snatched at the pacifier, but Tommy held it just out of reach.

"That's not nice." Luke jerked the pacifier from Tommy's hand. He passed it off to Malin and scowled at his son. "You need to be nice to your sister. What would Jesus think about that?"

For a moment, Tommy stared at the ground. He used the toe of his red and white tennis shoes to draw circles in the damp earth. "Just tryin' to help." He looked up and shaded his eyes. "I'm gonna go slide."

"Okay." Relief hit Luke as his son ran off. He pushed the stroller to the nearest park bench and flopped down. Ashley and her boys were meeting them, and Luke was glad the park wasn't crowded. He didn't want to work hard to keep an eye on Tommy. Today he needed to talk to a friend without distractions, and Ashley was still one of his closest. She would sort through the broken pieces of his life and help him make sense of them.

He was about to check behind him for his sister's van when he saw Tommy pick up a handful of sand and throw it at the slide. Then as the boy at the top of the slide came down, Tommy picked up another handful and threw it at the child.

Luke stood and cupped his hands around his mouth. "Hey!"

Tommy turned toward him, eyes wide. He opened his hands, and two more handfuls sifted to the ground. "What?"

"Come here." Luke felt worn-out. Being a lawyer was nothing to raising kids.

His son produced a full-faced pout and marched back. "Slides are better with sand!"

Luke willed himself to keep from yelling. "What about friends?" He put his hand on Tommy's shoulder and looked straight into the boy's eyes. "Are they better with sand too?"

"It was a big storm." Tommy's tone was whiny, something else that had been worse since the troubles between Luke and Reagan.

Luke gritted his teeth. "Did the other boy know that?"

"Um . . ." Guilt shadowed his eyes. "Maybe no."

"That's what I thought." Luke pointed at the other child. "You're going to go back and tell that boy you're sorry. Then if I see you throw another handful of sand, you'll be sitting beside me the rest of the afternoon."

Tommy blinked a few times, the way he did when he wanted to garner sympathy. "Yes, Daddy."

Luke watched him return slowly to the playground and approach the other child. At the same time he heard Ashley's voice behind him.

"Go ahead, boys. I'll be here with Uncle Luke." She walked up and hugged him. "How are you?"

"Frazzled." Luke led her back to the bench.

Ashley peeked in the stroller at Malin. "She's sleeping."

"Which is amazing in light of Tommy's constant efforts to keep her awake." Luke settled back onto the bench beside his sister. "We've been here ten minutes, and I'm already exhausted."

"It's not easy, raising kids."

"I never realized how much Reagan did all day." He crossed his arms and watched Tommy as he ran to greet his cousins. He smiled at Ashley. "Hey, congratulations on the baby."

"Thanks." She sat sideways, one knee pulled up onto the bench. Her pregnancy was showing a little, and she looked healthier than she had since losing Sarah. "We figured we'd call people rather than do the big announcement this time. Especially because Landon made a quick trip to see his grandpa in Wisconsin."

"Makes sense." Luke glanced at his sister. "Is it hard? I mean, are you ever afraid?"

Ashley smiled, but the worry showed in her face. "Very. It's a daily struggle. At least until our ultrasound next month."

They were quiet for a few seconds. Cole and Tommy walked Devin to the swings, and Cole helped him into the seat of one of the smaller ones.

Luke slid to the edge of the bench, ready to run to the boys if they needed help. "Is Devin okay on the swings?"

"Definitely. Cole knows how high he can go. He's a really good big brother."

"Hmm." Luke eased back once more. "Wish I could say that about Tommy. He and Malin are constantly at it. Makes me wonder how Mom and Dad raised us to be so close."

"Remember what they always said." Her voice softened. "'The people sitting around you at the dinner table are the best friends you'll ever have.' I find myself telling Cole and Devin that all the time."

"They believe you?" Luke was baffled. Could it really be that easy?

Ashley laughed. "It takes constant reminding, but yeah, they believe us. Or maybe it's because Cole was older when Devin came along. By then he'd wanted a brother for so long he could hardly stand it."

The kids stayed near the swings for a few more minutes and

then moved to a section of sand. With the happy sounds of their boys drifting across the playground and Tommy seeming under control, Luke took a long breath. "It doesn't look good for Reagan and me."

"That's why I'm here." Ashley reached out and squeezed his hand. "You can't give up; you know that." She released his hand. "Tell me what's happening."

Luke stretched his legs. The pain grabbed his heart and held on. "I'm not sure how it all started, but it got worse last month." He paused. "We were honest with each other."

"You told her about Randi."

"All the details." He laced his fingers behind his head. "Then she told me hers."

"Hi, Mom!" Cole shouted from his place on the sand. "Look at our mountain!"

"Wow!" Ashley stood and grinned at him. "It's huge!"

"As huge as a dinosaur!" Tommy jumped in place a few times. "We're gonna make it bigger!"

The boys went back to work, and Ashley sat down. Her expression went blank. "*Her* details?"

Luke pictured his front porch steps and Reagan and the firefighter bidding each other good-bye, laughing and sharing a hug. Luke wanted to respect Reagan's privacy, but she had given him permission to talk about the situation with Ashley. Luke bit the corner of his lip and tried to pick a starting point. "She became friends with a local fireman."

Something flickered in Ashley's eyes. "Did she . . . have an affair?"

Across the way, Luke glanced at the boys building their mountain of sand taller still. Then he let the story come, how Reagan had met the guy when Tommy got his head stuck between the railings of the banister and how eventually that led to a friendship, then to something much more.

"When she told me the truth, I said some things I shouldn't have.

How she should've learned her lesson with me." He shrugged, out of answers. "Nothing's been the same since."

Ashley sighed. "What'd she say before she left?"

"That maybe we should make a plan when she got back. She didn't mention a divorce attorney, but that's what she meant." Even saying the words doubled the hurt in his heart. "Mom would be so disappointed." Defeat rang in his voice. "Lately I've been thinking . . ."

Laughter from the boys carried to where they were sitting. Ashley and Luke looked their direction and saw Cole, Tommy, and Devin kicking apart the hill of sand and flopping into it as if it were a pile of snow.

Ashley smiled, but as her eyes reconnected with Luke's, her expression grew serious. "Thinking what?"

Luke took a breath and held it for a few beats. "That Reagan and I never should've gotten married. We made a mistake; we had a child. But that doesn't make it right to compound the problem by rushing into marriage. Being around Reagan . . . I don't know, it's like I always feel guilty. Even before I started looking at other women."

Ashley stared at him, her expression incredulous. "None of this is Reagan's fault." Frustration sounded in her voice, but she kept her tone even. "You loved her so much then. You talked about marrying her long before September 11."

"That was the day, wasn't it? The day everything changed."

"Because of your choices." She slid to the edge of the bench, more passionate than before. "That's how it is, Luke. We make our decisions, and then we have to live with them. It was that way for me, and it's that way for you. The key is always the same for any of us." She brought her tone down some. "There will be consequences, but if we seek God, we'll find redemption. That's where our hope lies. You know that."

Luke had figured his sister would set him straight, and in some ways that's what he needed. But here and now her reply grated on him. "I'm forgiven; I get that. But what am I supposed to do with the guilt? I never feel good enough around Reagan, and now . . . now she doesn't want things to work out anyway."

"And you're still not seeing a counselor?"

"She doesn't want to." He hesitated. "I'm not sure either of us does."

"Luke . . ." Ashley sounded shocked at his admission. "Listen to yourself. Of course you need counseling. You can't walk out on this marriage. . . . You can't."

Irritation built like so many small pebbles in his soul. "People do it all the time." His answer surprised even him. How far had he come from the days when he was the perfect Baxter, the son any father would be proud of? He rested his forehead in his hand and tried to find a point of reference, some way back to the person he used to be.

There was none. The words that had spilled from his heart were exactly what he was feeling. People gave up on their marriages all the time. Why not him and Reagan? He waited for the verbal barrage from Ashley, the one he most certainly deserved. He lowered his hand and looked at her.

Ashley exhaled and straightened so she had a clear view of the kids. "Why did you ask me here?"

He stared at the sky, at the building clouds, and shook his head. "I can't make sense of any of it. I thought maybe you could help."

Ashley put her hand on his shoulder. "Then listen to me. When Reagan gets home, tell her you're not ready to give up. Tell her the two of you need counseling." She gave him a hug. "Get on your knees and beg her if you have to, but don't just say nothing. Silence is the fading heartbeat of relationships."

"Daddy, come here! Quick!" Tommy hopped around at the base of the monkey bars. "Help me!"

At the same time, a cry came from Malin's stroller. "Mommy!" She always woke the same way, whiny and ready to fall apart if she wasn't picked up immediately.

Luke stood and went to her. "It's okay, baby girl. Daddy's here."

As he unbelted her and lifted her into his arms, he couldn't help but think that very soon this might be the norm. The children alone with him, Reagan back at her separate home waiting for her turn. The thought hurt his soul with a guilt that cut deep. He brushed his cheek against his daughter's. "Let's go find Tommy."

"Tommy!" She held out her hand and gave Luke a crooked grin. Her expression changed, and she reached back toward her stroller. "Poppy." She hesitated, and this time her grin was forced. "Peese!"

"Not this time." He gave Ashley a look. "Poppies are for naps only, sweetheart."

"You're a good dad." Ashley fell in beside him as they stepped down into the sand and walked to their boys. "Now you need to remember how to be a good husband."

Luke stopped himself from saying that it wasn't as easy as she made it sound. They reached the boys, and Luke transferred Malin to Ashley's arms so he could lift Tommy to the first rung of the monkey bars. Devin was content to run alongside the boys as they swung from one end to the other for the next fifteen minutes. The temperature was dropping, the sun moving lower in the sky, and after a few turns on the slides, it was time to go.

Ashley didn't bring up Reagan again, but as they reached their cars, she buckled her boys in their seats and then returned to Luke and hugged him. As she pulled back she kept her hands on his shoulders. "You're a Baxter. You'll do the right thing; I know you will."

"I don't feel like a Baxter." He didn't want to bring down the mood, but he had to be honest.

"Hey …." She hadn't looked at him this seriously since the day she connected with him on the campus of Indiana University to tell him he was the father of Reagan's baby. "Being a Baxter doesn't mean you're perfect." She looked deep to the places the two of them had shared since they were very young. "We bend and sway; we go through trials and temptations and heartbreak. But Baxters don't break, and we don't walk away. We keep getting up and dusting ourselves off and turning to God. As many times as it takes."

Luke couldn't think of anything to say. Instead he congratulated her again on her pregnancy and told her he'd pray for her, though the words sounded trite in light of the way he wasn't praying or trusting God about his marriage.

Long after Luke was back at his dad's house, after the four of them had eaten hamburgers and chips and settled down in front of Tommy's current favorite movie, *Toy Story*, Ashley's words about being a Baxter stayed with him. What had she said? *"Silence is the fading heartbeat of relationships."* Wasn't that it?

The movie played on as Malin nestled in her grandpa's lap and Tommy stretched out on the floor beside them.

Luke stared out the window at the silhouette of the barren oak trees not far from the house. How far had he fallen from God's best for his life? from his role as a loving husband, one who could lead Reagan in the ways that were best for both of them? If his mother could've heard his conversation with Ashley today, she wouldn't have recognized her youngest son.

"You've Got a Friend in Me" was playing cheerfully in the background, but Luke tuned it out. *I've fallen so far I'm not sure if I remember how to get up, God.* He gripped the edge of the sofa and closed his eyes. *Reagan hasn't called. It's like we've already walked away.*

My son . . . The answer whispered deep within him, a whisper so strangely loud it drowned out every other sound in the room. *You must remember. The righteous will live by faith.*

By faith? Luke opened his eyes. It was part of a verse his parents had taught him when he was going into middle school. Back then living by faith used to be like breathing. Now he couldn't even remember what it felt like to be that guy. *How, God? How do I live that way?*

This time there was no answer, no reassuring sense that God was even there. Only the haunting truth that Ashley had already spelled out. If silence was the fading heartbeat of relationships, he and Reagan weren't only in trouble.

They were terminal.

CHAPTER EIGHT

REAGAN STEPPED OUT of the cab and pulled her rain jacket more tightly around her shoulders. She handed the driver a ten-dollar bill. "Keep the change."

The man leaned toward the passenger window. "I wait, miss?"

"No thanks." Reagan glanced at the stone structure of St. Paul's. "I might be a while."

The man nodded and turned his cab back into the steady stream of traffic. Never mind that early spring was the rainiest time in New York. The weather did nothing to change the pace and flow of the city.

Reagan climbed the stairs to the chapel. This was the place, the tiny church on the border of Ground Zero in Manhattan's financial district, the one that withstood the force of the terrorist attacks on September 11 and became a gathering place for firefighters and police officers in the months afterward. Back then, weary volunteers could come to the chapel for a nap on one of the wooden pews or a hot meal or a conversation with a counselor.

It was Sunday afternoon, the last church service of the morning long since cleared out. Reagan wanted it that way. She'd already attended church earlier with her mom, and her flight back to Indianapolis didn't leave for a few hours. St. Paul's had been her mother's idea.

They'd spent the weekend talking about Reagan's marriage to Luke. Until yesterday, her mom had no idea that Reagan was also guilty of indiscretion. Reagan half expected her to agree that divorce really was the only option.

But her mother's reaction was nothing of the sort. She stared at Reagan for a long time, the emotions in her eyes changing from shock to disappointment and finally to an intense pleading. "Let the past be the past. You can't walk away from your marriage." Her voice held a controlled intensity. "You made a promise to God and to Luke."

"Promises that both of us have broken." Reagan's clipped response sounded sharp and thoughtless.

"Marriage takes work. Your father and I figured that out a few years into it." Her mother stood and crossed the room, taking the seat next to Reagan. She put her hand on Reagan's knee. "It's not too late. Not with God."

Reagan wasn't so sure. She patted her mother's hand and changed the subject. They talked about the early days, when Reagan and her brother, Bryan, were kids and life seemed headed toward a wonderfully happy ending. Back before September 11. Now her brother was married and living in New Jersey, and her dad had been gone for six years.

Though the topic of Reagan's marriage came up again several times that day, her mother was careful not to lecture. At the same time, her message to Reagan was clear, and she summed it up when Reagan left the apartment today after an early lunch. "The only way to make a marriage work is to never even think about saying the word *divorce*."

Reagan moved through the narrow door at the front of St. Paul's and stopped just inside. The last time she was here, memorabilia from the tragedy at Ground Zero had filled the small church all the way around the inside perimeter. Now, though, the displays were sparse and sanitized. The bulk of letters, keepsakes, and mementos found in the debris of the collapsed Twin Towers had been set aside for use in the not-yet-created official memorial site. The pretty chapel felt more like it was going about its business, as though even here in the shadow of the memory of the Twin Towers, life had moved on.

A small table stood to the left in the corner beneath a window. On it were photos of firefighters and businessmen and women, each with a note scrawled across the bottom or a letter tacked to one side. Next to the photo of a young man in a suit and tie, a note read, "Miss you, John, with every breath." And beneath the picture of a rugged firefighter, "Our hero and friend forever and always."

Tears stung Reagan's eyes. She blinked and turned from the table. She and Luke had attended a Sunday morning service here many years ago. The pastor had been a friendly man who seemed to understand that many of those in attendance were visitors.

"You'll notice," he said at the beginning of his sermon, "our pews are not nicely kept and neatly polished." He paused, his eyes filling with a depth that could only come from living through a tragedy like the terrorist attacks. "Rather they are scraped and battered, worn from the boots of firefighters and the holsters of police officers. The way they will stay, as a reminder to all who enter the doors that this chapel made a difference in some of the darkest days of our country's history."

Reagan slipped into one of the empty pews. She ran her fingers along the scarred, uneven surface of the bench beside her. Marks made by men like Landon Blake and countless other firefighters who searched through tons of debris looking for the remains of victims. Victims like her father.

The overwhelming sense of loss fell upon her again. Her father had done nothing more than go to work that Tuesday morning. There had been no closure, no warning . . . . no time for good-bye.

Reagan dropped slowly to her knees. She folded her hands and bowed her head, her eyes closed. That was wrong, wasn't it? There had been time for good-bye, but she'd lost the opportunity for one single reason. She was in the act of breaking her greatest promises to God and her parents. Too busy making out with Luke on the sofa in her Indiana University apartment to be bothered with a phone call from her dad. His last phone call to her.

Anger built and swirled, covering her heart like a cold, dense fog. Of course she and Luke weren't doing well in their marriage. When had they ever worked through the way Reagan felt about losing her father, the way she had to live forever with the truth that she'd missed her final conversation with him? Sure, she'd forgiven herself . . . but what about Luke? Had she ever really forgiven him for his part in that terrible day? Luke never should've stayed that night, never should've crawled up next to her while she slept on the sofa during *Monday Night Football*.

She still hung her head, but now she clenched her teeth and felt hot tears pool against her forearm. The choices made back then weren't only Luke's fault; they were her own. But she and Luke never talked about that time, how their failings had cost her that last conversation with her dad and how her pregnancy with Tommy had left her unable to have more children.

Her anger swelled and consumed her. How could her mother tell her to keep God at the center of her marriage when she and Luke hadn't relied on God since September 10, 2001?

She envisioned her dad, the way he must've looked at home in his La-Z-Boy recliner that Monday night, intent on commiserating with her on the Giants' loss.

Dad, I'm sorry. I should've picked up the phone. . . .

There was a touch on her shoulder, and Reagan jumped. She lifted her head and used her wrists to wipe the tears from her cheeks.

An elderly man stood at her side, his expression concerned. "You okay, miss?"

"Yes." Her answer was quick. Embarrassment brought a sudden heat to her cheeks. "I'm fine. Sorry."

"It's okay. I work here at St. Paul's. I lost my daughter in the Twin Towers." His lower lip quivered. "It's a pain that never goes away."

"No." Reagan's heart went out to the man. She thought about the daunting list of victims, each with his or her own story, each with unfinished business. "There was no time for good-bye."

The man shook his head. "Not for any of us." He seemed to understand that Reagan wanted to be alone and gave her shoulder a gentle squeeze. "I'll be in the back if you need me."

When he was gone, Reagan lifted her gaze to the front of the chapel. Light streamed in from the stained glass windows, and a stunning cross hung on the wall behind the altar. Above it stretched a banner from one end to the other that read, "In His redemption there is hope!"

Reagan read the sign again and again. Fresh tears gathered in her eyes and made the letters blurry. Was that what was missing for her and Luke? Redemption? The redeeming power of Christ, the hope-giving transformation that could come only from God?

She sniffed and dabbed beneath her eyes again. In the weeks and months after September 11, she had refused to even think about what had happened that Monday night with Luke. She moved home and refused Luke's calls, pressing forward through the days and nights of hoping that maybe somehow her father would be alive, then through the funeral when it became clear he had been killed in the collapse of the Twin Towers.

Months passed and there had been Tommy's birth, the tragedy of how she had nearly bled to death and the knowledge that she couldn't have more children. Not long afterward Luke appeared at her door, stepping back into her life as if they'd never been apart.

In the years that followed, never had she and Luke as a couple truly sought God's forgiveness for the mistakes they'd made. So maybe that was why a part of her had remained numb to everything that mattered—Luke, the Lord, and even life. She was angry with herself, angry with Luke, and unable to make peace with her feelings.

Of course her marriage was in a shambles.

Reagan read the words once more. *In His redemption there is hope!* She had no doubt the message was true, but there was a problem. Too much time had passed since Luke's and her decisions that distant September 10. If her angry heart and bitter regrets were any indications, if her marriage was any sign, the future held no hope for either of them. The fact was, they no longer deserved God's redemption.

But rather His rejection. His everlasting, unending rejection.

CHAPTER NINE

ASHLEY GRABBED HER CAR KEYS and stepped out back where Landon and Cole and Devin were sorting through a bucket of nails. She smiled at the picture they made—Landon, the dad Ashley had always known he would be, loving and kind, strong and tenderhearted.

He grinned at her. "This time we're finding the strongest nails in the bucket."

"Good idea." She laughed and walked a little closer. A thunderstorm had come through last night, and the winds had ripped down a section of the boys' tree house. It was Saturday, and Landon had the day off. He and the boys planned to spend a few hours not only fixing the tree house but making it better than before. She stepped into the shade from the tree and peered up at the broken branch that had done the damage. "The winds were stronger than I thought."

"Not to me." Cole looked up, his hands plunged into the bucket of nails, his blond bangs pushed to the side. "That's why I brought Devin into your room."

Ashley tried to keep from grinning. "Yes, Coley . . . so nice of you to look out for Devin." The truth was, Cole had scurried to her room during thunderstorms since long before she and Landon married five years ago. Now, though, since he was a big nine-year-old, he liked to say he was looking out for his little brother. Ashley didn't mind, and neither did Landon. Storms were the perfect time for kids to sleep in the middle.

"You're going to your dad's to paint?" Landon brushed his hands off on his jeans. The smears of dirt on his cheek only accentuated the ruggedness of his face, and Ashley felt the familiar attraction, the way his nearness caused her breath to catch ever so slightly at the back of her throat.

Instead of answering him, Ashley slowly touched her lips to his. "You look good with dirt on your face," she whispered close to his ear. "You always have."

"Oh yeah?" His eyes sparkled. "Maybe I'll cut back on my showers."

She tried to think of something witty to say, something to keep their little game going, but she began to laugh. "You're a goofball; you know that?" She kissed him again.

"Goo-ball!" Devin toddled over and tugged on Landon's hand. "Up, Daddy!"

Landon chuckled and swung Devin onto his hip. "Where were we?"

"Painting." Ashley put her hand on Devin's back and then touched his soft, downy hair. "Just for a few hours. I have an image I can't stop thinking of."

"Well, go paint it." Landon nodded to the tree. "We boys have our work cut out for us."

"We might make another floor if we get the time." Cole came up and hugged her around the waist. "When you get back, come out and see it."

"I will." Ashley looked at Landon again. "Thanks." She hesitated, loving the depth and emotion she saw in her husband's eyes.

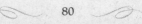

"For what?"

"For letting me paint."

"Are you kidding?" He grinned and kissed her one last time. "Painting is like breathing for you. If you didn't want to go, I'd drive you there myself."

A question rushed at her. Where would she paint when her father sold the Baxter house? Would he include a room at his new house, or would she simply have to find another place, a corner of the living room or a spot in the garage maybe? But she couldn't bring herself to share her concerns. While the house remained on the market, at least for now, she could still return to her old bedroom, where her easel stood and images came to life without effort.

Ashley bid them good-bye and headed for her van. They were under a tornado watch today until noon. After that the sky was expected to clear up, the way it often did in mid-March. She held tight to the wheel but instead of making the turn to her dad's house, she went left and headed for the cemetery.

She'd been nauseous for days leading up to the weekend, but this morning for the first time she felt well enough to be out, strong enough to take stock of her feelings and fears. They'd had their first ultrasound, and the baby's heartbeat was fine. Same as Sarah's had been. Now they would have to wait two weeks until the next appointment, when the test would show whether this baby was developing normally or if . . .

The thought hung in her mind, unfinished. She stared up at the sky and refused to give in to her fears. The clouds were already breaking up, the threat of a tornado waning. She thought back to the headlines this morning and the follow-up story about the Bloomington tornado two years ago. The town had come back, the article said. Houses were restored and memorials set up for those who lost their lives. The article even talked about the infant who had been found unharmed in her crib on the front lawn of her home, her family's sole survivor. The child had been adopted by a local couple and was doing well.

Ashley sighed and leaned back into her seat. She kept one hand on the wheel and the other tenderly against her stomach. She'd spent a little longer than usual reading her Bible this morning, and a verse from Psalm 130 had jumped out at her: "Put your hope in the Lord, for with the Lord is unfailing love and with him is full redemption."

That's what God planned for His people. No matter what the difficulty or loss, whatever the sin or moral failing, full redemption was possible in Christ. It had been true for the town of Bloomington after the devastating tornado and true for the Baxter family time and time again. No matter what the health of her unborn baby, His redemption would be true for Ashley too.

She pulled into the parking lot and cut the engine. Cemeteries were reflective and quiet and necessary. But so sad at the same time. She watched a middle-aged couple standing arm in arm near a tombstone marked by a small American flag. Had they lost a son or daughter in the war, or were they visiting the grave of a parent, a military veteran?

Ashley turned away and stepped out of her van. She walked slowly, taking several minutes to reach the bench near the graves of her mother and her infant daughter. She stooped to brush the dirt from the flat stone that covered Sarah's grave. "Hold her close, God . . . please." She stopped herself from asking that the baby inside her might not go through the same ordeal or that the child might be a girl. God knew these things, and there was no end to the prayers they were sending up on behalf of their baby. But here death was so real and present that Ashley could barely remember to breathe. Her voice was strained by the swell of sorrow inside her. "Hold my little girl. And tell Mom I miss her."

The only answer was the verse again: "Put your hope in the Lord, for with the Lord is unfailing love and with him is full redemption."

Ashley stood and regarded her daughter's tombstone a moment longer. For those who believed, there could be no place where the hope of salvation was felt more than at a cemetery. Christ died to redeem those who loved Him and so to promise an eternal life where His people would be reunited once more.

Therein lay the ultimate hope of redemption.

She moved a few steps to the left, bent down again, and brushed off the dirt from her mother's stone. Her dad's wedding plans were moving forward, the June date set. Elaine was wonderful; there was no denying that fact. Ashley agreed with her siblings that the marriage was the best possible option for their father. In some ways their relationship was another example of God's unfailing love. The same way the picture of Landon with the boys at the base of the old oak tree was.

She stood and pressed her hand to the small of her back. She was definitely showing now, enough that her jeans no longer fit. Today she wore comfortable clothes she could paint in—knit pants and a button-down cotton shirt over a long-sleeved shirt. She gave a last look at the graves and then turned back to the van.

The sunny blue sky was proof that the tornado danger had passed. She slipped on her sunglasses as she pulled out of the cemetery parking lot. All the while she was consumed by the Scripture, by the truth and certainty of God's redemption. If a theme had run through her life, that would be it. Not just for her but for the whole Baxter family.

Ashley was halfway to her dad's house when another idea hit her. She took the next right and worked her way through a residential neighborhood until she arrived at the Sunset Hills Adult Care Home. How much time had passed since she'd been here, since she'd checked in on her old friends, if any of them were even still alive? She'd been busy with Devin and then dealing with the impending loss of Sarah, and life had gotten too busy for the sweet people at Sunset Hills.

She parked, and halfway up the walk, she noticed the window Irvel used to look out when she was watching for her forever love, Hank. Irvel had found redemption, no question about it. She had loved God and Hank until her dying day, and now . . . now the

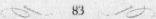

two of them were probably sitting on the bank of some heavenly river, basking in the glow of God's love and light.

Ashley's heart soared at the possibility. She reached the door and knocked quietly since it wasn't quite lunchtime and the residents would probably be napping.

The door opened, and a pretty African-American woman smiled at her. "Can I help you?"

She doesn't know me, Ashley thought. She returned the smile. "I'm Ashley Baxter Blake. I used to work here."

Immediately recognition flashed in the woman's eyes. "Oh yes, I know who you are. I'm Myrna." She held open the door and gestured for Ashley to come in. "Everyone's asleep."

"I figured." When Ashley was inside, she shook the woman's hand. "Nice to meet you. I was driving past and I had to stop. Just to check on the old place."

"Things are good." Myrna's expression held admiration. "The Past-Present theory is still being used. The results always impress the doctors."

The news brought a lump to Ashley's throat. How wonderful that the owners of Sunset Hills were intent on continuing the work Ashley had researched and started here, the idea that a person with Alzheimer's responded best if allowed to live in the place of their past where they were most comfortable. Dear Irvel, whose husband, Hank, had been dead for years, had been happiest believing that Hank was merely out fishing with the boys.

Myrna pointed across the room, where two people were asleep in the reclining chairs. "There's Bert. Remember him?"

"Of course!" Ashley kept her voice low. She took a few steps toward the sleeping patients. "What's he doing out here? He . . . he never left his room except at the very end before I left and then only for meals."

Myrna allowed a quiet laugh. "He's Mr. Social now. Comes out at breakfast full of stories about his horses, and then he and Helen watch *The Price Is Right*."

Ashley was overcome with joy. The legacy of what God had given her to do here lived on in the lives of people who otherwise might be anxious and distraught. She glanced toward the hallway. "Can I have a look at the rooms?"

"Sure." Myrna waved her off. "I'll be in the kitchen. I've got some baking to do."

Ashley looked back at Bert and Helen. God's faithfulness was evident here too. No wonder she'd felt the need to stop by this afternoon. She tiptoed out of the room and quietly walked down the hallway. The room where Irvel had slept held a new patient, of course. Someone Ashley hadn't seen before.

Beyond it was Bert's room. Ashley stopped in the doorway and there it was, the old saddle Ashley had bought him. It was still standing at the foot of his bed, and on top of it was a worn polishing rag. Clearly Bert was still shining his saddle, continuing to find purpose in doing the one thing that had defined him as a younger man. Ashley smiled even as tears blurred her vision. She blinked them back and peered into Helen's room. The framed photo of her daughter, Sue, as a teenager still stood on the nightstand near her bed.

Ashley felt her heart brimming with joy. God had mended her heart in her time here at Sunset Hills Adult Care Home, and He'd done something else. He'd taught her how to love again. The fact that her touch on the place remained was yet another gift from God.

She headed to the kitchen, and there in the dining room was the painting she'd done of Irvel, the one of the old woman sipping peppermint tea at this very table.

Ashley thanked Myrna and promised to stop back in sometime with her family. Then she left and this time drove without stopping. Along the way she passed a car being driven by Bailey Flanigan, and as the two waved at each other, Ashley noticed that Tim Reed was in her passenger seat.

Happiness hit her as she turned the opposite direction toward her father's house. *Joseph* had been cast and was well into production. Katy and Dayne had never looked happier. Bailey was the lead narrator for the musical, and her brother Connor was Joseph. The Flanigan kids' experience with CKT shone in every rehearsal so far. Already the creative team could tell the show was going to be something special. And not just the show but the friendships that were coming from it.

Tim was helping with the choreography, and though he was careful to keep his distance from Bailey during rehearsals, where he was in a leadership role, Ashley had a sense that the two were seeing each other away from CKT. Ashley smiled to herself. Tim was good for Bailey, the way Landon had been good for her. But Bailey was smarter than Ashley had been at that age. She would recognize the benefits of a guy like Tim and in the process spare herself the heartache Ashley had lived through.

She turned onto her dad's street, and as she pulled into the driveway she stopped, studying the old place. The Baxter house. From this vantage point, she wanted to savor the slant of the roof and the expanse of the covered porch, the windows and the way she knew exactly what lay on the other side of each of them. But only one thing captured and held her attention—the bold For Sale sign. Ashley felt her chest tighten. Her father had told them he was getting interest from people. One couple was close to making an offer.

Maybe this was the reason she was feeling so emotional, so caught between yesterday's redemption and tomorrow's uncertainty. When the house was gone, nothing would be the same. Without the expanse of grassy field and the stream out back, without the familiar walls and windows, memories of every chapter of life would fade. Ashley willed herself to look past the For Sale sign to the stand of maple trees along the front side of the driveway, trees that had seen the Baxter kids go from making free throws to making families of their own.

Slowly she removed her foot from the gas pedal and eased up

the driveway to her familiar parking spot. Once inside the house, she heard her father tinkering in the kitchen. She set her purse down. "Hi . . . it's me."

"Ash! Hi." Her dad's voice held a warmth that was his alone. "Did you come to paint?"

"I did." She walked into the kitchen. Her dad was tightening a screw on the hinge of the refrigerator door. "Must be home project Saturday again." A light bit of laughter tickled her throat. "Landon and the boys are making repairs on the tree house."

"The door kept popping open on its own." He had a screwdriver in his back pants pocket. "I've just about got it figured out." He glanced out the window to the backyard. "Next it's the garden. The weeds are coming to life a lot faster than the zucchini."

Ashley watched him. He could easily be mistaken for a decade younger than his actual age, in his sixties. She leaned against the corner of the wall. "Tell me about the house."

Her dad looked up, and in his eyes the answer was painfully clear. "The couple was back for a third time this morning. They're talking to their lender on Monday."

Ashley's knees trembled at the news. In that case, an offer could be in her father's hands by Monday. The sale was getting close.

Her dad must've known the information was hard for her because he held out his arms. "Come here."

She went to him, the way she had done so many times before. In his embrace she would always be that little girl who couldn't get enough time playing outside with Luke and that teenage girl no one ever seemed to understand. No one but her daddy. And she would always be the grown woman who had made peace with her past and with her mother, weeping at the graveside service after her mom's death. Safe and secure and convinced that the world would go on—that's how she felt then and now.

"I know . . . We'll get through it." She eased back and her eyes met his. "But this house belongs with us. I just wish there was some way . . ."

"Me too, honey." He kissed her forehead. "Me too." He moved back to the fridge and returned to work on the hinge.

Ashley poured herself a drink of water and headed toward the stairs. "I'll find you outside when I'm finished."

"Okay." He looked up again, and there was fresh concern in his eyes. "How are you really? You look tired."

"I'm okay." She lifted the corners of her lips. Her father had enough on his mind without worrying about her. "Praying for the baby, and I don't know . . . sort of nostalgic, I guess. Probably just the house." She felt her smile become more sincere. "I'll be fine."

She took the stairs slowly, aware that her father was right. She was more tired than usual; with her previous pregnancies by now she was usually feeling lots of energy. *It's not a sign,* she told herself. *Everything is fine. It has to be.* As she walked into her old bedroom, the sense of sadness lifted. Her easel was up and on it, a new canvas, clean and vast and screaming with possibility.

The air was stuffy, so she crossed to the window, unlatched the lock, and slid it open. A sweet-smelling breeze filled the room, and Ashley felt herself relax. Yes, everything was going to be fine. She sat on the stool in front of the canvas. A part of her wanted to take her paints and easel out front and capture the house one last time before it belonged to someone else.

But that wasn't the image in her mind, the one she'd talked to Landon about earlier. She took one of the sharp pencils from a jar on the table beside her easel and touched it to the canvas. She moved her pencil in smooth, fast strokes, allowing the image to come to life in a preliminary form. This was sometimes the most difficult part of creating a painting, making sure the rough sketch matched the picture in her head.

Minutes became half an hour, and finally Ashley set the pencil down, stood, and stepped back. What she saw filled her heart with joy, because this was one of those rare times when the markings on the canvas were exactly what she'd been seeing in her mind. Two women—one older, one younger—walking together at sunset on a path near a stream. And in the arms of the older woman a newborn baby, bundled in blankets. The faces of both women turned down, marveling at the child in the midst of a setting that showed God's creation bursting with life all around them.

Sometimes the image in Ashley's head was one only God could've given her, and that was the case with this painting. Ashley arranged her paints and imagined the mix of colors, the vibrant streaks of yellow and green and blue in the stream and the pinks and oranges in the sunset overhead. The painting would have the only title that could possibly have fit, the title that summed up the Baxters like no other word ever could.

Redemption.

CHAPTER TEN

JOHN SETTLED INTO THE BOOTH and glanced at the front door just as Elaine walked in. Another thunderstorm was sweeping through Bloomington, and Elaine closed her umbrella before scanning the restaurant and spotting him. A smile spread across her face.

They'd been having lunch every Friday afternoon for the past few weeks, using the time to talk about the coming wedding. They both looked forward to the time as a special break from the week, a chance to let their excitement build about a future that included creating a home together.

John watched her walk to the table, and he stood, kissing her lightly on the lips and taking her raincoat. "Pretty stormy out there."

"The radio said there's a tornado warning a few counties over." She was breathless as she sat down across from him.

It was always this way at springtime, and John didn't mind. Back when he and Elizabeth were raising their children, they would sometimes pile into the car and drive to the lake, where they could get a better view of the thunderstorms that rolled across this part of the country each spring. He kept that detail to himself. "So, how are you?"

"Good. I had a nice visit with my kids." Elaine wore a pretty lavender blouse, and her eyes shone. She was retired, so every few weeks she took a few days and visited her children and grandchildren. "The kids are growing up so fast."

"They do that." John had spent time with Elaine's kids and grandkids over dinners at her house, and he was grateful for their overwhelming acceptance of his pending marriage to Elaine. Though her daughter lived in northern Michigan and her son in Indianapolis, John could picture times when all of their combined children and grandchildren might get together for a picnic or a dinner. "I told you about the house, right?"

"The couple backed out. That's the last you told me."

"They couldn't swing the loan." At the time, John had been relieved. He needed to sell the house, but another few weeks without a sale was okay with him. "There's a new couple now. They're older, looking for a place where their grandkids can visit."

Elaine rested her forearms on the edge of the table and searched his eyes. "Is that hard?"

He smiled at her, feeling the ache that would always be there at the thought of letting go of his house. "I won't lie to you. It's hard. Someone else sitting on the front porch. Someone else's little grandson hunting frogs near the pond . . . It's definitely hard."

The waitress approached them and dropped off two ice waters and a promise to return shortly.

When she was gone, Elaine's expression became more intent. "I'm not asking you to sell the house. You know that."

"Of course." John let the hurt from earlier pass. After all, Elaine had just sold her house a week ago. He took a drink of water and kept his eyes on her. "I couldn't do that to either of us, have us start out a life together surrounded by memories of my past."

"It would take a while, but we'd get used to it." Elaine reached for his hands. "We'd make new memories."

For a moment, John actually considered the possibility. After all, Elaine had loved Elizabeth too. Their new marriage might not be hurt by the history in the old house, the fact that those were the rooms where John and Elizabeth had raised their children and welcomed grandchildren.

But just as quickly the idea fell flat. He could see himself having coffee with Elaine at the kitchen table in the Baxter house. But loving her? Being a husband to her? No, he could never make a new life with Elaine in the place where he had loved Elizabeth. The idea was crazy.

He gave her a sad smile and squeezed her hands. "You don't know how much that means to me, that you'd consider living there."

"I'm serious. No matter what you've told yourself or anyone else . . . that house is a lot more than walls and windows." She released his hands and took hold of the menu. Her smile was sincere. "My house had only belonged to me since I became a widow. It doesn't hold nearly the importance as yours. I saw that from the beginning."

"We need a new place." John was finished considering the idea. "But thank you." He picked up his menu, and after they had both ordered, he pulled a checklist from his coat pocket. "I made a few phone calls this week. The church is open for June 21, like we hoped."

Elaine looked relieved. "I'm so glad. We couldn't miss the big Fourth of July picnic at the lake."

Originally they'd chosen the following Saturday for their wedding, but with a weeklong honeymoon, they wouldn't be back in Bloomington until after the Fourth. Even though Erin and Sam's move back to the area had been postponed to the end of June, it still meant the entire Baxter family would be together for the big Fourth of July picnic at Lake Monroe for the first time in years. When they realized that, they switched the wedding to the twenty-first, and now he had the church confirmed for the date.

"Pastor Mark?"

"He's available." John put a check mark next to the pastor's name on the list of items he'd taken care of that week. Mark Atteberry had been there through so many family events, including the celebration of Elizabeth's life and her homegoing to heaven. Now he had agreed to officiate the wedding between John and Elaine.

"The reception? Did you talk to Katy and Dayne?" Elaine's body language told him she was relaxed and comfortable talking about the wedding plans. They weren't a first-time couple worrying about every detail. The ceremony and the reception would be simple. The conversation between them felt more like two people talking about a dinner party than a wedding.

"To quote Dayne, they'd be honored if we'd have it at their house. Katy said she'd have a casual dinner, and we shouldn't give it another thought." He felt the familiar gratitude in the fact that he had not only connected with his firstborn son but they were now neighbors and friends as well.

"Sounds beautiful." Elaine allowed the excitement to show on her face. "I can't wait."

"And I think I've worked out the specifics on the honeymoon." John tapped his pencil against the pad of paper and took a drink of water. "We talked about a road trip, bed-and-breakfasts from here to upper Michigan."

"Yes." A softness appeared in Elaine's eyes. "That'd be wonderful."

"I've got a pretty good route mapped out." John explained how they would travel from Indiana to Ohio, where on their third night they would stay at a beautiful bed-and-breakfast rife with Civil War memorabilia. "Jennie Wade was the only civilian killed in the Battle of Gettysburg, shot accidentally in her sister's kitchen while baking bread for the troops." He checked his notes. "The love of her life died nine days later. It was a tragic story." The owners of the bed-and-breakfast had allowed their home to be a tribute to Jennie Wade and to the love she'd held for her young soldier. "It seemed too special to pass up. What do you think?"

"I like it. Bed-and-breakfasts have so much more personality than a hotel." Elaine linked her fingers around her glass of water. A clap of thunder shook the restaurant, and the lights flickered. She looked out the window for a moment, then back at John. "We're spending a night on Mackinac Island too . . . before we come back?"

"Yes." He made another check mark on the pad of paper. "Got that all taken care of."

"We're stopping to see my kids on the way home, and then back to Bloomington for the Fourth. I can't imagine a nicer honeymoon, John."

He felt the same way. They made a plan to look at houses this weekend, and the rest of their lunch passed quickly.

After sharing coffee, they went their separate ways, and John reported to the hospital to make his rounds. He was working only three days a week, allowing the younger doctors to take on more of the load. But he still had patients in the hospital, and Friday afternoons were a regular time for him.

The nurses and several other doctors greeted him as he walked into the intensive care unit on the third floor. Two of his patients had undergone bypass surgery and were recovering in the cardiac ward of the ICU. They were getting around-the-clock care from their cardiologists and the ICU staff, but John liked to check in on them too. On his way down the hall, he scanned the patient dry erase board that listed the names of those currently filling the various rooms. One of the names—Angela Manning—caught his attention and stopped him cold.

He read the name again and tried to remember where he'd heard it before. Then like a slap in the face the answer hit him. Angela Manning was the name of the college girl behind the affair that led to the murder of his daughter Kari's first husband. The events replayed in his mind, the details just as sad and sorry today as they'd been seven years ago. Tim had been a professor at Indiana University, having an affair with Angela Manning, one of his students. Only at the same time, Angela was being stalked by a crazy student on campus, a guy addicted to drugs and steroids, paranoid and suffering from mental illness. He was the first one to tell Kari that her husband had been cheating.

Then like some sort of wild soap opera, three weeks after Tim announced he was moving out, Kari discovered she was pregnant. Even though Tim had cheated on her, she wanted him to leave Angela and give their marriage another chance. Some of her sisters recommended that she divorce Tim, but Kari stuck to her promise to God and to Tim. She wouldn't leave him no matter what.

Eventually her prayers and diligence paid off. Tim returned to her, repentant, intent on going back to church and living his life right, being a husband to Kari and a father to their unborn baby. But the stalker college kid had other plans. On a fateful night in the months before Kari gave birth, Tim stopped by Angela's apartment to tell her that things were finished between them. The college kid was waiting outside. He aimed his gun at Tim and fired. The bullets hit Tim squarely in his chest, and he bled to death there on the sidewalk.

The jury didn't buy the insanity defense, so the kid was sentenced to life without possibility of parole. Turned out the guy was very clear-minded once he was off the massive steroids he'd been taking. Meanwhile Kari gave birth to Jessie, and Ryan—Kari's high school sweetheart—became the friend Kari needed as a single mother grieving the loss of her husband. Eventually their friendship led to the beautiful marriage Kari and Ryan shared today.

But John never knew what happened to Angela Manning.

One of the doctors from his practice was walking up. John stopped him and pointed to Angela's name. "What's she in for?"

"It's a sad story." The man shook his head. "Suicide attempt. She's one of mine."

Suicide? John felt the adrenaline release through his veins, felt his heart rate pick up. "Really?"

"Last night she took a bottle of sleeping pills and tried to end it."

"Hmm . . . sad." John's mind raced. "Is she . . . is she in a coma?"

"Not anymore. She's groggy, but she'll be okay."

John looked toward the young woman's room. "I think I'll check on her, if you don't mind."

"Go ahead." The man glanced at his notes. "Tell her I'll be in a little later."

As his colleague moved down the hall, John paused at the doorway of Angela's room. *Dear God, I know You too well to think this is a coincidence. Let me see her the way You see her.*

I am with you, my son.

Reassured that he wasn't operating in his own strength, John walked in and crossed the room to the side of her bed. Angela was sleeping, but even with her eyes closed, her appearance looked haggard. Her hair was pulled into a ponytail, and dark circles pressed deep into the gray skin beneath her eyes. As John studied her, a handful of conflicting emotions hit him from either side. At one time she had been a beautiful woman. John had seen her picture in the news and on TV after the murder. But here . . . she looked like she'd aged twenty years. And no wonder, with the guilt she must've been living with. He was still trying to believe this was really her.

Here was the woman who dared sleep with a married man, the woman who cared nothing for Kari or the life Tim had back at home. But for the woman lying in the bed before him, Tim would probably still be alive, still married to Kari. John swallowed, trying to keep his anger at bay and get a grip on his feelings. Then, almost as if God was leading his thoughts, he suddenly saw her not as an adultress but as a broken child. She couldn't have grown up dreaming she would be the paramour of a married professor when she was older. And whatever demons she'd battled in the years since that time, they'd led her here, to an attempt on her own life.

Angela moaned slightly and turned her head from side to side. As she did, her eyes opened, and she squinted at him. It took nearly a minute before she seemed truly aware of her surroundings and the fact that a doctor was standing beside her. "You're . . . you're not my doctor." Her voice was flat, utterly void of emotion.

"I work with him. He wanted you to know he'd be in a little later." An overwhelming sympathy came over John. He felt his expression soften. "How are you?"

"My head hurts." She was still squinting, still acting a little bewildered. "I tried to kill myself. . . . I couldn't even do that right."

John wondered again at the odds of him walking by at just the right time, stumbling across her after all the years that had passed. "I firmly believe there's a reason why you didn't die." The compassion in his heart grew. She was someone's daughter, a woman who had believed a lie from the devil and so had paid with her life in a number of ways, and now, by nearly dying from an overdose. John put his hand on the bedrail. "I'm going to recommend inpatient psychiatric care for you, admission to a Christian facility downtown."

The lines around her eyes relaxed a little. "Are you a Christian?" Disdain sounded in her tone and filled her expression. "Seems like there's a Christian around every corner these days."

John felt a surge of anger, but he resisted it. The young woman should be dead. She had no room for mocking the kindness of a stranger. Still, she wouldn't be here if she weren't being deceived. He exhaled, steadying himself. "Yes, I'm a Christian." A strange and outrageous idea hit him. "Listen . . . once you're established at an inpatient facility, we have a group of women at church who make visits to people who are struggling. Would you be open to that?"

A laugh devoid of any humor slid between her lips. "Look, Doctor, you don't know me. My family's from Boston, but I left for a degree at the university. Found my way into a personal nightmare, a pile of debt, and what turned out to be a worthless job. Never figured a way back to Boston." Her eyes closed for several seconds, and when she opened them, her look was harder than before. "If you can find someone in Bloomington who wants to talk to me, more power to you." Her eyelids fluttered and she yawned. "What'd you say your name was?"

John hesitated. Would she know his name? Did she have any details about the wife of the man she'd had the affair with? If she knew John's identity, she might shut down and order him out of her room. Either way he had to be honest. He opened his mouth to answer her question, but her eyes were closed. "Angela?"

A soft snoring sound came from her.

John realized he was holding his breath. He exhaled, turned, and left the room. Once he was outside, he thought about what he'd dared to ask her. Whether she would want a visit from one of the women's ministry volunteers. The thing that made the idea outrageous was that he wasn't thinking of any random volunteer.

He was thinking of his daughter Kari.

CHAPTER ELEVEN

THE HOUSE WAS ALIVE with the sounds of *Joseph and the Amazing Technicolor Dreamcoat,* and Jenny Flanigan loved every moment. In the next room Connor was singing "Close Every Door," one of his Joseph solos, and Bailey was adding the backup vocals. Jenny stirred the pitcher of iced green tea, poured herself a glass, and was walking toward the kids as Jim burst through the back door with Ricky in tow, the two of them laughing. They'd been practicing baseball, and their cheeks were red.

The volume from the next room rose, and Jim made an exaggerated show of putting his hands over his ears.

Jenny made a face at him and jabbed him lightly with her elbow. "Don't you hear it?"

"Are you kidding?" He produced a mock look of pain. "People half a mile away can hear it."

"Not the volume." She rolled her eyes. "The music, our kids' voices filling the house." She closed her eyes and swayed to the sound. "It's the soundtrack of our lives."

"It's a loud one." He chuckled. "I'll give you that."

Jenny giggled and pulled on his sleeve. "Come listen to them. They sound really good."

"Yeah." Ricky grinned at him. "They do sound pretty good."

The three of them went to the next room just as Connor's song was coming to a close. His voice had matured in recent years to a rich tenor, with a powerful sense of vibrato that complemented the song.

Jenny leaned in close to Jim. "I don't care how well the kid can throw a football. He can definitely sing."

The teasing from a moment ago faded from Jim's expression. "They both can." He slid his arm around Jenny's waist. "I'm impressed."

Ricky lost interest as Connor and Bailey began working on another number. He ran upstairs with a promise to return with his baseball cards. "I think I have one worth a hundred dollars!"

Jim gave him a thumbs-up, and then he nodded at his oldest two kids. "Wow . . ." There was appreciation in his voice. "The play's going to be great."

"Thanks." Bailey blushed slightly. "We're excited about it."

"Yeah, thanks." Connor stuck his hands in his pockets. "We have a lot of scenes to block still." He blew at a wisp of his dark hair.

"You'll get it." Jenny put her hand on her son's shoulder. This was his first leading role, and he was taking the responsibility seriously.

Ricky raced down with the baseball card. "See! Here it is!" He thrust it at Jim. "Whadya think? It's a collector's item."

Jim studied the card. "Could be. Keep it in a safe spot. We'll check the Internet after dinner." He looked out the window. "Today's too nice to be inside."

"Unless you're rehearsing." Bailey grinned at him, then nudged Connor. "Which we still have to do."

"Hey, Dad, let's go throw a tennis ball to Reggie. He loves that."

Jim grinned. "How about me and your mom watch?"

Ricky thought for a second and then shrugged. "Sure!" His eyes danced the way they often did. He was so full of life and light, and out of all their kids he was the one most upset whenever anyone in the family was in trouble or needed discipline. "I like it when everyone's happy," he would say.

This was that kind of day, and Jenny basked in it.

Connor was finding the next song on their rehearsal CD as Jim reached for Jenny's hand and led her toward the front door. "Another episode of the Ricky and Reggie show."

Jenny laughed, loving Jim beside her, the way he made her feel protected and precious at the same time. He was a couple weeks into the initial coaches' meetings with the Colts and thrilled with the challenge. Just this morning, Ryan Taylor had announced Jim's resignation to the team, and one of the junior varsity assistants was being promoted to take his spot.

With his busier schedule, Jim had been conscientious about finding time to talk with Jenny, something both of them needed. They walked to the double recliner on the front porch and sat down, still holding hands.

Jim sighed. "I love this view. Have I ever said that?"

"Every time we're out here." Jenny snuggled close to him. Sunshine warmed their faces, and the hint of jasmine from a row of plants at the base of the porch wafted up and around them.

Ricky ran into view, using his T-shirt to carry six or seven tennis balls. "This'll give him some exercise. Here, Reggie! Here, boy!"

Their old Lab came barreling up, stopping short of Ricky and dancing in place, anxious for the first ball.

Inside the house, the kids were singing again and Jim knit his brow, curious. "They sound wonderful. When did that happen, anyway? I mean, just the other day they could sing and dance like the other kids, but they didn't stand out."

"I know." Pride warmed Jenny's insides. "I have a feeling God's going to use those kids in a very visible way." She rested her head on his shoulder. "So . . . tell me about the meeting."

"It was good." She felt him tense a little. "I wasn't looking forward to it." He was quiet for a moment. "Those kids mean a lot to me."

Jenny waited, the way she'd learned to do years ago when she and Jim were dating. He would share his heart and soul with her anytime, but she had to listen. Otherwise she could dominate the conversation and walk away knowing nothing new about the man she loved.

"Taylor said something that made me feel good. The guys are still committed to stay away from drinking."

"Really?" Jenny had wondered how the team was handling the no-alcohol mandate. It was one thing to hand a list of rules to a bunch of teenagers. But after Cody's near-death incident with alcohol poisoning, Jim and Ryan had given the team an ultimatum: stay away from alcohol or be kicked off the team. Period. At the time Jim had wondered if he was reaching the kids or just preaching at them. Jenny was grateful that the players had responded. "Ryan has to be happy about that."

"He is." Jim shrugged. "The guys are okay with me leaving. They have Ryan, and they're used to working with him. The transition should be easy for everyone."

"Everyone except you." Jenny turned so she could see his expression. "You'll miss those guys."

"I will." Jim's face was relaxed and unlined. He was the picture of peaceful confidence. "The pro players aren't much different from the high school guys. Bigger and more talented. More at stake. But they still have to work hard, still have to stay away from partying."

Jenny hadn't thought of it that way. "You made the right choice." She slipped her arm around his broad shoulders. "That much is already obvious."

"For now." His grin was easy. "In pro football your job is only as good as your win-loss record. But as long as God lets me stay, I couldn't agree more. It's where I'm supposed to be." He winked at her. "Besides, I think Ryan might consider having me back if I'm ever out of work."

Fifty yards down the gentle slope of the front yard, Ricky flung one tennis ball, then another and another. "Go, Reggie! Get the balls!"

Jim shaded his eyes, watching their youngest son. "I keep thinking how great it'll be for the younger boys, getting to hang out at the Colts training facility this summer. Falling in love with the game."

A twinge of concern shot through Jenny's veins. "Seeing up close how violent the game can be." She gave him a wary look. Ricky had been born with a heart defect and had undergone emergency surgery as a three-week-old. He was fine now, but he still needed checkups every other year. She exhaled slowly. "It'll always be hard for me to watch Ricky in a football uniform."

"Which is why—" he kissed the top of her head—"we hold on loosely. Life is meant to be lived. God would never want a kid as active as Ricky to stand on the sidelines."

"You're right." Jenny knew the appropriate answers when it came to worrying about her kids—whether it was her anxiety over watching Bailey drive off for rehearsal in a downpour with Connor belted into the passenger seat or watching the boys run full force into an opposing player during a soccer match. Her concern for the safety of their children was something she had to take to God often. She could only imagine being the mother of a soldier serving in Iraq, the way Cody's mother was. Cami Coleman had served time for drug charges, but she was out now. From everything Jenny had heard, she was staying clean. Finally committed to being a good mother for her grown son.

Jenny patted Jim's knee. "That reminds me. I talked to Cody's mom yesterday. She hasn't heard from him in more than a week."

"It's a war." Jim didn't sound overly concerned. "It's probably hard to find time for writing letters more often than that."

"True." Jenny crossed her arms, remembering the conversation. "She said something that seemed a little strange. Apparently Cody is considering moving to the West Coast when he returns to the U.S."

Jim nodded slowly. "Cody talked to me about that once a long time ago. Before he lived with us. I guess he always wanted to live in Southern California. Close to the beach."

"Hmm." Jenny didn't want to voice her thoughts, but she didn't need to.

Jim shot her an understanding look. "Him and Bailey?"

"Well . . ." Jenny squirmed a little. "Him and all of us. He's like family, so I guess . . . I figured he'd come back here when he was done. I know that's the impression Bailey had." She hesitated. "I haven't told her yet."

"Cody's still a kid." Jim brushed his fingertips against her cheek. "I've never been convinced he was right for Bailey for a lot of reasons."

"Me neither." Jenny could hear the uncertainty in her voice. "Until last summer . . . before he left for training. There was something special between them."

Jim leaned forward and planted his elbows on his thighs. "She's only eighteen. There's lots of time for love in the years ahead."

Jenny smiled. Bailey was their only daughter, the little girl who'd had her daddy wrapped around her finger since the day she took hold of his thumb in the hospital nursery. He was never comfortable talking about Bailey and the various boys who had shown her interest at one time or another. "You know how we've always told Bailey she's one in a million?"

"Because she is." He put his arm around her shoulders. "That girl might have a messy room and run late once in a while, but she's everything we prayed she'd be."

"She is." Jenny felt the familiar fondness for their daughter. "I guess that's why I like Cody. Even as a friend for Bailey. He has a look in his eyes when he's around her, like he adores her. Cherishes her, even." She met her husband's eyes. "Almost as if he's the only friend she has who truly sees her as one in a million."

Jim thought about that for a few seconds, but before he could respond, they heard the phone ringing inside the house.

Jenny sprang up. "I'll get it. The boys' soccer tryouts are probably over." Just inside the front door she slipped into her office and grabbed the cordless receiver from the phone on the desk. "Hello?"

"Jenny?" The voice on the other end sounded too distraught to recognize, muffled and thick, as if the person had been crying.

In as much time as it took to breathe in, Jenny imagined a dozen horrific possibilities, reasons why someone might be calling the house sounding so broken. One of the boys had been severely injured at soccer or something had happened to one of the CKT kids or . . .

"This is Jenny." She steadied herself against the edge of the desk. "Who's this?"

"Cami Coleman."

Cody's mother. Jenny clutched the phone to her ear and bent over her knees. *Please, God, not Cody. Don't let anything be wrong with Cody . . . please.* Her heart slammed in her chest, and she worked to find even a whispered voice. "What . . . what is it?"

"I just got word; I had to call." Cami was sobbing now, her words hard to understand.

Jenny held her breath and shook her head. It wasn't possible. The charming kid who had hung out at their house since he was a freshman in high school had to be okay. War was dangerous, but Cody was resourceful, right? "Please talk to me." The panic in her voice was matched only by the pain on the other end of the line. "Is he hurt?"

"I'm not sure."

They were the best words Jenny had heard since she answered the phone. Hope coursed through her, but her heart still pounded. "What did they tell you?"

The sound of two quick sobs came across the line. "He . . . he and three of the guys from his platoon are . . . missing in action." Another few sobs and then a stifled wailing sound. "I don't know what to do."

Missing in action? Jenny paced to the far end of the office. She stared out the window to where Ricky was still throwing the ball to Reggie. Her mind raced, trying to make sense of this new and terrible detail. "Did they say anything else?"

"Hardly anything." Cami's sobs were quieter now, but she sounded like she was shaking, giving way to a fear that must've known no limits. "Cody and the guys were checking on a deserted building, and they were . . . they were ambushed. At least that's what they think. Someone reported seeing two Iraqi off-road vehicles speed down a back alley a few minutes after the guys went in."

Jenny struggled to draw a complete breath. "And then?"

"That's all." The cry returned to Cami's voice. "They haven't heard from them in three days."

Jim walked through the front door and saw Jenny standing at the far corner of the office. He hurried to her side. "What happened?" he mouthed.

She covered the receiver. "Cody . . . he's missing. . . ."

"Jenny, I don't know what to do." Cami's fear verged on panic.

A million possibilities raced through Jenny's mind. "Pray." She shielded her eyes and leaned her forehead against Jim's chest. "God knows where Cody is. They'll find him. We have to believe that."

Before Jenny hung up the phone, she prayed with Cami and reiterated that Cody's superiors were probably looking for the missing men even at this very moment. "We're here if you need us. Any hour—I mean it."

The call ended, and Jenny set the receiver back on the base. Then she turned to Jim, and for a few seconds they stared at each other. She could see in his expression a reflection of her own. Jim took her hands in his, never breaking eye contact.

Jenny told him what she knew, but before she was finished, Bailey and Connor appeared at the office door. Bailey's face was pale, her mouth open just enough that Jenny had no doubt her daughter had heard at least some of the conversation. Suddenly the scene was like a flashback to when they found Cody in their guest room, unconscious from alcohol poisoning.

Back then they hadn't known if he would live or die, but they were determined to do what they could to help him. This time that wasn't possible. Cody wasn't within reach, where they could find him and take him for help.

He was lost in a raging war halfway around the world.

※

Bailey had heard her mother answer the phone, and she turned down the music, just in case the call was for her. When she heard it was Cody's mother, she moved to the edge of the room and listened more carefully. That's when her mom asked about whether Cody was hurt.

All along she'd known Cody was in danger, driving through the streets of Iraq and constantly dodging death traps or roadside bombs. She heard the concern in the lines of his letters and e-mails, and she was more aware when news reports talked about casualties of the war. But as the phone conversation continued, Bailey realized a truth she'd been denying since the day Cody left.

He really might never come back.

Her mind went numb, and her legs felt weak and wobbly.

Connor had obviously heard too because he came to her and whispered, "Cody's mother?"

Bailey nodded and put a finger to her lips.

By the time the call ended and Bailey and Connor walked into the office, she understood most of what had happened. Cody was missing; the rest was just details. She went to her parents, and the three of them hugged for a long time. "They'll look for him, right? I mean, they have to find him." She peered up at her dad. "Isn't that what happens?"

Bailey had seen her dad look truly scared only a few times— when their family learned that Ricky had to have heart surgery and when Cody was knocked out on the floor after drinking. But no question her dad was afraid now. He swallowed and looked at

Bailey's mother, then back at her. "When a soldier is missing . . .
he isn't always found."

"They call them MIA." Her mom's voice was shaky. "It means
missing in action."

Connor stood a few feet away. "Should we . . . can we call someone? the governor or something?"

Bailey glanced at her parents, but their faces told her they
couldn't call an official or write the president for that matter.

Connor leaned against the wall and hung his head.

Guilt surrounded Bailey like a winter fog. She'd been hanging
out with Tim lately, and she'd even mentioned it in one of her last
letters to Cody. She cared for Cody, of course. But her feelings for
Tim had grown stronger, and she wanted to be honest about that.
What would Cody care, anyway? He didn't have those sort of feelings for her, right? He was the one who'd always told her to date
someone like Tim, someone she would have more in common
with. But she still felt confused once in a while. After all, not a day
went by when she didn't think of Cody.

Bailey bit her lip. "Did . . . did she say anything else?" She moved
away from her parents and folded her arms. "Did his last letter say
anything new?"

Another layer of sadness colored her mom's eyes. "Just that he's
thinking of moving to the West Coast when he gets back."

"What?" Bailey felt her heart react to the news. Cody hadn't
mentioned living in California since he was in high school. "Why
there?" She tried not to let her feelings for him creep into her voice.
"Why not here?"

"I don't know." Her mom's voice filled with tears. "First . . . they
have to find him."

"Come on, guys." Her dad held out his arms. "Let's pray for him."

The four of them looped their arms around each other's shoulders. In the tight circle, the numbness began to wear off, and in its
place Bailey's heart hurt. "I'll start." Her throat felt tight. "Dear God,
You know exactly where Cody is right this second. So please, Lord,

protect him from anything bad. If he's—" Her voice broke. "If he's scared, please give him peace." She could manage only a strained whisper as she finished. "We can't lose him, God. Please."

Connor prayed and then their mom. By the time Dad finished up, Bailey wasn't the only one crying. They held on to each other for a little while; then Bailey hurried out of the office and up the stairs to her room. How could she let herself fall for Tim when Cody was in Iraq fighting for the country, for freedom from terrorists?

Her freedom.

Bailey flung herself on her bed and reached beneath it for the box of letters she kept there. As she opened the most recent one, her tears were so strong she couldn't see the words, so she folded it and placed it back in the box. She buried her face in her pillow and let herself cry. *Please, God. Please let him be okay.*

She heard no response, but then she didn't really expect one. Not right here in the quiet of her room. The answer she wanted wouldn't come until the phone rang with the news that Cody was found unharmed. Maybe they'd let him come home early because of the ordeal. But what if . . . ?

Bailey felt sick, and she rolled onto her side. *I can't lose him.* She remembered how it felt talking to him late into the night last July and walking beside him through the trees behind her family's house. The look in his eyes when he told her good-bye. An image came to her mind: Cody being found and coming home only to leave for the West Coast. Another wave of tears came over her, and she realized that as terrible and selfish as it was, she wasn't crying only because Cody was missing.

She was crying because they'd both moved on. The bond shared back then was gone forever, and there was no way back to last summer.

.Whether Cody was found or not.

CHAPTER TWELVE

EVERY FAMILY DINNER at the Baxter house had a different feel to it these days. A sense of finality. John and the others rarely talked about the fact, but the sense remained anyway. Their days in the old farmhouse where the kids had grown up were numbered.

It was the last Sunday in March, and another tornado watch had passed over earlier today. So far no twisters had touched down, and forecasters were saying the rest of the spring figured to be less volatile. John was glad. There was enough going on in the family without the concern of a tornado hitting town again.

John had cooked up barbecued spareribs, and now he picked the last one off the grill and placed it on the heap with the others. He grabbed both sides of the metal tray, carried it inside, and set it on the kitchen counter.

In the next room the adults were rounding up the children. Tommy and Malin weren't here because Luke was by himself tonight. Apparently Reagan wanted time alone with the kids. The family had tried to talk to Luke, and Kari had made a few phone calls to Reagan, but their marriage was still in deep trouble. What with that and the pregnancies of Katy and Ashley, between the sale of the house and his impending marriage to Elaine, John spent much of his alone time on his knees.

Brooke stepped into the kitchen. "Need a hand?"

"Thanks." John pointed to the cupboard. "Can you get the plates?"

"Sure." She took down a stack of dishes and grabbed a handful of forks. "Did I tell you about Hayley?"

"No." He braced himself. His granddaughter had hit a few speed bumps lately on her long road to recovering from her near drowning a few years ago. Her reading progress had stalled, and the school's learning specialist had diagnosed her as dyslexic. "She's not worse?"

"Not at all." Brooke's eyes danced. "They're trying a new reading technique on her, and in just a week they're seeing progress! Even with her dyslexia."

In a heartbeat, John was back in the hospital with Brooke and Peter after Hayley's accident. No one had expected her to pull through, and if she did, it seemed clear she might spend the rest of her days blind and brain damaged. In what was a low point in his journey of faith, John had asked God to simply take her home. He hadn't prayed for a miracle or asked the Lord for the impossible. Then over time Hayley made a series of unbelievable turns for the better. This was one more.

John hugged Brooke. "That's wonderful, honey."

"I know." Brooke pulled away and reached for a stack of napkins. "I think God has a few more surprises in store for us in the months ahead." She grinned. "I'll keep you posted."

They called for help, and working as a team they moved the dinner and dishes to the dining room table. Elaine poured ice water into the paper cups. "I love that Sunday dinners aren't too formal."

Ryan Junior walked along at her side. "What's *formal*, Grandma?"

Mixed emotions welled in John's heart at RJ's use of the term.

Lately the young kids had taken to calling Elaine by the name that once belonged to Elizabeth, and John was grateful. After all, she was about to be their grandmother, no question. But at this point it still felt bittersweet.

"Huh?" RJ hovered near Elaine's arm. "Tell me what *formal* is."

Maddie stepped between RJ and Elaine and put her hands on her hips. She gave her younger cousin a slightly condescending look. "It means nice china plates and cups and very serious manners." She shared a smile with Elaine. "I like that Sunday dinners aren't formal too." She cut in front of RJ and grinned. "I'm sitting by Elaine."

John and Elaine exchanged a smile, and after everyone was seated, John prayed. As soon as he said, "Amen," four different conversations broke out. Ashley and Katy were sitting by each other, talking about their pregnancies and laughing about Katy's craving for fried mushrooms and plain yogurt.

At the other end of the table Cole was pointing to his spareribs, explaining to Devin and RJ that "Pigs have ribs too, so that's what we're eating tonight. Pigs' ribs."

Elaine covered her mouth to keep from laughing.

"Craziness." John spoke low near her. "Wild, happy craziness."

"It's wonderful." She passed the platter to Peter, who served Maddie and himself, then passed it on.

John was waiting for the salad when Kari caught his attention. She looked more tired than usual, and he wondered if she'd been sick. In a rush he remembered that tonight was when he had planned to pull her aside and tell her about Angela Manning. If she wanted to step in and help, then so be it. If the idea was too much for her, then she could simply know that the woman was struggling deeply, and she could join him in praying for her.

But now . . . John doubted himself. Maybe Kari was better off never hearing about her again, never having to go back even for a few hours to that terrible time in her life.

The dinner played out, the conversations happy and loud around the table. Brooke waited for a break to announce that she had looked in on a very special little baby at the hospital a few days ago.

"Her mother was a struggling college girl. She was going to have an abortion." Brooke looked straight at Ashley. "But she came to Sarah's Door instead."

The look on Ashley's face told everything she was feeling. She closed her eyes for a few seconds, clearly moved. Then she took hold of Landon's arm and pressed her forehead into his bicep. For a few seconds no one laughed or rejoiced or even dared to speak. It was a sacred moment, and everyone at the table seemed to understand. Because of Ashley and Landon's heartache from Sarah's brief life, a baby had been saved. When Ashley looked back at the others, her eyes were damp. But they were also shining with joy.

Cole glanced from his mother to Brooke and back again. "That's because of Sarah, right? Because of that place you put together with Sarah's name on it?"

"Yes!" Ashley laughed, and even though the sound held a hint of sorrow, the others silently rejoiced with her, the looks in their eyes proof that they too were celebrating the newborn who had been spared because of Sarah's brief life.

The night was full, and by the time the adults started getting the kids' coats on and saying their good-byes, John still wasn't sure whether he should tell Kari. He was waffling with the idea when she found him in the entryway, where he was helping Hayley with her pink jacket.

She touched his elbow. "Can I talk to you?"

John's heart skipped a beat as he straightened, puzzled. Sometimes God took the guesswork out of what he was supposed to do next. This seemed like one of those times.

❧

Kari needed reassurance. Ever since hearing about Ashley's pregnancy, she'd been worried sick that her sister's newest baby might also have anencephaly. The thought kept her awake at night, and for the past week she hadn't slept well. She kept remembering little Sarah and the heartbreak of that day. Her fears were so strong that she finally shared them with Ryan but only with him. As if by telling her dad or Brooke or any of the others, she might somehow make the possibility more real. Her fears, combined with the fact that Annie was eight months old and teething, meant Kari was up off and on throughout the night. The combination was leaving her exhausted.

Ryan had prayed with her every day and reminded her that the Bible advised not to be anxious about anything. The reminder sent Kari back to Philippians chapter 4—a section of her Bible she'd worn out back in the days when her first husband left home. Reading about the peace that passed all understanding helped, and next week she planned to start with the Scripture before turning in at night. Even still, yesterday she'd googled the possibilities of a repeat incidence of anencephaly and she'd found conflicting reports, nothing that would help her sleep better.

After Kari shared the results of her Internet search with Ryan, he'd come up with the only idea that made sense. "Talk to your dad. He's probably thinking about it too."

So Kari had determined that she'd find her father alone for a minute or two and ask him his thoughts on whether Ashley was at risk again. Ryan had taken the kids out to the car, and when Kari and her dad were far enough away from the others that no one could hear her, she turned to him. "I didn't want to talk about this, but Ryan said I should."

Her dad looked concerned. "About what?"

"Ashley. Her pregnancy." Kari felt a chill pass over her arms, and she ran her fingers over the goose bumps. "I'm so worried. I looked on the Internet and tried to find the odds of having two babies with anencephaly. But every Web site says something different." She paused, searching his eyes. "So what is it?"

For a beat, her dad looked a little stunned, as if her question truly surprised him. Then he pulled her into his arms. "Honey . . ."

He released her and studied her face. "Is that why you look so tired?"

Kari stared at her feet, and a sigh came from her throat. "Yes." She lifted her eyes. "I'm scared to death for her. Ryan thought you might know the odds."

"I can give you the medical answer." He took hold of her hands. "Research shows the chance of recurrence to be as high as 5 percent."

"One in twenty?" The panic nagging at her a little more every day instantly doubled. "That's higher than I thought, so how in the world is Ashley handling this when—?"

"But with God the odds are a hundred percent." Her dad's tone was kind but firm.

"What?" Kari wanted so badly for this baby to be healthy for Ashley. "That's a terrible thing to say."

"Listen . . . what I'm saying is with God the odds are a hundred percent that this baby will turn out exactly the way He planned." He gave her a sad hint of a smile. "Just like Sarah."

A gradual dawning came over her. Why hadn't she thought of it that way? All her life she'd struggled with worry and often for good reason. A verse she'd memorized as a teenager came to mind. "'Who of you by worrying can add a single hour to his life?'" She smiled at her dad. "Is that what you mean?"

"Exactly." The seriousness stayed in her dad's expression. "Obviously it's a scary situation for all of us. None of us wants Ashley and Landon to go through that again." He gave her one more hug. "Ultimately, though, it's up to the Lord."

Kari felt the truth working its way through her, leveling her nerves and reminding her of a number of verses all underlining her father's wisdom. The goose bumps faded, and she took a deep breath. "I still need you, Dad."

"I'm glad." His eyes grew more concerned. "There's something I need to talk to you about too."

This time Kari resisted her tendency to immediately assume something was wrong. She gave him her full attention. "Yes?"

He hesitated, clearly wrestling with whatever he had to say. "When I was at the hospital the other day, I visited with a young woman who had tried to kill herself."

"How sad." Kari wasn't sure why her dad wanted her to know, but she felt for the woman, so distraught that she didn't feel life was worth living.

Her dad took a step closer. "The woman was Angela Manning."

The name caught her by surprise. Her mind raced, leaving her breathless. "Angela? Tim's Angela?"

"Yes." He took her hands again, lending her his strength. "She looks terrible. Whatever demons she's battling, she's losing." He went on to say that Angela was being sent to the Christian inpatient facility he had recommended, and she was open to having visitors from their church's women's ministry. "Anyone could go talk to her, but I thought I'd tell you in case . . ."

Kari sucked in a breath. A replay of the images of that time in her life was flashing across her heart, making it hard to think clearly. But in that instant she knew exactly what her father had in mind. That maybe the visit should come from her. "Wow." She felt the chill on her arms again. "I don't know." She tried to imagine the possibility. "I . . . I guess I need to talk to God . . . and Ryan."

"I'm not asking you to see her. I just thought you should know."

"Okay." She nodded, still trying to comprehend the news. "I'm glad you told me."

They talked a few more minutes, and then Kari joined Ryan and the kids in the car. She was quiet on the way home, sorting through the various aspects of the idea. Kari had wondered now and then what had happened to Angela Manning and what it would be like if they ran into each other at the market or the library or downtown at one of the boutiques near the university. Over time, Kari convinced herself that Angela must've moved as far as she could possibly get from Bloomington. But now she knew the truth. Angela was still here and struggling so much under the weight of her choices that she no longer wanted to live.

After they got home and the kids were in bed, Kari sat next to Ryan at their kitchen table. He wasn't immediately in favor of the idea. "You'd be welcoming a lot of old pain back into your life." He leaned over and kissed her, brushing his knuckles softly against her cheek. "I like the idea of praying about it."

That night Kari felt no anxiety as she lay down to sleep. Her father had helped set her straight about Ashley's pregnancy and the fate of her baby. Instead her thoughts were consumed with the choice laid out before her. She had asked God for a ministry of helping women, and God had given her just that. Kari had acted as a sounding board and friend, a mentor of sorts, first to her own sister Erin and then to several women from church.

But there was a difference. Each of those women had been discouraged in her marriage and feeling unloved or betrayed. That was definitely not the case with Angela. Whatever God asked of her, Kari was willing to do, and if God could use her to lead Angela to a saving relationship with Christ, then so be it. But if God wanted to use Kari that way, Ryan was right. A meeting with Angela would not come without great pain and sadness. Because Angela wasn't only the woman who had gotten involved with Kari's husband.

She was the woman whose deceitful lifestyle had led to his murder.

CHAPTER THIRTEEN

THE DREAM WAS THE SAME three times in the week leading up to Ashley's ultrasound. She and Landon and the boys would be on a strangely deserted beach under ominous storm clouds, staring out at the sea, when a wave would rise up taller than the rest. Higher and higher and higher the wave would build until it towered over Ashley and her family.

"Run!" Landon would scream.

They scrambled to their feet, Devin in Landon's arms and Cole running alongside them. The wave grew higher and closer, and no matter how fast they ran, the sand kept them from getting farther ahead of the wave. For what seemed like hours they would keep running, staying barely a few feet away from the deadly wall of water, until finally Ashley would sit bolt upright, gasping for air, her eyes wide with terror.

Landon would spend the next half hour calming her down, and somehow she'd fall asleep again. But the image of her family about to be overtaken by certain death, desperately outrunning a tidal wave, remained in her waking hours as well.

Now finally the day had come, and in a few hours they'd have their answer. Either they'd be thrashing about in a sea of heartbreak or they'd find higher ground. Ashley's heart pounded hard, and the first few miles of the trip she kept pressing her fingers to her wrist, checking her racing pulse. But halfway to the doctor's office, Ashley's heartbeat was so wildly fast she stopped checking it. The numbers were only making her more anxious.

She stared out the window and remembered her conversation with Kari earlier this morning. "I've never been more afraid in my life," she'd told her sister.

Kari had reminded her about the verses in Philippians and how the Scripture provided God's people a formula for peace. Now Ashley did the one thing she could do. She silently repeated the words from Philippians.

"You okay?" With his left hand, Landon had a tight grip on the steering wheel.

"Fine." She crossed her arms and rested them on her belly. "Everything'll be fine." She looked out the window and began once again. *"Rejoice in the Lord always. I will say it again: Rejoice! Let your gentleness be evident to all. The Lord is near."* This was not the first time she'd drawn from these verses, so the words came from her soul with little effort. *"Do not be anxious about anything, but in everything, by prayer and petition, with thanksgiving, present your requests to God. And the peace of God, which transcends all understanding, will guard your hearts and your minds in Christ Jesus."*

She stopped there and marveled for a minute. The peace of God truly did transcend all understanding because only by God's peace was she able to take this ride to the doctor's office without weeping every mile of the way. This was the road, the very same path they'd taken the day they first found out the bad news about Sarah. Now here she was taking it again and with no guarantees about what awaited them at the other end.

"You sure?" Landon reached out and took her hand. "You're quiet."

"Reciting Philippians." She smiled at him. "Every time I read about the peace that passes understanding, I feel the truth of it spreading over me like . . ." She looked out at the blue sky. "Like sunshine, I guess."

"Really? You're not nervous?"

Ashley felt her smile fade. "I'm not nervous. I'm scared to death. But God's giving me enough peace that I'm still sitting here, taking this ride." The corners of her mouth lifted a little. "I'm here and I'm breathing, and right now, that's enough."

He brought her hand to his lips and kissed it. "I wish the next hour was behind us."

Ashley angled herself toward him. "It's like this ultrasound is all that stands between us and our baby's future, like if we can get over this mountain, the rest'll be easy."

Her words made him chuckle. "It's never easy."

"I know." She too allowed a rare bit of tender laughter. "With a child, there's always another mountain." She shifted, putting her back against the seat once more. "Makes it hard to let them go to school each morning."

"Absolutely."

They reached the doctor's office, and at the sign-in counter they were greeted with the news that their doctor wasn't in today. One of her kids had the flu, and she'd stayed home. For an instant Ashley considered turning around and coming back when their doctor was in. She'd been with them through the journey of Sarah's diagnosis and her birth. This was no time for someone new.

But Landon nodded at the receptionist, and with a light touch on the small of Ashley's back, the two of them took a seat in the waiting room.

"I don't want a new doctor," she whispered. Panic was shouting at her from the other side, making it hard for her to concentrate on the Scripture.

"Any doctor can do the test." He kept his tone low to match hers.

"'Rejoice in the Lord always,'" she mumbled. "'I will say it again: Rejoice! . . .'"

"What?" Landon looked worried about her.

"Philippians." She glanced at the doorway of the waiting room as a nurse appeared. "Trying to stay sane."

"Ashley?" The nurse smiled in their direction.

Ashley stood and tried to make her legs walk without shaking. She linked her arm through Landon's, and together they followed the nurse.

The entire walk, she felt like she'd fallen into one of her dreams. She could practically feel the mist from the tidal wave closing in on them. *Breathe,* she ordered herself. *Help me to breathe, God.*

Daughter, My grace is sufficient for you.

The voice breezed across the landscape of her heart, giving her just enough strength to make it to the examination room. She sat on the edge of the table, and the nurse gave her the routine about changing into a gown. When they were alone and Ashley had changed clothes, she held Landon's hand but neither of them spoke. The test would do all the talking needed.

Ashley slid her feet beneath the sheet, and after barely any time, the doctor knocked and then entered the room. He was an older gentleman with white hair and kind eyes. Ashley liked him immediately.

After he introduced himself, his expression grew even more compassionate than before. "I know your history." He looked from her to Landon. "Let's get on with the test. Then we can put aside any fears you might have about this baby."

Any fears? How about constant fears? she wanted to say. How wonderful that this doctor understood how she was feeling. But now it was time, and that meant . . . that meant the answer was coming. Ashley felt light-headed, and she gave the doctor a vague smile. "Yes, let's get it done."

Landon stood at her side, but he remained quiet. Ashley looked at him, deep into his heart, and she knew he was praying. Whatever the answer today, they would get through the coming months and years together. They would cling to their faith and their family because God would not abandon them now. No matter what the test revealed.

The doctor wheeled the ultrasound machine and the attached monitor to the other side of Ashley's bed. He lifted her gown just enough so the bump of her stomach showed. He squirted a blob of warm gel onto her stomach. Then he took the machine's probe and used it to spread the gel evenly over her abdomen. Immediately, the sound of the baby's heartbeat filled the room.

Okay, here we go. . . . The familiarity of the routine made Ashley feel sicker than before. She closed her eyes for a moment. *"Do not be anxious about anything, but in everything, by prayer and petition . . ."*

"Let's see if we can get a look here." The doctor's voice was gentle and soothing.

Ashley studied the monitor, not quite sure what they were look-ing at.

"Is that the baby's spine?" Landon took a step closer, his attention locked on the screen.

"Yes, exactly." The doctor sounded happy. Happy was good. He shifted the probe, and what looked like toes came into view. "These are your baby's feet and legs. All very normal and healthy."

Ashley moved her tongue along the dry roof of her mouth. The probe was going in the wrong direction. They weren't worried about the baby's feet and legs but the head. The skull. She held her breath.

"Let's take a look at the other end of the baby's spine."

Ashley ordered herself to exhale. The other end was where the spine met the baby's head, the place where neural tube defects could be seen, the place where a problem would be seen if there was—

"Good news." The doctor's tone never changed. "No neural tube defects for this little one."

Ashley felt the tears. No neural tube defects! No anencephaly, no death sentence for the child growing inside her. She turned her head to the side and let her tears spill onto the pillow.

Landon bent down, kissing her tears and pressing his cheek to hers. "Thank You, God," he breathed against her hair. "Thank You."

The doctor was still moving the probe over Ashley's stomach. "We really don't expect to see something like anencephaly recur. But you have nothing to worry about now." He slid the probe another few inches. "Well . . . look at that. Would you like to know if you're having a boy or a girl?"

Ashley and Landon had been so concerned about the health of their baby that they hadn't even discussed whether they wanted to know. But now Ashley couldn't help but wonder if this baby might be a girl, the daughter she could picture herself raising. She turned to Landon, and they both nodded.

The doctor chuckled quietly. "His legs are not quite together. No question this little one's a boy."

For an instant, a crushing weight of disappointment hit Ashley square in her chest. So that was that. This child would not be the daughter she so wanted. But just as quickly she rejoiced at the news. Another boy! A healthy boy to play with Devin and Cole and to fish with his daddy and play in the tree house. A wonderful, endearing, rambunctious little boy.

She put her hand over her mouth and squeezed her eyes shut as again her heart shifted. Again her emotions waffled. So there would be no little girl to fill the empty places Sarah had left behind. Ashley had been granted a daughter once but not this time. And since she wasn't sure if they'd have another child, the news meant there might never be another girl. No daughter whose hair she might brush, who would share secrets with her on a Friday night after a date with a boy. No girl whose heart would be like her own and no one to buy dresses for when prom time came around. No daughter to plan a wedding for.

"A boy!" Landon kissed Ashley's cheek and wiped her tears with his thumb. "A healthy boy!"

His tone gave him away. She looked into his eyes, and there she saw the same fleeting disappointment. Somehow, though, as they stared at each other, the hint of sorrow vanished for both of them. God had granted them a healthy baby boy. Ashley smiled, and it made her giggle with relief and joy. Everything truly was going to be okay. She was going to be the mother of three marvelous boys.

The doctor completed the test. "Everything looks perfect. He's a long baby. Probably wind up a basketball star." He gave them a final smile as he headed for the door. "I'll have the results written up for your charts, and we'll print off a few photos you can take with you."

"Thank you." Landon straightened. "Today could've gone a lot differently."

"Yes, well, I'm happy for you." He nodded as he reached the door. "Go celebrate the news."

"We will." Landon turned to Ashley as the man left. She pulled her gown back down and sat with her legs over the edge of the table. He took her in his arms and clung to her. "He's healthy, Ash."

Her relief was still working its way through her heart and mind and into her body. No more fears or worry. This baby was healthy, and he would be protected by his older brothers, surrounded by cousins and in the same grade at school as Katy and Dayne's baby.

Suddenly Ashley could hardly wait to get home. Her dad was at their house watching Devin, and by the time they had lunch and returned home, Cole would be back from school. The boys were going to be crazy with excitement about the news.

She and Landon went to an Italian restaurant near the university, and the happiness from earlier magnified so completely in Ashley's soul that she couldn't quit smiling. They talked about the reaction their sons were bound to have, and they bounced around a few names.

The only thing they didn't talk about was that initial instant when they were both crushed by the same momentary heartache, when it became clear that this baby would not be a girl. Landon had so looked forward to Sarah. Neither of them dared voice that they hoped this child might be a girl too.

But the hope had been there for both of them. That much was clear in the moments after the doctor's announcement. Not now, though. In the wake of all that today's test could've shown, in light of the disaster God had allowed them to steer clear of, they had nothing but pure bliss and gratitude over the news.

They walked along a strip of boutiques, holding hands and enjoying the sunshine on their faces, and Ashley called Dayne. "We had the test!" Her voice told him the obvious—that the news was good. "He's perfect. Completely healthy."

Dayne exhaled hard. "That's wonderful! Katy and I have been praying every day."

"Thanks." She still loved the fact that she had an older brother and that they could share moments like this. "The doctor thinks he'll be tall."

"Wait . . . wait!" Dayne laughed on the other end. "He? It's a boy?"

"Yes!" The happiness in Ashley's voice was real. "The boys are going to be thrilled."

If Dayne was thinking about whether Ashley and Landon were disappointed about not having a girl this time around, he didn't say so. Instead he let out a celebratory shout and reiterated that the news was the greatest answer for the whole family. "It's so amazing, the idea that God is growing a baby inside you." He calmed down some. "Katy and I aren't going to find out about the boy-girl part. We want to be surprised."

They talked a few minutes more, and then when the call ended, Ashley slipped her phone into her purse. "The others can wait. I just had to tell Dayne since Katy and I are due about the same time."

"July ought to be some kind of celebration." Landon stopped and peered into the shop they were passing by. It held baby clothes and vintage baby furniture. He grinned and entered the small store. "I want to buy him his first outfit."

"That's so sweet." The dizziness Ashley felt now had nothing to do with the anxiety that had plagued her since she first took the pregnancy test. It was a giddy breathlessness that came from know-ing the love of her life was strong by her side and that together they were about to welcome the addition of a healthy baby.

Landon seemed to know where he was headed, and as he reached the first rack of clothing, Ashley understood why. Stenciled on tiny blue one-piece pajamas were the words *My daddy's a firefighter*. He held it out and admired it. "Perfect."

As Ashley ran her fingers over the soft blue outfit, she could almost see her newborn dressed in it, ready for a peaceful night's sleep. She put her arm around Landon's waist and gave him a hug. "I feel like I can breathe again . . . knowing he's okay."

"Me too." He held the pajamas close to his chest as he took them to the counter. By the time they paid, walked to the truck, and drove home, the boys were both out back with Ashley's dad, carrying separate buckets and searching for critters in the shrubs that ran along the fence.

In case the news was bad, they hadn't told the boys where they were going or anything about today's test. Ashley greeted her dad first, and again tears filled her eyes. She hugged him around his neck. "The baby's fine. Perfectly healthy."

"Thank God." The relief in his smile told them he had probably been more concerned than he let on. "We've all been praying."

"I know." Ashley kissed his cheek. "Guess what else? It's a boy. We found that out too."

There was a hint of bittersweet sadness in his eyes but only for a moment. "A houseful of boys. What an adventure."

Landon grinned as he looked at Cole and Devin, still crouched intently near one of the bushes. "He has no idea what kind of fun he's in for."

"Mommy!" Devin dropped the bucket he was holding and ran to her, his arms open.

Ashley bent low and caught him in a hug. "Hey, little guy, whatcha doing?"

"Catching frongs! Big frongs!"

"Actually—" Cole was at her side, showing her the inside of his bucket—"they're not frogs. They're toads. And I caught the big one, not Devin." There at the bottom was a grumpy-looking toad bigger than Ashley's fist.

She reached in and touched the toad's bumpy skin. "He's a beauty."

"Yep." Cole nodded. "Papa and I are teaching Devin how to find the beauties."

"Spent ten minutes tracking him down." Ashley's dad chuckled. "Cole's a master."

"Let me see him." Landon took a step closer, and the boys scrambled to him. They hugged his legs and spent another minute inspecting Cole's toad. Then Landon exchanged a look with Ashley, one that asked if now was a good time to tell the boys their news.

She nodded.

"We took Mommy to the doctor today for a test on the new baby."

Instantly Cole turned his attention on them, his eyes wide and frightened. "Is the baby sick . . . like Sarah?"

"No." Ashley put her hand on Cole's back. "He's very healthy."

"Good." Maturity and wisdom shone in Cole's eyes, and he stood a little straighter. Almost as if the joy of this baby's health was tempered by the memory of losing his little sister. "I asked God that nothing bad happen this time."

Devin seemed bored with the conversation. He reached into the bucket and patted Cole's toad.

At the same time, Cole realized what Ashley had just said. "If he's a he . . . then is he a boy?"

"Yes." Ashley laughed. This was the part she was most looking forward to, telling Cole and Devin they were about to have another brother. "In a few months we're going to have three brothers."

Cole grinned and gave her dad and then Landon a resounding

high five. But after a few seconds, his smile dimmed. "Except—" he looked at Ashley—"I really wanted a sister. Really bad." He shrugged. "I was used to the idea, 'cause I could take care of her and stuff."

"You'll take care of another little brother." Landon's tone was subdued. "The same way you're so good at looking out for Devin."

"True." Cole studied Devin, who was still stooped down admiring the toad. "I am pretty good with Devin. So maybe boys are the best for our family."

A slight pang stung at Ashley's heart, but she smiled at her oldest son. "That's right. That's how we're going to look at it."

Devin straightened his chubby legs and held up both hands, his head cocked to one side. "My frong?"

"Your frog is still out there somewhere." Landon tousled the boy's blond hair. "You'll find him, buddy. Cole will help you."

"Yeah, I'll help you find a *toad*." Cole put his arm around his little brother's shoulders as they headed toward the back of the property. "Lucky for you I'm the best toad catcher in town."

Ashley laughed. "No confidence issues for that one."

"Definitely not." Landon took her hand, and they watched their boys return to the hunt.

"A boy will be good for them." Her dad stood shoulder to shoulder with Landon. "This place is a boy's paradise."

"And Cole really does make a great big brother." Landon chuckled. "The kid's a natural leader."

Ashley didn't add her comments to the mix. Everything they were saying was true, of course. Another boy would be a delightful wonder, a tremendous blessing to their family, and, yes, the three boys would have a magical childhood together. Ashley could already see them playing in the tree house and running through the shallow water along the shore of Lake Monroe, defending each other on the playground at school, and cheering each other on during basketball season. Staying close through their teenage years.

But for just a moment longer she grieved the piece of their family that didn't seem meant to be. The one who would've worn a long blonde ponytail and split her time catching toads and playing with dolls, the teenage girl every boy who came through the house would silently marvel at. A girl who would exist only in Ashley's heart and soul.

Cole and Devin's sister.

CHAPTER FOURTEEN

DAYNE SAT IN THE BACK ROW of the theater, the same place he'd sat the first time he came here what felt like a lifetime ago. As long as they produced CKT shows out of this building, the back row would be his favorite place. He crossed one leg and settled back in his seat. From here he could watch the kids and Katy without being a distraction. Especially tonight.

It was Monday of dress rehearsal week, the night that always required the most work, at least according to Katy.

"Usually by the end of the first dress rehearsal, I'm ready to contact the ticket holders and give them their money back," Katy had joked with him as they arrived at the theater earlier. "So we'll see what this one brings."

Now the rehearsal was winding up, and Dayne was surprised at the outcome. *Joseph and the Amazing Technicolor Dreamcoat* was a musical in the truest sense. No dialogue whatsoever except for whatever was written into the songs of the characters and the narrators. Dayne and Ashley had come up with a number of creative sets, and by now the backstage crew knew when to rotate a certain piece and when to move a set off so another one could be brought onstage.

The songs were smooth, and the costumes looked sharp and eclectic. Depending on the scene the kids wore a mix of bell bottoms and tie-dyed shirts, jeans and cowboy hats, or poodle skirts and penny loafers. Bailey did a phenomenal job as the lead narrator. She wanted to pursue acting and musical theater, and clearly she had the ability. Still, Dayne half hoped she'd change her mind, go into something safer where she wouldn't have to risk losing herself.

Connor was easily as talented as his sister. His rich tenor filled the theater as he played Joseph. During the rehearsal Dayne got so caught up in the story he forgot he was watching a run-through. There was Joseph, reunited with his brothers and connecting with his father after a lifetime of being apart.

In the shadows of the back row, Dayne pulled his baseball cap down low on his brow. Suddenly he wasn't watching Joseph run into the arms of Jacob. He was sitting on a bench at the park across the street, watching his father climb out of his car and walk toward him. For the very first time.

God had given him his heart's desire that day, brought him back together with the family he'd been separated from. Because the God of Joseph was the God of Dayne Matthews and John Baxter. The God of all of them. A God whose promises and faithfulness were certain even if seeing them come to be took a lifetime.

The song ended, and the kids onstage held their final pose.

Katy climbed the stairs and held her arms straight up in the air. Her voice rang with victory. "That was the best CKT Monday night dress rehearsal ever!"

A loud chorus of cheers came from the kids, and it took a minute before Katy had their attention again. Dayne stood and moved slowly out of his row and down the center aisle. This was one of his favorite parts, listening to Katy talk to the kids, hearing her work her gift of direction on what already seemed like a great show. He took a spot off to the side in the front row and gazed at his wife.

They were halfway through April, which meant she was six months along. She wore a flowing maternity top and stretchy pants, and her stomach looked like she was hiding a perfectly placed basketball.

"You know what they say," he'd told her the night before. "When you carry the baby out front, it's usually a boy."

"Oh, okay . . . now you're an expert." Katy laughed. "Wasn't that a line in one of your movies?"

He tried to keep a straight face, but he broke. "How'd you know?"

She kissed him on the lips and let her face linger near his. "Because there's no truth to it."

Ashley was having a boy, so a boy would be nice for them too since the two cousins would be the same age. But it didn't matter. He just wished July would hurry and get here. Dayne readjusted his baseball cap and watched Katy flip through her yellow notepad.

"Connor . . . on the scene where the brothers are groveling, I need you to work the stage a little more." Katy made a sweeping gesture with her hand. "You can storm to a brother on one side and then spin around and track down another brother at the opposite side. We need to see your indignation and anger."

"Okay." Connor was hanging on every word, same as the others.

"And, Sydney, you're playing the bratty younger narrator, and you're doing a great job." Katy walked closer to the girl. "But I want to see you doubt yourself once in a while. So go ahead and sing those big notes, get in front of Bailey and Julia, and be a show-off. But then you have to get a sheepish look—" Katy made a nervous face while she glanced over her shoulder—"like that . . . so we see that you're aware you might've overstepped your boundaries."

"Good." Sydney nodded. "I like it."

Pride for his wife warmed Dayne to his core. Katy had no idea how good she really was. She could've become a director for the big screen. But she didn't want any sort of fame. She would use her talent here, and that would be enough. More than enough.

That night back at their lake house, Katy was tired and they turned in almost as soon as they got home. The nights were still cool, but April had brought warm enough temperatures that Dayne left their patio door open a few inches. The breeze felt refreshing as it drifted over them.

They were lying side by side, talking about the show and all Katy hoped to accomplish in the coming week before Friday's opening night, when she sucked in a breath. "Oh . . . wow, I really felt that."

"The baby?" Dayne's heart picked up its pace. She'd been feeling flutterings and movement for several weeks, but every time he laid his hand on her belly the baby was still.

"Feel this." Katy took his hand and laid it on the right side of her swollen stomach.

Dayne spread his fingers over her bare skin, and at almost the same time he felt a soft jabbing motion against his palm. "I felt it! That's amazing."

She giggled. "I know. Sometimes I lie here and try to imagine whether it's an elbow or a knee."

"Or a foot." He shifted his hand, and again something pushed against him. "That definitely felt like a foot."

"She's a feisty little thing." Katy's eyes danced. "'Cause you know what they say . . . if you carry straight out in front, then it's definitely a girl."

Dayne didn't care if it was a boy or a girl. The only thing that mattered was that here in this moment he was having his first contact with a child who would always be a part of his life. His baby. He leaned in close to Katy's stomach. "Hi." His voice was as soothing as he could make it. He looked at Katy, uncertain if he was talking loud enough or if she thought he was crazy.

"Go on. She can hear you."

Dayne gulped. Nothing in all his life had prepared him for how this felt, feeling his unborn child moving beneath his fingers. "This is your daddy. You're a very loved little baby. And we can't wait to meet you." The baby moved again. "Jesus is with you. He picked you out just for us."

After a minute or so, the baby grew still. Katy stroked Dayne's hair. "You must have the golden touch. You're going to be the best daddy ever. I mean, look at that—you helped her fall asleep."

"*He's* a good boy. He knows it's nighttime." Dayne loved this, the way he could mirror her teasing, and neither of them took the matter seriously. He was about to give another reason why the baby would no doubt be a boy when the phone rang. Dayne looked at the clock. It was nearly ten. "Strange." He shifted to the nightstand and picked up the receiver. "Hello?"

"Dayne, it's Bob." His friend sounded happy and upbeat. "Didn't wake you, did I?"

"Not at all." Dayne leaned against the headboard and grinned at Katy, who had turned onto her side so she could see him. "You won't believe this. I just felt my baby move for the first time."

"You're pregnant too?" Bob chuckled at his own joke.

"Very funny." He ran his fingers through Katy's hair and allowed himself to get lost in her eyes. "I guess it's old hat for you veterans. But for me . . . I had my hand on Katy's stomach, and the little guy kicked me. It's like a miracle."

"Actually it is." The laughter faded from Bob's tone. "And, no, it never gets old. We're expecting our third in December."

"Really?" Did either of them ever imagine life going this well back when they were at the missionary boarding school? back when everything seemed confusing, at least for Dayne? "God gives us so much more than we deserve, doesn't He?"

"Definitely." Bob hesitated. "That's sort of why I'm calling. It looks like we're getting a furlough in June, and we might be able to stay until Katy's due date. If you're up for company, we'd love to spend a few days with you."

Dayne's heart soared. "Absolutely. Stay as long as you want." There could be no more fitting friend than Bob Asher to pay them a visit and take part in the celebration as Katy's due date drew near. Bob, after all, had led Dayne into a saving relationship with Christ at a time when he and Katy never would've survived otherwise. Time and again when life was out of control, Bob was the one with the wisdom, Scripture, and prayer support to help turn things around.

"I can't wait to meet your little one."

"That's a photo I want framed on the mantel." Dayne felt the emotion from the day well up inside him. "My best friend holding my baby. Because without you . . ." He couldn't finish the sentence.

"Hey, don't go getting all mushy on me." Bob laughed, but he sounded sentimental also. "I was just in the right place at the right time. God's the One who changed you."

They talked for a few more minutes, and then Dayne remembered something. "Hey, I need you to pray for Luke."

Bob knew well the bad decisions Luke had made last fall and how they had hurt Dayne. "I wondered how his marriage was going."

"Not well. They're talking about a divorce."

A sigh came across the phone line. "The devil never gives up, does he?"

"Not for long." Dayne explained how fault lay with both Luke and Reagan and how that had complicated the situation. "But isn't that the whole point of being a believer? We might make the worst mistake of our lives, but we learn from it and still find forgiveness and grace?"

"Exactly." A sad ripple of laughter filled the space between them. "Maybe you should've been a missionary after all."

"I think I am." Dayne considered all that lay ahead, the trials and triumphs that were bound to come in a group as big as the Baxter family. "Maybe we're all supposed to be missionaries in our own way."

"You're on to something there. And of course I'll pray." He paused. "Keep me posted."

The call ended, and after Dayne hung up, he noticed Katy had fallen asleep. He tenderly pulled the covers over her shoulders, tucking the sheets in close to her chin. She was the picture of true beauty, resting peacefully, her skin smooth and unlined, her blonde hair fanned out on the pillow, their baby growing inside her.

He was about to slide in under the sheets next to her when the phone rang again. Before it could wake Katy, Dayne grabbed it from the base and clicked the On button without checking caller ID. "Hello?" He kept his voice low, slightly baffled. Did anyone know it was a weeknight?

"Oh, Dayne . . . this is Kari. I'm sorry I woke you." She sounded troubled.

"No, it's fine." Dayne covered his mouth so he could keep the noise level down. "Katy's sleeping; that's all."

"Okay, I'll keep this short." She exhaled in a way that conveyed her weariness. "I'm meeting with Angela Manning tomorrow. She's the woman who had the affair with my first husband. She tried to kill herself, and now she's in a psychiatric hospital." She took a shaky breath. "I'm going to tell her how with Jesus she can find hope and forgiveness."

"That'll be tough." Dayne had heard the story from Ashley, but he didn't realize the woman had resurfaced in Kari's life. "Does she know who you are?"

"No. And I think I'll leave it that way, at least for now. That's why I'm calling. Ryan thought I should ask everyone to pray so everything that happens tomorrow is about bringing glory to God and not because of my own curiosity or because I want to pay her back or anything else."

"Got it. I'll pray and I'll tell Katy in the morning."

"Thanks." Kari paused. "That means a lot."

When the call ended, Dayne eased himself onto his back without disturbing Katy. He studied her in the moonlight, and his words to Bob replayed in his mind. He wouldn't want to be a missionary in a foreign country, though he deeply respected that his adoptive parents and Bob's family had been called to such an important ministry. But what he'd said earlier was true. Dayne didn't need to leave the country to be a missionary, to pray for his family and act as a light whenever a situation arose. He could be a missionary right here in Bloomington.

The way his sister Kari was about to be.

❧

Kari couldn't draw a full breath as she entered the lobby of the downtown psychiatric hospital, but she could feel the prayers of her family holding her up, giving her strength with each step.

She reached the front desk and introduced herself. "I have an appointment with Angela Manning."

For a moment, the receptionist looked at her strangely, as if maybe she recognized Kari and knew the connection she had with Angela. But then she managed the slightest very serious smile. "That's very nice of you, volunteering your time." She picked up a telephone receiver, pushed a button, and hesitated. "Kari Taylor is here. Can I send her back?" Another pause. "Okay, thanks."

"They're ready for you." The receptionist studied Kari again. "Visits like this . . . we find it makes a big difference to these women. Gives them hope that once they get out of here, they'll connect with people who will help them continue growing in their faith." She pointed down a hallway. "First door on the left. They'll bring in Angela in a few minutes."

"Thank you." Kari appreciated those words. They were a confirmation, the additional reassurance she needed. She followed the woman's directions and sat at one end of a sofa anchored beneath a picture window.

Kari wasn't alone for long before the door opened and suddenly there she was, standing next to a man in a white coat. Her eyes were dead and empty, and she wore a look of bored indifference. Kari studied her, and she couldn't help but wonder how Tim could've chosen the woman standing in the doorway over what he'd had at home with her. She resisted the sudden resentment welling within her. *I'm not sure I can do this, God.*

You can do all things through Me, for I will give you strength. . . .

Yes. Kari exhaled. *That's true.* Last week she and Ashley had discussed the virtues in the fourth chapter of Philippians, and Kari had read it a number of times in the past week. Along the way, in addition to the wonderful message about God's peace, Kari had rediscovered the thirteenth verse: "I can do everything through him who gives me strength."

"Kari?" The man led Angela into the room. "I'm Dr. Montgomery, and this is Angela Manning."

"Nice to meet you both." She stood and shook the doctor's hand. "How long do we have?"

He checked the clock on the wall to her right. "A half hour?" He looked at Angela. "How does that sound?"

She shrugged. "Fine. There's nothing else to do." She gave Kari a look that bordered on suspicious.

"Very well." The doctor smiled, undaunted by her comment.

Kari had submitted an outline of what she planned to talk about to Dr. Montgomery, and then she'd spent fifteen minutes on the phone with the man while he explained that she needed to keep to her outline. "Not every inpatient facility allows this type of lay counseling. We do, however, because we know you've undergone training, and because you're the type of friend she'll need when she gets out. But it's important you don't say anything to contradict the help she's getting here."

The only part of his directions that made Kari struggle was the part about being a friend. It was one thing to come to this place and talk to Angela about how she'd seen Jesus work in the lives of hurting women. It was another to be Angela's friend. For now, Kari was certain God wasn't calling her into that type of a relationship with Angela, but at the same time maybe Kari could connect the woman to a group that would befriend her.

After the doctor was gone, Kari took her seat again on the end of the sofa and motioned for Angela to sit in the closest chair. As she came closer, Kari smiled at her. *Don't think about who she is,* she told herself. *This hurting and broken woman was created by God. That's all that matters.* "I'm Kari." She shook Angela's hand. "Thanks for talking with me."

Angela crossed her legs. "I don't know why you'd come."

Kari decided to start at the beginning—how she'd had a troubled marriage and how she hadn't known what to do next. "I was raised with a strong faith, but not until my life was turned upside down did Jesus Christ become truly real to me."

Angela leaned back slightly. "What does that mean, *real* to you?"

Kari's nerves relaxed a little. She could do this. She could share the message of Jesus with this woman no matter how their paths had crossed so many years ago. "See, having faith isn't just believing in a list of rules. It's about having a relationship with God."

A flicker of interest showed in Angela's eyes. "Explain that."

And Kari did. For the next several minutes she talked about Jesus, how He wanted a friendship with His people and how that relationship always started with forgiveness. "Because we're all sinners. All of us have things in our past that separate us from the Lord. Things He wants to forgive us for."

Angela was silent for a few seconds. Then she shook her head slowly. "He won't forgive me for my past. I've done things that no one could forgive. Things that haunt me."

In that instant Kari knew that Angela had to be talking about her relationship with Tim. Which was why Kari was here—because in the end, before his violent death, Tim had found forgiveness and healing. Now it was Angela's turn.

When their meeting was almost finished, Kari pulled a new Bible from her purse and handed it to Angela. "You tried to kill yourself because you didn't think life was worth living. But Christ died on the cross to give you a vibrant, joyful life." She nodded to the Bible. "You can read about it there."

Angela appeared stunned. "I've never . . . had a Bible." When she looked at Kari, some of the indifference from earlier was gone. "Where should I start?"

"The book of John. It's in the New Testament at the back." Kari took the Bible again and flipped to the first page of John. "Start here."

They had maybe another minute, and Kari knew what she was supposed to do next. She set the Bible down on the sofa. "Can I pray with you?"

Angela hesitated, and it felt like maybe she would say no. But then in a voice that was strained from new emotion, she whispered, "Yes . . . thank you."

Here was the moment Kari had dreaded and feared. *Please, God, be with me.* She took hold of Angela's hands. The hands that had wrongfully touched Tim and loved Tim, even though he was married. The hands that had welcomed him into her apartment time and again, the hands that had tried to keep him from returning to Kari, even when Tim learned Kari was pregnant. A feeling of repulsion choked Kari and made it impossible for her to pray.

But then she remembered something else. These were also the hands that had tried to commit suicide.

Kari found her voice. "Dear Lord, be with Angela this week. Let her see You in her counseling sessions and in the group therapy. And let her hear Your leading as she reads the book of John. Help her know that no one—" she swallowed the tears building in her— "is beyond Your forgiveness. Because Your sacrifice was enough for all of us. No matter what. In Jesus' name, amen."

As they finished praying, Dr. Montgomery stepped into the room. "Well?" His smile was warm and peaceful. "How'd it go?"

"Good." Kari released Angela's hands. She was shaking, but she'd done it. She'd come here and met with Angela and even held her hands. "I'll be back next week if that's okay."

Angela nodded, her expression markedly different than it had been thirty minutes ago. Now she looked more like a lost child, baffled at why someone would take the time to help her. She picked up the Bible from the sofa and held it close. "I don't get this, why you're here." Her tone wasn't exactly kind, but it was warmer than before. "Anyway . . ." She raised the Bible a few inches. "Thank you. And I guess . . . I guess we'll talk next week."

As Kari left the facility, everything around her seemed to be bursting with new life. Flowers and patches of grass and new leaves that she'd missed coming in colored the scene in a way that made her want to break into song. God was faithful beyond anything she could imagine! He had brought new life to her, even when her whole world felt ripped apart by Tim's unfaithfulness and then by his death. But now she had Ryan, Jessie, RJ, and Annie, new life and new hope. Sharing that new life with the very woman responsible for nearly destroying her wasn't something Kari could do in her own strength, and therein lay the beauty of it. Her visit with Angela today was proof that God was and that He lived and that He was still working today.

And something else. She really could do all things through Christ who gave her strength.

CHAPTER FIFTEEN

CODY COLEMAN CLUNG to the rusty bars and peered into the darkness of the hot, dank room. It was late, though Cody wasn't sure if it was midnight or two in the morning or four. With no windows in the building, they'd lost all sense of time except what their bodies told them. And since the others were sleeping—each locked in his own cage—Cody could only assume it was late.

He couldn't stand upright in the metal box, and his spine ached because of it. Some moments he wanted out of the cage so badly he could picture losing it. Truly losing it. Banging his head against the ceiling of the metal box and screaming from the insanity of it.

Instead, every time Cody felt like he was going to go crazy from the confinement, he talked to God. He had known about the Lord a number of different ways and times. As a teenager he'd heard the Flanigans talk about God, how Cody couldn't expect his life to go well if he didn't first find that all-important faith in Christ. And after his near-death experience from drinking, he'd gone to those alcohol meetings at the Flanigans' church and found a very real relationship with Jesus.

But the Lord had never been more alive to him than right here, locked in an Iraqi holding room, trapped in a five-by-five metal cage.

"I know You're here, Jesus." He whispered the words because there was something about hearing his own voice that helped him stay sane. His mouth was dry, but he couldn't drink from the water bowl on the dirty floor of the cage. Not yet. He needed to ration the water in case his captors forgot to bring more. He ran his tongue along his gritty gums. "There's a reason I'm still alive. I know that." He gripped the bars more tightly. "Please send help. Get us out of here so I can figure out why You spared me."

Cody pressed his head to the top of the cage, fighting the wild desire to stand tall and straight. Even for a few seconds. His head hurt from the pressure, and finally he sank to the floor. He eyed the water bowl in the corner. Maybe just one small sip. He picked it up, grateful for the cover of darkness so he couldn't see the dirt and bugs at the bottom of the bowl. He dipped his tongue into the cool liquid and lapped up a few quick drinks. This was what his life had become these past few weeks, nothing more than an animalistic existence. The way his captors wanted it to be.

He pulled up his legs and planted his elbows on his knees. They were bonier than before, and he wondered how much weight he'd lost. Once a day angry Iraqi insurgents burst into the room and flipped the lights on. They would bark things at the men that none of them understood, and they'd shove a tray of something like cold oatmeal into each of their cages. No vegetables or fruit or meat and no utensils. Sometimes they'd poke the butts of their guns into the cages, jabbing at the prisoners for fun.

The first time one of his captors did that to Cody, he grabbed the man's gun and tried to wrestle it away. But that only attracted the attention of the others, who hurried over and joined in the attack. Before it was over, Cody was on the floor, blood pouring from his head, almost unconscious from the blows.

When the men finally left, Cody had the wherewithal to apply pressure to his bleeding head. After a while, he ripped a piece of material from the inside hem of his pants and applied it to the wound. The bleeding stopped and he fell asleep, his head pounding. When he woke up the next day, his buddies told him they were surprised he'd lived.

"They wanted to kill you, man," Carl told him. Carl was in the cage opposite Cody's. "If they come back at you again, fall sooner. Maybe that'll make 'em stop."

Sure enough, later that day the Iraqis came back, jabbing their guns at Cody and trying to break open his head wound. Cody fell to the back of his cage, careful to keep his damaged scalp out of reach. Without the game of seeing Cody fight back, the men gave up and turned their attention to the other prisoners. When each of them chose to cower in a corner, the Iraqi men quit fighting, pointing at the Americans and laughing at them.

Cody ran his fingers over the spot where the wound had long since healed. He lowered one hand and felt along the floor for the rock, the small one with the pointy edge. In the cover of darkness, he had used it to scratch lines into the bottom of the cage. One line for every day they'd been in captivity. He ran his fingers over the lines now and counted again. Twenty-two.

He could hardly believe they'd been here so long. Certainly someone had to know where they were and that they needed help. He rested his forehead in his hands. They never should've been caught, for that matter. They'd been searching an empty building when the insurgents had burst in through two different back doors. Had they run, they might have all escaped because Cody was pretty sure that only two of the Iraqi men were armed.

But Carl had turned his weapon on the men and fired, killing one of them instantly. And that was that. Thirty men rushed at the Americans, and guns or not, the sheer number of them was overpowering. In a matter of seconds, Cody and his comrades were in handcuffs and being dragged to a series of waiting Jeeps.

The air in the building tonight felt hotter than usual. Hot and dense and thick, like an airless cloud. Cody breathed in, but the sensation left him feeling like he hadn't breathed at all. Where was the air in this place? Or maybe his captors had done something to fill it with carbon monoxide. Maybe that was how they were going to die, slowly through suffocation.

Cody had the sudden desperate need for even the tiniest bit of fresh oxygen. He sucked in through his nose, but the inhalation brought no relief. This had happened before, right? More than once since they'd been locked up. He had the sure feeling that the hot cement walls were getting closer, closing in on him. Death dug its fingernails into his shoulders and poked at his back and ribs. Was this the end? Was he going to fall unconscious, unable to breathe in the boxy cage? Was there really enough air in the building to keep four men alive?

He opened his mouth and sucked in as deep as he could. Then he did it again and a third time. "Come on, lungs . . . find the air!" he hissed, not wanting to wake the others. "Help me breathe, God!" His heart pounded in his chest, screaming at him that if he didn't get a full breath soon, it would be too late.

Then he had an idea. He lay down on the metal floor and pushed his legs up the far wall. Only in this position could he stretch his arms over his head and fully extend his spine.

As he did, finally . . . finally a single breath filled his lungs, making him believe once more that he might survive. Lying there like a human letter L, his legs stretched up along the far wall, he realized what he'd known before. The breathing thing was all in his head. Yes, it was hot and stuffy and oppressive, but if he stayed calm, if he forced himself not to think about what he was breathing, then he'd be okay. His captain had talked often about mental toughness. Now Cody understood why.

When his heartbeat returned to normal, he sat up again. He felt shaky and exhausted from the effort of breathing, but he wasn't tired enough to sleep. From the corner of the room he heard the scratchy sound of mice or maybe rats as they scurried along the

floor, the way they did every night. Whenever Cody and his buddies were given food, the Iraqi men scraped a few spoonfuls onto
the floor in the corner. It was a way of assuring that the mice or rats
would stay, irritating the Americans, making them crazy.

Cody blocked out the sound. There was a reason he stayed
awake long after the others were asleep. He needed this time so he
could think about creating an escape.

Every day after their captors brought in the trays of porridge,
they would go to each of the cages one at a time and in broken
English ask a few simple questions. "Who are you? What your
name? What your rank?"

The reason they had to ask was thanks to Cody. When they were
first brought here, they'd been locked in their individual cages and
left alone in the dark for nearly a day before the first water and
food appeared. During that time, Cody had an idea. The first thing
the insurgents would do was take their names and insignia from
their uniforms. In that way they could flash the scraps of material
in front of news cameras, boasting that they had possession of
American prisoners.

But if they destroyed their own stitched names and insignia
first, the Iraqis would have nothing. The floor of the room where
the cages sat was made up of dirt and small rocks. Cody instructed
the others to reach through the bars in their cage and sift around
until they found the sharpest rock. Then he told them to use the
rock to slice off the part of their uniform that bore their name
and insignia. It took more than an hour for the guys to get that
far and another two hours using the sharp edges of their rocks
to shred the pieces of material. By the time they were done, all
that remained of those pieces of their uniforms was a small pile
of threads.

When their captors came in next and flipped on the lights, it
took them only a few minutes to realize what the men had done.
That's when they began shouting at them and jabbing them with
the butts of their guns. After that the questions were a regular

part of the visits. "Who are you? What your name? What your rank?"

Over the last few days, an idea had begun to take form. But Cody would need every detail worked out before he could share it with the others, before he could even begin to imagine acting it out. He leaned his head against the back of the metal box. However it happened, he had to get out, had to escape. Whether someone came for them or not.

He had to get out of here and back home so he could see the one person he'd dreamed of seeing every day since he left the United States.

Bailey Flanigan.

Her last letter ran through his mind again. She'd mentioned that she was spending more time with Tim, and she didn't have any real reason not to. No one else had feelings for her, at least not that she could tell. As soon as he read her words, Cody understood why she had written them. In every letter he had made a point of telling her that she should be dating someone like Tim, someone she would have everything in common with.

So finally she'd taken Cody's advice, but he detected at least a little bitterness in the tone of her letter. Did she really think he didn't care for her? that he didn't hit his bunk every night wishing he were back in Bloomington, where maybe they could've become better friends . . . and one day maybe even something more?

Her written words had hurt so much that in his last letter to his mother he'd told her he might just move to the West Coast. Why not? Bailey deserved someone like Tim—Cody truly meant that. Especially with him in Iraq for the next year or so. But he could hardly move back to Bloomington at the end of his tour and watch her head toward a serious relationship, maybe even a marriage, to someone else. If Bailey was falling in love with Tim, then the place for Cody was on the opposite side of the country—as far away from her as he could get.

At least that's how he'd felt when he wrote the letter. Later he began to doubt himself. If he cared about Bailey, why hadn't he told her? Maybe she really had turned to Tim only because she no longer thought Cody was interested. Either way, he owed her the truth at least. He had been planning to share his true feelings with her that night when he returned to his bunk. Only he never made it.

A thousand times he'd written the letter anyway, penciling it with his thoughts across the tablet of his heart. So when the time came, he would remember everything he wanted to say, and the letter would simply pour out of him. *Dear Bailey,* he would write. *You have to understand something. I've been telling you to see other guys like Tim Reed for one reason only. Because you deserve someone like that and I'm not there. But don't for a minute think that means I don't have feelings for you. I do. I have ever since that night after Bryan left when we talked. . . .*

There would be more to the letter too. He would tell her of his plans to get out of Iraq alive and come back to Bloomington, not California. His plans to get a college degree and let God bring life once more to their friendship. Plans that included her at every level. He would apologize for not making himself clear, and he would ask her to understand the things he'd said before.

The entire letter was already written.

Cody slid to the floor of the cage, curled up on his side, and closed his eyes. Hunger pangs twisted at his insides, and a few feet away the sound of scurrying scratchy feet echoed in the darkness. He ran his hands over his bony shoulders and elbows. Yes, he had the letter memorized. Now he had to find a way out of here.

Because only then could he finally get the message from his heart to hers.

❧

There had been no word on Cody, no sign of him or his buddies. They were still listed as missing in action, though his superiors told

Cody's mother that they had a few leads that seemed promising. Either way, the fact that he hadn't been found took away some of Bailey's thrill that Friday.

It was opening night for *Joseph*, and Bailey and Connor were driving to the theater earlier than the rest of the family. Call time was six o'clock—an hour ahead of the show when all actors had to report to the theater—but the doors didn't open to the public until half an hour later.

Connor turned to her. "You're thinking about Cody." It wasn't a question.

"He should be here." Bailey kept her eyes on the road. The radio was turned low, and ahead of her she recognized the Reeds' car. The theater was only a few miles away.

"It's hard." Connor held a big paper bag filled with supplies he'd need for the run of the show. "He joined the army because he wanted to, because he thought it was right."

"It was right. And it's right for our country to stand strong against terrorism." She hesitated, feeling confused. "I'm just saying he should be here."

After a few minutes of silence, Connor raised his eyebrows in her direction. "Care if we warm up?"

Bailey felt her shoulders fall an inch. "I'm sorry." She gave him a weary smile. "It's opening night. It doesn't help Cody for us to head into the first show feeling all gloomy."

"No." Connor had his iPod connected to the car's radio. He scrolled through a list of songs, and the sound of "Joseph's Coat" filled the space around them.

They began to sing, warming up their voices, and as they did, the promise of the story lifted Bailey's spirits. God was in control of all things at all times for all people. Maybe Cody had been thrown into a pit for now—like Joseph had been—but God knew the plans He had for Cody. She would do her friend no good by spending these days worrying.

She reached the theater and parked, and together they grabbed their things and climbed out of the car. As they headed across the street to the old theater, they heard someone behind them.

"Wait up!"

Bailey turned and saw Tim, his arms full of two flats of bottled water. As he reached her and Connor, the three of them slowed to a walk. At the side door, Tim stopped and looked at Connor. "Uh . . . why don't you go on in, okay?"

Connor looked confused at first, but then he seemed to understand that Tim wanted to talk to Bailey alone. Connor did as he was asked.

When they were alone, Tim faced her and set the water down. "I wrote you a letter." He pulled an envelope from his back pocket and grinned. "It wouldn't fit in a text. I thought maybe you could read it before you go on tonight."

"That's really nice." The gesture was so thoughtful. Sure, they'd been spending time together and texting a ton, but Tim hadn't ever spelled out his feelings for her. There was no way of even telling if he saw her as more than a friend. Butterflies danced around in her stomach, and she was grateful for the growing darkness overhead, glad he couldn't see the color in her cheeks.

"I know I'm in a teaching role, and I can't really talk to you once everyone's here. But I wanted you to know what I'll be thinking out there in the audience." He gave her a quick hug. "You're going to be amazing tonight, Bailey. I can feel it." He released her, but their eyes met and held. "I'll be praying for you." He bent down and picked up the flats of water. "Got to get these to the refreshment people." He smiled at her one last time, then headed up a set of stairs toward a different door than the one actors used.

Bailey watched him go, and before he went inside, he stopped and looked at her once more. Chills ran over her arms and down her spine. Was this really happening? Was he really falling for her?

She ran down the steps to the greenroom entrance and glanced at her watch. She had time to read his letter, but not in the greenroom with everyone watching, wondering what was so important.

Instead she darted down a hallway and into the dark, empty kitchen. She hit the light and moved to the corner where no one would see her even if they passed by the open door.

The letter wasn't long, just one page, one side. The butterflies doubled as she opened the piece of paper and held it up.

> Bailey,
> I guess I have two things to tell you. I figured I'd do a better job if I wrote them. Otherwise I'd chicken out and never say this. Anyway, first, I want to apologize. I know I've never been that easy to understand, and I'm sorry about that. It was never because of you. I always liked you. From the time we were in Tom Sawyer together.

Bailey balanced herself against the rickety old refrigerator in the corner of the kitchen. She had dreamed of getting a letter like this from Tim, hoped for so many years that he might really be developing feelings for her. But Tim had been so flaky in his attention toward her. Glad to see her one day and able to get through an entire CKT practice without so much as a hello another time. After a while she'd given up. Cody was living with them by then, and he was becoming the friend Tim had never really been. But now . . .

She found her place and kept reading.

> The problem is the drama that comes with CKT. The drama offstage. I don't want people knowing who I like or talking about whether we're an item. All that garbage. So I tried dating a few girls from church, but . . . okay, you guessed it . . . they only made me think about you more. Truthfully, I still don't know if I want a girlfriend. It's not bad being single. You can probably agree with that. But if I did want a girlfriend, you'd be the girl. I wanted you to know. I don't have feelings for anyone else.

Bailey's excitement fell off by a percentage. It wasn't bad being single? Was that supposed to make her feel good about whatever they were building together? She pursed her lips and finished the letter.

> Anyway, the second thing is that you've really come a long, long way in your ability as a stage actress. I know CKT is about more than the stage—that's true for all of us—but the growth I've seen in you as a singer and actress has been incredible. You could really do this for a living even. Out of all the kids in CKT, I think there are only a handful of us who have a future at it. Lately I have to say you're definitely one of those.
>
> It makes me dream that maybe one day you and me and Connor might all be living in New York City and being a light for God. I really think it could happen. I guess that's all. I wanted you to know before you go onstage tonight. You're blowing me away with your role as narrator. So go break a leg! I'll talk to you later after the party when no one's around to gossip about us.
>
> Your friend,
> Tim

Bailey made a face. She read the letter once more all the way through and tried to figure out what she was feeling. Once, when she was sixteen, her parents had taken them to a fancy steakhouse in downtown Indianapolis. For weeks her dad had built the place up, telling them that the steak was better than any he'd ever eaten. Amazing broccoli casserole and potatoes and salad and bread. When they finally reached the restaurant that Sunday evening, the whole family was ready for the best dinner of their life.

Only, when Bailey was halfway through her broccoli, she lifted a forkful to her mouth and there, stuck between two pieces of broccoli, was a dead fly. Bailey dropped her fork and had to excuse herself to the bathroom so she wouldn't be sick. She never did end up tasting the steak or finishing her meal. Everything good about it was ruined by a single dead fly.

That was how she felt now. Okay, so Tim was admitting he liked her. Something she and her mom had talked about and something she had at times dreamed about. But he was also saying he was truly happy having no girlfriend at all. Then the part about her skills as an actress? His compliment felt cheap and . . . Bailey couldn't quite figure out why it bothered her. Maybe because he came across arrogant, saying only "a handful of us" had a future at theater. And how about the part where he didn't want to be seen with her? A guy should be willing to stand up to the gossip and look the other way. Who cared what people said? As long as he didn't show her any affection or extra attention when he was in the role of teacher, there shouldn't be a problem. But he hadn't blamed his leadership role as the reason. He'd blamed the offstage drama. Why did it matter so much?

She frowned at the letter, folded it, and placed it back in the envelope. As she walked to her place in the greenroom in the base-ment of the theater, and as she found her costume on the back of her chair, she couldn't help but think of the one person who never would've said such a thing.

Cody.

But then . . . Cody wasn't interested in her. If they ever found him and rescued him, if he ever made it back to the United States safely, then he was moving as far away from her as possible. So maybe there was some merit to Tim's idea of moving to New York City and pursuing a career in musical theater.

Her thoughts were so confused that by the time she started to apply her stage makeup, she could no longer remember the words to the opening song, a solo she was scheduled to sing. She hung her head and gripped the edge of the table where her mirror and makeup were spread out. *Please clear my mind, God. Tim's right, anyway. Being single really is better—at least for now. And please . . . wherever Cody is, be with him. Help the people looking for him so he can be found. Thank You.*

She lifted her head, and Connor was standing beside her. "You okay?"

"I'm fine." She stood, and at the same instant the words to the song came back to her. "I just need to get onstage."

Connor wanted to ask her about Tim, about what was so important that he had to talk to her alone outside. She knew her brother well enough to see that in his eyes. But instead he only smiled and patted her back. "Yeah. Me too."

The hour passed quickly, and she and Sydney and Julia formed a small cluster and went over their key songs. With every word, every note, Bailey felt herself drawing closer to the part, owning her role as narrator. And with every minute that passed, all thoughts of Tim and even Cody left her.

They circled up in the greenroom, the entire cast holding hands. Katy placed herself in the circle and grinned at the group. "You all look wonderful. God is really going to use this show. I can sense it." She looked up at the cement ceiling and exposed water pipes. "Let's sing."

Singing a song of praise to God was one of the CKT traditions Bailey would miss most when the next three weeks of shows were finished. Emotion built in her eyes as the song started. "'We love You, Lord . . . and we lift our voice . . .'"

Bailey held on to each word, each refrain. While preparing for the show, she hadn't given much thought to the obvious. She was eighteen now, and this was the last show until summer. Which meant Bailey could try out for the fall and winter shows next year, but after that she'd be too old to perform with CKT.

Softly and with beautiful harmonies, the song continued. "'. . . to worship You, O my soul, rejoice! Take joy, my King, in what You hear. May it be a sweet, sweet sound in Your ear.'"

When the song ended, Katy led them in a brief but powerful prayer. As they took their places, as Bailey, Sydney, and Julia walked onto the stage to begin the show, Bailey was overwhelmed by the truth in what Katy had told them. The message of Joseph was a lasting and powerful one.

Now it was time to share it with the people of Bloomington.

CHAPTER SIXTEEN

KATY FOUND HER SEAT UP in the balcony, the place where she always sat for opening night. Only this time she didn't have to watch the door for signs of Dayne or wonder if he was coming or what he was doing out in Hollywood. He was right here beside her. She leaned into his arm. "I'm a nervous wreck."

He smiled at her. "You have no reason. These kids could take this show to Broadway. They're way beyond prepared."

She relaxed some and placed her hands on her rounded stomach. The baby had been particularly active today. "Really? You think they're ready?"

"Absolutely."

The houselights were still up, and Katy looked back toward the lobby. There on the wall were portraits of Sarah Jo Stryker and Ben Hanover, the two CKT kids killed by a drunk driver a few years ago. With the new start-up of CKT, the newspaper had done another article on all the theater group had gone through and how they had pulled together after the deaths of Sarah Jo and Ben and then again with the near loss of their theater.

Katy settled back in her seat.

"What're you thinking?" Dayne gripped her hand, his warmth and strength a constant support.

"What it took . . . all we've gone through to be here tonight." Her emotions were running high tonight, and Katy was certain they'd stay that way. "The Hanovers are here. Sarah Jo's mother too." She stared at the stage, at the thick velvet curtains stretched across the front. "Apparently the drunk driver wrote to both families. Mrs. Hanover told me a few minutes ago."

Dayne's expression reminded her that he too had been a part of that sad time. "What did he say?"

"He's changed. Gave his life to God and joined a Bible study in prison. He's actually mentoring a few guys." She squinted at the stage and envisioned sweet Sarah Jo playing Becky Thatcher in *Tom Sawyer*, singing in all her glory. "Every day he thinks about the kids he killed. He said he'd spend the rest of his life trying to make something good of himself. In their memory."

"Makes me wonder . . ." Dayne's attention was on the stage also. "How much of that came from your visit."

"Hmm." Katy hadn't thought about that. "Could be. He was pretty shaken up that day." She remembered that afternoon, the day she took a group of CKT kids to jail so they could see the young man responsible for the deaths of their friends. Bailey, Connor, Tim, and a dozen others took turns greeting the guy and forgiving him. "I guess something like that could change a person."

"Because without God none of you could've done that."

"True."

They were silent for a minute, lost in thoughts of the past.

"Did you ever imagine . . . ?"

"I'd be here on a night like this?" Katy peered at him. "Never."

The houselights went down, and darkness draped the theater. A hush fell over the crowd.

Katy touched her lips to Dayne's and held his gaze. "Thank you," she whispered.

He searched her eyes. "I should've done it sooner."

She smiled.

A spotlight appeared at center stage, and all eleven of Joseph's brothers filed out. Working in character and with great comedic timing, they informed the audience that it was time to turn off cell phones and there would be snacks at intermission.

. Katy was still thinking about Sarah Jo and Ben, the drunk driver, and something Ashley had told her. She'd been reading from the book of Psalms, and she'd come across a verse about God's redemption in all things. His faithfulness. It was true for the tragedy CKT had gone through in losing two precious kids, and it was true in the trials she and Dayne had survived.

Katy remembered the phone call she'd gotten from Rhonda earlier today. "Tell everyone to break a leg," Rhonda had said. And then she'd shared about how happy she was, how she and Chad were loving their work with CKT and loving each other most of all. Their wedding had been moved to August because that was the soonest they could get the church they wanted, but their relationship was getting stronger all the time. "It's like a dream. Sometimes I can't believe this is my life."

Indeed. A warmth filled Katy's soul. The music began, and the three narrators took the stage, Bailey leading the way. If there was one message Katy hoped people would take away from the production of *Joseph*, it was this: God was faithful. He was a redemptive Father and Creator, and He always kept His word.

Dayne had a framed Scripture in his newly decorated office at their lake house. It was from John 16:33. "In this world you will have trouble. But take heart! I have overcome the world."

"A reminder," Dayne had told Katy, "that life doesn't always have a happy ending. But in the end, if we believe, we all win anyway."

She reached for his hand, loving the way her fingers felt woven between his. CKT was theirs, and it always would be. This was how they could truly love the kids in their community with the gifts God had given them. Along the way, they could teach kids about

God, the way the story of Joseph taught them. That when God's people were suffering in the midst of a trial, they needed only to remember what Joseph remembered, the truths that kept him sane during his days in Egypt.

God loved them, and God was in control.

The show was over, the bows about to begin, and Ashley couldn't stop smiling. Opening night was everything she'd hoped it would be. Bailey, Sydney, and Julia were brilliant as narrators, and Connor's performance as Joseph brought tears to her eyes. Sarah Nordlund also did well, and more than that, her mother reported that during Sarah's time among the CKT kids, her diabetes didn't make her feel quite so different.

But the most touching part for Ashley was seeing Cole onstage for the first time, watching him sing with the ensemble, his hands outstretched. If Ashley had her way, this would be the first of many CKT plays for Cole and one day maybe for Devin and their newest little boy. It didn't matter the size of the role, just that the kids took part at all. In *Joseph*, Cole was playing the son of Joseph's brother Simeon, and in the weeks leading up to opening night he had asked her a number of questions about the Bible story of Joseph.

"You know, Mom, I'm kinda like Joseph," Cole deduced one night after another question-and-answer session.

"How's that?" Ashley was feeding Devin in his high chair, and Landon was at work.

"Well, my life was really great, but I didn't have my dad. It took a whole lot of waiting before God brought us all together."

During the curtain call, Cole's group of actors took the stage first to a rousing round of applause. Ashley joined the others on their feet. She rested one hand on her belly and put her other arm around Landon. They would be an all-boy family, but that didn't mean they'd spend their lives entirely in a gym or on a field. Maybe there would be these moments too, when her love for the arts lived clearly in her sons.

Landon had Devin in his arms, and the boy clapped as loud as anyone. "Coley!" he cried over the noise of the cheering crowd. "My Coley!"

The next group came onstage and the next, and finally the lead actors took their bows. Then the entire cast raised their hands to the light booth and then to the band—their way of giving credit to the ones who made the show possible. They finished by doing something that set CKT apart from other theater groups. They raised their hands straight up, shining eyes lifted toward heaven.

Ashley felt a rush of sweet sadness and unfathomable joy. Yes, it was all thanks to God. The theater, the show . . . and the fact that like Joseph, Cole had a daddy and not one brother but two.

The lights came up, and the kids filed down into the audience.

As soon as Cole had a chance, he ran to them. He hugged Landon first, then her. "Did you see me? I was right up front in that one song."

"We did." Ashley hugged him.

All around them kids were greeting their parents and congratulations were being handed out. Cameras were everywhere as cast members took pictures with their family members who had come to see the show. Ashley could see that Brooke and Kari and their families were making their way through the crowd toward them.

"Hey, buddy!" There was no hiding the pride in Landon's expression. "You were great!"

"Thanks. I still like baseball and basketball better. But guess what? They're doing *Peter Pan* in the summer, so I'll probably try out again."

Ashley could almost picture Cole as Michael or John, one of the Darling children in *Peter Pan*. Her happiness spilled into a laugh, because she didn't need to wonder any longer. There would indeed be more nights like this.

Devin strained against Landon's arms. "Devin down!" Landon

released him, and he rushed to his big brother. He raised his hands in the air. "Coley!" Then he flung his arms around Cole's waist.

"Hey, Dev." Cole rubbed his head. "You liked the show?"

Devin hopped around Cole in response, and Cole laughed, the way he often did these days when he was with his younger brother. "You know what I was thinking?" Cole turned teasing eyes to Ashley and then to Landon. "If Joseph could have so many brothers, maybe I could too." He shrugged. "We already have two, so we're on our way."

Ashley laughed harder. "You're lucky to have two."

Cole grinned at her. "Yeah, I know." He looked at Landon. "It was worth a try."

The rest of their family gathered around then. Ashley's dad and Elaine were there and Luke and Reagan and the kids. Even in the happy theater crowd, Ashley could tell things were still strained between her younger brother and his wife. She put the thoughts from her head. This wasn't the time to think about that.

Cole made his way around the group, accepting hugs and congratulations from everyone and taking a dozen photos with them. Hayley and Jessie seemed somewhat shy around Cole, as if they were a little starstruck by his performance.

Even Maddie told him what a good job he'd done. "Next time I'm gonna try out too," she told him. "Because girls are better dancers."

"And boys are better baseball players." Cole winked at her.

For the first time Maddie had no retort. She hesitated and then her face lit up and she grabbed Cole's hand. "Let's go say hi to Aunt Katy and Uncle Dayne."

The crowd was thinning, most people already headed off to Burgerland for the opening night party. Ashley talked a few more minutes with her sisters and Reagan while the guys chatted a few feet away.

Finally Landon came up beside her. "We better go. The burgers'll be sold out."

Ashley was about to round up the boys when a couple and their son walked over. The boy was in the show, one of the middle school actors onstage, but his family was new to CKT and Ashley hadn't gotten to know them well. She wasn't even sure of the woman's name. Ashley and Landon turned toward them, and Ashley thought they looked strangely tentative, nervous almost.

"Hi." The man took a step forward and shook Landon's hand. "We're the Franklins. I'm Tom." He put his arm around the woman. "This is my wife, Carol, and our son, Bobby."

The name sounded vaguely familiar, and Ashley figured it was from working with the cast list.

"I'm Landon." He smiled. "Nice to meet you. The kids were great tonight, huh?"

"Yes, but . . . well . . ." Tom looked to his wife and then back at Landon. "My wife and I . . . Can I ask . . . are you a firefighter?"

"I am." Clearly Landon was equally curious about where the conversation was headed.

Carol put her hand on her son's shoulder. "We wanted to thank you."

Tom cleared his throat. His lower lip quivered. "See . . . . Bobby was the boy from the apartment fire seven years ago."

Ashley's mind raced, and the floor beneath her seemed to turn to liquid. "You mean—" she looked at the boy—"he's the one?"

"He is. He's twelve now." Tears filled Carol's eyes. "I didn't put it together until I saw your husband enter the theater with you. We knew the man's name was Landon Blake and that Blake was your name." She turned to Landon. "When we saw you tonight we recognized you."

"From your picture in the paper." Tom looked deep at Landon, to the vicinities of his heart where only a father could relate. "Bobby's our only child. We can't have more." He bit his lip. "I don't know what we would've done if . . ."

Carol stepped away from her son and gave Landon a hug. Bobby shook Landon's hand and uttered a quiet thank-you. He was polite, but he seemed embarrassed by the moment. He moved off to talk to a few girls near the snack stand.

Tom shook his head, his brow lowered from the obvious intensity of his feelings. "You risked your own life for my son. We sent you a letter to the firehouse, but . . . we always wanted to find you and thank you."

Ashley's eyes filled with tears, and she blinked so she could clearly see the boy. Bobby from the show was the one? that boy? The fire had been one of the most dangerous in Bloomington history, affecting an apartment complex and threatening the lives of a dozen people. Landon had found the boy unconscious on the second floor. For a while he'd tried to buddy-breathe. He would take a gulp of air from his mask, then place the mask over the boy's face and repeat the pattern. But eventually the smoke and heat were too much for Landon, and he passed out with the mask firmly over the boy's face.

The resulting smoke inhalation nearly killed Landon, but his heroism did three things. First, it saved the life of the shy twelve-year-old standing a few feet away. Second, it brought Ashley back to Landon. If he hadn't been near death after that fire, she wouldn't have held a vigil at his hospital bedside, and she wouldn't have allowed herself to admit what had been true forever—that she loved Landon Blake.

A chill passed down her spine. The third thing was just as dramatic. Landon's injuries in that blaze delayed his ability to move to New York City and fight fires with his buddy Jalen. And because of the delay, Landon wasn't where he would've been—trudging up the stairs of the South Tower in lower Manhattan on September 11 when the whole thing collapsed.

They talked for a few more minutes and then headed for the van. Cole was singing "One More Angel in Heaven," one of the play's funnier songs. But Ashley and Landon hadn't said a word to each other since the family walked up to them. Not until they had the boys belted in and they took their seats did Landon lean back and stare straight ahead. He made no move to start the engine.

"I don't even know what to say." He looked at Ashley, his jaw slack. "God used me to save that kid, but afterward He saved me twice. Know what I mean?"

"I do." Her voice was somber, filled with awe. "His ways are far too complicated for us."

"Yeah." Landon pulled the keys from his pocket and slipped them into the ignition. A sad smile tugged at his lips. "Because not everyone comes out alive."

He was thinking of Jalen, of course.

Jalen's parents had let Landon stay in Jalen's New York apartment over the several months after 9/11 when Landon worked almost without stopping looking for his friend's remains in the rubble of Ground Zero. He sifted through ash and human remains right up until the afternoon when Jalen's body was discovered. After that he came back to Bloomington wanting only one thing. A relationship with Ashley.

She was about to ask whether Landon had heard from Jalen's parents lately when his cell phone rang. He pulled it from his pocket and checked the caller ID. His expression darkened as he opened his phone and held it to his ear. "Mom, what's going on?" The engine was running, but he still hadn't moved the van. Now he rested his forearm on the steering wheel. "A few hours ago, then?"

Ashley crossed her arms and watched him. The news couldn't be good. Landon's grandpa Westra was still very sick from his heart attack, clinging to life in the ICU. The family was planning a trip there as soon as the show run was finished. Now watching Landon's part of the conversation, Ashley was pretty sure that this was the call they'd been dreading.

"Okay. I'll call you tomorrow. Thanks for letting me know. . . . I love you too." Landon turned to Ashley as he slid his phone back into his pocket. He hesitated, his chin quivering. "He's gone."

"Oh, Landon." She closed the distance between them and hugged him. "I'm sorry."

"What happened, Dad?" Cole poked his head between the two front seats. "Is something wrong?"

Landon sighed and eased back from Ashley. His eyes were dry, but the heaviness in his voice was heartbreaking. "Grandpa Westra died." He managed a weak smile for Cole. "Remember him?"

"Yes." Cole's shoulders sank. "I liked him a lot. He was really nice."

Ashley put her hand on Cole's shoulder and turned to Landon. "Is there a service?"

"Something small and simple. It's set for Tuesday morning. We can catch a flight out Monday and come home Wednesday."

"Good." Ashley sat back in her seat and buckled her belt. "I'd like us all to be there."

"Me too." Landon put the van in drive and turned out of the parking lot.

Ashley covered his hand with her own. "We can skip the opening night party if you want."

"It's Cole's big night." Landon glanced over his shoulder at their son, and even with his damp eyes, his voice was filled with pride. "I wouldn't want to be anywhere else."

The party lasted until nearly midnight. After they were home and the boys were in bed, Ashley found Landon sitting in the dark living room alone, staring out the front window. Quietly she took the seat next to him, nuzzling up against him, her arm around his shoulders. This was one of those moments when love didn't need words.

Ashley tried to imagine being married for seventy-six years. Andrew and Effie must've been so close, their hearts so tightly woven together that when one breathed in, the other felt life in his or her bones. Andrew had been well when Effie died, well enough that he wanted that last night in their bed together. But with his

Effie dead and buried, life had slowly begun to ebb from Andrew. His broken heart could be alone for only so long.

"He wanted this." Landon turned to her. "The moment Grandma was gone he wanted heaven."

"His body wouldn't let him stay here without her." Ashley studied her husband; then she put her hand alongside his face and kissed him. A kiss that told of love and longing and heartbreak. A kiss that understood there would never be enough time together in this life. But even so, God had a happy ending right around the corner for those who believed. Ashley and Landon knew the lesson personally, as Andrew and Effie had. Or as Ashley's grandmother used to say, "All this and heaven too."

The kiss lingered, and even in the shadow of great loss, Ashley felt herself smile.

All this and heaven too. Indeed.

CHAPTER SEVENTEEN

LUKE WOKE UP to sunshine streaming through the window of his old bedroom on the second floor of the Baxter house. The play last night had offered a glimmer of hope between him and Reagan, but still here he was. He rolled onto his back and stared at the off-white ceiling. It could use a coat of paint, but it didn't matter now with the house on the market.

He sighed and closed his eyes. Reagan had at least agreed to bring the kids and meet him at the play. Luke drove by himself, straight from work. Mostly because he wasn't sure she'd actually come and he had promised Cole he'd be there to see his first performance. So when Reagan showed up, Luke took the action as a good sign. But other than polite, functional conversation, she didn't talk to him once during the play, and when it was over, she seemed uncomfortable.

"You're staying at your dad's?" Her question sounded more like a statement. She had Tommy by the hand and Malin in her arms.

Tommy tugged on her coat sleeve. "Are we sleeping over at Papa's? Huh, Mommy, are we?"

"Shhh." Her tone was just short of harsh. She shot their son a look and then turned back to Luke. "I'm taking the kids home." Her eyes were empty and cold. "I thought the space could do us good."

Luke was about to argue with her, but his anger wouldn't let him. How dare she bring the kids to the show as if she were willing to take a positive step forward in their relationship only to turn around and basically tell him that her trip to the theater had nothing to do with him?

He kicked his legs over the edge of the bed and sat, slouched. He caught a glimpse of his reflection in the mirror on the opposite wall and cringed at the dark circles under his eyes, the defeat in his face. Anyone could see he was a broken man. Part of it was that sleep didn't come easily these days. Reagan was hinting about getting a divorce a little more every time they talked. Any week now she was going to stop hinting and simply serve him with papers.

That's where their marriage was headed.

He stood and stretched, then slipped on his T-shirt and sweatpants. He went to the window and looked out at the familiar landscape, the basketball court, where he and Ashley had played all those pickup games when they were kids. Maybe if he could find a way to buy the old Baxter house, he could bring Reagan and the kids here, and by the very virtue of all the happy times the walls in this house had seen, they would find love again. How could a family not be loving and happy here in this place?

Luke blinked and gradually dismissed the thought. He opened the window and lifted his gaze to the blue beyond the trees. *I'm losing everything. I don't know how to stop it from happening.*

A breeze rustled the branches outside, but there was no distinct answer, no clear direction that might help him avoid the carnage ahead. What kind of kid would Tommy grow up to be if they got divorced? And what about Malin? Had they adopted her from China to bring her up in a broken home? Splitting time between

Reagan and him, the kids were bound to feel lost and rejected. Especially compared to their cousins.

I'm at the end of myself, God.

There was no quiet whisper or shouting voice telling him which way to turn. But he had the overwhelming sense that he should go downstairs, that in the early morning hours he might find his father at the kitchen table. He brushed his teeth and headed down, feeling the weight of his loneliness and failure with every step, every breath.

Sure enough, his dad was at the table drinking coffee and reading the Bible.

Luke was in his socks, and his steps had been quiet. His dad didn't see him there at the bottom of the stairs, which gave Luke the chance to study him. Really study him. A sad, silent laugh rattled around in his chest. He was asking God for help, but when was the last time he'd spent a morning like this? up before anyone else, exploring God's Word and seeking wisdom for the day? He leaned against the stair railing. This was the exact picture his dad had always made in the early morning. No wonder Luke had been raised in a home of goodness and grace, love and laughter. His dad's deep devotion to God had created that type of home for his kids.

"Luke!" His dad's smile was full and welcoming, without any of the disgust or discouragement that he would've been justified in having. "You're up early."

"Couldn't sleep." He rubbed his head and padded over to the table. "You sure I won't disturb you? I can come back in a little while."

"Not at all." He patted the spot on the table across from him. "I finished a few minutes ago. I was just looking up a few verses."

"Oh." Luke sat down and rested his forearms on the table.

"Want coffee? There's more in the pot."

"No thanks." Lately coffee made his heart race. Probably because he was in a near constant state of anxiety already. The last thing he needed was caffeine. "You have a minute?"

His dad chuckled in a tender sort of way. He eased his fingers around his coffee cup. "It's not quite seven in the morning. My schedule's pretty open." His smile faded. "You didn't say much about Reagan last night."

Luke felt his anger at the situation rise again. "Not much to say. She didn't talk about it." He lifted his hands, discouraged. As he sat back, he put one arm over the back of the chair next to him. "The show ended, and she told me she was taking the kids home. She thought it'd be better if I came here. So we'd have more space between us."

Concern creased his dad's forehead. "Then things aren't any better."

"They're worse." He held his breath for a few seconds and then released it slowly. As he did, his anger left him. The seriousness of the situation was suddenly glaring. "I'm losing her."

"Son." His dad folded his hands on the table in front of him and looked at him. "A marriage isn't something you lose. It's something you work to keep . . . or it's something you willingly let go."

"Where does that leave me?" Luke wanted his dad's advice, but how could he understand something like this? "I don't want to let go, but Reagan's finished." He worked to keep his frustration from spilling into his voice. "Things are a mess."

"They are." His dad's answers were slow and thought out. "Maybe you need to go back a ways . . . to where the knots first began."

Luke narrowed his eyes. "When we moved to Indiana?"

"No." His dad paused, his gaze kind but intense. "September 10, 2001."

"Dad . . ." The last thing Luke wanted was to rehash the past. "We're over that. We made a mistake. We moved on."

His dad took a long sip of his coffee and then set the mug back on the table. "Moral failure is more complicated than that." He folded his hands again. "You think you're past it, and in some ways you are. God forgave you. You moved on. But if you took a walk back to that time, you'd see there were probably aspects you didn't deal with."

Luke wasn't sure he was tracking with his dad. "I apologized to her, if that's what you mean."

For a moment, his dad looked out the window, his eyes distant. As if he were seeing a scene from long ago. "I know about moral failure. Obviously." He set his jaw. "The whole time your mother was pregnant with Dayne, those months when she lived at the girls' home, I must've apologized a dozen times. I felt like it was all my fault. It wasn't until after your mother came home, after she'd been forced to give him up, that I took her for a drive and asked for her forgiveness."

"It's the same thing."

"No." His answer was kind, but it came quicker this time. "*You* give an apology. Forgiveness can only be given by the person you've hurt."

The words swirled around in Luke's head and hit their mark. Suddenly he could see the events of that fall even more clearly than he'd seen them back then. Monday night—when he and Reagan crossed lines that had defined them—was too late for anything but regret. And the next day he was trying to think of how he could face her when the news came screaming across the campus. New York City was under attack, the Twin Towers on fire.

Luke closed his eyes for a few seconds. He had been shocked like everyone else, and as the towers collapsed, the last thing on his or Reagan's mind was their compromise from the night before. A sharp breath filled Luke's lungs, and when he opened his eyes, he felt different. "I never thought about it like that."

"I hadn't either." His dad picked up his coffee mug and held it with both hands, his elbows planted on the table. "Not until I needed to."

Since his marriage began falling apart, since the tangles became bigger and more complicated than either of them knew what to do with, Luke had often imagined himself in the middle of a pitch-dark tunnel. The kind that winds for miles underground, with twists and turns and a limited amount of oxygen. Often Luke felt like he'd never see daylight again.

Until this moment.

Adrenaline pushed through his veins, and he worked to keep from being too hopeful. "You think it would help if I asked for her forgiveness?"

"Think about all Reagan lost after that day." His dad's tone was gentle, but he seemed to have thought this through before today. "Her purity, which she intended to keep intact until her wedding day. She went from being a single college coed to a single mother and all the stigma that comes with."

Luke could hardly argue.

"She lost her independence, and in the process of having Tommy, she lost her ability to have more children."

Each bit of loss hit Luke like a hammer to his stomach. And his dad hadn't even touched on another sad truth. Reagan also lost what would've been her last conversation with her dad. Because that was when . . . when everything went wrong.

"I know you were both responsible for what happened that night. Moral failure rarely happens in a vacuum." His dad set the cup down and pushed back from the table a little.

"But I had a responsibility." What was wrong between him and Reagan was clearer than ever. "I never should've let things get out of hand. So maybe this is what we've been missing. Because I never asked her to forgive me."

His dad stood and motioned for Luke to follow. "I need to move the sprinkler." He opened the door between the dining room and kitchen, and once they were out back, Luke fell in beside him. The day was already warm, and though a few puffy white clouds hung along the horizon, the sky was clear. Like Luke's thoughts.

"Can I make a suggestion?" His dad slipped his hands in his pants pockets and glanced at Luke.

"Please." Luke was kicking himself for not having this talk with his dad sooner. The man had so much wisdom. But then, it was a wisdom born of experience.

"Don't rush home and ask for her forgiveness." He stopped next to the rosebushes Luke's mother had so dearly loved. His dad absently pulled off a few dead leaves and ran his fingers over the buds, each bursting with life. They continued walking. "Be thoughtful about your words so Reagan knows how much her forgiveness would mean to you. Maybe take her someplace, somewhere away from home. Since you've been fighting a lot there."

"Okay." Luke's mouth felt dry. He didn't want to blow this chance. "What about until then?"

"That's easy." He smiled, and as they walked he put his arm around Luke's shoulders. "Serve her. Encourage her. Be kind even if she isn't kind in return."

Luke had to be honest with himself. As cold and distant as Reagan had been, that part would be harder than asking for her forgiveness. He looked over his shoulder at the rosebushes, and he could almost see his mother, almost feel her walking on his other side. He allowed a quiet laugh. "That's what Mom would say. Basically, love her."

"It is." His dad stopped and nodded slowly. He too looked back at the roses. "I miss her so much."

For a few beats they stood there. Days like this, Luke still couldn't believe she was gone. As if he almost expected her to be waiting for them back in the house. They set out toward the far edges of the yard, and once his dad had moved the sprinkler, they took the same path to the house again. "You're really going to sell it."

His dad stopped again and seemed to survey the property. "I'll miss everything about it. The way it looks in the glow of a sunrise and the way the shadows fall against it at sunset. Every memory, every room." He gave Luke a sad smile. "The smell of your mother's roses coming through the open windows and mixing with whatever was cooking in the oven."

Luke swallowed the emotions building inside him. "Maybe I

should try to buy it, move Reagan and the kids closer to the rest of the family."

They started walking again. When his dad finally responded, his voice was thoughtful, filled once more with that familiar seasoned wisdom. "The house is wonderful, but it isn't walls and windows that make a home. I learned that from the fire." He glanced at the corner of the house near the garage, the place where last fall's blaze had started. "Go see about making things right with Reagan. That's where you'll find your home."

For a few more minutes they talked about the different buyers who had come through and made offers and how the soft market wasn't helping. "The buyer's out there." His dad opened the back door and held it for Luke. "It'll all happen in God's timing."

Like everything about life, Luke thought.

He took half an hour to gather his things and chat a little longer with his dad, and then he headed home. Reagan wasn't expecting him until late Sunday. The time apart was good for them; at least that's what they had agreed. But if he was going to find ways to serve and encourage her, he needed to go back today. Before another minute passed.

As he drove, one bit of advice from his dad kept replaying in his mind. *"Go see about making things right with Reagan. That's where you'll find your home."* At the time, Luke meant to ask exactly what his dad meant. A home was made of memories and magical moments, seasons shared and years of love and laughter. What did making things right have to do with that?

Luke stared out the windshield at the road ahead, trying to relate the two. Then, as if God had dropped the answer straight to his heart, the connection was obvious. Part of what made up the memories in a family were times like this when everything was falling apart. Some of the best memories made in the Baxter house had come from the days when he and Ashley found their way back to being not only brother and sister but friends. Times when his mother was sick and his father cared for her around the clock.

The family meetings when they were little, when their dad would sit them down to talk. Luke and the others always dragged their feet as they came together, but at one time or another they all admitted how much better life felt once they worked through their differences. Looking back, those discussions were part of what made the tapestry of their lives so rich, so memorable.

With God's help, if he could find the words to ask Reagan for her forgiveness, then one day years from now this terrible time in their marriage would be only one more streak of color across the picture of their past. Part of the richness of life together.

He looked at the clock on his dashboard. He would be home in less than ten minutes, and for the first time in months the thought didn't discourage him. He and Reagan could love again, couldn't they? If there was true forgiveness? He imagined for a moment how it would feel walking the hallways of his house without the tension he felt there now or what it would be like to sit down to dinner and look into the eyes of his wife, knowing what they'd survived.

So his father's words made perfect sense. Luke didn't need the Baxter house to have a sense of love and shared memories and a history rich with hope and healing. He needed to go to Reagan and take his father's advice.

And in that way, one day the place he was headed wouldn't be merely the house he shared with Reagan and the kids.

It would be a home.

CHAPTER EIGHTEEN

K ARI HAD BEEN PRAYING for Angela Manning every day since her father first mentioned her a month ago, and something unexpected had happened. God wasn't only helping Angela; He was helping Kari understand grace and mercy like never before.

She parked her car, climbed out, and headed for the front door of the psychiatric facility. This was the fifth straight Tuesday she'd made the trek, and each time she came with less fear, less anxiety. She still wasn't sure if her visits made a difference, since Angela was receiving inpatient counseling around the clock. But whenever Kari prayed about her visits, the answer seemed to be the same—there was a reason. However complicated and unclear.

God was walking with her through this strange counseling relationship, and Kari had been surprised many times. By the fact that she'd survived the first encounter praying with Angela, holding her hand, and managing to stay discreet about her identity as Tim's wife. And also by the strides Angela made from week to week. Clearly Angela was wounded and drowning in guilt. The counseling seemed to be opening her up to the idea that there was still hope for her, that forgiveness was possible with Christ.

The woman at the front desk smiled. "Hello, Kari. Angela's looking forward to your meeting. You can go on back."

Kari thanked her and walked to the small room where she met with Angela.

After a minute, the door opened and Dr. Montgomery stepped inside. "I have good news." The familiar calm marked his voice. "Angela is progressing very nicely. She's agreed to stay until we think it's safe for her to leave. Which may be sooner than we thought." Gratitude warmed his eyes. "It's been a while since I've seen a patient so fully embrace the message of the gospel. And I believe your visits are a big part of that."

Kari wasn't sure what to say. Dr. Montgomery was giving her exactly what she needed, a confirmation that her time with Angela was helping, even in some small way. "Thank you. That means a lot."

"You're a volunteer, caring for a stranger. That illustrates Christ's love more than anything we can teach her in here." He smiled. "Angela will be here in a minute or so."

When the doctor was gone, Kari stared absently at the rich blue-striped wallpaper. There was one problem. Angela wasn't a stranger. Maybe it was time for Kari to tell her about their shared connection to Tim. She was still considering the idea when Angela walked in. She was holding her Bible, the one Kari had given her.

"Hi." Angela's voice was still marked by shame but not as much as before. "Thanks for coming." She took the seat opposite Kari. "I asked Dr. Montgomery to tell you how I've been doing. I'm . . . I don't know. I'm learning things I never thought about before." She folded her hands on her lap, and a new sense of peace emanated from her. "I can actually feel the love of God, if that makes sense."

"It does." Kari slid to the edge of her seat, reached out, and touched Angela's shoulder. "I've been praying for you every day."

"I don't know why." The hardness in her face and eyes was being replaced by a transparency that hadn't been there before. "I mean, you don't know me or anything. But I appreciate you, Kari. Really, I do."

Kari had brought her Bible, and now she directed Angela to the back of the New Testament. "We're going to read from the sixth chapter of Ephesians." Kari helped her find the right spot, and they took turns reading out loud and then discussing the meaning in the verses.

"The armor of God . . ." Angela closed her Bible as they finished. "It's like He knew we'd be in a battle here."

For a moment, Kari was back in the house she'd shared with Tim, watching him walk out for a life with his mistress. A life with the woman sitting across from her. "Yes, battles are a real part of life." She pointed out that according to Scripture, strength for the battle came only through Christ, and when the time came for Angela to go home, it would be crucial for her to connect with a church.

Angela thought for a minute. "Sometimes I'm so . . . ashamed, I guess. Because I wound up here." She glanced down at her hands, and when she looked up again, her eyes were clouded with guilt. "I'm telling strangers things I'd blocked out of my mind for years."

A twinge of anxiety hit Kari, and she had the urge to run. "It's important to open up in counseling. I'm learning that I have to be honest about my past before I can let God direct my future."

Their half hour was up, and Kari stood. Only then did she realize she was trembling. She went to shake Angela's hand, but the woman stepped closer and hugged her instead. Not the sort of casual huglike greeting people pass out at church. But a desperate, clinging hug that said much about Angela's need for a friend.

As she drew back, Angela's eyes welled up. "I think I'm close. You know, to giving my life to Christ. I thought you should know."

The admission filled Kari with a rush of joy and gratitude. After all, this was the reason she'd come—to share a Bible and the saving grace of God with this woman who had so harmed her.

"That's the best news." Kari smiled at her, and a knowing reso-nated deep within her. For Angela was no longer the other woman. She would soon be a person made brand-new by Jesus.

A few minutes later when she was back in her car, Kari finally exhaled. She couldn't be a friend to Angela because she could never tell her the complete truth. They would meet one more week, and then Kari would encourage Angela to connect with a women's ministry at one of the local churches. By then she'd be ready—at least it seemed that way. Kari would check with Dr. Montgomery next time just to be sure.

On the way home, Kari felt trapped in the past. Images of Tim on their wedding day and their first Christmas together and a dozen other days gone by flashed in her mind.

RJ and baby Annie were at her father's house, and he'd told her to take her time. At the next light she turned right instead of left and drove just out of town to the cemetery.

It wasn't often she came here, not by herself anyway. She and Brooke and Ashley would stop by on special days, their mom's birthday and the anniversary of her death. But today Kari wanted to do something she hadn't done in a long time. She parked her car and climbed out. The afternoon was warm and sunny, with none of the usual spring thunderheads hovering on the horizon. She took the narrow paved path that meandered onto the grounds, and then she veered off it through the manicured grass to where her mother was buried. She couldn't come here without stopping by this spot first.

The stone was simple, with her mother's name engraved at the bottom. Kari bent down and dusted off a few grass clippings that had settled on top. "Mom, you wouldn't believe what happened today. . . ." Her voice was a whisper, filled with a sorrow that would always be there. She hesitated, then stopped at the grave of her niece Sarah.

Kari moved on another twenty yards until she reached the place where Tim was buried. Sometimes her life with Tim felt like it had happened to another person, as if she and Ryan had been together forever. But here, looking at Tim's tombstone, the past was both vivid and real.

She brushed a residue of dirt off Tim's stone. For a long time she stared at the marker, at her first husband's name etched across it. As she did, the vividness of the past gradually faded, and Kari felt peace come over her. She lifted her face to the sky and closed her eyes. *You are amazing, God. You see us through whatever battle comes along.*

I have loved you with an everlasting love, My daughter. . . .

The gentle response blew lightly across Kari's soul, and she set off for the car without looking back at the gravestone. God had a plan in all things, a way to survive the battle however fiercely it raged. Even on a day like this . . . when He reminded her of His great love for her.

Kari breathed in the sweet spring air, and the freshness of the feeling replaced the sadness of yesterday. She would see her commitment to Angela through, meeting with her one more time. Someday soon, Angela would commit her life to Christ—Kari was confident. Then God would lead Angela to a church where she could truly begin this next chapter of her life. And sometime in the near future, thoughts of Angela would no longer bring her pain and heartache.

They would bring her closure.

CHAPTER NINETEEN

IN ALL BAILEY'S DAYS at Clear Creek High, she'd been to only a couple of dances with groups of friends, but tonight was her senior prom, and she was taking Tim. Bailey couldn't stop thinking about all the times she'd imagined going with Tim to a dance like this one. She had circled May 17 on the calendar the first week of school, and now it was finally here.

Bailey looked in the mirror. Her floor-length dress was silky aqua green with thin shoulder straps and a gathering of material at the center, just above her waist. It was elegant, and her mom said it clung to her in all the right places without being formfitting. She tilted her head and studied her shoes. Whitney had loaned them to her, and they were perfect. Silver open-toed sandals with one-inch heels.

She stepped back from the mirror and glanced out the window. Like every day since they received the news, only one thing made today less than perfect. Cody was still missing.

Bailey passed her nightstand on the way to her bathroom and paused long enough to brush her fingers against Cody's last letter.

Please, God, You know where he is. She looked out her window again and tried to picture her friend captured in some Iraqi prison. *He needs Your help. Give the guys looking for him the wisdom to know where to look. You're his only hope.*

She waited a moment, but there was no answer, no distinct Scripture or sense of knowing to reassure her that Cody would be okay. Bailey turned slowly from the window and sighed. As she did, she noticed her mom standing in the doorway to her room.

"Thinking about Cody?" Her mom's tone was understanding.

"Yes." Bailey touched her hair. The curlers were nearly cool, but she wasn't in a hurry. Tim wouldn't be here for another half hour. She met her mother's eyes. "I wish they'd find him."

"Me too." Her mom stepped inside and sat on the edge of Bailey's bed. A few seconds passed before she smiled. "You look beautiful. Absolutely breathtaking."

"Really?" Bailey came closer. "The dress doesn't make me look too big?"

A light bit of laughter came from her mom. "Honey, you couldn't look big in a potato sack. The only thing more beautiful than you in that dress is the person God's made you on the inside."

"Aw, Mom . . . that's sweet." She leaned down and gave her mother a hug. "Thanks for knowing just what to say." She straightened. "I can't think about Cody tonight."

"No. Tonight's for you and Tim."

"Connor says it isn't fair prom's only for juniors and seniors." She giggled and walked the few steps into her bathroom. "He wanted to bring Rachel."

"Yes, well, he'll have to wait."

"I have a feeling Rachel will still be around in a few years." Bailey gave her mom a grin. "But me and Tim? I mean, who saw this coming?"

Her mom laughed. "I think you and Tim are the only ones who didn't."

"Yeah . . . maybe." Bailey moved close to her bathroom counter and carefully undid one of the rollers. A section of her light brown hair tumbled down, the curl perfectly set. "Still . . . I don't know what he's really feeling. If he sees this as a fun night out or if he's ready to be open about liking me."

Her mom could still see her from the place where she sat on the edge of the mattress. "He might not know just how much, but he likes you. That much has always been true."

"I don't know." Bailey undid another two curlers. "That's sorta what he said in his letter, but I'm not sure. I hope you're right."

"I've seen the way he looks at you. He's liked you for a long time, but for the last few years he's been very careful."

"That's what he says. About the offstage drama at CKT." Bailey glanced in the mirror at her mother. "I don't know why he cares so much."

"Because gossip could ruin the experience of CKT." Her tone was more thoughtful. "He has a point."

Bailey finished with the rollers and eased her fingertips up into her hairline so her hair hung in a curtain of curls. Then she used a handful of bobby pins to lift the crown off her forehead. When she was finished, she turned and stepped back into her bedroom. "What do you think?"

Her mom stared at her with admiration. She rose and took hold of Bailey's hands. "You look like an angel." She leaned in and kissed Bailey's cheeks. "I've never seen you more beautiful."

Her mom stayed as Bailey applied a bit of blush and eye makeup, and then they went downstairs, where her dad and the boys were having burgers. As Bailey drifted down the stairs and into the kitchen area, the action around the raised bar came to a standstill. Her dad stood and simply watched her, his mouth open.

"Come on, guys." Bailey giggled as she did a slow pirouette. "Say something." She faced them, her hands out to her sides. "Do you like it?"

"Wow." Ricky set his burger down. "You look like a movie star or something."

Justin studied her dress. "Sort of like a mermaid."

"Yeah, a pretty one." BJ grinned at her.

"Some people think mermaids really live off Grand Bahama Island." Shawn's eyes grew wide. "I read that in my shark book."

Her dad still hadn't said anything, but he made his way to her side. "For a moment there, I had a vision of the future." He touched his hand to her elbow and looked deep into her eyes. "My little girl ready for me to walk her down the aisle." He kissed her forehead. "You're stunning, Bailey. All grown up."

Of all the compliments she'd gotten in the last few minutes, this was the most tender. Her dad struggled with the fact that she was getting older. But here he seemed to have no choice but to admit that she was becoming a young woman, that someday soon she would leave home and find her way. Bailey looped her arms around his neck. "I'll always be your little girl, Daddy."

He smiled at her. "And you'll always be my princess."

There was a knock at the door, and Ricky let loose a low whistle. "Tim's here!"

BJ grinned at his brothers. "Ooooh . . . Bailey's going on a date!"

She rolled her eyes at them as she smoothed her dress. "Okay, guys. Enough." She glanced at her mom. "How do I look?"

This time an excited urgency filled her mother's eyes. "Perfect!" She pointed toward the front door. "You can't leave him standing there."

Bailey's heart skipped a beat as she hurried toward the door, her delicate heels clicking on the tile floor as she went.

Halfway to the entryway she heard her father instructing the boys. "No funny business, okay? You don't want to embarrass her."

The boys laughed in response, but Bailey heard all of them agree that of course they knew better than to make the moment awkward for their sister.

She reached the door, slightly breathless, and stopped. Once more she adjusted her hair and her dress; then she took a breath and opened the door.

Since she'd known him, she'd seen Tim as larger than life, the guy who ruled the stage at CKT and praised God through his music with an undivided heart. But standing in front of her now, dressed in a black suit and tie, a boxed corsage in his hands, for the first time Tim looked nervous and uncertain.

"Hi." She heard the shyness in her voice as she stepped back and made room for him.

He followed her inside, and his eyes filled with an awe she hadn't seen there before. "Bailey, you look beautiful."

"Thanks." Heat flooded her cheeks, and she lowered her chin. As she looked up at him, she had the strangest feeling, as if this were the first time they'd really seen each other. "You look nice too." She wasn't sure whether to hug him or not, and after a few seconds the opportunity passed. "I have your boutonniere in the fridge." She motioned for him to follow her, and he did.

In the kitchen, the boys pretended to be busy with their burgers, but each of them said a quick hello to Tim and watched all that happened next.

After her parents greeted Tim, Bailey took the single white rose from its clear plastic bag and brought it to him. "I'm . . . I'm not really sure how to do this."

"It goes on the right side." Her mom swapped a look with her dad. "Isn't that it?"

"I think so." Her dad leaned against the stove, his arms crossed. He grinned at them. "Just be careful with the pin."

After a few attempts, Bailey managed to gather enough of Tim's suit jacket so she could thread the pin through without poking him.

Midway through her efforts, her mom took their picture, and she took another when the flower was finally neatly in place. "I talked to your mom." She smiled at Tim. "I told her I'd take lots of pictures."

"Good." Bailey giggled and gave Tim a hesitant look. "Right?"

He laughed. "Sure. My mom's the same way, so I'm used to it."

They took pictures for the next ten minutes, while Tim gave her a pretty wrist corsage and as they posed on the foot of the stairs in the entryway and again in front of the living room fireplace. Finally it was time to leave, and Bailey's parents walked them out to the front porch.

Laughter tickled Bailey's throat as Tim opened the door for her. She spoke in a voice only he could hear. "I feel like Cinderella going to my first ball."

He paused, searching her eyes. "Only so much more beautiful than Cinderella ever dreamed of being." He held her gaze a few moments longer and then hurried around to the driver's side. Once inside his car they waved good-bye to her parents and drove off.

This year's prom was in one of the reception halls at Indiana University. A dinner was catered for the couples, and a local band provided music. Whereas other school dances held in the gymnasium tended to be marked by dirty dancing and dark lighting, the prom was different. Elegance was expected, and an instructor would be available to give couples lessons in several classic dances.

Bailey was glad. She avoided the other dances, the ones that no chaperone could seem to control. But tonight with Tim would be a dream. She settled back into her seat and stole a glance at him. He had never looked more handsome, and the cologne he was wearing was something she recognized, something that she sometimes smelled in her dad's *Sports Illustrated* magazine.

As they drove, Tim seemed to relax. "Is this weird? Us going on a date after all these years?"

"No." Bailey's voice was soft. "Not really." She wasn't sure what he was getting at, but she didn't want to share her feelings without first knowing what he was thinking.

Then he did something that took all the guesswork out. He reached over and took gentle hold of her hand, giving her a quick look. "Being with you tonight . . . it's all I could think about since you asked me."

From that moment on, Bailey didn't have to wonder about what Tim felt for her, and suddenly she understood why he'd looked nervous on her front porch. He was as unsure about her feelings as she was about his.

The rest of the night was magical, like something from a favorite movie. They sat with two other couples who had been involved with CKT at one time, and for the first half hour they worked as a group with the dance instructor. For the next few hours they waltzed and two-stepped and even tried the tango. Before the dance was over, they had their picture taken by the professional photographer, and they shared one last slow dance.

In Tim's arms, Bailey was overcome by emotions. This was Tim Reed, who she'd admired from a distance for so long, here before her, holding her just so and moving her across the dance floor. But a part of her felt like she was back on a CKT stage acting out a scene from a story that didn't really belong to her. Bailey blocked the emotions from her heart and tried to stay in the moment. She could sort through her feelings later.

When the music stopped, Tim led her back to their table and helped place her wrap around her shoulders once again. Before he took her home, they stopped for ice cream at Renaissance, a cute little spot a block off campus. They talked about *Joseph* and the way the community had responded to the show by packing the theater for three straight weekends.

Tim was sitting across from her, and he gave her a flirty look over the edge of his malt glass. "Because of you . . ."

"What?" She allowed a happy ripple of laughter. "They came for Connor. He was Joseph."

"No, no." He sat up straight and reached for her hand. "They came to see Bailey Flanigan. Best narrator ever!"

"Maybe they came to get a glimpse of Tim Reed, former CKT star."

They both laughed. "The real reason is Dayne Matthews. The town might be getting used to the idea that the country's top superstar is running a kids' theater in Bloomington, but they still want to be around him."

Bailey loved this, the way they shared so much of the past. In lots of ways, she and Tim had grown up together, going through many of the same highs and lows over the years.

Eventually the conversation turned to their plans for the coming fall, since Bailey was graduating.

"You going away to some big university?" Tim kept his tone light, but the question was a serious one. His expression told her that much.

"I've thought about it." She angled her head and studied him. "How do you like IU?"

"I love it." He shrugged. "I'm doing a double major, music and business. It has everything I need, and I can still help out with CKT."

Bailey nodded slowly. "That's what I've been thinking. I mean, I'd love to go to New York City and audition for a show; you know, dance every day for a living. But until then, I'm probably going to stay here. I got my acceptance a month ago."

"Really?" Tim didn't hide his excitement. "To IU?"

"Yes." She laughed at his reaction. "Like half the kids around here."

Bailey had talked about college with her parents shortly after New Year's, and they'd all agreed that IU was her best option for now. It was a major university with all the right degrees and opportunities, and it would allow her to live at home instead of in a dorm. At the same time she would continue with voice and dance lessons and watch for auditions in New York City so when the time was right, she could take a shot at the dreams that were beginning to take shape for her.

But Tim didn't ask about any of that. He seemed happy enough to hear that she was probably staying in Bloomington. At least for now.

By the time they finished their ice cream and Tim took her home, it was a few minutes before midnight.

"Well—" he put his arm around her shoulders as they walked up to her front door—"I got you home before twelve."

"Yeah . . ." Her voice was soft, and she felt the same shyness from earlier again. They stopped just before the entryway. "Wanna come in?"

"I better not." Tim took a step closer, and his eyes sparkled with the reflection of the full moon. "I have to study for finals."

Bailey nodded. "Are they pretty intense?"

"Very." He chuckled and slid his hands into his pants pockets. "Nothing like high school."

She tried to think of something to say in response, but his eyes distracted her and in a heartbeat she knew what was about to happen. He was going to kiss her! Tim was going to kiss her good night right here on her front porch beneath a sky full of springtime stars.

He took another step closer and brought his hands up to either side of her face. "You know what?"

"What?" Bailey couldn't breathe, couldn't think or move or analyze what was happening. He was so near all she could do was listen to him take his next breath.

"I used to wonder what it felt like to fall . . . you know, really fall."

She felt dizzy, and she leaned a little against his hands to steady herself. "And?"

Tim looked deep into her eyes. "Now I know." He pulled her slowly into his arms and hugged her for a long time. As he did, she circled her arms around his waist and wondered if he could feel her racing heart. Then, as he pulled slightly back, he brought his lips to hers, and for the sweetest few seconds, he kissed her. Not a kiss of passion or desperation but a kiss that told her he meant what he'd said. He was falling for her, the same way she was falling for him.

As he moved back, there were more stars in his eyes than in the whole expanse of sky above them. "I'll call you this weekend."

She folded her arms to ward off the chill his absence left behind. "I . . . I had a great time tonight."

Tim paused, and his face lit up in a smile. "Me too."

Before Bailey could think of a way to make him stay longer, he got into his car and pulled away.

When he was gone, she went in and found her parents in the kitchen. They were sitting side by side at the bar, drinking coffee. Whatever they'd been talking about, the atmosphere felt casual, and Bailey knew they'd waited up for her.

"So . . ." Her mom smiled at her. "By the look on your face I don't have to ask how it went."

Bailey pulled up the first open barstool and grinned. "It was amazing."

"How amazing?" Her dad took on a mock look of concern.

"Don't worry." Bailey stifled a giggle. "We're not engaged or anything."

Her dad sighed. "That's good. Because you can't get married for another ten years. At least."

"Daaad." Bailey made a silly face at him. "You worry too much."

"Only when my little girl's heart is on the line."

Her mom put an arm around her dad's shoulders. "Never mind your father. He gets crazy when he thinks about you on a date with any guy." She kissed his cheek. "Even Tim."

They all laughed, and Bailey told them about the night, about the dance instructor and learning the different steps and how the hours had melted away. This was a tradition she'd had since she was very young, sharing everything that mattered with her parents, especially her mom. It helped her sort through her feelings to share them this way. Never mind that most of the kids at school did their best to avoid their parents. Bailey would always consider them her closest friends.

When they were done talking, Bailey headed upstairs, and after washing her face and brushing her teeth, she studied herself in the mirror. There was something different about her eyes, her expression. She stepped back and angled her face. Was this how it looked to be falling in love?

Is Tim the one, God? Is this the beginning of something that could last for always? Often when she talked to God she could hear His response—either she'd feel a gentle nudging toward one direction or another or a Scripture verse would come to mind. But tonight, the question that hung alongside the stars in the night sky of her soul was met with no answer.

She fell asleep thinking about Tim and the dance, but her dreams were of a football receiver dressed in a dirty army uniform and running from a pack of angry Iraqi insurgents. She woke up gasping for air, Cody's face as vivid in her mind as if he were standing in front of her. She lay there in bed, wondering why that had happened. Why after a perfect date with Tim did she spend the night having terrible dreams about Cody?

Adrenaline rushed through her veins, and she had the urge to find her mother and let her know that something was wrong with Cody. Otherwise why was he so strongly on her mind? She was about to climb out of bed when her bedroom door opened and her mom walked in. Bailey bolted up in bed, her eyes wide.

Only then did she realize how upset and serious her mom looked, and suddenly Bailey wondered if she was still in the dream, if all she had to do was wake up and she'd be back in that happy place where she was last night after saying good-bye to Tim.

"Mom?" Bailey swung her legs over the edge of the mattress, her heart pounding. "It's Cody, isn't it?"

Her mom wrinkled her brow and slowly sat on the corner of Bailey's bed. "Did . . . did you hear my conversation?"

"No." Bailey swallowed hard. Her heartbeat was so fast and hard she could barely talk. "I . . . I dreamed about him, that he was running from someone."

Her mother's expression told Bailey that the dream and the news she was bringing were somehow connected. She put her hand on Bailey's knee, never breaking eye contact. "They found him."

"Cody?" Bailey let out a cry, but she didn't dare breathe. Not until she heard the other details. Her words tumbled out in a pinched whisper. "He's alive, right? He has to be alive!"

"He is." Her face looked pale, and fear left a shadow over her eyes. "He escaped his captors and was running toward a convoy of U.S. troops when he was shot."

Shot? Cody was shot? Bailey squeezed her eyes shut and tipped her head back. *No, not Cody.* She couldn't stop herself from picturing him lying on some Iraqi street. Her breathing came faster, and she opened her eyes, desperate for some sort of news she could hold on to. "How bad is it?"

"I don't know." Her mom's eyes welled up. "He was rescued by two U.S. soldiers, but he lost a lot of blood. His mom said the situation was critical."

"No!" The word came out as a single cry. Cody was just here, just standing in their doorway hugging her brothers and her parents and telling her good-bye. He was promising that he'd be back soon and that everything would be okay. He couldn't be critical. Panic scrambled her thoughts, and she fought for clarity. "What else?"

"That's really it." Her mom hung her head for a moment. "We'll know more in a few days, I guess." She met Bailey's eyes again. "If . . . if everything goes okay, he'll be flown back to Washington state, where he's based, and stay there until he's well enough to come home."

"Until when?" Bailey felt sick to her stomach.

"His mom said six weeks. Maybe longer."

There was only one thing left to do. "Pray with me, Mom. Please."

They held hands and her mom started, asking God to use His healing touch on Cody and to spare his life from the injuries. She thanked Him that Cody had escaped and asked that they might have peace and patience as they waited for further word.

Bailey prayed next, and as she did Cody's face was there again, clearly in her mind the way it had been when the two of them walked through the forest behind the Flanigan house. She also asked God to heal Cody and to bring him back home. "Soon, God . . . please bring him home soon."

When they finished, she and her mom hugged for a long time. Only after her mother had gone back downstairs and Bailey was left alone in her room did she realize something that told her much about her true feelings. Hours after one of the best dates in her life, news about Cody's injuries should've saddened and shocked her and left her desperately praying for him. After all, Cody was one of her closest friends. But the feelings she had now went beyond concern for an injured friend. She had a longing for Cody like nothing she'd ever known before.

And that longing made her doubt everything she'd felt just twelve hours ago.

Even if last night was practically perfect.

CHAPTER TWENTY

WITH TWO MONTHS LEFT in her pregnancy, Ashley felt bigger than a house. Her fears about this baby had eased, even if they hadn't completely disappeared. It was the last Saturday in May, and in a few hours she and her sisters would meet at Kari's house for Elaine's wedding shower.

Ashley stretched her lower back and made her way around the edges of their bed, pulling up the sheets and straightening the blue and white comforter. She and Landon and the boys were about to walk to the park, and she didn't want to leave the room messy.

She smiled to herself as she fluffed up the pillows. Funny, with Sarah she hadn't noticed any of the usual aspects of being pregnant. Not the largeness or the sore back or her tendency to straighten and organize that had come with her other babies.

With Sarah the nine months were all about enjoying her while there was still time. Every day had brought them closer to her birth, closer to her death. So Ashley's focus had been entirely on the baby inside her and not on her own changing body. This time was more normal, something Ashley was grateful for. Though she enjoyed feeling her little boy move about inside her, she was anxious for his birth.

"You about ready?" Landon poked his head in through their bedroom door. He wore a baseball cap, shorts, and a T-shirt. "The boys are ready to bust the door down."

"Almost." She straightened and stretched her back once more. "I'm feeling it today."

"I bet." His tone was tender. "The humidity's got to be at 70 percent."

It had rained the last four days straight but not today. The temperature was supposed to rise above eighty, and sometime late this evening thunderstorms were predicted. But for now it was sunshine and blue skies, even with the humidity. The boys weren't the only ones itching to get out of the house.

She found a loose maternity top and struggled into a pair of stretch shorts and white Keds.

Devin no longer needed his stroller on walks to the park, so today he and Cole held hands and stayed a few feet in front of Ashley and Landon.

Landon put his arm around her waist and slowed his pace to hers. "Is he moving much?"

"Earlier." The heat was making her forehead damp, and she dabbed at it with the back of her hand. "It's hard to tell when I'm walking. I think the motion usually lulls him to sleep."

Landon shifted the bag of sports gear up a little higher on his shoulder. "I have a feeling he'll be a lot like Cole. Curious and full of life." Landon lifted his face toward the sun and breathed in deep. "We're so blessed. You know?"

"We are." Ashley no longer felt the twinge of sadness that this baby was a boy and not a girl. No one could've replaced Sarah anyway.

They reached the park, and the boys gathered around the sports bag Landon had been carrying. Inside was a wooden bat for Cole and a plastic Wiffle bat for Devin, along with a few baseballs and

Wiffle balls. Cole was playing Little League this spring, and his coach had nominated him for the local all-star team. They agreed that Landon would pitch to Cole twenty yards away, and Ashley would pitch to Devin.

She took Devin by the hand, and when they were a safe distance apart, she tossed him a series of pitches with the lightweight plastic balls. He hit nearly all of them, and a few went to the place where Landon and Cole were playing.

"Hey!" Landon grinned at Devin. "You're a little slugger!"

"He learned it from me." Cole thrust his chest out. "Right, Dad? He learned it from me!"

"He must've." Landon laughed and caught Ashley's eye. "His humility too."

"What?" Cole cupped his hand around his ear.

"Nothing." Landon flashed a grin at Ashley. "Let's gather up the balls, and I'll pitch another round."

The hour went by quickly, and Ashley couldn't help but see the scene the way it would look a year from now when she'd have her third son in a stroller. Would he love sports, or would he have a passion for singing and theater like the kids at CKT? Or would he enjoy doing both, the way Cole did? Maybe he'd be a math whiz or a science kid. Whatever God had planned for him, He was working out the details day by day, knitting her baby boy together inside her.

They got home with enough time for Ashley to get ready for Elaine's shower. It was at two o'clock, and afterward, she planned to spend an hour at her dad's house working on the painting, the one that was still so strong in her heart. The images were taking shape a little more every time she worked on it. The two women showing a great connection with each other as they walked the path ahead of them. She was nearly finished now, which was good because the image was always on her mind.

Ashley stepped into the warm shower and let the water wash away her strange sadness. This was a day of celebration, one she needed to embrace. She closed her eyes and pictured the gift she'd bought Elaine. Much thought had gone into choosing the contents of the wrapped box sitting on her kitchen counter. In the end, she'd decided to give Elaine a set of beautiful etched wooden frames. In the card, Ashley had written a letter telling Elaine how God had brought her into their lives. The frames, Ashley wrote, were so that her dad and Elaine could start filling their new home with the memories they'd make together as a couple.

All week leading up to this afternoon, every time Ashley thought about the party, she checked her emotions. "I'm really okay about this," she'd told Landon a few times. "My dad's fiancée is having her wedding shower this weekend, and I'm handling it."

But as Ashley finished her shower and slipped into a pale floral maternity dress, as she found the right shoes and blow-dried her hair, she felt the familiar doubt creeping back. She was halfway to Kari's house when she realized that what she was feeling wasn't doubt but sorrow. The deep sorrow that still came with missing her mom. Strange, because after her mother's death, a well-meaning family friend had told her something at the funeral that had stuck: "The pain will lessen with time."

The sentiment was something Ashley had heard echoed several times in the years since, but so far it hadn't held even a slight bit of truth. Not for her, anyway. There was the initial grief and shock after her mother was gone and buried. The realization that she would never walk through the door again, never join them around the table for a family dinner. Never hold her grandchildren again. But then a different type of sadness hit. The knowing that without a determination to hold tight to yesterday, the ever-pressing tide of the present would wash away the vividness of every beautiful memory.

And something more. The understanding about what a long time it had been since she'd felt her mother's touch or heard her voice and what a long time it would be until they would hear or feel her that way again in heaven. All of that combined made for an aching loss that sometimes felt stronger than ever.

Ashley focused on the road. That's what she was feeling today, nothing but the usual sadness over missing her mother and the knowing that came with it. Especially on a day like this one, when there would be no need for a wedding shower for her father's fiancée if only her mother were still alive.

A sigh rattled up from Ashley's heart. Elaine was wonderful. There was no reason to arrive at the party feeling less than happy about her father's pending marriage. She focused instead on her baby and all she still had to do to ready the nursery for his arrival. By the time she parked in front of Kari's house, her sadness was tucked away in its proper place, in the basement of her soul.

Kari met her at the door, and after a hug her eyes lit up. "Did I tell you?"

"Tell me what?" Ashley set her gift down on a table near the entrance.

"About Angela." Excitement brimmed in Kari's voice. "She gave her life to the Lord. She's not the person she was. Seriously."

Ashley stared at her sister for a moment. How could she and Kari even be related? Kari was so much kinder than she was. "I don't know how you do it, meeting with the woman your husband had an affair with." She leaned against the cool wood-paneled wall and caught her breath. "I couldn't handle it."

"If God asked you to handle it, you would. I know you, Ash."

She wasn't sure, but she smiled at Kari and shrugged. "You're my hero. Let's just leave it at that." She hugged her sister again. "Is everyone here?"

"Brooke's running a few minutes late. Elaine and Katy are in the living room. Reagan can't come. Tommy's sick." She dropped her voice. "I'm glad we're doing this. I think it means the world to Elaine."

Ashley smiled at Kari. "I agree. It was a good idea."

They were still standing by the front door when Brooke arrived, and the three of them joined the others in the next room. Ashley and Brooke took turns hugging Elaine and Katy. Once the greetings were finished, Kari announced that it was time to eat. She'd made tortilla roll-ups and fruit salad for the occasion, and after they'd filled their plates, they used the next half hour to catch up on the latest news.

"My kids and their families will definitely be here for the wedding." Elaine looked pleased. "My daughter wanted to be here today also. She sends her love."

Ashley crossed her legs at the ankles and adjusted her plate on her knees. That was something else she didn't spend a lot of time thinking about. The fact that after her father married Elaine she'd have stepsiblings. She smiled at Elaine. "Tell them we're glad they'll be here for the ceremony."

Brooke put her fork down and let out a gasp. "I almost forgot. Dad called me on my way here. He has an offer on the house. He asked us to pray that this time it wouldn't fall through."

Ashley stared at her half-eaten lunch and felt herself lose her appetite. It was bound to happen, of course. In fact, the sale of the house *needed* to happen for her dad and Elaine to afford the new house they'd bought. But still the news landed like a couple of bricks in her stomach.

"I understand you and John have found a place." Katy was still able to cross her legs. She looked much smaller than Ashley. At least it felt that way. The two of them had gotten even closer during their pregnancies, talking often about the physical changes they were going through and allowing themselves to dream about the future, the way Ashley had done with Kari before she learned Sarah's diagnosis.

Katy's question sparked a description from Elaine. "It's a farmhouse, smaller than the one he's in now and with much less land. Just half an acre, enough so we can plant a vegetable garden."

Ashley tried to embrace the image. "That's nice."

"It's closer to town and not far from the university. All that and it's just a short walk to the park." She smiled, and a warmth filled her eyes. "We plan to do a lot of walking."

This was the part about Elaine that Ashley loved most. She would keep their father happy and healthy, bringing him the friendship and companionship he deserved in the next few decades of his life. They were both healthy and fit, and they shared the same interests. Truly Elaine was a gift from God, nothing less.

As lunch wound down, Kari explained that rather than play shower games, they would go around the room and talk about their own love stories and what God had taught them through the journey of time. "We thought it would be good to remind ourselves of how important marriage is to each of us and maybe help you get to know us a little better at the same time."

Elaine's expression held gratitude for Kari and each of them. "I think it sounds wonderful."

Brooke went first. She talked about meeting Peter in medical school and how at first they seemed too competitive for each other. "Actually, that problem followed us into our marriage. Before Hayley's near drowning, some of Peter's feelings about me came to the surface. He really questioned my ability as a doctor." Her eyes held some of the pain of that time in her life. "After Hayley's accident, God worked out all those feelings. Peter finally realized we weren't in competition, and it was possible for both of us to be good at what we're gifted to do. Every time I look at Hayley, I'm reminded of the healing God's done in our lives—not just for our daughter but for our marriage." She paused and met Ashley's eyes. "I guess God's taught me that miracles don't always look the way we expect them to look. But that doesn't make them any less miraculous."

"I knew some of those details but not all of them. Not the deeper pieces about your marriage." Elaine looked at Brooke with a genuine sincerity. "Thanks for telling me."

Brooke nodded and took a sip of her iced tea. "Who's next?"

"I'll go." Katy set her plate down on the table next to her side of the sofa. "My story's sort of obvious. The tabloids captured most of it."

"And none of it." Ashley smiled. "They never really knew either of you."

"They didn't, I guess." Katy talked about seeing Dayne for the first time and the adventure that followed. It took several minutes before she reached the part about meeting up at the theater the day before last Christmas. "In the weeks before that I was pretty sure we were finished." She put her hands on her round belly. "But God had other plans."

"You could write a book with all He's taught you over the last few years." Kari pulled her knees up onto the chair where she was sitting. "Wouldn't you say?"

Katy laughed. "Probably. But one thing stands out. Even if the whole world thinks otherwise, you have to expect the best of the people you love. I knew Dayne. I absolutely knew him. But I let myself be tricked into thinking the worst of the man I loved. I'll never do that again."

Just for that moment, Ashley was glad Reagan wasn't here. The fact was, she'd expected the best of Luke and he'd let her down. But even then there was something to what Katy was saying. In the process of forgiveness, people needed to think the best of each other also. Otherwise there could be no progress at all.

"In some ways I feel like you a little," Kari told Elaine. "Because I had two love stories." She gave a sad smile to each of her sisters and Katy. "All of you know about Tim and how that ended." She turned her attention to Elaine again. "But I'm not sure you know about my past with Ryan."

"Not really." Elaine was caught up in the stories, gripped by the details that would now make up part of the fabric of her family life as well.

Kari explained how she and Ryan were childhood sweethearts and how after he went to college on a football scholarship, things grew distant between them. He was playing for the pros when he suffered an injury that nearly paralyzed him. What happened next involved a strange and sad set of circumstances. Kari went to the hospital. When she asked a nurse if she could go into Ryan's room, the nurse said that his girlfriend was with him. "I thought the girl she was talking about was someone other than me. So I left and never looked back."

After that, since she and Ryan hadn't been talking much in the year that led up to his accident, they simply moved on with their separate lives. Ryan fought back to health and took a position coaching, and Kari fell in love with and married Tim. "The timing was so interesting, because Ryan came back into my life before Tim's death. While Tim was still having the affair. But I knew with everything in me that God didn't want me falling for Ryan while there was still a chance that Tim and I could work things out in our marriage."

Eventually Ryan made a determination to stay in New York City, where he was coaching for the Giants. Even after Tim's murder, Ryan came to visit Kari only once, when Jessie was born. After that it was nearly a year before God made it clear that the two of them belonged together.

"God's taught me so much over this journey. I guess most of all that love is a decision. I didn't give up on Tim, and he found forgiveness before his death. I'll always be grateful for that." Kari's voice was thick with emotion. "But I also learned that I need to pay attention to God's prompting, to the quiet, gentle way He speaks to us in our everyday life."

Ashley was trying to figure out how to condense her story into a few minutes when suddenly it was her turn. "I was afraid to love; that's what it came down to. Landon always knew it, and he loved me anyway. Something I'll never understand."

She drew a deep breath and started at the beginning. "I was rebellious and difficult. I dressed differently, acted differently. I went against everything the Baxter family stood for." She had nothing to hide now, no reason to soften the reality of the story.

"Landon fell for me in high school, but I thought he was too safe, too clean-cut."

Her sisters knew her story, but Katy had never heard all the details and neither had Elaine, so she included every aspect of what happened next. "I went to Paris with sheer defiance in my heart. I connected with one of the top art galleries, with the goal to have them look at my paintings."

But that never happened. Instead she'd met up with one of the premier French artists of the day. His interest in her had nothing to do with her artwork, and soon their friendship became an intimate and forbidden affair. "He was married." Ashley's voice was heavy with the pain that still came from remembering that time. "But in his circles married men had affairs all the time, so I let him convince me that our relationship was normal."

When Ashley learned she was pregnant, he turned mean. "He told me he didn't want to see me again and that the abortion clinic was down the street." A shudder worked its way down Ashley's spine, and goose bumps broke out along her arms. "I went there. . . . I almost did it."

Quiet hung over the room, and Ashley could feel the love and support coming from everyone gathered around her. "Only God could've grabbed me out of that place and sent me back home." Her eyes filled with tears as she looked at her sisters. "I felt like my family could never accept me, especially Luke. But he came around eventually."

Ashley explained that in the years after Cole was born, she was unable to feel or forgive herself, unable to fully love or find the energy to paint. But all that changed when she began working at Sunset Hills Adult Care Home. Helping the Alzheimer's patients reminded Ashley of something she'd forgotten. Every day she was making memories that she would fall back on one day when she was relegated to a nursing home. She was especially touched by Irvel, a woman whose love for her husband continued in a very vivid way, despite the fact that he had died many years earlier.

"My heart was healing, and Landon had come back into my life, but I was so confused." She sighed and laced her fingers over one knee. "Not until 9/11 did I really understand how much I loved him. And then . . . well, then the real struggle began."

Once Ashley was able to identify her feelings for Landon, she convinced herself that he deserved someone better than her. "On top of everything else, I had a huge health scare, a misdiagnosed positive reading for an HIV test." She dabbed her eyes. "I could never have put Landon through that."

Finally, Landon returned from New York, and Ashley learned that her health was fine. "After that, there was no turning back. I'll love Landon until the day I die. I pray that if God takes him before me, I'll have the sort of beautiful memories Irvel had of her dear Hank."

Kari wiped at the corners of her eyes too. "All of us were so grateful when you and Landon got married. I think Mom and Dad prayed about that every day for two years." As soon as Kari mentioned their mother, she looked at Elaine. "I mean . . . that's how strongly they felt about Ashley and Landon as a couple."

"It's okay, remember? You can include her when I'm around." Elaine's voice was calm and full of a sweet sense of peace. "Ashley's story is beautiful, and it very much involves your mother. I believe God let her live long enough to see that wedding. It meant that much to her."

Ashley's throat felt thick, and she was quiet for a few seconds. Her emotions were high anyway, and now with Elaine showing such grace and understanding, it was all Ashley could do to keep herself from breaking down. She studied the woman seated across from her, the one who would soon marry her father. And before she might change her mind, she stood, crossed the room to Elaine, leaned down, and hugged her. When she could find her voice, she whispered the words pressing against her soul. "Thank you for letting us keep our mom . . . even when you're here."

Elaine stood. For several seconds she clung to Ashley. "I wouldn't have it any other way."

Eventually the moment passed, and Ashley returned to her seat. Around the room came the sound of sniffling.

Finally Brooke faced Ashley. "You didn't tell us what God taught you along the way."

It took Ashley a few seconds to realize Brooke was kidding, and by then a chorus of laughter had begun and was building with contagious fervor throughout the room.

Ashley allowed her own joy to mingle with the others'. The lessons God had taught her were so obvious they hardly needed to be restated. In some ways it was the same lesson He had taught all of them, the one Ashley had read about in Psalm 130 two months ago. For by putting their hope in the Lord and His unfailing love, they had all found the redemption they'd so desperately needed.

Ashley maybe most of all.

CHAPTER TWENTY-ONE

BRILLIANT BLUE FILLED THE SKY outside John's open bedroom window as he woke. It was early, just past six, but already there was the familiar sound of birds in the trees adjacent to the house. John squinted at the sunlight streaming into the room, the sort of bright sunshine that marked early summer mornings and new beginnings. Fitting, he thought, and as he did he slowly began to realize that this was Saturday, the day he'd looked forward to and in some ways feared since he proposed to Elaine.

Today was his wedding day.

He made no sudden move to get out of bed. There was too much to think through, too much to consider first. He breathed in deep and took stock of his room. This was the very last time he would wake up here. Tonight he and Elaine would leave for a honeymoon road trip, stopping at bed-and-breakfasts between here and northern Michigan, and when they returned home, they would begin life in their new house. They had closed on it three days ago, and already they'd purchased new bedroom furniture.

He stretched his arm to the empty side of his bed and ran his fingers over the smooth, cool sheets, the place where Elizabeth had slept beside him all those years. After today he wouldn't wake up alone again, and suddenly he felt like he was standing on the edge of a cliff about to free-fall into a vast and unknown chasm. How could he walk away from the home he'd made with Elizabeth, from the memories the old place held and from the bedroom they'd shared?

Then just as quickly his fears subsided. Last night they'd had a simple rehearsal, and afterward they'd gone to their new house, walking through the rooms deciding which of their existing sofas would look best against which wall, then going over the plans to have his kids help with the move once the honeymoon was over. They ended the night by sitting outside on the new glider they'd bought for the front porch.

Now John could feel his heart rate return to normal as he remembered the conversation from last night.

"It won't be easy for either of us, starting over again." Elaine's eyes had given him a transparent look straight to her heart. "We're going to need time to work through all the changes."

Her words gave him the greatest sense of relief. "I thought . . . I was the only one feeling that way."

She smiled. "It would be easier for both of us to keep things the way they were, living out our lives in the comfort of the past."

"But easier isn't always better." He put his arm around her shoulders, his eyes still focused on hers.

"Exactly."

The conversation faded from his mind, and he eased himself up to a sitting position. Elaine understood. This morning she was no doubt going through the same mix of emotions, excited about the future and yet deeply aware of all that had brought them to this day. The closure that would come because of it. The heartache and loss they'd both survived was one reason they'd found a friendship in the first place, but today their overriding joy was bound to mingle, at least in part, with some of that same hurt.

The wedding would take place at four this afternoon, followed by a dinner reception at Katy and Dayne's. The invitation list wasn't quite fifty people—family and a few close friends. John had lots of time between now and then, and he already had his day mapped out. Breakfast and Bible time at the dining room table; then he would spend a few hours in the garden, tending to Elizabeth's roses.

The buyer had closed on the Baxter house nearly a week ago now. John had until the second week in July before he needed to be completely out, enough time to move the furniture he was keeping into the new house, time to let his kids go through what remained in case there was anything they wanted. But it was important that he turn over the house in good condition with the rose garden and yards manicured and attractive, the way he and Elizabeth had always kept it.

Erin and Sam, who would move to town next weekend, had asked for the bedroom furniture, and John was glad. Even after so many decades, the old pieces were in great shape, and at least now the sentimental set would stay in the family.

Slowly John slid his legs over the side of the bed, and as he did his eyes fell on the photo of him and Elizabeth, the one that sat atop the dresser in the corner of the room. The portrait that had brought him such comfort in the months and years since her death.

Without warning, a sense of gut-wrenching betrayal dug its claws into his shoulders and refused to let go. He could never replace what he'd shared with Elizabeth, so why was he about to try? How could he stand in front of his family and friends and pledge a lifetime of love to another woman?

He stood and took measured steps across his room to the dresser, and almost in slow motion he reached out and took hold of the framed photo. Elizabeth's eyes seemed to be looking straight at him, loving him unconditionally, bringing no judgment even today. "Elizabeth, darling, I didn't want it to go this way." His voice was so soft it barely made any sound at all. "I promise I still feel you here with me, as real as if you were standing at my side."

For a long time, he studied the photo, memorizing it, allowing the image to burn itself even more deeply into his heart. He would keep the picture, the same way Elaine would keep photos of herself with her deceased husband. But would he ever have a moment like this again, where he could look at her eyes and long for her the way he did right now? Or would that be another betrayal, the kind that went against Elaine?

The weight of his emotions and the burden of responsibility that came with choosing to remarry pressed in against him from every side. He set the photo back on the dresser and opened the top drawer. This was where he kept his own copy of Elizabeth's book of letters. After making one for each of the kids, it had taken little time to put one together for himself. Not that he'd leave it out on the coffee table at their new house, but he wanted it handy.

He pulled it out and tenderly carried it back to the edge of his bed. He sat down, the book on his lap, and opened the front cover. *I need to read something from her, something to help me shake the awful sense that I'm doing something wrong by marrying Elaine, that I'm somehow hurting her. . . .*

John began flipping through the pages of the book. Many of Elizabeth's letters had helped him over the years since her death, but right now he wasn't sure where to turn, which page would contain the assurance he needed.

He took hold of a section of pages and stopped at a letter near the back of the book. Elizabeth had used floral paper, and the vividness of her handwriting stood out more sharply on this one than the others. His book did not contain copies of her letters but the originals. He ran his thumb over the page and with great reverence began at the top.

My dearest John,

He closed his eyes and willed himself to remember her voice, the songlike quality of her tone and the hope that rang out from her soul with every word. When he could hear it again, when her voice was so clear it was as if she were sitting beside him talking to him, he opened his eyes and continued.

> Ever since I got sick again, I've felt more inclined to write to you. I bring this silly pad of paper with me so that when I'm hooked up to the chemo I have something to take my mind off the treatment. Whenever I place my pen to the paper, my heart turns to you. I've told you before that I believe with all my heart God will heal me. Eventually I will be whole and well again. I'm convinced. But I think you and I both know that healing can happen here . . . or it can happen in heaven.
>
> I'm not trying to be negative with this letter, but if God chooses that my healing doesn't happen until heaven, there are some things I want you to know. First, that you've given me a life of love I never could've had otherwise. My greatest dreams about marriage pale in comparison to the decades you've created for the two of us. I understand that as you've looked to God for wisdom and leadership, He's equipped you to be the man you are. Without our Lord none of this wonderful journey would've been possible. So let me just say here that I am grateful for the privilege of loving you, the privilege of being loved by you, and I will remain grateful as long as I live.

John looked away from the scrapbook page and turned his attention to the open bedroom window. The blue was deeper now, the rays of sunlight a warmer golden color. *The privilege was all mine, Elizabeth. All mine.* With her words filling his mind and heart, he truly could feel her beside him, sharing a morning together one last time. He looked back at the letter and found his place.

> Secondly, I want to give you a very special gift, John. The gift of choosing life for yourself no matter what happens with me. I know I've written to you about this before, but I think it's worth repeating. Deuteronomy tells us that God sets before His people life and death and that He urges us at every turn to choose life.

It was the same message John had seen in another of Elizabeth's letters, the same Bible verse. God must've been making a great impression on Elizabeth to make sure he knew her heart, that she would want him to embrace life—even if that life didn't include her.

> You see, love, I'm choosing life right this minute sitting in this chair with the chemo dripping into my veins. I want to live because I want to grow old with you. I want to live to see the birth of our future grandkids and great-grandkids. I want to see the story of our children's lives unfold in the decades yet to come.

The wording stopped there, but the ending felt strangely abrupt. Was it possible the letter continued on the other side? Typically Elizabeth used a second piece of paper rather than write on the back of a single sheet. But John had the sudden strange sense that this letter was the exception. He eased his thumb beneath the tape at the bottom of the page, and when he'd broken through it, he carefully lifted the page.

Sure enough, there was more to the letter on the back. John felt his breathing quicken as he rotated the book so he could read the writing. He began at the top.

> But I also know that God might have another plan for me. If He does, then you must continue with the same fervor for life that we shared as a couple. What I'm saying is you must choose life. I would never want you to waste away in the shadow of all that was. Not if I'm no longer here to be a part of your life. In that case, you must embrace new adventures and new friendships, and you must follow where those friendships lead. If it means remarrying someday, then remarry. And do so with a full and whole heart, knowing that somewhere in heaven I'll be cheering you on.

John's breath caught in his throat, and he read that last section again. *If it means remarrying someday, then remarry?* He wasn't sure how it was possible, but he was convinced he'd never read this letter before, not in its entirety. The book probably held more than a hundred notes and letters from Elizabeth, so somehow he must have overlooked the back of this one.

But to find it here . . . today . . . A shiver came over him, and he found his place once more.

> I hope you understand the tone and intention behind this letter. I won't give it to you right away but only if it seems fairly certain that God is planning to heal me in heaven and not here. Until then I will continue to choose life, and I will believe that you will do the same. Whether I'm here or not.
> With all my love,
> Elizabeth

With great care, John straightened the sheet of paper and closed the book. Then he did something he'd done often throughout his life when his desperate need for Christ was so pressing he could hardly draw a breath and when the realness of God's miraculous presence was so strong he could do nothing but cry out in praise.

This was one of those times.

He dropped to his knees at the foot of his bed and buried his face in his hands. The oppressive weight of betrayal was gone completely, and in its place his heart and soul were filled with a joy that knew no limits, a joy that was supernatural. *God, my Lord, You are so faithful, so kind and good. I asked for a sign, and You answered me in a way that leaves me breathless.*

My son, love is of God. . . . Anyone who loves is born of God and knows God.

John was overcome by the presence and Spirit of the Lord, sheltering him, surrounding him like a cloud of love and peace that was simply beyond anything he'd ever felt. The response was straight from Scripture, from 1 John, and in it was proof of God's love for him but also of God's endorsement of love between His people. Especially married love between a man and a woman, equally determined to serve Him.

Thank You, God . . . that You would create the universe and send Your Son to die for me and still have time to lead me to that letter. . . . Thank You.

As John opened his eyes, as he stood and returned the book of letters to the top dresser drawer, he felt a happiness he hadn't felt in years. He would never forget this moment or the way God met him here on the morning of his wedding day.

He went to the window and breathed in long and deep. This was his wedding day! He was going to marry his best friend and begin a life that would take them into their twilight years loving and serving and trusting God together! Great joy welled within him and swelled his heart to nearly bursting. God had brought Elaine into his life, and God had given him the gift of certainty about his decision to marry her.

And something else. The knowledge that somewhere in heaven, Elizabeth was cheering him on.

CHAPTER TWENTY-TWO

LUKE HAD TAKEN EVERY DETAIL of his father's and Ashley's advice, and in a civil conversation with Reagan, the two of them had agreed to take an hour or two before his father's wedding to talk. It was just past ten o'clock in the morning when he and his family arrived at Ashley's house. She and Landon had agreed to take Tommy and Malin for as long as they needed.

"Okay, kids, Mommy and I need you to be very good for Aunt Ashley." Luke looked over his shoulder at the two of them, both buckled into their car seats. Already this morning Tommy had flown into a full-blown temper tantrum because Malin found his favorite robo-dinosaur and broke off the tail. He sat with his arms crossed, eyes still puffy from his earlier crying. Luke maintained his patience. "I need to hear 'Yes, Daddy' from both of you."

Malin went first, uttering a mournful repetition of the words, and then Tommy followed. But his tone made it clear he wasn't happy about anything that had happened today. Not the dinosaur, not Malin, and not the idea of being dropped off at his aunt's house, where he would need to behave.

Luke didn't dwell on the moment. Reagan opened her car door and began helping Malin out of her seat, and Luke did the same with Tommy. Ashley and Cole met them at the front door.

"Hi, Tommy! I got the bin of LEGOs out." Cole grinned at his littler cousin. "We can build a whole city if you want."

The sour look left Tommy's face instantly. He struggled to get down, and as soon as his Spider-Man tennis shoes hit the ground, he ran to Cole. "It could be a space city! A space city with dinosaurs!"

Gratitude filled Luke and calmed his nerves. "That kid of yours is a keeper." He reached Ashley and gave her a side hug. Her belly was too big for anything else. "Hey, thanks. . . . I mean it."

Reagan allowed a faint smile in Ashley's direction. "We really need this time."

"I know." Ashley kissed Reagan on the cheek. "We'll be praying for you guys."

"We should be back before noon." Luke stepped back while Reagan set Malin down. "Is that okay?"

"Plenty of time to get ready for the wedding." She smiled, and the joy in her expression seemed genuine. She'd come a long way in her acceptance of their dad's marriage. "Until then we'll just have playtime."

Devin appeared at the door, and after a few seconds, he and Malin ran off into the house.

"Thanks again, Ash."

"Are you kidding?" She grinned at Luke. "Tommy gives us more entertainment than we usually get in a solid week around here."

They all laughed, and Luke put his hand on the small of Reagan's back as they walked to the car. The gesture came naturally, and it wasn't until they reached the bottom of the sidewalk that Luke realized the small victory they'd just experienced. Because this time Reagan hadn't pulled away.

It's a good sign, right, God? Please let it be a good sign. He uttered the prayer silently as he took his spot behind the wheel. There was no answer, but that was okay. God was with them today. Luke knew because he'd spent the last few weeks praying about this moment, making sure—like his dad had advised him—that he had thought through everything he needed to say. Even more importantly, waiting for a time when Reagan was open to talking. Something she'd been opposed to when he brought it up the first time.

It was only through repeatedly asking her and by allowing God to give him patience and kindness toward Reagan that finally she had agreed to the meeting they were about to have.

He filled his cheeks with air and exhaled through pursed lips. As he did, he turned to Reagan. "Thank you for doing this."

"It means a lot to you. I understand that." She buckled her seat belt and looked at him. She didn't exactly smile, but the gentleness in her eyes was something he hadn't seen in a very long time. Her tone suggested that she felt indifferent about the benefits of the pending talk, but Luke refused to let that discourage him. At least she didn't sound hurt or angry, something that had marked nearly all their conversations since Christmas.

Luke opened the console between the two front seats and pulled out a Chris Tomlin CD he had burned for the ten-minute drive ahead. He slipped the disc into the stereo and turned the music up just loud enough so the words could fill his soul. "Strength will rise as we wait upon the Lord . . . . We will wait upon the Lord. . . ."

The truth in the message magnified the hope he felt for the coming hours, and he sang along as he drove. At some parts, it was hard to keep his hands on the steering wheel when all he wanted to do was reach them high to heaven, to the God who could still turn his terrible mistakes into a triumph. If only Reagan would forgive him.

Praise music was a funny thing. After failing as a husband and a Christian, Luke had felt like a hypocrite listening to music like this. But now because of something Ashley told him, he understood differently. Music like this was balm to the soul, a reminder of a perfect God, especially in times of imperfection. So Luke had learned to let the music help him focus not on his own inabilities but on the Lord's great capabilities.

Reagan shifted in her seat so she could face him. "Where are we going?"

"To the university." He didn't want to tell her exactly where they were headed. "I have a spot in mind."

She studied him for a moment. "You've really thought about this."

"Yes." The flicker of hope fanned into a bright flame. Luke reached for her hand and gave it a gentle squeeze. "You have no idea how much."

Two more songs played out before they reached the parking lot, the one that sat adjacent to the apartment building where Reagan had lived when the two of them started dating. Most kids had gone home for the summer or had things to do on Saturdays, so there were only a few other cars in the lot.

Reagan rolled down her window and stared out at the apartment complex. Then she turned to Luke. She looked puzzled. "This is where you want to talk?"

"Here. Where it all began." Luke had so much to say that for a few seconds he hesitated, not sure where to begin. But then he forced himself to start with the reason he'd brought her here. "I wanted to find a place that would help us remember the reasons we fell in love. I thought about Lake Monroe and the softball fields on campus, and I thought about the stadium or the creek behind my parents' house."

Her eyes held a light that hadn't been there before.

"All those places had a better atmosphere, but I thought if we were here, it would help me remember not only how much I loved you back then—" his voice was thick as his eyes met hers—"but how much I let you down."

Reagan tilted her head. "You let me down with Randi Wells." Her words were not accusatory, just matter-of-fact. "Here . . . here was where you were loyal."

"No. I knew what God wanted of us, yet that night—" Luke looked straight to her soul—"I allowed things to get out of hand. I let you down, and I've never . . ." His emotions got the better of him, and he hesitated, waiting for the strength to continue. "I've never asked for your forgiveness about that."

Reagan's expression changed, and the hurt in her eyes became so raw it was painful to look at her. She settled back into her seat and folded her arms tight across her chest, her attention once more on the apartment. "I don't like to think about it."

"Me neither." Luke was making progress, but he still had so much more to say. "But the fact is, I blew it that night. I loved you and I wanted to spend my life with you, but I acted outside God's plan for both of us, and because of that I let you down."

Her eyes grew distant, and tears spilled onto her cheeks.

"I'm sorry that this is taking you back. But if we don't go to the past, I don't think we'll find any way to keep things together for the future." He leaned over and lightly brushed the tears off her cheeks. "Please, Reagan . . . I have more to say."

She sniffed, and when she turned to him, she looked like a brokenhearted little girl. "I'm listening."

Luke remembered his father's words. "Moral failure always comes with a price. Until I take responsibility and go back and deal with that part of my past, there can never be real growth. Not for me or for us."

She gazed at him, fresh tears in her eyes. "You don't have to say this."

"Yes, I do." He reached for her hand again, and though she didn't pull away, he felt her stiffen beneath his touch. *Help me, God. Open her heart so she can hear what I'm trying to say.* "Reagan, please . . . listen to me."

A quiet sob shook her. She leaned her head back against the seat. "Go on."

"My actions that night caused you a great deal of loss, and I'm not sure I've ever acknowledged that." Luke remembered running up her apartment stairs that Tuesday, September 11, knowing that the Twin Towers had collapsed and that her father had most likely been buried in the rubble. The pain of the memory sliced through him like a knife. "Because of me, you missed out on the last conversation you would've ever had with your dad. You had to go home believing you'd let your dad down, when he had thought the world of you. He had admired you for taking a stand on purity and for keeping the promise to wait until you were married, and all of a sudden because of me you had to accept that you'd broken that promise."

Reagan sniffed three times and brought her free hand to her face. "You didn't let my dad down. I did that. You . . . you can't take all the responsibility."

His heart hurt for her, but he needed her to understand. "That isn't true. It was my job to care for you and treasure you. But that night . . . that night I wasn't thinking about you or what was best for you or the fact that you were a precious gift from God. I was thinking about myself."

"Luke . . ."

"There's more." He swallowed hard. He'd never meant any words more than these. "You went back home, and in the process of having our son, you lost the ability to have more children. You lost your self-respect before your family and your church friends, and you lost your freedom. You lost the girl you'd been because in such a short time you had to become a mother."

Reagan lowered her hand. Her tears came harder now, as maybe the sum of all he was saying was finally hitting her.

"I'm responsible for all of those losses. Every consequence that came from my own moral failure." Luke let his forehead rest against hers. "And until now . . . until now I've never asked for your forgiveness." His voice dropped to a whisper. "Please, Reagan, I beg you. Forgive me for failing you that way. I'm so sorry."

For a few seconds she remained unmoving, and he wondered if maybe she was going to refuse him. But then he felt her break, felt her arms come up slowly around his neck and her body surrender against his. "If only . . . I would've answered the phone."

In that instant Luke knew that Ashley and his father were right. This was where the problem between them had started, and it was where they needed to begin if they were going to work things out. He ran his hand along her back, holding her, clinging to her. "It was my fault. Forgive me." He pressed his face against hers. "I've failed you so many times, but from this moment on I promise I'll never fail you again. I love you."

Reagan wiped her cheeks and looked at him. "I believe you. I really do." A series of deep sobs shook her shoulders, but she didn't break eye contact. "I forgive you. But . . . but will you forgive me too?" She breathed out slowly. "Forgive me for all you lost because of that night?"

"Baby, of course I forgive you." He put his hands on either side of her face. "And thank you for coming here today, for listening to me."

"We need to get counseling."

His heart soared. "Definitely."

"Because I love you too. I don't want to lose us."

Her eyes were red and swollen, but in them Luke saw true forgiveness and hope, the redemption they'd both been unable to find before today. Suddenly Luke knew that after today they would never talk about leaving again, that they would get counseling and find again the faith that once bound them. They would tend to the behavior issues of their kids and build a life together day by day. Luke was certain because now he saw in Reagan the tenderness and presence of the Holy Spirit and something else, something he hadn't known if he'd ever see in her eyes again.

He saw the girl he'd first fallen in love with.

CHAPTER TWENTY-THREE

THE ENTIRE FLANIGAN FAMILY was invited to the wedding, and Bailey was told she could bring Tim as her date. She was in his passenger seat as they followed her parents' Suburban to Clear Creek Community Church, and though Tim was singing along to the radio and making casual conversation with her, Bailey was quiet.

Weddings had a way of making her think about the future.

She stared out the window at the trees that lined the boulevard, trees that had been barren and snow-covered what felt like a few days ago. Now that she had graduated, she had a better understanding of what her parents had always told her about time. Basically that she shouldn't blink, because the seasons had a way of running into each other, faster and faster all the time.

"What are you thinking about?" Tim turned the radio down and smiled at her.

"Nothing." Bailey kept her tone casual, her smile easy. Her thoughts were still trying to line up in order, so there really wasn't anything to share with Tim. Not yet, anyway. "Just life and how quickly it goes."

"Like the fact that you're all grown up and graduated?"

"Yeah . . . I guess." She turned the radio back up. Her graduation party had been small but wonderful. A few friends from school and a houseful of CKT kids. Her parents had given her a memory book with photos from her life and school days, and her mom had put together a movie on her MacBook. The combination of the photos and video and the music her mother chose made it a tearjerker. Bailey would treasure it always.

Tim was once again involved in the song on the radio, focused on following her parents. Bailey glanced at him, and again she wondered if five years from now the trip to the church would be theirs. Was that the way God was leading her? She leaned against the car door and straightened her navy blue skirt. Since prom her friendship with Tim had been moving right along. He hadn't kissed her again, but she was glad. She wasn't ready for something serious, and no matter how they felt about each other, she had the feeling he wasn't either.

They arrived at the church, and Tim parked next to her parents. She was glad for Mr. Baxter, glad he'd found someone to love after all the years of missing his first wife. Her parents said the wedding would be simple, certainly not like Katy and Dayne's wedding.

Tim's eyes looked warm and kind as he walked beside her, and halfway to the door of the church he took hold of her hand. Her brothers were behind them, and she knew she'd hear about it later, but she didn't care.

Inside, Bailey saw the Baxter family gathered on the right side of the church. Katy and Dayne were cuddled up close to each other, and Bailey smiled at the picture they made together. That's what she wanted. Someone who would love her as much as Dayne Matthews loved Katy, a guy who would fly across the country for a few minutes with her. Someone willing to let God lead in every aspect of their relationship.

They found their seats and the guests grew quiet as the music began, something traditional played by the organist at the front of the church. Pastor Mark Atteberry stood near the center aisle just below the altar, with Mr. Baxter next to him. Bailey wasn't sure, but it looked like Mr. Baxter's eyes were a little wet. Then all his grown kids joined him. Bailey glanced at the single-page program and read their names—Dayne, Brooke, Kari, Ashley, Erin, and Luke. She looked up. Their stories weren't entirely clear to her, but she knew they'd been through a lot together. They were a beautiful family.

Bailey let the music fill her heart, and for a few seconds she closed her eyes. What would her siblings look like years from now all grown up and dressed in fancy suits? What would her mother wear, and how would her dad handle giving her away? Most of all, who would be waiting for her at the front of a church someday?

Without meaning for it to happen, her mind turned to Cody. He was in Washington now, recuperating. His mother hadn't given them many details, and neither had Cody. But he must be doing pretty well because he was writing again—twice, anyway. His letters weren't long like before, and he didn't talk about his feelings much. Almost as if he wanted to create distance between the two of them. In his first letter he thanked her and her family for praying and said he hoped to be back in Bloomington around the first of July. He also said that he'd changed his mind about moving to the West Coast, and he was going to live with a few of his friends from the Clear Creek football team. The good guys who would never consider partying.

Okay, great that he had a plan, but Bailey wondered why he wasn't coming back to live with them, and she asked as much in her first letter to him once she had his new address. His response had hurt, though she wasn't sure she understood exactly why. He wrote that he needed to make his own way in life, just like she needed to make hers. *"You're grown up now, Bailey. You need the freedom to live your life and fall in love without me hanging around in the background."*

Beside her, Tim ran his thumb along the side of her hand and smiled at her.

She returned his smile just as the music changed. But as they stood and faced the center and as Ms. Denning made her way down the aisle, Bailey couldn't shake the thought of Cody. He wanted only to be her friend, and Bailey was sure that's where things would stay. Besides, maybe the war had changed him. It did that to a lot of guys. At least that's what she'd read.

But as much as she cared for Tim and as great as it felt to know he had feelings for her, she had to be honest about one thing. When she asked herself who would be waiting for her at the front of a church someday, Tim's face wasn't the one that came to mind, no matter how crazy that was. Rather, the image that filled her heart in that moment was one that belonged to a dark-haired football player. The face of Cody Coleman, who maybe still meant a lot more to her than she was willing to admit.

Even to herself.

Like her sisters, Ashley wore a deep brown satin dress that fell softly to well below her knees. Hers had to be specially made to accommodate her growing stomach, and now, standing in front of their family and friends, Ashley made sure to bend her knees just a little so she wouldn't pass out. She'd been having false contractions all day, probably because of the emotion of the day, having Tommy and Malin at the house until lunchtime, then hearing from Luke and Reagan that they'd reached a breakthrough and that now they were committed to making their marriage work.

All that and now this.

She drew a slow breath and steadied herself. On either side were her siblings and to her far right was her dad, looking handsome and far younger than his sixty-some years. They were all here, all six of them and their families, and Ashley couldn't help but think that very soon they would all be together for more than special occasions and the once-in-a-while Christmas.

Erin and Sam and their girls had flown in for the wedding and to close on a house they'd found back in December. It was a two-story in a newer development, not far from Ashley and Landon, which meant that she and Erin could meet often at the local park and begin to make up for so many years apart. For that matter, they could meet with Kari and Katy, Reagan and Brooke too. All of them were raising kids, needing the friendship and camaraderie of each other.

The music switched to a wedding march, and Ashley willed herself to exhale. This was it . . . the moment she'd been unable to fathom for such a long time. For an instant she felt a hint of anger or maybe just an intense sadness. If only her mother hadn't gotten sick again . . .

But just as quickly the moment passed, and Ashley watched as Elaine came into view. She wore a short-sleeved off-white silk dress that came nearly to her ankles. Her grayish blonde hair was styled in a way that flattered her face, and in her hands was a bouquet of white roses cut from her mother's flower garden.

At first Ashley hadn't agreed with the idea. But her father had explained it. "Your mother wrote me a letter giving me her blessing about this day, as if she somehow knew my life might include the chance to love again. The roses are one way to acknowledge that your mother—her love for both me and Elaine—is very much a part of this new life we're beginning together."

And so each of the girls held a single rose from their mother's garden.

Ashley stared at the roses and then lifted her eyes to Elaine's. As she did, Elaine looked straight at her, and even from halfway down the aisle, Ashley felt her love as clearly as if she'd shouted it for all their guests to hear. All at once Ashley relaxed. *Thank You, God. Thank You for Elaine and thank You for letting my dad find love again.*

She looked away, turning her attention to her father. He was smiling, bursting with joy, even as tears gathered in his eyes. Ashley felt her own eyes grow damp, and then once more her gaze fell on the white roses in Elaine's hands. Her mother wasn't really gone. She would stay in their hearts always, and when her name came up in conversation, Elaine would join them in talking about her. That her dad would fall in love with someone so kind and dear, someone who had been a friend of her mother's . . . Ashley could ask for nothing more.

Elaine reached the front of the aisle, and her kids took their places on her other side.

Pastor Atteberry looked first at Ashley's father, then at Elaine. "This is not the kind of wedding that comes along every day. And I am in a very unique position. For I knew each of you when your first spouses were still alive." He paused and looked at their dad. "I watched you honor your wife, John, loving her through health and in the end through great sickness." He turned to Elaine. "And I watched you love and respect your husband until he drew his final breath. I know that if you'd had your way, neither of you would be standing here now. God's plans don't always match ours. But God does promise that those who love Him will have life to the full—now and forever." His smile filled his face. "John . . . Elaine . . . I believe this marriage is God's way of giving you life to the full even after all you've separately lost."

Around the church, several people dabbed their eyes, and next to her Ashley felt Kari do the same thing. Ashley had figured she would weep through the entire ceremony, weighed down by memories of her mother and unsure about what this next stage in their life as a family would look like.

But instead she felt the peace and certainty that Pastor Mark was right. They had loved much and they had lost, but they were Baxters and they stuck together even in the darkest times. Over the years, their family had always come out with more love on the other side of whatever trial they'd faced. Their father's marriage to Elaine was further proof of that fact. Today wasn't about losing the past or jeopardizing the future; it was about overcoming sorrow with triumphant joy.

She blinked back happy tears as the ceremony wound down, as Pastor Mark led them through the exchange of vows and rings, and as he introduced them to the congregation. Their story was still being written, and as her dad and Elaine walked up the aisle toward their new lives, Ashley rejoiced in all the next chapter would bring.

Because that's what Baxters did.

CHAPTER TWENTY-FOUR

KATY HAD SLIGHT contractions all through the wedding, but afterward she compared notes with Ashley. False contractions, Ashley had told her. Braxton Hicks, nothing more.

Now Katy and Dayne pulled into the garage at the lakeside house for the reception, and her heart raced as she scanned the list of last-minute details. "You talked to Tim's mother about starting the coffee?"

"Yes." Dayne grinned. "And about putting the sherbet in the punch and about warming up the quiche in the oven and about breathing every so often."

She poked him in the ribs with her elbow. "Seriously . . . that was her car in the driveway, right? Hers and Lori Farley's?"

"They're here and they know exactly what to do." He touched his lips to hers, and his kiss gave her a welcome distraction. He breathed the next words against her skin. "Everything's going to be fine. It's just a dinner reception."

"I know." She exhaled and put her hand on her round stomach. "I'm giving myself false contractions worrying about it."

Dayne straightened and stared at her, fear gathering in his eyes. "False? How do you know?"

Katy laughed and pulled him close again, returning his kiss. "Because Ashley said so. And she should know."

He didn't look quite sure. "The books talk about that, don't they? False contractions?"

"Yes, dear." She giggled. "To quote my favorite guy, 'Everything's going to be fine.'"

They kissed again, and then they heard the sound of more cars pulling up in their driveway. "Yikes." Katy drew back and opened her door. "Come on. We have a party to throw."

Dayne hurried around to her side and lightly took hold of her elbow, guiding her up the three steps to the garage door. "You tell me if they stop being false, okay?" he whispered into her ear as they entered the kitchen. "I want to be the first to know."

She smiled, and before she could wonder if things were under control, she saw her two friends working away in the kitchen. They looked calm and controlled. Katy exhaled, relief stopping her short. This was the nicest party they'd thrown since they'd moved into the lake house, and she wanted all the details to line up. She walked the rest of the way into the kitchen. "You two are great."

Tim's mom was at the sink, and she grinned at Katy. "How was the wedding?"

Katy felt a softness come into her eyes. "Beautiful. Everything the family thought it would be." There was a knock at the front door, and Katy motioned in that direction. "I'll get it."

Dayne was already opening the door by the time she reached the entryway. Brooke's and Kari's families were on the porch, and Luke and Reagan and their kids were walking up the drive, with more cars arriving. Dayne held the door open wide. "Come on in!"

For a few seconds, Katy stood back and watched him. The picture he made welcoming his family into their home grabbed at Katy's heart and drew her instantly back to a time she didn't think about much anymore. Dayne's car accident. And right there, with Brooke, Peter, Maddie, and Hayley all talking at once and the laughter of Kari and Ryan behind them, Katy was suddenly in Los Angeles at the rehab center. Back then, Dayne hadn't thought any of this would happen. Not the return of his health, not his marriage to her, and certainly not his relationship with his family.

That had been a critical point for the two of them, a time when Dayne had needed God more than ever. But here they were . . . God's promises evident at a single glance. Tears stung Katy's eyes, and she shook her head. This wasn't a time for sentimental reflection. It was a celebration. She took hold of Maddie's hand. "Come on, girls." She grinned at Hayley. "Let's get some punch."

"You're pretty, Aunt Katy." Hayley's eyes shone with the sweet innocence that always marked her smile. "And you're gonna have a baby!"

"I am." Happiness filled Katy's heart. It wouldn't be long now. Just a couple more weeks. "The baby's going to be your cousin."

"Remember that, Hayley? I told you Aunt Katy and Uncle Dayne's baby was going to be another cousin." Maddie gave Katy a grin. "I hope it's a girl cousin!"

The conversation continued on into the kitchen, and after the girls had their drinks, Jessie and RJ lined up for theirs and soon all the cousins had cups of punch.

Katy ushered them outside onto the back deck. The evening was warm, and a chorus of frogs provided the perfect background. After Katy flipped a switch near the back door, soft piano music added another layer of atmosphere.

"That's the most balloons ever." Erin's daughter Chloe walked toward the railing. "How many, Aunt Katy? A million?"

Katy surveyed the white helium balloons she and Dayne had tied to their porch railing before the party. She covered up a laugh. "Maybe a little less than a million."

Cole did a quick survey of the balloons. "It's thirty-six. Exactly."

Maddie rolled her eyes. "You're such a know-it-all."

"Only because I really *do* know it all." Cole puffed out his chest.

Then just as quickly he relaxed his posture and giggled. "Not really. My dad knows a lot more than me."

Jessie, who was becoming as much a talker as Maddie, joined in with a story about a boy whose sister got married and everyone at the wedding released a helium balloon and how the bride didn't want anyone to throw rice or even birdseed because she didn't want birds "leaving their lunch" all around the wedding party. She was barely taking time to catch her breath, still wrapped up in the details of the story, when Dayne opened the patio slider.

Cole pointed to a tree halfway between the house and the lake. "An eagle's nest! Seriously, guys, come look!"

The kids scampered after him, and Katy turned her attention to Dayne.

"There you are." He walked outside, and behind him was Bob Asher, Dayne's missionary friend who had been there through the crisis moments in Dayne's journey. In the rush of the wedding she'd almost forgotten that the Ashers were coming into town today too. "Bob . . ." She closed the distance between them and threw her arms around his neck. As she pulled back her voice broke. "It's been too long."

"Way too long." He put his hand on Katy's shoulder and smiled. "I believed Dayne's story would end up this way. And that you would be the reason."

Katy took hold of both his hands and studied him, this man whom God had used to intervene for Dayne so many times. She remembered the flowers Dayne had sent her when he returned from his first visit to see Bob in Mexico. The card had read *"I once was lost but now am found"*—Dayne's way of telling her he'd given his heart to God, that he no longer wanted to handle life alone. Now Katy looked deep into the faithful soul of Dayne's friend. "How can I ever thank you?"

Bob shook his head and tried to say something, but instead he hugged Katy again. "God did it," he whispered. "What can I say? Dayne's my best friend."

A shy-looking woman came through the open doorway. She was dark-skinned with kind brown eyes, and there were two young girls standing close behind her. The woman gave a slight nod. "Hello, Katy." Her Spanish accent was heavy. "I'm Rosa, Bob's wife."

The tears Katy had held off earlier stung at her eyes once more. She'd met Bob in Cancún when he officiated her wedding, but this was the first time she'd seen his wife and children.

"The girls are so tall." Dayne stepped up and introduced Bob and Rosa's daughters, both of whom seemed as shy as their mother.

For several minutes the four adults talked about the family's furlough from their missionary work in Mexico and how they hoped to be in town for Katy's due date.

"You're staying with us the whole time." Katy looked at Dayne. "Right? You told them?"

Bob laughed and put his arm around Rosa's shoulders. "I remember what it was like getting ready for our first baby. We'll give you your space." He turned to Dayne. "I got in touch with Pastor Atteberry. You were right. He's thinking about taking a mission trip to Mexico next summer, so we'll stay here a few days and then move in with him." He gave Katy a kind look. "But thanks for your offer. We have only three weeks; then we need to head to our home church in Los Angeles for the last month before going back to Mexico. We just hope we don't miss the baby."

Katy put her arm around Dayne's waist. They still hadn't decided on a name, but they had time for that. The important thing was that so far the baby was healthy and Katy was too.

She had talked to her parents, and though they were too ill to make the trip, as soon as the baby was a few weeks old, Katy and Dayne were planning a trip to Chicago. So everyone who loved them could see the miracle of life God had brought out of all the years of uncertainty and heartache.

"Look, Uncle Dayne!" Cole was standing against the deck railing pointing to what appeared to be an enormous nest. "He's getting ready to fly!"

The group turned in the direction of Cole's voice just as a bald eagle lifted gracefully from the nest, flapped its powerful wings a few times, and took off over the lake. For a moment, the laughter and conversation on the back deck fell completely silent and all eyes watched the stately bird, each adult and child in awe of the beauty before them.

Katy smiled at the majestic picture the eagle made against the blue sky, and she held on a little tighter to Dayne. Because the miracle of God's presence wasn't only in the eagle but in every person gathered here this evening.

And in the struggles and victories, in the life stories that had brought all of them this far.

The reception was exactly how John had wanted it, simple and casual and marked by the deep family love that the Baxters expected from one another. Dayne and Katy's house was filled with close friends and family, the rooms ringing with the sounds of the children's laughter and the conversations that marked the friendships his grown children shared. Elaine's adult kids had found their place among the mix, and as John went back for another cup of coffee, he saw them and their spouses talking with Ashley and Landon in the living room.

Ashley spotted him, and she broke away from the group. "Dad, can you get Elaine? I have something for her. A wedding gift."

John wanted to ask, but he held back. "Okay. We'll be here waiting." He found Elaine outside, and together they returned to the living room just as Ashley came through the door. She was carrying an oversize flat box wrapped in gold and silver wedding paper.

"Here." Ashley handed the gift to Elaine. "It's for both of you." She gave Elaine a hug. "But you most of all."

Elaine's eyes glistened as she smiled at Ashley. Then she sat down on the arm of the nearest chair and balanced the gift on her lap so she could open it. Inside was one of Ashley's gorgeous paintings, a picture of two women walking along a curved path through a beautiful parklike setting. One woman was older, the other younger, and their arms were linked.

Ashley looked at Elaine through teary eyes. "It's you and me. Getting to know each other. Going through life as friends."

Elaine studied the painting for a long time. "It's lovely. I'll treasure it." She returned the cover of the box and set the gift on the fireplace hearth. This time the hug came from her. "And I'll treasure you even more."

John watched the two women caught in an embrace. Ashley's love and acceptance of Elaine was the greatest gift she could've given either of them. Greater even than the precious painting.

He would thank Ashley later. For now, he left them quietly talking, and he went to the kitchen to fill his coffee cup. As he did, he stared out the window at the group of kids on the back deck. They were looking at something, a bird in the sky, maybe. John watched them, how they stared motionless for a few seconds and then returned to batting at the balloons and giggling and talking all at once the way kids did. For an instant, he thought about Elizabeth, how she would've loved a party like this, a time when everyone was happy and healthy and together.

Then just as quickly, the thought passed and he glanced over his shoulder to where he could still see Elaine. She and Ashley were laughing, and even from the kitchen he could see the sparkle in her eyes. Her soft blonde hair was streaked with gray, but she looked a decade younger than her sixty years and very beautiful. Funny, he thought. Her appearance had nothing to do with his decision to spend the rest of his life with her. At this point in life, companionship and a shared faith were so much more important.

John was anxious for their honeymoon, glad that in an hour they'd set off not only to their bed-and-breakfast road trip but to a new life together. He let the thought roll around his heart for a minute, and he smiled. Gone was the sense of betrayal and sadness he'd felt earlier today. Elaine was his wife, and he didn't only enjoy her presence and company. He wasn't only glad for her friendship and camaraderie; he felt something much stronger, something he'd fully acknowledged to Elaine long before this day.

He loved her.

CHAPTER TWENTY-FIVE

A BREEZE MADE THE HUMIDITY bearable as Kari stood outside the church with Annie on her hip.

"Mama!" Annie put her chubby hands against Kari's face and grinned. "Hi, Mama!"

"Hi, Annie girl!" Kari kissed her daughter's cheeks. "This is the big day. Everyone'll be here." She bounced Annie up a little higher and scanned the parking lot. "Any minute now."

Sam and Erin had flown back to Texas a week ago after their dad's wedding, then spent the next few days packing their belongings in a U-Haul truck. The plan was for them to get into town today and for as many family members as possible to go home after church, change clothes, and meet at Erin and Sam's new house to help them move in.

Erin had called last night with the update. "We should be there right about nine in the morning. Sam and I figured we'd meet everyone at church."

Kari had passed the good news on to the rest of her siblings, and later that night she'd heard from her dad. "Elaine and I will be home tomorrow afternoon." He sounded happy and rested. "We'll meet everyone at Sam and Erin's."

Kari loved days like this, when everyone came together for a common goal.

She brushed her hair back from her face and squinted at the far entrance to the lot. Just as she was about to grab her cell phone from her purse and call Erin, she spotted a long U-Haul. The truck pulled in, and behind it was a white van, clearly the one Erin was driving.

"They're here!" Kari kept her squeal low since behind her the church doors were open.

"Here!" Annie raised her hand.

Again Kari kissed her cheek. She was such a happy baby, such a blessing in their lives. Kari was watching her sister's family find parking places near the back of the lot when she felt a tap on her shoulder. She turned around, and there, with a stricken look on her face, was Angela Manning.

"Kari . . ."

"Hi." Kari wasn't sure what to say. Two things were obvious. Angela was upset about something, and clearly now that she was out of the psychiatric hospital she'd taken Kari's advice and was attending church. But of all the churches in Bloomington, Kari hadn't expected her to visit Clear Creek Community. During their Bible study time, Kari had never mentioned where she attended, because she didn't want things to get awkward for either of them. She gently touched Angela's elbow. "Something's wrong?"

Angela's mouth opened and stayed that way for a few seconds while she searched Kari's eyes. "Why?" Her voice was barely loud enough to hear and full of pain. "Why didn't you tell me?"

Kari's heart skipped a beat, and she racked her brain. Did Angela know who she was? And if so, how had she found out? Kari's mouth felt dry. "I'm . . . not sure what you mean."

"I wanted to send you a card, to thank you for talking to me." She covered her mouth with her hand, and tears slid down her cheeks. She shook her head and fought for control. "I'm sorry. I

Just . . . I can't believe this. Your name kept sounding familiar, and finally I googled it and . . ." A sob came over her, and the sorrow contorted her face. "I know the truth. I . . . I know who you are."

Dear God, what am I supposed to do now? Kari held tight to Annie and tried to steady herself. She should've said something from the beginning, but now what? Annie seemed to sense something was wrong, and she laid her head on Kari's shoulder and stuck her thumb in her mouth. In the distance, Kari could see Erin and Sam and their kids walking from the van and the moving truck, starting out across the parking lot. She only had a minute or so to resolve the situation. She looked intently at Angela. "I'm sorry. I guess I didn't know how to—"

"No." Angela looked practically frantic. "No, you can't apologize to me! None of this . . ." Another sob caught in her throat, and she pressed her brow with her thumb and forefinger. "It's not your fault. When I figured it out, I wanted to run, forget about God and having a new life, because what sort of person—" her voice fell to a strained whisper—"does what I did?"

Compassion filled Kari's heart. "That was in the past. I knew it, and I knew God wanted me to tell you about Him." She shrugged and smiled. "It's okay. Really."

"It's not. It'll never be okay. But I realized something." Angela looked intently into Kari's eyes. "If God's love could convince you to study the Bible with me . . . me of all people . . . then God's love was big enough to give me a new life. Even big enough to forgive me. It's a love I can't begin to understand."

Kari was overwhelmed by the significance of the moment, the miracle of it. Her body began to tremble. She thought about how far God had brought all of them since Tim's affair, his murder, and she reached out and hugged Angela. "Yes . . . the love of God really is all that." She eased back. "Our pastor likes to say that if we could completely understand God, then He wouldn't be God. But the fact is, He's beyond our understanding. His love's that way too."

Angela seemed to notice Erin and Sam and their girls, smiling and laughing and coming their way. She sniffed and took a step back. "I'm not sure this will be my church, but I had to tell you that I knew the truth." She smiled, and through her tearstained face a deep regret filled her expression. "I'm sorry, Kari. You'll never know how much."

Then Kari said the words her parents had taught her to say, words that were crucial for healing to begin. "I forgive you."

Angela's expression changed, and the regret faded. In its place were gratitude and peace that Kari had never seen there before. "Thank you." Without another word, Angela nodded and then turned and walked back into the church.

At the same time, from ten yards away Kari heard Erin's joyful cry. "We're here!"

Sam looked happier than he had in a long time. He grinned at Kari as they walked up. "Even on time for church."

"Yeah." Chloe's eyes were wide. "Daddy hates being late for church."

They all laughed, and Clarisse reached up and took hold of Kari's free hand. "I wanna sit by you."

"Me too." Heidi Jo and Amy spoke at the same time, and they both scampered to Kari's other side. The girls wore sundresses, their hair in matching ponytails.

Erin gave Kari a hug. "I can't believe we're really here. It's like a dream." Her face glowed, and her happiness was contagious. "Is everyone inside?"

"Everyone but Dad and Elaine. They'll get back later today." She heard music from inside. "We better go! Cole and Maddie are singing with the kids' choir."

With that they headed into church, the girls giddy, whispering about this being their new home, and the adults excited about sharing a Sunday service. Because this was the way all of them had always wanted life to be. The Baxter family and their spouses and kids going through life together, worshiping God together.

Not just for now but for a lifetime of Sundays.

The worship band started off with a Jeremy Camp song about walking by faith even when sight wasn't possible. Ashley sat with Landon in the back of three full rows filled with her family. The music grew and filled the church, and the words touched Ashley's heart with their relevance. "I will walk by faith even when I cannot see because this broken road prepares Your will for me. . . ."

Ashley felt Landon take hold of her hand, felt his fingers ease between her own. She closed her eyes and let the words wash over her. The message was so completely true. When she was alone in Paris or when her life was on the line because of her health . . . even last year when they lost Sarah, with Landon by her side she had learned to walk the journey of life with faith in God alone.

But that wasn't all. Because the truth was, the broken road she'd walked over the last ten years had indeed prepared her. She opened her eyes and caught a glimpse of Kari whispering to Erin two rows up. For a second, Kari's profile looked almost the same as their mother's.

Ashley lifted her gaze to the plain wooden cross at the front of the church. One of the letters her mother had written to them, a letter Ashley hadn't read until her father gave them their scrapbooks, said basically the same thing as the song. "So often," her mother had written, "only in weakness do we reach out to God, and only as we reach out to God do we find the strength He always intended for us, the strength for whatever comes next."

The song ended, and another one began. Ashley surveyed her extended family filling the pews in front of her. After the kids' choir, the children would leave for Sunday school, but for now everyone was together. Ashley looked past Landon to Cole and Devin.

Cole turned and whispered to Landon, "I think it's time."

"It is." Landon slid his legs to one side. "Go ahead. You'll do great."

Ashley leaned closer and put her hand against Cole's cheek. "You can do it. Don't be nervous."

Cole held her gaze for a moment, then gave a firm nod to both of them. With that, he hurried out the right side of the pew, waited for Maddie to slip out of her row, and the two of them hustled down the aisle at the same time as other children left their seats. All of them met up front near the sweet, gray-haired choir director. She organized them into a line, and when the second song ended, the band waited while the kids walked onto the stage in single file.

The kids' choir was something new at Clear Creek, and Cole and Maddie had tried to talk their other cousins into joining them. The way Erin's and Kari's kids were straining in their seats, looking excitedly at Cole and Maddie, Ashley had a feeling the others would get involved soon enough.

The choir director sat down in the front pew and held out her hands. As she did, the children quieted down, their attention completely on her. With that, the band began to play "This Little Light of Mine." Ashley felt her heart swell with pride as the children's voices rang out across the church. How different Cole's life would be if it weren't for her parents and Landon, if it weren't for God's mercy and love. Would he even have a light to shine for all the world to see?

The song was well under way when Maddie took a step forward and raised her voice louder than the others around her. Ashley watched, confused. Before she could wonder if her strong-willed niece was about to sing a solo, Cole took hold of her arm and pulled her back into line. For a moment it looked like a fight might break out right between the verses. But then Maddie grinned at Cole and linked arms with him.

Midway through the second verse, Ashley felt the baby inside her kick hard against her ribs. She smiled and put her hand on her stomach. Ashley and Landon had finally settled on a name for their newborn son: Isaac James. Isaac because this child felt like a gift from God, the way Isaac was for Abraham in the Bible. And James because Ashley and Landon both loved the message of James in Scripture—that the testing of one's faith developed perseverance.

Through the past year, the truth that perseverance developed hope had become even clearer to them. This new little boy was definitely a ray of hope for their family.

By the time the kids' song ended, Cole and Maddie ran back down the aisle to their seats looking like the best friends everyone knew they would someday be. Cole took his spot beside Devin, breathless from the performance. "How was that?"

"Great!" Landon rubbed his head, his voice a soft whisper. He winked at their son. "I like how you kept Maddie in line."

Cole rolled his eyes. "Someone has to." He seemed to be bursting with some sort of information. "Mom, guess what?"

"What?" The band was launching into another song, but Ashley wanted to hear what was on his mind.

"When I was singing, I could picture Grandma and baby Sarah watching." His smile became tender and heartfelt. "From their window in heaven."

Ashley smiled. "I can picture that too. We'll talk more later."

He nodded, and all of them turned their attention back to the front of the church. Ashley picked up the church bulletin from the spot on the floor where she'd set it. As she did, she scanned the top of the front cover for the title of the message. A chill ran down her spine as she found what she was looking for. She leaned into Landon's shoulder and motioned for him to read it too. He did, and his eyebrows rose in surprise. He put his arm around her and leaned his head against hers.

The sermon today was on the very Scripture she'd been so taken with lately, Psalm 130. And the title was as simple as the truth they'd all found along the journey of life, along the walk of faith. It was just one word, but it spoke volumes

Redemption.

CHAPTER TWENTY-SIX

THE FLANIGANS WERE SPREAD throughout the house and yard, getting ready for their big Fourth of July party, and Bailey was dusting the woodwork in the family room when she heard a knock at the door. She dropped her dust rag on the coffee table and brushed her hands on her jeans.

"I'll get it!" she yelled. It wasn't quite noon, far too early for any of their friends to be here yet. The party didn't start until five, when their dad would set up at his built-in barbecue out back and start grilling six dozen burgers. Bailey hurried down the hall to the entryway. It couldn't be Tim. He and his family were in Colorado on vacation. Cody had been delayed, and his mother had told them it could be another week before he'd be home.

She tucked a wisp of her long hair behind her ears and hurried to the front door. Probably just the mail lady making the trip up the drive because once again the Flanigans had too much mail for the mailbox. She opened the door, and almost in slow motion, her heart skittered into a strange rhythm and her head began to spin. It took a few seconds for her to grasp what she was seeing, and by then the guy standing with crutches on her front porch was already shifting, clearly nervous from the awkwardness of the moment.

"Cody . . . I can't believe it's you." Bailey found her voice, but at the same time she realized something was terribly wrong. The look in Cody's eyes was not the same easygoing kindness that had been there before. Instead there was an intense sadness, a shame almost.

"I just got into town." He came closer. "I guess you can see now . . . why I haven't written all that much."

His words confused her, and she was about to ask him to explain himself when something strange and out of place caught her attention. She looked down, and she suddenly understood. She kept herself from gasping or letting her hand fly to her mouth, but that didn't lessen the shock tearing through her insides.

He hadn't lost his whole leg, the way another injured Bloomington soldier had. But from the left knee down, Cody had a prosthetic lower leg.

"It's okay." Cody shifted his weight to the other side. "You don't have to say anything. You weren't expecting this." He looked at the ground, then back at her. "I asked my mom not to tell you."

Bailey felt sick to her stomach. She grabbed on to an image of Cody lying on the ground in a busy street in Iraq, his leg torn to shreds. "Can you come in?"

"For a minute. My mom's expecting me." He entered the house, and after the door was shut, he leaned against the wall.

Bailey noticed he was putting weight on the prosthesis, and he barely walked with a limp. The crutches must've been because he was still healing. She swallowed hard, not sure what to say. "Does it hurt?"

"Sometimes." Cody flexed the muscles in his jaw, his expression stoic. "I'm okay. I can walk and drive, and pretty soon I'll be running again. Don't feel sorry for me."

"Okay." Her answer was quick because she didn't like the tone between them. Her pity and his lack of emotion. She kept herself from looking down. "You came home early."

"I worked it out so I can finish my rehab in town. I didn't really want to go to the West Coast anyway." For the first time since the door had opened, his eyes grew the tiniest bit softer. "I came here first because I have to tell you something."

Bailey hated the way things felt so distant and awkward between them. Her palms were damp, and she rubbed them against each other. This was Cody . . . the same Cody who had been their neighbor and slept on their sofa and lived with them. The Cody who had raced her down the footpath at the lake and walked with her in the woods behind her house the day he left for the army. The Cody she still thought about every day. So why did things feel so weird?

He set his crutches a few feet away in the corner near the front door and took a deep breath. "Every day in Iraq, every day I was at war, only one—"

"Wait . . ." She blinked, and before he could say anything else, she held out her arms. "I haven't seen you in a year. Don't I get a hug?"

Cody opened his mouth like he might ask her to wait, but then his shoulders sank and after a few seconds he took a half step forward. Without any words and with the most gentle touch, he slowly pulled her into his arms. The hug lasted longer than Bailey expected, but she couldn't let go, didn't want the moment to end. Never mind his leg, Cody was here and he was going to be okay. That was all that mattered.

Bailey pressed her hands against the muscles in his back and kept her head against his shoulder. He still smelled the same, the faint mix of cologne and fresh shampoo and laundry soap. She breathed it in. "I missed you." Her words were so soft, she wasn't sure he could hear them. But that didn't matter. "I was so worried. I wasn't sure . . ." She squeezed her eyes shut. It felt so good being in his arms, having him back in Bloomington. All of it was a start, the beginning of a bridge that would span the gap left by time and war and whatever nightmare Cody had been through in the last year.

"I missed you too." His whispered reply spoke straight to her heart. When he stepped back, he looked a little more like the football hero who had walked out of their house last summer. But the change in his eyes remained.

Bailey studied him and tried to understand what the difference was, a determination maybe or a hardness. She didn't dwell on the fact. At least now they'd erased some of the distance between them.

Cody ran his tongue over his lower lip and seemed to gather his thoughts. "I came here first because I had to. Out there only one thing kept me going." He hesitated, but his eyes stayed fixed on hers. "The idea that if God allowed it, I might see you again."

Bailey was suddenly light-headed. What had he just told her? That seeing her again was all that kept him going? Was he serious? Did he have feelings for her after all? She reached out and took hold of his hand. "I . . . didn't know."

"That's my fault." He hung his head for a moment and seemed to study the place where their hands were joined. When he looked up, his eyes were bright with the emotions that seemed to be trying to break through. He gave her hand a tender squeeze. "Don't get me wrong. I meant what I said in my letters. You and I will only be friends." A slight smile tugged at his lips. "God has someone better for you. I know that."

"How?" Her heart thudded against her ribs, and she shook her head. "How do you know?"

His fingers were still in hers, but he leaned back against the wall again, almost as if he was trying to put distance between them. "I'm okay with you and Tim. I always knew you'd find a guy like him . . . a guy like you."

A sense of betrayal wrapped itself around the moment, and Bailey released the hold she had on his hand. She crossed her arms. "Tim and I . . . we're not serious."

He held up his hand. "Bailey, don't . . ." He forced a slight smile. "It's okay. I didn't come here to make you feel guilty. I just wanted to thank you for giving me a reason to stay alive."

She hated this, the way his homecoming felt more like a terrible good-bye. "I thought . . . from your letters . . ." She searched for the right words, but her head was spinning. "You talked about moving to the West Coast, and I thought . . . you didn't really care about me anymore."

"That was never the reason." Cody looked at his crutches and then down at his leg. "About my time in Iraq . . ." His voice grew with an intensity he'd never shown her before. "I will never, ever regret going. Even if I wouldn't have made it back, I believe in this. What we're doing over there is good. It is."

Bailey could hear a defensiveness in his tone, and she understood. The media had been down on the war for some time now. Even so, opinions from soldiers—as far as she'd heard from her dad and from friends—all sounded very much like Cody's. She relaxed her arms to her sides. "I'm glad you feel that way."

"Freedom is worth defending. Here or there. I'd be there still if this . . . if I hadn't gotten hurt." He shrugged, and some of his intensity faded. "But about us . . . let's be real. I couldn't expect you to . . ."

She waited for him to finish his thought, but he never did, and suddenly she thought she understood what he wasn't saying. Though neither of them had talked about his injury, now there was no way around the topic. "Are you talking about your leg?" She glanced at his crutches, and as she did, a sense of anger gathered around her confused heart. She stood a little taller. "Because maybe you're not giving me enough credit."

"Don't get mad." He sighed and cocked his head, looking more like the Cody she remembered. "I didn't come here to make you angry."

"Listen." The uneasiness she'd felt earlier faded. Since he brought it up, maybe it was time to say everything she'd felt since he walked through the door, since she noticed his crutches. "You could've lost your leg in an accident, and that wouldn't have changed who you are. But your injury came because you're a hero." Her voice rose, and she forced herself to bring it back down. "Lots of people talk about freedom, but you did something about it. Please don't think I see you differently now. That isn't fair." Her tone grew softer, and she stepped closer to him. "I missed you every single minute you were gone."

He looked like he wanted to argue with her, explain again how he had to pull away from her life because of Tim or because of his injury. But the air around them changed, and the attraction between them was undeniable. For a few seconds, Bailey thought he might kiss her, or if he didn't, that she might kiss him. But instead he drew her into another hug, this one washed in a sense of desperation.

"I don't know," Cody whispered against her hair. "Everything's so different."

"Nothing's different." Bailey's heart pounded so hard that she was sure he could feel it. She moved back just enough to look into his eyes, and the connection she felt left her breathless. "Can't we at least have what we had before?" She leaned against his chest. "You were my best friend when you left here."

"Bailey—" his breath warmed the top of her head—"I want you to have the best."

"I do." She held him a little tighter. "I have my arms around him right now."

They stayed that way for a few more heartbeats before Cody released her. "I need to go see my mom."

"Come back for our party." She hated the thought of him leaving so soon. "My family can't wait to see you."

He hesitated, this strange new battle clearly taking place in his head and heart. But in the end he sighed and nodded. "Okay." He kissed her forehead, same as he'd done a year ago when he left. "I'll be your friend. We can at least have that."

It was a victory, one that Bailey could settle for. Especially in light of the fact that he'd come ready to cut things off with her— all so she could have a better life without him. She shivered at the thought and walked him to the door. She didn't want to think about Tim or the future or the all-consuming attraction she felt for Cody. He was her friend, and for now that would have to be enough.

As he left, as he climbed into his car and drove off, Bailey was struck by a very certain fact. Cody might've lost his leg, but he hadn't come home any less of a man.

He'd come home more of one.

Jenny was walking along the upstairs hallway when she glanced down over the staircase railing and saw Bailey hugging a young man. It took her a moment to realize that the guy was Cody, and at the same time she saw the crutches and the prosthetic leg.

Cody's leg . . . I had no idea, no way to prepare Bailey. She pressed her fingertips to her lips, her eyes glued on the couple in the entryway below.

Even as she stood there, an answer both certain and subtle breezed across the landscape of her soul. *Bailey is Mine. I have prepared her. I know the plans I have for her.*

Tears layered her eyes as she watched the two young people step back from each other and continue their conversation. In that instant, she noticed an attraction or chemistry between them, something completely undeniable.

Jenny slipped through the door of her bedroom, unable to watch the private exchange happening between Bailey and Cody. This moment was for them alone. The rest of the family would see Cody later.

Jenny trembled as she crossed her room to the wall of windows that faced the front yard. She bit her lip and leaned on the windowsill. The window was open, and she could feel the July heat building outside. So, Cody had lost part of his leg in the war. Why hadn't his mother told them?

The answer was obvious, of course. Cody never would've wanted them or anyone else feeling sorry for him. That wasn't his style. He must've asked his mother to keep quiet about his injury. He probably figured he'd take care of the news himself here . . . in person.

Where no words would be necessary.

Jenny gazed at the blue sky and at the cumulus clouds gathered along the horizon. Never mind about Cody's leg; it was wonderful to have him home again. *Thank You, God, for sparing his life. Thank You a million times.*

Relief took the place of the sick feeling she'd had since she'd first noticed Cody's leg. So many young men hadn't returned home from the war, but Cody was alive! He could get by without his lower leg. Thousands of soldiers managed with the same disability. She blinked at the open sky. Yes, of course he could get by. They were all blessed by the fact that he'd come home at all.

Jenny thought about Bailey and the emotions her daughter must be going through right now. She'd watched Bailey's growing friendship with Tim, but she had never felt quite right about the two of them, not as a couple, anyway. Tim was kind and talented, and he loved God. But not once had she ever seen Tim look at Bailey the way Cody had looked at her just now.

She released a slow breath. When Cody had gone away to the army, Jenny and Jim had in some ways been glad for the break it offered their daughter. Cody's past was so different from Bailey's that neither Jenny nor Jim had been able to see him as someone Bailey might date one day. But Cody had grown much in the past few years. And the bond between them a moment ago was breathtaking.

She squinted against the glare of the uncertainty ahead. *She's Your daughter, God. I know that. But please make Your path clear for her.*

Her prayer created a familiar echo in her heart, the same words she lifted to God often for all her kids. This time there was no answer, except one. A very strong certainty that in the days to come they might still see a lot of Tim. But they'd also be seeing more of a young man who might actually love their daughter. The handsome soldier who had fought with every breath.

The high school football player who had come home a hero.

CHAPTER TWENTY-SEVEN

As July Fourths went, this one wasn't too hot or humid. A light wind came off the lake and swept gently up the hillside where John and Elaine sat side by side watching the rest of the family set out their blankets and picnic gear and slather sunscreen on the kids.

John leaned back in his beach chair and pulled his baseball cap down so he could see despite the glare of sunlight against the water. He was grateful they'd made it back in time for the big picnic. Every year this event was one of the Baxter family's most special but this year maybe most of all. They were all living in one place now, the Baxter kids and their families close the way John and Elizabeth had once upon a lifetime ago prayed they would be.

He stretched out his arm and took hold of Elaine's hand. Two weeks after marrying her, they were still settling into their new house, still browsing furniture stores for odds and ends that would help make the place feel like a home. The sale of the Baxter house made him sad, but even more it gave him closure. Something he needed before moving on—he and Elaine both agreed about that. But most of all, they talked often about how they felt like they'd stepped out of a time of mourning and into a time of living. Truly living.

John savored the sound of his grandchildren laughing and playing and chattering on the grassy shore. Each wore a life jacket and sunscreen, and Erin's girls had matching colorful hats to keep the sun out of their eyes.

John turned to the place where Erin and Sam were setting up one of the picnic tables. With the help of the rest of the family, they had completely moved into their new house, and their four girls were already fast friends with their cousins, especially Jessie, Maddie, and Hayley. Malin had a while before she'd be old enough to join them, but even now Erin's girls circled her, oohing and aahing over Malin's new yellow polka-dot swimsuit and her Hannah Montana water shoes. Only Peter and Brooke weren't here yet, but they planned on arriving a little later.

John focused his attention to his grandsons a few yards away. Cole, Devin, RJ, and Tommy were already hard at work on what looked like a monster-size sandcastle. Cole had brought small rocks and raisins and uncooked spaghetti noodles to decorate the outside when they were done with the construction. From where he was sitting, John could hear him handing out instructions to his cousins.

"See, guys." Cole's face was a mask of concentration. "Build up the sides nice and smooth like this." He stopped and studied the work Tommy was doing. "Right. Just like that. This'll be better than any girl sandcastle ever!"

"Yeah!" RJ grinned big. "Boys are best!"

"You're smart for your age." Cole gave him a hearty pat on the back. "I always knew that."

A quiet chuckle echoed through John's chest. Cole hadn't changed since he was a little guy Devin's age. Talkative and confident, kind and competitive. He studied his oldest grandson and felt the familiar special fondness he had for the boy. Cole had spent a lot of time at the Baxter house during his early years when John had been the only father figure in the child's life.

John watched Landon and Ryan walk over to the boys and admire the foundation of the castle. Landon knelt and used a bucket to drag a pile of sand closer to Cole.

Cole threw his arm around Landon's shoulders and kissed him on the cheek. "Thanks, Dad! You're the best!"

A smile filled John's heart. Indeed. Landon was the best thing to ever happen to Cole. God had worked out every prayer ever spoken on behalf of Ashley and Cole. John shifted his gaze to his very pregnant middle daughter, sitting with Katy on a bench facing the lake and laughing her head off about something. Cole wasn't the only one to benefit. These days, Ashley's life and faith, her innate ability to love and find joy in a situation—all of it was nothing short of a miracle.

"She's beautiful." Elaine's voice was soft and thoughtful beside him. She was looking at Ashley too. "Even ready to deliver."

"Yes, she is. Katy too. They're both so healthy and happy." John sighed. "It could be anytime for Katy."

"I'm glad." Elaine squeezed his hand. "I can't wait."

There was no reason to think trouble existed for Ashley this time, so no one had discussed the possibility. Still, a hint of concern remained for John, because anytime a woman delivered a baby with a birth defect, there was a chance it could happen again. He ordered himself to relax. Never mind the past. Here in the warm early afternoon light, with every reason to rejoice and his family around him, John refused to dwell on his concerns. He smiled at Elaine. "There's nothing like a brand-new grandbaby."

They fell silent again, comfortable with each other. John gazed farther down the slope of grass and sand to where Kari and Erin stood at the water's edge, lost in conversation.

John studied his second oldest daughter and felt himself overcome with pride. After he had passed on the information about Angela Manning to Kari, he'd doubted himself more than once. He knew she had always believed that love was a decision, but that didn't mean she should be pressed into a Bible study with her first husband's mistress. Even so, Kari had taken on the challenge to meet with Angela and talk to her about the Bible, hoping to keep the connection between them a secret.

"But in the end, God worked it all out," Kari had told John last Sunday when he and Elaine returned home from their honeymoon. "Somehow knowing that I'd care about her even after what happened between her and Tim, it's like that made her believe in God all the more."

The Lord had blessed Kari's determination to love at all costs, something that she'd learned from her mother. The love Elizabeth had for people lived on in Kari; that much was clear. Like Elizabeth, Kari was someone they had all learned about love from over the years, and John had no doubts that God would continue to multiply that love for Kari and her family.

Dayne had been setting up another table, and now John watched him join Katy and Ashley. Even this many years later, there were still times when John had to remind himself that Dayne, one of Hollywood's leading men, was in fact the son he and Elizabeth had given up for adoption a lifetime ago.

That You would bring Dayne into our lives was beyond anything I could ask or imagine. But this? Dayne and Katy starting a family here in Bloomington? John felt a lump form in his throat. *You are truly good, Lord. We don't deserve all You've done.*

Jeremiah 29:11 came to mind immediately, the verse he and Elizabeth had drilled into the heads of their kids while they were growing up. John let the words fill his heart and mind. *"'For I know the plans I have for you,' declares the Lord, 'plans to prosper you and not to harm you, plans to give you hope and a future.'"* The picnic spread out before him was proof of that again and again and again.

"You're taking stock, aren't you?" Elaine's words were unhurried. She wore sunglasses, but she shielded her eyes as she looked at him.

"I am." He was warmed by the fact that she already knew him so well, that at times like this he was bound to survey his growing family and the way God had brought them through another year, another set of trials and triumphs.

"Look at Luke and Reagan." Elaine turned her attention to the couple, sitting on a log a little ways off from the group. Luke had his arm around Reagan's shoulders, and she had hers around his waist, her head on his shoulder. Elaine smiled. "I've never seen them look so in love."

"I have." John thought back to how things were before, back when the blonde college coed would join the Baxters for Sunday dinners, and after she left, Luke's sisters would talk about how smitten their brother was. The memory was bittersweet, tempered by the heartache and hurt of their separate choices after 9/11. He was suddenly overcome with thanks to God for all He'd done in the last few weeks. John cleared his throat, finding the words despite his emotions. "I prayed Luke and Reagan would look like that again, but I honestly wasn't sure."

"God is faithful." Elaine angled her head. "Even when we aren't."

"Yes." John breathed in deeply, filling his lungs with the fresh lake air. Again he surveyed his family, the adults and children. "That's the story of our lives, really. His mercy and grace, His love. Even when things don't go the way we hoped they'd go." He smiled at her. "Even then He has a good plan for us."

There was a sudden commotion of voices and laughter coming from the parking lot behind them, and John turned just as he saw Peter come into view. His son-in-law grinned and waved at the crowd of family members. "Hey, everyone! Come on up. We have a surprise for you."

John was still holding Elaine's hand as they stood and stretched. It took a few minutes, but eventually the whole group of adults and sand-covered kids was trudging up the hillside. As they reached the edge of the parking lot, the laughter and conversation fell to a hush. Standing a few feet from their van, Brooke and Peter and Maddie were gathered around Hayley, who was wearing a pink helmet.

Braced in Peter's hands was a pink two-wheel bicycle with white streamers and a floral basket.

For a minute, John's heart pounded. It was the bike that had stood parked in his garage since Hayley's accident, the one he'd given a picture of to Brooke while she sat at Hayley's hospital bedside. Brooke must've gotten it from his garage and cleaned off the layers of dust..Back then the gesture had been deeply symbolic for John because it represented a shift in his thinking. Initially after Hayley's near drowning he'd thought the child would be better off in heaven, but in time God had convinced him that as long as she had a heartbeat, he had to pray for his granddaughter's life. For vibrant, abundant life. That his prayers must be for a miracle and nothing less.

None of them had any doubts that God had granted them the miracle they'd asked for. She continued to make progress in every area of development, and always John was grateful for the reports. But even still, the idea of Hayley on a bicycle had always seemed far-fetched.

Until this moment.

Maddie jumped up and down, unable to contain her excitement. "Watch, everybody! Watch our surprise!"

Hayley grinned at the group of family watching her and then up at Peter. Her long golden hair and innocent eyes peering out from beneath the bicycle helmet made her look more like an angel than a child struggling with a brain injury.

"Go, Hayley!" Cole yelled from his place next to Landon. "You can do it."

Hayley pointed at Cole, her smile stretching from one ear to the other. She gave him a firm thumbs-up and then turned back to Peter.

A near silent awe came over the group as they watched Peter whisper something to Hayley.

She nodded, her face more serious than before. Then with motions only slightly slower than other children, Hayley took firm hold of the handlebars and swung one leg over the middle. Peter steadied the bike, and by using the pedals, Hayley slid herself up onto the seat.

Is she really going to . . . ? John had to remind himself to take a breath.

Again Hayley smiled at her dad and gave a firm nod of her head. With that, Peter jogged alongside the bicycle a few steps and then let go. Hayley wobbled a little at first, but then her determination took over, and she pushed herself forward and found her balance.

Hayley was doing it! She was riding a bicycle! John blinked back tears, his eyes glued to his granddaughter. *She's doing it, God. You told me to pray that she'd live, and now . . .* He couldn't stop the tears from rolling onto his cheeks, and he wiped them with the back of his hand.

A chorus of cheers came from the curbside, and Hayley maintained her balance even while shooting them another grin. She made a large circle around a planter at the end of the parking lot, and when she reached her family once more, she stopped and caught herself with her feet.

"Hayley!" Cole was the first to race over, both his arms raised over his head. "I can't believe it! You were awesome!"

"She learned from watching me." Maddie lifted her chin, but at the same time she caught her father's look. She smiled at Cole and released a nervous laugh. "Just kidding. Actually, Daddy taught her." She moved to the side and made room for Cole. She was practically bursting with pride as she patted her sister's back. "This is your big day, Hayley! Right, isn't this your big day?"

"I learned how!" Hayley beamed up at her father, and the two exchanged a high five. "That was my best, huh, Mommy?"

Brooke nodded, but clearly she couldn't speak. John saw the tears on Kari's and Ashley's faces too as the group moved into the parking lot and surrounded Hayley and her bicycle. Congratulations and words of encouragement came from every side.

Tommy worked his way to the place near the front. He looked determined. "Hey, now you can teach me, Hayley. I'm so tired of training wheels!"

Laughter rippled through the crowd, and they made way for Peter to lift the bicycle back into their SUV. Elaine and the rest of his family started back down the hill, but John waited for Brooke and Hayley.

Hayley spotted him from a ways off, and her face lit up. As she reached him, she held out her hands and took a running jump into his arms. She hugged him around his neck and leaned back enough to look straight to his heart. "That was good, right, Papa?"

"Yes." He nuzzled his face against hers and pressed his hand against her silky hair. "That was very, very good."

Hayley kissed him on his cheek. "Thanks for the bike. I like pink so much!" She flashed him a grin, then scrambled down and ran with Peter to catch her cousins.

John turned to Brooke. For several seconds they only looked at each other, the reflection of Hayley's painful past haunting both their eyes. Finally John pulled his oldest daughter into his arms and held her for a long time. They had so much in common, really. Their love for the medical field and their ability to handle things calmly, directly. And a long time ago in a hospital room with Hayley hooked to life support, they had both struggled with the same thing.

Believing for a miracle.

John stepped back and took hold of Brooke's hands. His voice was tight, but he managed. "You . . . you found it in my garage."

"I didn't think you'd mind." Brooke smiled through fresh tears. "We told Hayley it was from you. She's been practicing on one at school."

"Remember . . ." John was overwhelmed once more, and he stared at the ground as a quiet sob caught in his throat. "I was the first one who believed it could happen." He sniffed hard and pressed his palms briefly to his eyes.

This time the hug came from Brooke, and neither of them said a word. This was the way family was supposed to be—there for each other through whatever life brought, loving each other, supporting each other. And believing God for the best.

As the hug ended, John smiled at his daughter, and in awestruck silence they walked arm in arm down the hill to join the others. Everything that needed saying had already been said in a single picture. The image of their precious Hayley, who wasn't supposed to walk or talk or ever get out of bed, pedaling away on her pink bicycle.

A picture John would cherish as long as he lived.

CHAPTER TWENTY-EIGHT

THE BARBECUE WAS OVER and daylight was close to fading when Ashley began to take her contractions seriously. The big annual fishing contest between her dad and Landon was more than halfway finished, and the cousins were bunched together on a couple of fallen logs not far from the water. This year the kids were split between who they were rooting for. In the first few minutes of the half-hour contest, Landon had caught a fish so small his *own* cheering section burst into laughter. Since then her dad had snagged a twelve-inch bass. The stakes were same as last year— loser jumps in the lake with his clothes on.

Ashley noticed Katy and Dayne sitting on top of a picnic table, their feet on the bench. They were off by themselves, their heads close together, and whatever their conversation, it seemed intense. Ashley took a step in their direction. Maybe Katy wasn't feeling so good either. Earlier she had also been having what felt like contractions. Ashley looked back at the water. She wanted to find a spot close to the fishing action, but maybe if she wandered over to Katy and Dayne, the walk would distract her body from the tightening in her belly.

Already the day had been so full, with swimming and throwing a Frisbee and of course the sand castle contest between the boys and girls. She glanced back at Cole, sitting with Tommy and RJ and Devin and cheering for Landon. The child was so competitive. At one point during the sand castle building, he'd stood up, raised his shovel in the air, and shouted, "No one can beat this castle! Especially not a bunch of girls!"

After that Landon had gone over for a little talk with him. Ashley had watched from the hillside, and she saw Cole's immediate remorse. He really meant well. And Maddie never lessened her efforts at egging him on. Still, he needed to be gracious, whether he won or not. In the end, Landon had declared the boys' castle the biggest and most lifelike and the girls' castle the prettiest and most thoughtful.

Landon had no idea Ashley was having occasional contractions—at least she didn't think so. Earlier she'd seen him talking to her dad. The conversation looked serious, and Ashley figured Landon had questions about her pregnancy. But other than that, he hadn't seemed too concerned, and she hadn't wanted to worry him unless they became more regular. Now that they were, he was in the middle of the fishing contest. A half hour wouldn't make a difference.

Ashley trudged up the hill. As she reached Katy and Dayne, she saw they had a pad of paper between them, and Dayne was writing something down. His face looked drawn, his eyes anxious. He looked up at Ashley. "She's having contractions."

"Still?" Ashley took the spot next to her brother so he was in the middle. "You're writing them down?"

Dayne glanced at the paper. "Every eight or nine minutes for the last hour."

"They're not strong enough to be real." Katy stretched back and leaned against her hands. "I think I just need a little rest."

"You're due this week, so I don't know." Ashley gave Katy a wary look. "If they don't stop . . ."

"It could be time." Dayne swallowed hard. He looked at his watch. "It's been four minutes."

Katy allowed a light laugh. She motioned at Dayne but kept her attention on Ashley. "You don't happen to have a paper bag?"

It took Ashley a minute, but then she laughed too. "For Dayne?"

"In case he hyperventilates. I'd hate for him to pass out on the way to the hospital."

"Fine, go ahead." Dayne tossed his hands, feigning persecution. "Mock me. I can take it."

Ashley was about to say something to her brother, something about never being too safe when it came to babies, when another pain grabbed at her midsection and held tight. She sucked in her breath and held it, leaning back in an effort to relieve the contraction even a little.

Dayne turned to her. "Don't tell me . . . you too?"

A worried look flashed in Katy's eyes. "It's too early. You aren't due yet."

Gradually the pain eased and Ashley exhaled. She caught her breath, fighting the wild tears inside her. "Three weeks away." She breathed out more slowly. "Early . . . but not too early, I guess."

"So what are you saying?" Alarm replaced the laughter in Katy's tone. "You've been having contractions since we talked earlier?"

"On and off. Not regular enough to tell Landon." Ashley sat a little straighter, stretching her torso, trying to get comfortable. "I keep thinking maybe they're false."

"But not if they're regular and they keep getting—" Katy squeezed her eyes shut, and her hand went to her rounded stomach.

"Another one?" Dayne sounded almost panicky. He poised the pen over the pad of paper and checked his watch. "That's seven minutes." He stood up. "I'm getting Dad."

From down the beach came a loud cheer, and the three of them turned to the sound. Ashley watched their father steady himself and then reel in a struggling fish that had to be at least twenty-four inches long.

The kids seated on that side of the competition jumped up, cheering and squealing and chanting, "Papa . . . Papa . . . Papa."

"Looks like the contest might be over." Katy's contraction had come to an end, and she sounded tired but not nearly as worried as Dayne. She slid her feet slowly to the ground. "Let's go watch the last few minutes."

They walked down the hillside and reached the sandy shore.

Landon appeared to get a bite. "This is it! I can feel it!" He dug his heels into the sand and focused all his attention on the movement in the water thirty feet out. "Come on, baby!"

Cole bounded to his feet, his hands cupped around his mouth. "Get in here, you stubborn fish, and you better be huge!"

Then with everyone watching, the fish on Landon's line jumped into the air. It was easily the biggest fish of the day. But as it flopped in the air, it pulled free of the hook and swam off in the other direction.

"What?" Landon reeled in as fast as he could, but it was no use. He let his hands fall to his sides. "That's plain old wrong."

Ashley laughed quietly to herself.

Cole was still staring out at the place where the fish disappeared, his expression frozen in shock. He tossed his hands in the air and looked over at his grandfather and then at the girl cousins supporting him. "You all saw it. So that counts, right?"

"No." Maddie giggled. "You have to *catch* the fish. Not *look* at it!"

"And . . ." Peter raised the stopwatch he'd been holding. "Time!"

"That's it!" Maddie ran around in small circles, and the other girl cousins followed her lead. "Papa wins! Papa wins!"

Ashley winced. She could only imagine the battle ahead.

Cole put his hands on his hips. "That's not fair, 'cause we had the biggest—"

Landon walked up a few feet onto the beach and set his pole on the ground. He moved to their son's side and messed up his blond hair. "Papa won fair and square." He shrugged. "You win some, you lose some."

"Yeah, but—" Cole lowered his voice, but his determination remained—"you lost last time."

"Here's the good news." Landon pointed out at the lake. "That big ol' fish is still out there. And next week you and Devin and I'll come back and catch him for sure."

Cole hesitated, but a smile crept up his face. "Okay. Let's do that." He giggled and gave Landon a light push toward the water. "Plus, now we get to watch you jump in the lake!"

"Lake . . . lake . . . lake!" The girl cousins formed a half circle a few feet up the sloped shore.

Just as Landon took a deep breath and ran straight into the water, Ashley noticed Katy get hit by another contraction. Dayne put his arm around her and supported her, but he looked ready for the trip to the hospital. Ashley heard Landon hit the water, and she glanced back to the shore as—like last time—he ran out until the water was a little past his waist, and then he flopped back and disappeared beneath the surface. When he came up, he held his hands high, his face full of exhilaration. "Papa's the winner!" he shouted.

But at that moment, Landon looked at Ashley, and he must've caught the concern on her face because his expression changed and he moved quickly out of the water in her direction. "Ash . . . what is it?" He was breathless, drenched from the lake, his tanned skin covered in goose bumps.

Ashley nodded at Katy. "Contractions. We're both having them."

Landon wiped the water from his face and tried to wring out his T-shirt. "Why didn't you tell me?"

"I . . . I kept thinking they were false." Ashley gave Landon a weak smile. "I'm not so sure now."

"That was a big one." Katy looked pale as she turned to Dayne. "Maybe we should have it checked."

"You too." Landon was still dripping, so Cole ran a towel to him. He wrapped it around his waist, but his eyes never left Ashley's. "You don't look good."

Ashley felt clammy, and her heart was pounding. "I need to sit down."

Her father must've heard what was happening, because he set his pole down and made his way over. When he reached them, he looked from Katy to Ashley. "You're both in labor?"

"I know." Ashley bent over slightly. "Crazy, huh?"

"How long?"

"Off and on all day." Ashley gripped Landon's wet arm. She looked at her sister-in-law. "I think it's the same for Katy, right?"

"Pretty steady for the past four hours." Katy winced. "I think they must be real."

Brooke walked over with Peter right behind her. "What's happening?"

"Contractions." Dayne's eyes were wide. "For both of them."

The group talked about the situation for another minute, and before either Ashley or Katy could have another contraction, Ashley's father, Brooke, and Peter agreed that a trip to the hospital was necessary.

"What about the picnic? We have to pack up our things."

"We'll get it. Don't worry about a thing." Peter looked at Dayne and then Landon. "You guys go. We'll take care of the kids and your stuff, and we'll all meet at the hospital."

The decision was made quickly, and Ashley was glad. She bid a quick good-bye to Cole and Devin, and as Landon helped her up the hill and into their van, she had another strong contraction. Landon helped her buckle her seat belt, and he was out of the parking lot headed for the hospital with Dayne and Katy right behind them by the time the pain subsided.

Ashley slumped down, exhausted. "What if . . . I waited too long?"

"You didn't." Landon's jaw was set. "Everything's going to be okay."

She looked straight ahead and tried not to remember the last time they headed for the hospital for the birth of a baby. But even so, her eyes blurred with tears. She reached out and worked her fingers between his. "Landon . . . please." She blinked a few times and looked at him. "Pray for little Isaac."

Without hesitating, he began praying. "Lord, You know our hearts and You know our concerns." His knuckles were white from the tight grip he had on the steering wheel, his clothes still wet from the lake. "Be with Ashley and give her peace, and please . . . please help our little boy be okay. And not only our baby but Katy and Dayne's baby too." A tense chuckle came from him. "This is a wild day. We won't get through it without Your help. Thank You, God. In Jesus' name, amen."

"Amen." Darkness was falling over Bloomington, and in the distance a burst of fireworks filled the sky. Ashley watched the reds and silvers swell and fade. "Looks like we're going to miss fireworks this year."

"The kind in the sky, anyway." Landon managed a grin. "How're you doing?"

"Okay." She looked at the spot in the sky where she'd seen the fireworks. Maybe if there were more, the display would help take her mind off the pain. But as the next burst of color appeared on the horizon, her body seized up and she was overcome with pain. Not five minutes had passed since the last one. She gasped. *I'm so afraid. Please, God, let us get there in time. Please help my baby. . . .*

If ever Ashley wanted a clear, audible answer from the Lord, it was now. But He gave her something just as helpful—a Scripture that had brought her peace time and time again in the days since she and Landon first reconnected. *"Rejoice in the Lord always. I will say it again: Rejoice! Let your gentleness be evident to all. The Lord is near. Do not be anxious about anything, but in everything, by prayer and petition, with thanksgiving, present your requests to God. And the peace of God, which transcends all understanding, will guard your hearts and your minds in Christ Jesus."*

The words spoke deeply to Ashley's soul. She focused intently on the baby growing inside her. How long had it been since she'd felt him move or kick? She dismissed the question as soon as it hit her. *"Do not be anxious about anything, but in everything, by prayer and petition, with thanksgiving . . ."*

She had two more contractions before they reached the hospital, and by then Landon was on his cell with Dayne. Katy's were getting stronger, but they were no closer together. If Ashley weren't in so much pain, the situation would almost be comical. Both of them going into labor at the same time, rushing to the hospital caravan-style.

Landon helped Ashley out of the van, while right behind them Dayne did the same with Katy. Inside the emergency room waiting area, there were only a few people seated in chairs—a man with an Ace bandage around his ankle and an exhausted-looking woman with a sick child in her arms. But no one seemed in critical condition, and the staff behind the desk responded quickly to the arrival of two pregnant women in advanced labor.

It took twenty minutes before they were registered and taken to separate rooms. Ashley had time for a quick good-bye before she lost sight of Katy. By then, Katy's contractions were coming every five minutes, and Ashley's had slowed, but she seemed to be in more pain. As she and Landon were set up in a labor room and a nurse hooked her up to a monitor, Ashley stretched out on the hospital bed and silently recited the verse again. *"And the peace of God, which transcends all understanding, will guard your hearts and your minds in Christ Jesus." Please, God, give me Your peace. Let my baby be okay . . . please. Be with Isaac James.*

"We'll let the monitor pick up the next few contractions." The nurse was young, but she seemed adept. "Use the call button if you have any concerns."

When the nurse was gone, Landon stood at the side of her bed, the way he had when Devin was born and of course when she had Sarah last summer. His clothes were drier now but still damp as he stroked her hair and whispered to her. "We've been here before. You can do this."

And she could; she knew that. God was with her—she could feel His presence. But even still something about this delivery felt different from either of the last two. With Devin, she'd gone into labor during a tornado and her blood pressure dropped. He'd nearly been born in the basement of the Baxter house, but she'd made it to the hospital in time to have a C-section. Then with Sarah, they'd known what terrible loss awaited them in the hours after her birth. But this time . . .

Ashley was hit by another contraction. She worked with it, releasing short bursts of air while the pain grew and peaked. As it tapered off, her thoughts picked up where they left off. This time there seemed to be something very wrong, something in the severity of the pains. But whatever was going on inside her, the situation was shrouded in the unknown. At least it felt that way.

A few contractions passed before a doctor and a nurse finally made their way into the room. The doctor apologized and wasted little time as he conducted an exam and asked Ashley questions about her contractions. As he finished, he crossed his arms and his brow lowered in concern. "You're definitely in labor, but the baby's transverse. Sideways. That would explain the severity of your pain." He looked at the monitor again. "So far the baby's heart rate looks good, but if he doesn't turn on his own, or if I see any sign of stress on the baby, we'll have to do a C-section pretty quickly."

"How . . . ?" Landon looked concerned. "How will you know . . . if he becomes stressed?"

"The nurses can read your wife's monitor at their station." He gave a firm nod. "As soon as we see any sign of struggle, we'll be on it. I promise you that." He smiled at Ashley. "A lot of times babies turn on their own. We have to give him time for that to happen. At least as long as his heartbeat stays steady."

With that the doctor asked if they had any questions, and when they didn't, he excused himself with a promise to be back often.

Again tears blurred Ashley's eyes. "I don't like this." Her voice cracked. "I knew something was wrong. Can't it ever just be easy?"

Landon pulled up a chair so his face was closer to hers. "With you—" he kissed her cheek—"nothing worthwhile ever is."

Two hours passed slowly, but with every exam the news was the same. The baby was still transverse. Ashley survived the terrible waiting and intense pain with God's strength and the support of Landon and because the baby's heartbeat remained unaffected. The doctor offered her an epidural, but he felt fairly sure that the medication would increase the odds of a C-section. So rather than that, Ashley tried to endure. She felt strongly that a traditional birth would be better than a C-section, since traveling through the birth canal was better for a baby's lungs. Even if she had undergone the surgery before. That was different, of course. They had known Sarah wouldn't survive, but this baby was supposed to be healthy.

At least up until now.

Once in a while Landon would leave long enough to get an update on Katy in the room four doors down. He kept Ashley at least a little distracted with a constant stream of information. Katy's exam had gone better than Ashley's. She was dilating, and the contractions were progressing fairly quickly.

Ashley's dad, Elaine, Cole, and Devin were gathered in the waiting room watching a John Wayne movie. The rest of them had gone back to Kari and Ryan's house.

As Ashley's most recent contraction let up, she readjusted the cold cloth on her forehead and nodded to Landon. It was eleven o'clock, and they hadn't had news from the other room in almost an hour. "Please . . . find out how Katy's doing."

Landon looked doubtful, but he didn't hesitate for long and Ashley understood why. Her next contraction couldn't be far off. He hurried out of the room, and after less than a minute he returned, his face lit up. "The doctor said it'll be anytime. Katy's been taken into delivery."

"No problems?" Even in her own haze of pain and uncertainty, Ashley was grateful for Katy and Dayne. After all they'd been through, the birth of their firstborn would be the sweetest highlight of their life together.

"None." Landon took his place beside her again.

A smile came over Ashley, and she closed her eyes. "I think . . . when the doctor comes back in . . . we should ask how much longer." She opened her eyes and searched Landon's face. "A C-section wouldn't be so bad, right? I've done it before."

"Of course not." He took the cloth from her forehead and waved it around, trying to cool it down again. After a few seconds he patted it gently to her cheeks and neck, and then he set it once more on her head.

She was about to ask how Cole and Devin were doing when the doctor walked into the room and closed the door behind him. He took a deep breath. "That last contraction was harder on your baby." He glanced at a clipboard in his hand. "His heart rate dipped more than I'd like. If I see it again, we won't hesitate. As you know, we can deliver the baby by C-section very quickly if there's a problem."

He performed another exam, and this time there was good news and bad. The baby had turned and was head down in the birth canal. But because he'd been in the wrong position for so long, Ashley wasn't dilated whatsoever. The doctor explained the situation to them. "You'll need several more hours of labor to get to the point of delivery. Now it's a question of how much the baby can take."

"Why wait?" Landon had slid to the edge of his seat, his back straight, body tense. "Let's go ahead with the C-section now."

"We will if there's any further concern." The doctor's expression was more reassuring than before. "Like I said, we'll watch very closely. We still want to avoid a C-section if possible. If the conditions are right, a natural delivery is always best for the baby's lungs."

When he was gone, Ashley's tears came in earnest. She rolled slightly onto her side and held out both hands to Landon. "I'm not sure I can do this." She was exhausted and tired of waiting. "I'm trying to feel God's peace, but I'm not sure . . ."

"You don't have to feel it." He cupped his hands around hers and kissed her fingers. "God's here no matter how we feel."

His words comforted her, and she held on to that truth and to one very certain fact. However the delivery took place, every contraction brought them that much closer to the moment they'd been looking forward to for months.

The beautiful, miraculous first look at their newborn son.

CHAPTER TWENTY-NINE

As Dayne rushed into the delivery room alongside the gurney, as Katy squeezed his hand and fought another wave of contractions, he was overwhelmed by one very amazing detail. Their baby was about to be born on the Fourth of July. The day God had brought him into this family. The timing seemed too spectacular to be a coincidence, and the joy in Dayne's heart made him feel like he was floating.

Katy was panting, her face twisted in pain. She groaned when the attendants parked the gurney and the doctor positioned her legs for delivery.

Dayne leaned close to her face. "I'm here, honey. It's okay."

"I have to push!" Her face was red, her eyes wide. "I feel like I have to push!"

"Just a minute." The doctor was adjusting the sheet across her stomach and checking the baby's progress. "All right, Katy . . . wait for the next contraction, and then you can push. Any minute now."

Any minute? Dayne felt a layer of sweat break out across his forehead. His heart banged around in his chest, and he felt like his knees might buckle. *Dear God, help Katy. . . . Be with our baby. . . .*

The very first breath of life is from Me, dear son . . . the first and the last.

Dayne felt the gentle response deep in his soul, in a place where he knew the answer could've only come from God. He thought about Ashley's baby Sarah and how her life had been a direct picture of this truth. That life was God's to give and His to take. The certainty of that fact took all the worry out of the moment.

"Dayne, I can feel it. The baby's coming!"

"You're doing great." He put his arm around her shoulders and supported her. As he did, he whispered near the side of her face, "You can do this, sweetheart."

The doctor nodded and looked up at her. "Okay, you can push. Push hard, Katy." In a mirror that hung behind the doctor, Dayne could see the top of his baby's head. The doctor sounded calm and in control. "Keep pushing . . . a little more. That's it, good." The contraction ended. "Rest for a minute. The baby's almost here."

Katy was completely out of breath. She leaned against Dayne's shoulder. "Hold me up. I need you."

"I am. I won't leave." Dayne's heartbeat tripped into double time. The rest of his life would be changed by the next few minutes. "I can see the head."

She tried to see the mirror, but another contraction was already hitting her and clearly she needed all her strength to push. This time, the baby's head made it out, and on the second half of the contraction, the little body slipped into the doctor's hands.

"Congratulations!" The doctor's voice rang through the room. "You have a little girl." The doctor waited a few seconds, and at that instant, their daughter's first cry filled the room.

The miracle of it all was more than Dayne could take in. Tears welled in his eyes, and he leaned over and tenderly kissed Katy's lips. "Can you believe it? God gave us a daughter!" The words sounded like they were from a script, like this was a scene from some incredible movie.

Their little girl's cries tapered off, falling to little more than an occasional whimper.

The nurse smiled at Dayne. "You can cut the cord." She motioned to the spot across from her. "Here. I'll show you where."

Dayne looked at Katy, and he noticed that there were tears streaming down her cheeks. She smiled and nodded at him, silently telling him that she would be okay. He blinked so he could see clearly. And then, for the first time, he looked full into the precious face of his daughter. Whether she could see him clearly or not, she looked at him. Straight at him. And the connection ran through Dayne like nothing he'd ever felt.

"Hi, little girl." His voice gained strength. "You're a miracle."

"Hurry." Katy sounded weak but anxious. "Bring her to me so I can see her."

Dayne leaned over her and followed the nurse's instructions as he cut the baby's cord.

The nurse placed a clamp on it and finished wiping the infant clean. Then she wrapped her quickly in a blanket and handed her to Dayne.

It was another first—the first time he would ever hold his baby girl in his arms. There would be so many other times along the journey of life. The long nights when Katy needed a rest, the times when Dayne would wrap her in a towel after a bath, and the night before her first day at kindergarten when she needed her daddy to help her not be afraid. He would hold her anytime she skinned her knee and anytime anyone dared to break her heart.

But of all those times, this was the very first.

Dayne brought her close and kissed her feathery soft cheek. "I'm your daddy, honey. I'm so glad to meet you." He carried her gently, carefully, as if she might break if he rushed or held her too tightly. Then in the sweetest moment of his life, he lowered her into Katy's arms. Tears slid down his face as he looked at her. "She's beautiful. Just like you."

A soft gasp came from Katy as she looked at their daughter.

"Dayne . . . this feeling." She lifted her teary eyes to him. "I've never imagined anything like it." She studied their daughter, and a quiet sob filled her throat. "I can't believe from that first day of seeing you at the theater . . . that God would bring us to this . . . this moment."

"She's perfect." He reached out to the baby at the same time she worked her arm free from the hospital blanket, and as Dayne touched her tiny hand, she took firm hold of his little finger. His baby girl, holding his hand, and Dayne felt that little touch to the center of his heart. He met Katy's eyes. "What's her name?"

Katy smiled, looking more beautiful than ever before. "I like your idea."

"From last night?" He looked at their daughter. "Hey, I think you're right. It fits her."

"Sophie Kathleen." Katy beamed at the infant in her arms. "I love it. Elegant and sweet and . . . and so girly."

Dayne studied her dainty nose and sweet little lips. "She looks like a Sophie." With his free hand he touched his fingers to her fine, damp hair. "It doesn't look very dark."

"No." Katy grinned. "I think she's gonna have my blonde hair."

The nurse came back. "I need to weigh and measure her." She held out her arms, and Katy handed the baby over. "Just a few minutes and you can have her back." She looked at Dayne. "You can go tell the family in the waiting room if you'd like. They're welcome to come in."

Dayne waited until the nurse walked away before touching Katy's face. "I've never loved you more."

"Or you." She cupped her hand around the back of his head and slowly pulled him to her. "I can't believe we're really here."

He kissed her again, and as he drew back, he motioned to the door. "I'll go tell the others."

Katy nodded. "We'll be here."

He tried to take a complete breath, but his chest was too tight, too full from the joy and love that knew no bounds. He pictured

Sophie Kathleen's sweet face, her innocent eyes, the sound of her cry. His daughter, given to him on the Fourth of July.

As Dayne left the delivery room and headed down the hall to his father, as he tried to imagine his baby in his dad's arms for the first time, he remembered the way he'd felt that July 4 a few years ago. After a lifetime of wanting a family, after looking for the Baxters and finding them, after knowing about them and longing for them, it was on Independence Day that he'd been with them for the very first time.

And now, on the same day, God had given him a precious child, a daughter who would be his always, even long after she was grown up and moved away. For though time would one day take her from him, Dayne was sure of one thing.

That little girl would never let go of his finger.

Just after midnight the doctor made his decision. By then Ashley was almost delirious from the exertion of the contractions and barely able to concentrate on what was happening around her. She was in the middle of another series of pains when the doctor came in and checked her again.

"It's time," he announced. "I don't like the baby's progress. We'll take him by C-section."

"Landon." She held up her hand. "I'm afraid."

"The doctor said it'll be fast." He walked beside her, and as they entered the hallway, Dayne appeared from one of the rooms. "We had a girl. Sophie Kathleen. Seven pounds, three ounces. Twenty inches long." Dayne was grinning so big his smile lit the space around him. But then he seemed to notice the urgency of the moment, and his expression changed. "Is . . . everything okay?"

"Yes." Landon's voice was firm, no room for doubt. "Tell your dad they're doing a C-section."

Dayne stopped and watched them go. "We'll be praying."

Ashley felt another contraction bear down on her, and she held on to the thought that everyone would be praying. The pain ripped into her and racked her body for what felt like a full minute at least. When it let up, she couldn't quite catch her breath. "Landon . . . help me!"

"You're okay. Everything's going to be okay." He was right beside her as they wheeled her into a brightly lit room and a group of people seemed to surround her, all of them working on her at once.

Someone came up to her opposite Landon and asked her to roll onto her side. "We're giving you an epidural, Ashley. You'll feel a lot better after that."

In the recesses of her mind she knew what they were going to do, that they were going to insert a needle into the fluid around her spine, and she could hardly wait. Maybe then she could focus on what was happening and how her baby was doing. *My baby boy, Jesus . . . please let him be okay. Please . . .*

The response came over her gradually, a warmth and a peace, and at the same time Ashley realized that the epidural was probably taking effect. The doctor was asking her to roll onto her back again, and he was explaining something about feeling a slight tugging and discomfort and saying that the baby would be born in just a few minutes.

"How are you?" Landon was stroking her hair. "Talk to me."

It took a minute or so, but Ashley finally realized the pain was gone. Completely gone. She was exhausted but she could breathe again, and the truth about what was happening around her hit her like a splash of cold water. She was about to give birth to their son! She opened her eyes wider than before. "I'm . . . I'm much better." Now nothing could stave off the excitement growing inside her.

At that moment, another medical person covered her mouth with an oxygen mask. "Just for a few minutes," he assured her. "We want you to be strong."

Ashley's fear returned, so she looked at Landon. As long as she could see his eyes, everything would be okay. It had to be. God wouldn't bring them this far only to have something happen to their baby.

A couple of nurses erected a screen below her chest, a barrier so she couldn't watch the operation taking place. The situation was just like when Sarah was born, but Ashley refused to see it that way. This was different. It had to be different. The ultrasound had shown that their son was perfectly healthy. *Give me Your peace, God.*

The doctor was right. She felt a series of tugs and pulls but no pain. The pain was behind her for now but not the strangeness of the moment. She was on a slight decline, her head lower than her shoulders, the oxygen mask still in place. Landon moved down by her knees so he could watch the surgery. A few minutes passed while Ashley watched her husband, her strong firefighter, the man who had loved her for so long. With God and Landon she could get through anything. That much time had already proven.

Suddenly the doctor peered at Ashley over the screen. "Were you expecting a boy?"

Ashley stared at the man and sucked in hard on the oxygen streaming into her mask. She nodded and thought how strange the doctor's comments were. Of course they were expecting a boy. The doctor had seen her charts by now, right?

Landon looked as confused as she felt, and then his mouth opened. "Ash, it's a girl. I'm serious."

Her mind raced, and she shook her head. No, the baby wasn't a girl. Why would Landon say such a thing? She motioned to one of the nurses and pointed to the oxygen mask. She needed to talk but she couldn't until . . .

Tears were in Landon's eyes, and he came a step closer to her. "The baby's a girl, Ash. She is."

The technician took the mask from Ashley's face as Landon's words hit their mark. He was telling the truth. The ultrasound was wrong about this one thing, and now . . . "We have a daughter?"

"Yes."

The sound of the sweetest melodic wailing filled the room, and

Ashley tried to make herself believe it was all really happening. God had given them a girl? After all this time preparing for Isaac James, the whole nine months God had been preparing her for a gift too wonderful to take in. Ashley held out her hand and Landon took it, but she couldn't tell whether she was laughing or crying. Her emotions were too overwhelming to rein in and figure out.

They had a daughter.

The next few minutes passed in a blur. The baby was taken to a table, and Landon cut the cord, and all the while the doctor was stitching Ashley up, talking about how ultrasounds weren't perfect at determining sex, even with as far as technology had come.

"I love when this happens." He chuckled. "Do you have a name for a girl?"

"A name?" Ashley only wanted to hold her, but the doctor made a good point. "Landon, we don't have a name."

The nurse was cleaning up the baby, then weighing and measuring her.

Landon came to Ashley's side and took hold of her hands. "I do."

Ashley searched his face. "You do what?"

"I have a name for her." He ran his thumbs over the tops of her hands, the way he'd done since the first time they'd acknowledged their feelings for each other. "I never told you, but back before the ultrasound I had a name I liked if the baby turned out to be a girl."

A sense of awe swept over her at the wonder of the man standing before her. "You did?"

"Yes." He smiled. "I didn't want to say anything because . . . well, you were so intent on making sure the baby was okay. It didn't seem right to talk about names until we knew." A quiet laugh came from him. "I never for a minute thought the test might be wrong about it being a boy."

"Me neither." Ashley felt someone come up behind them.

"I have your baby girl for you." The nurse held a blanketed bundle. She carefully placed the baby in Ashley's arms.

And then . . . only then did the reality truly hit her. She looked into the face of their infant and tears choked her, kept her from speaking. This little girl would have everything Sarah never could. She was whole and healthy and bursting with life. When Ashley could find the words, she ran her fingers along the side of her daughter's face. "She looks a lot like Cole."

By now, Devin was taking on his own look, more like Landon. But this baby definitely had Cole's eyes and nose.

"She does." Landon softly stroked her head. "No one's going to believe it."

Ashley used her shoulder to dab at a trail of happy tears. "How are we ever going to explain this to the boys?"

"I'm not sure." He looked deep at her, his eyes glistening. "God knew. . . . He always knows." He swallowed, struggling to keep his voice. "He knew you needed a daughter."

Ashley thought of all the moms who wanted a daughter and never got one. For that matter, the women who wanted any kids at all but couldn't have them. "No, Landon." She smiled at him through her tears. "I didn't need a daughter. I'll never deserve her or you. But since God has given me the people in my life . . . I'll spend the rest of my days being grateful." Her voice fell to an emotional whisper. "Thankful with every breath."

He moved closer, and he kissed their daughter on her forehead. Then he kissed Ashley, and the feel of him, this wonderful man and all he'd brought to her life, moved her to a level of love she'd never felt before. "God is so gracious."

Landon's eyes grew wide. "That's it . . . her name!"

The baby let out a few soft cries and turned toward Ashley. She was hungry, and Ashley could hardly wait to feed her, to feel the connection that only existed between a mom and her newborn baby. But first she giggled at Landon. "Gracious? That's what you want to call her?"

"No." He laughed, but it faded as a new depth came into his tone. "Janessa Belle. I looked it up when you first told me you

were pregnant. Janessa means gracious. And Belle—" he grinned—
"means beautiful. Like her mother."

Janessa Belle Blake. Ashley let the name play in her mind for a
few seconds. It was beautiful and lyrical and strong all at once.
"I like it." She was touched to the core that he would've thought
up a name for a girl and that he would've kept the idea to himself
until they knew more. Just in case the Lord had different plans for
the outcome of this little one. "Gracious." Ashley was brimming
with joy. "What could describe her presence in our lives better
than that?"

Landon nodded, and in his eyes Ashley saw the man she almost
walked away from. "Thank you, Landon, for putting up with me . . . .
for waiting until I came to my senses."

His smile held an ocean of meaning. "I never could've loved
anyone else."

They stayed that way, sharing the magic of the moment, not
wanting to let it go, until finally Janessa's cries grew louder. "I'll
feed her. You go tell everyone and get the boys."

He hesitated long enough to study their daughter once more.
Then he left and Ashley had no trouble coaxing her baby to eat.
Janessa was sure and determined, and Ashley had a feeling she
would be strong-willed, that she would stand up for the weak and
less fortunate, and that her life would make a difference in the
world. A difference for God.

Landon stayed away for several minutes, long enough for Ashley
to finish feeding. All the while she couldn't help but think of the
plans God had for the little girl in her arms. These thoughts were
still filling her mind when the sound of voices came from the hallway. Trailing Landon were Cole, Devin, Ashley's father, and Elaine,
all of them talking at once.

Cole pushed his way ahead and ran to the side of her bed. "Is
it true? We have a sister?" He couldn't possibly have looked more
excited.

"It's true." She smiled at Landon. "This is Janessa Belle."

"Janessa! I love that name." Cole looked at Devin. "Whadya think? Isn't Janessa a pretty name?"

Devin had his fingers in his mouth, and he was clinging to Ashley's father's pant leg.

"She's beautiful, Ashley." Her dad touched her shoulder and stared at Janessa. "What an amazing surprise."

"She looks just like you." Elaine smiled at Ashley. "Congratulations."

"I still can't believe it." Ashley thought for a moment how much this would've meant to her mother, knowing that Ashley had survived the loss of Sarah and that now she would indeed have a daughter. "A boy would've been wonderful, but . . . I don't know, I guess I just can't believe she's really here."

Devin had taken a few steps back, and now he bent his chubby legs and his head way down to look under the hospital bed. When he straightened, he held up his hands and turned to Ashley. "Where he?"

She reached out for her younger son. "Who, buddy?"

"Baby Isaac." Devin shrugged and looked over one shoulder and then the other. "Where?"

Cole's expression said he wasn't sure whether to lecture Devin on the academics of what had happened here or to wonder about the issue himself. After a few beats, he turned to Landon. "Yeah, what happened to him, Dad?"

"He never was." Landon was clearly touched by the boys' confusion. "The doctor thought Mommy was carrying a baby boy, but they were wrong."

"Oh." Cole gave a knowing nod, and then he turned to Devin. "So it was always Janessa all along. Understand?"

Devin put his fingers back in his mouth and turned his attention to the baby in Ashley's arms. He was still confused, but in time they would all get used to the idea. There was no third son, at least not for now.

Her dad and Elaine and Landon began talking, Landon recounting every detail of the delivery.

Cole leaned over the bed and patted Janessa's head. "Know what?" he whispered to Ashley.

"What?"

"I really wanted a baby sister." He looked very serious. "After my last sister went home to Jesus, I asked God if He could give me another one. I wanted a baby brother really bad. But I wanted a sister more."

Ashley felt her happiness swell. Cole had shared his thoughts so succinctly, so simply. She put her free arm around her oldest son's shoulders. "That's exactly how I feel, Coley."

"Katy and Sophie are doing well," her dad announced. "Dayne wanted me to be sure and tell you."

A new reality hit Ashley. All during her pregnancy with Sarah, she had longed for the relationship her daughter would have with Kari's girl—the way they would grow up together and be best friends and attend the same school, the same class. They would get ready for kindergarten and middle school and high school together, and in a blink of an eye they'd be getting ready for prom. Every season in between would be one they would share. And now that very scenario would be true, but not with Kari's daughter. With Dayne's.

Which made the miracle of Janessa's birth even more dramatic and the presence of her mother all the more real. Without her mother's desperate prayer that she might meet her firstborn son, none of them might've ever known Dayne. So their mom's faith and God's goodness hadn't only brought about the gift of Dayne in their lives. But now this . . .

A best friend for Janessa Belle.

CHAPTER THIRTY

By now everyone knew about the surprise. Everyone but Ashley.

The Baxter family was putting final touches on the pink decorations and waiting anxiously for the guests of honor to arrive. John and Dayne were out back flipping burgers. Elaine was inside slicing tomatoes and lettuce with Brooke and Kari, while Erin and Katy were on the front porch watching Cole, Tommy, RJ, and Devin catch toads. The rest of the men were playing horseshoes in the side yard, and the other kids were playing tag out back.

John closed the lid on his barbecue. "We're just about ready." He brushed away a curl of smoke and smiled at Dayne. "You getting any sleep?"

"Not a lot." Dayne chuckled. The faint circles under his eyes were a telltale sign of the newborn at his house. "But you know what? I love those late nights more than anything. Katy can feed her, but then it's my turn. Me and Sophie, sitting in the rocking chair while the rest of the world sleeps."

"Yes, I remember those days." John felt the decades melt away and his smile become more nostalgic. "You're right. There was nothing quite like that."

"I know how quickly it'll be over." He shrugged and handed John the plate of sliced cheese. "I guess I'm determined to drink in every minute of it."

They talked a few more minutes about how well Katy and Sophie were doing.

"Katy told me that being a mom is the role of a lifetime." Dayne grinned. "The role she was born for."

John opened the grill and placed a slice of cheese on each burger. Any minute now he was bound to hear from Landon. Five days had passed since the babies were born, and finally this afternoon Ashley and Janessa were being released from the hospital. John wasn't sure he could wait another day. Not with the surprise baby shower they had planned.

He turned the gas burners off and went back in the house for the tray of sesame seed buns, Ashley's favorite. He and Dayne were arranging them on the platter when his cell phone rang, and in record time he had it open. The caller ID said it was Landon. "You're on your way?"

"Hey, we were just driving by. Thought maybe you'd like to see Janessa for a few minutes." Landon's response didn't really make sense, but that was to be expected because Ashley was sitting next to him.

John laughed, then explained how the details of the party had fallen into place, giving Landon time so that his next words were believable.

"Well . . ." Landon sounded hesitant. "We were just going to stop by for a few minutes, but if you've got dinner . . . I guess. I mean, we can't stay out too late."

John chuckled again. "Okay. We'll be ready."

Dayne waited until John had clicked the phone off before shaking his head. "Ashley has no idea, does she?"

"Not at all." John's head was still spinning from the way everything had come together. "I worked out all the details with Landon."

Dayne looked out over the backyard toward the stream behind the Baxter house. "It reminds me of the surprise she gave to me and Katy when she got everyone together to give our lake house a makeover." His laugh was quiet, lost in the memories of that time. "You and Landon pulling this off . . . it might be even better. Summer will be over before Ashley believes it."

Dayne held the tray while John slid one burger after another onto an open bun. When the tops were in place, he carried the towering pile into the house. More than half the furniture remained, but the house no longer felt like his. He and Elaine were happy in their new home, and a few days ago when the title to the Baxter house changed hands, John had felt a sense of closure.

Several of the pieces of remaining furniture were going home with his kids today, and a few things would remain. The two dining room tables, for instance, the main one and the one he and Elizabeth had bought six years ago to accommodate their growing family. Both tables fit in the dining room and were set up for the big surprise party. John surveyed the dining room, decorated in pink streamers and balloons, pink plates and cups.

Yes, the tables would stay. And though John wouldn't host another family party in this house, every inch of table space would be needed for future parties here. The parties he and Elaine would attend as guests, with full hearts for how God had worked out the details. The way only God could have.

John walked slowly from the dining room to the family room, where he had gathered so often with his kids and, in the last decade, with his grandkids. How wonderful that the old walls would see another generation of love and laughter.

Elaine came up beside him and slid her arm around his waist. "You're glad, aren't you?"

"About the house?" He turned to smile at her and felt the subtle thrill from the truth that was still working its way through his conscience, the fact that Elaine was his wife now. "It's all I can think about." He looked through the front windows to where the kids were playing near the pond. "It's like something from a dream."

"Hmm." Her voice was gentle against his soul. "You're not sorry you sold it?"

John put his arm around her shoulders and drew her close. "Not for a minute. Whether we spend time here or not, we needed our own place." He gave her a tender kiss. "A new start."

Elaine's smile told him she wasn't surprised by his answer. "I love our house."

"Me too." He led her slowly toward the front door, and together they stepped out on the porch. The girls had wrapped pink streamers around the railing and the posts, so there was no mistaking that the house was the site of a baby shower.

Together they watched as Maddie and a group of the girl cousins came running over to the pond. "Let's see what you caught, Cole!"

Elaine leaned her head on John's shoulder. "I love your kids."

"They feel the same about you." John breathed in deep the smell of summer in the air. "Ashley and Landon should be here any minute."

"It'll be the best surprise ever." They watched Cole hold a softball-size toad up high over his head.

"This one's king of the pond!" Cole crouched back down at the water's edge. "That's why we have to let him go. No one else is big enough to be king." He released his catch just as a van pulled into the driveway. Cole noticed his parents' arrival instantly. "Hey! They're here! Everyone get on the porch for the surprise!"

As Landon steered the van up the drive, a slight pang stung at John's heart, a mix of bittersweet loss and the excitement of newness and change. Elaine was perceptive, asking him about the sale, because of course it was on his mind. This was where he and Elizabeth had raised their children, the rooms and yard where their kids had run and played and grown into adults. They had staged weddings and wakes on the property, and they had used this house to welcome one grandbaby after another.

John uttered a quiet sigh, even as the group gathered on the porch for the big surprise. The years would take them far from this time, from this transitional moment. But no matter who owned the Baxter house, this much was true—as long as he had breath in his lungs, a piece of John's heart would remain here. The walls held a million memories because this was the place where they came together, where they became people of faith and loved God and each other, where they battled tragedies and handled trials and celebrated triumphs. John would hold on to all of that. For in this old house they had become who they were and would always be.

The Baxter family.

From the moment Landon made the phone call, Ashley had smelled something fishy. Her father wanted them to stop by the Baxter house because he happened to have dinner ready? Shouldn't he have been with Elaine at their new house? And what was he doing cooking at the old place, anyway? What about the new buyer? Even after Landon explained that her dad had made some sort of arrangement not to vacate the Baxter house for a few more weeks so he could find a home for the old furniture, Ashley was still wary.

"If we're going for dinner, we should at least get the boys." Ashley was confused. "I mean, they're waiting for us with Kari and Ryan back at the house."

"Dinner won't take long." Landon kept his eyes on the road. "Besides, your dad wants you to look over some furniture."

That point had finally convinced her. Over the next few weeks, while finding a routine with the new baby, Ashley might not have time to make this one last trip to the house. But now, as they turned in to the driveway, Ashley saw half a dozen cars parked near the garage and her family spread across the length of the covered porch. She looked at Landon, adrenaline pushing its way through her. "What's going on?"

He grinned, his face masked in mock innocence. "Everyone wanted to see the baby. What can I say?"

They reached the top of the driveway, and Ashley saw the pink streamers covering the porch railings. She looked along the porch at everyone standing there—Kari and Ryan, Brooke and Peter, Erin and Sam, Dayne and Katy and their baby, and Luke and Reagan. Near the porch steps all the kids were clustered together, grinning and jumping up and down, as if they were ready to run out to Ashley and Landon the moment their parents gave them permission.

"A party? You knew about this?" She put her hand on Landon's shoulder. The gathering touched her more than she could put into words. They had come together the last time she and Landon had a baby to help them grieve a too-early death. But now . . . they had gathered to help Ashley and Landon celebrate life. A final celebration at the Baxter house. She was choked up when she turned her attention to him again. "You're always like this. Surprising me in some crazy way or another."

Landon's eyes sparkled, and he still looked like he was up to something. "Let's get out."

Landon lifted the sleeping Janessa from her car seat and cradled her in his arm. He walked around to the passenger door, and with his free hand he opened Ashley's door and gingerly helped her down onto the ground. She was healing faster than she had after Sarah's birth. That, or maybe she was so happy she didn't notice the pain as much. Even so, she held her stomach with one hand as Landon put his arm around her and led her back around the van.

Then, when they were in full view of the others, he stopped and faced her, his back to the gathering twenty yards away. With Janessa tucked in close to his chest, he touched his fingers to Ashley's face and searched her eyes. "You have the most beautiful hair." He ran his hand along the back of her head. "Has anyone ever told you that?"

Her heart melted. "Only you, love." She was touched but a little bewildered. She looked beyond him to the crowd on the porch. "Everyone's waiting. . . ."

"Tell her, Dad!" Cole shouted from his place at the top of the porch steps. "I can't wait another minute."

A chorus of laughter came from her family, and Ashley shifted her attention from Cole back to Landon. "Tell me what?" She was drawing a blank, but then all at once she realized what was happening. This wasn't a simple gathering; it was a party. "Is it a surprise baby shower? Is that what this is?"

Landon put his hand on her shoulder and studied her for a long moment. "After my grandpa died, I received a letter from him. Something he wrote to each of us grandkids."

The sounds beyond them faded, and she focused on Landon, on trying to make sense of the story he was telling. "You . . . never mentioned it."

Landon framed her face with his fingers. "Ash, the letter came with a check."

Her head was spinning, and the ground beneath her feet felt suddenly unstable. She looped her arms around his waist and swallowed hard. "A check?"

"A very large check." Landon lowered one hand to his pocket. Then, before Ashley could make sense of where the story was going, he pulled out a set of keys and handed them to her. "The Baxter house is yours. I bought it for you."

As Ashley stared at the keys, her heart began to race. This couldn't be happening. It was a dream. It had to be a dream. She tried to remember how to breathe. "How could . . . ? How did you . . . ?" She leaned into Landon's free arm so she wouldn't collapse. "Are you serious?" Her words were muffled against his shoulder. "You bought it?"

As if they could all hear what she was saying, across the porch every one of her family members began to clap. Kari nodded to Cole, and he flew down the steps with Devin right behind him.

"We're home, Mom!" Cole ran to her and hugged her around

her waist. Devin did the same with Landon. "Can you believe it?" Cole was bursting with the news. "We get the house and the pond and the basketball court and the stream out back and every single toad and the roses and . . ."

He was still talking, but Ashley couldn't hear him, couldn't think or feel or see anything but Landon, the marvelous man still holding both her and their daughter in his arms. The world would always see Landon and his peers as heroes for the way they rushed into burning buildings when everyone else was rushing out. And there was no doubt his profession made him a hero. But to Ashley, his most heroic efforts would always be the ones he'd made on her behalf.

And now this. Buying her the Baxter house so they could spend the rest of their days here . . . in the place that would always be her home.

Ashley thought about the grandfather Landon had lost, and she was certain of one thing. Grandpa Andrew Westra would be very proud of the way Landon had spent his money.

She drew a breath, filled her lungs with the sweet country air around her. The reality of what he'd done was beginning to sink in, and she drew back, a little steadier than before. "If I'm dreaming—" she kissed Landon on the lips—"don't wake me."

"With you all of life is a dream," he breathed against her skin, and his warmth, his nearness made her light-headed again.

The others hurried down the porch steps and headed their way, everyone congratulating them at once. Elaine took Janessa from Landon, and once his arms were free, he wrapped them around Ashley. She didn't know the details of the sale, but she could hear them later. Cole had already said the only thing that mattered. They were home. Finally and forever.

"Isn't this the best news?" Cole was back at her side again, one arm around her and one around Landon. "Me and Devin could barely contain ourselves."

"I bet." Ashley kissed the top of Cole's head and then smiled at

Devin. "And, yes, this is amazing news." She grinned at Landon. "I can't believe it."

Landon eased back and grinned as they followed the group into the house. "Now you know why we had to come here first. We had to bring Janessa home, right?"

Ashley was overwhelmed with joy, overcome by the kindness of her husband and the love from her family.

"Come on." Kari ushered her toward the house. "You have to see some things."

Ashley took hold of Landon's arm as they crossed the threshold of their new home. She couldn't imagine what else she needed to see. Already it was surreal, walking through the front door and into a house that now belonged to her and Landon. She blinked back tears. If she let herself give in to her emotions now, there'd be no stopping them.

Cole led the way. He took them upstairs to Ashley's painting room. It was still set up the way it had always been—Ashley's old bed on one side of the room and her easel and paints in the middle of the floor on the other. "Look, Mom. There's something new." He pointed to a framed photograph that had been newly hung on one side of the window.

Ashley took a step closer. The tears came then, streams of them. It was the photo of Irvel and Hank, the one Irvel's grandson had given to Ashley at Irvel's funeral. Ashley had tucked it away in a drawer because the wall space in their old house was so limited. She turned to Landon and hugged him. "This . . . is the perfect place for that."

"I know." He kissed the side of her head. "You okay?"

She sniffed and laughed at the same time. "Never better."

"Good . . . there's more!" Cole tore out of the room and back down the stairs. Most of the group tagged along behind Ashley up to her painting room and now back down the stairs. But none of them could've known the significance of the moment as Cole led Ashley into the downstairs playroom.

There, hanging on the wall, was Ashley's painting of her mother in heaven, seated in a rocking chair, baby Sarah in her arms, surrounded by a field of vibrant flowers. Ashley brought her hand to her mouth, grateful that Landon was beside her, steadying her. It was exactly as she had pictured it when she created the painting. That it would hang in her children's playroom one day. But not just any playroom—this one. That had been her dream, even though it had been impossible at the time.

Landon pointed to another of Ashley's favorite wall hangings on the adjacent wall. It was a wooden plaque etched simply with this Bible verse: *"Nothing is impossible with God."*

Ashley was overwhelmed. "Landon . . . I don't know what to say." She looked at Janessa Belle in Elaine's arms, and fresh tears filled her eyes. The message was so very true. Nothing was impossible with God—something Ashley might've missed out on if it weren't for Landon's love and the prayers of her family.

Her dad stepped into the playroom and motioned out front. "The burgers are ready." His eyes danced as he looked at Ashley. "And there's a whole stack of presents in the family room for you to open."

"Presents?" The delight she felt spilled over into laughter. "So it *is* a surprise baby shower."

"Right." Cole beamed at Landon. "Dad's gift is the house."

They all laughed and moved into the dining room. Ashley looked out the window at the gravel path that led to her mother's rose garden. *Her* rose garden. She could scarcely take in the magnitude of all Landon had given her.

Just as they were about to sit down, Maddie raced in through the front door. "Hey, Daddy!" She looked wide-eyed at Peter. "Remember when I said a sunset has a million colors?"

Peter had Hayley by the hand, but he gave Maddie his complete attention. "When you were coloring that picture at Easter time, right?"

"Yeah, and guess what?" She ran back toward the front door. "Everyone come quick, because this sunset is just like the one in my picture. A million colors for sure!"

The kids were the first to dash out the door behind her, but the adults all followed. As they stepped onto the front porch again, they could see that Maddie was right. The sunset was breathtaking.

Ashley held Landon's hand. "I love you," she whispered. She could see the reflection of the vibrant sky in his eyes. "Thank you."

"I love you too." He looked deep to the places in her heart that belonged to him alone. "We're home . . . and we have each other." He smiled at her and then at the sky. "Even God is celebrating with us."

Ashley turned back to the colorful display, the pink and orange and blue streaks splashed across the sky. Somehow it seemed fitting that on a day like this, God would give them a magnificent sunset. The picture made her think of another painting, and suddenly she could hardly wait to begin it. The Baxter house, bathed in the colors of a sunset. But this time the people sitting in the porch swing wouldn't be her parents.

They would be her and Landon.

Yes, God's redemption was sure and true. Ashley would always remember that, and when she did, she would return to the place where God first saved her, where her heart would always rejoice in what God had done for all of them. One day there would be that great reunion, but until then, as Dayne's life proved, no amount of fame would be better than what they had together, right here in Bloomington.

Here, the hurts of the past were forgiven, and the life they'd found was more than any of them could've dreamed. They had family, and even if they didn't have forever, they would enjoy every day God gave them. Life was like a sunrise, full of newness and hope and opportunity, but in this, the summer of their lives, there was no more reason to long for someday. The hope and life they'd longed for was here. Now. Ashley remembered what Maddie had just told them, and she smiled at her new home, her family, and all the future held.

Because on a night like this, there really were a million colors in the sunset.

A WORD FROM KAREN KINGSBURY

Dear Friends,

And so we reach the end of an era, the final pages of a time in my life and yours when we have journeyed alongside the Baxter family. Together we have walked with them through trials and tragedies and triumphs, and we have watched God demonstrate His redemptive love time and time and time again. You are my friends, and I thank you for taking this marvelous adventure with me and with the Baxters.

First I must tell you that I'm not ready to say good-bye to the Baxter family. Here's the good news: you'll find them lurking in the background of my next series, which will involve a new family, but will be set—at least in part—in Bloomington! So make sure you visit my Web site often for details as they come about!

Maybe one day down the road I'll write about the Baxters as main characters again. I'd love to tell the story of Elizabeth and John's early days, and I would treasure the chance to check in with these fictional friends years from now to see how they're doing. God will make it all clear as time passes.

I must tell you, the loss of writing the last book in the Baxter family series didn't really hit me until I wrote about Hayley's pink bicycle. Most of you know that Hayley experienced a near drowning several years back, and medical experts did not think she would ever see, let alone walk or ride a bike. But in the book *Rejoice*, God convinced John Baxter to believe in life as long as God granted it. John's way of affirming Hayley's life was to buy her a pink bicycle and park it in his garage for the day when Hayley would be able to ride it again, so he could say he was first to believe it was possible.

As I was writing that scene, watching God's miraculous healing of Hayley come full circle, the closure overwhelmed me, and I truly wept for the fact that I had to end this saga with the Baxters. I've loved everything about writing these books—first the Redemption series, then the Firstborn series, and finally the Sunrise series. I tried to use *Sunset* to bring about closure for every aspect of the thirteen previous books. In every case, the message was the same.

God's redemption.

I pray that you will continue to go back to these books and share them with your friends and family. God has used these stories to do amazing things in the lives of readers. If you're one of those, please visit my Web site and drop me an e-mail. I'd love to hear how reading about the Baxter family has made a difference in your life. Definitely sign up for my monthly newsletter so you'll be the first to know what happens next.

As I've said before, I might start a Baxter update for those who want to know how these characters are doing now that we've reached the end of the series. Maybe a blog from Ashley's point of view or from Katy's or Dayne's or John Baxter's. In the meantime, I'll release new books, other Life-Changing Fiction titles that are already forming in my head and heart. These stories and my new series are so strong in my mind that I can't wait to share them with you.

That brings me to the most important part of this letter. You've watched as the Baxter family leaned on God for strength and wisdom, love and support. If you don't yet know the personal love and forgiveness of Jesus Christ, if this is the first time you're hearing about God and His powerful salvation, His plans for your life, please visit a Bible-believing church in your area and talk to the pastor about Jesus. You need to spend time in God's Word—the Bible—in order to know what the Lord wants from you and what He is offering. If you can't find or afford a Bible, please let me know. I'll send you one. Simply write *Bible* in the subject line.

If this book changed your life or led you into or back into a relationship with Jesus, please write to me and put *New Life* in the subject line. I'll be sure to read that letter and pray for you as you journey toward a deeper walk with our Lord.

Either way, I hope you take a minute and visit my Web site at www.KarenKingsbury.com. There you can see what books are coming up or connect with other readers and book clubs. You can leave prayer requests or take on the responsibility of praying for people. Readers often tell me they haven't found a purpose or meaning to their faith. Maybe they're on the go a lot or their circumstances keep them homebound. Remember, prayer is a very important ministry. It was prayer that turned things around for Dayne and Luke and little Hayley and so many other characters in this series. Your prayers—either in the midst of a busy day or as the main focus if you're homebound—could be crucial in the life of someone else. Visit the prayer link on my Web site and make a commitment to pray for the soldiers and hurting people who have left requests there.

In addition, I have two new pages on my Web site—one for active military heroes and another for fallen military heroes. If you know someone serving our country and you'd like to honor them, please click the appropriate links on the side of the home page and submit their photo, name, rank, and how people can pray for them. We can include more details if you have someone you'd like to honor on the Fallen Military Heroes page. The importance in our current war is not who is wrong or right, because war is complicated. However, the duty we all share is to honor and respect and admire our troops. They are heroes, and they deserve our utmost support and constant prayers.

On a personal note, my family is doing well, learning how to live without the constant joyful presence of my dad, who passed away a year ago. Life here at our house is a wonderful adventure of laughter and precious memories. This book releases on Austin's eleventh birthday, and at the other end of the age spectrum, Kelsey has graduated from high school and is in her first year of college—locally, so our time with her is ongoing for now. Something we're grateful for. The boys are moving quickly through middle school and on to high school, and Tyler is in his sophomore year at our Christian school. As always, I can feel the days moving too fast, and there's nothing I can do to slow the ride. But I am enjoying every minute, trying to remember the lessons from the Baxter family. I pray that this leaves you looking for new beginnings in life and believing that God will give you a beautiful sunset to mark your lasts.

Thanks so much again. I pray for you, my friends, and I am grateful for the time you spend praying for me and my family.

Until next time, blessings in His amazing light and grace,

Karen Kingsbury

www.KarenKingsbury.com

DISCUSSION QUESTIONS

Use these questions for individual reflection or for discussion with a book club or other small group.

1. What does a sunset represent to you? Tell about a time when you stayed outdoors and watched a sunset from beginning to end.

2. What area in your life do you most hope will have a brilliant ending? What steps would you need to take to do what you can to make sure that ending happens someday?

3. Describe the relationship between Landon's grandparents Andrew and Effie Westra. What do you think goes into having a long-lasting, beautiful love like theirs?

4. Landon desired to be like his grandfather. What character traits did Landon have that his grandfather also had?

5. Time and again with the Baxter family, love is shown to succeed despite trials. How can you love the people in your life better based on the lessons you saw acted out among the Baxters?

6. Were you surprised at Ashley's ultrasound results? Tell about a time when you thought you had all the answers, but God gave you a surprise instead.

7. What do you think God was trying to teach Ashley in *Sunset*? What has He tried to teach you with the unexpected events of your life?

8. Describe how Katy and Dayne felt, their Hollywood days behind them, as they set out to serve Bloomington with

CKT. What can you do to help kids find uplifting, faith-building activities in your community?

9. Talk about John Baxter's feelings when he watched his granddaughter Hayley ride her bike for the first time. Tell about a time when you were deeply touched by God's faithfulness.

10. Luke and Reagan have struggled in their marriage for some time, but in *Sunset*, Luke received advice from John and Ashley that he hadn't considered before. What was that advice? Talk about the power of asking someone for forgiveness and how that differs from an apology.

11. Do you need to ask someone for forgiveness? Describe the situation and why asking for forgiveness might be difficult. Or tell about a time when you did ask someone for forgiveness. What was the outcome?

12. Did you have any idea that the painting Ashley was working on represented her and Elaine? What was the significance of this gift?

13. Tell about a time when you gave a significant gift, one that fostered friendship. What were the results?

14. Throughout the Baxter Family Drama books, Landon was always seeking to surprise Ashley. In what ways do you try to incorporate thoughtful gifts and surprises into your relationships—especially your relationship with your spouse and children, your family, or your friends?

15. What were your thoughts about John and Elaine's wedding? Has anyone in your family remarried after the death of a spouse? What were the emotions you and the rest of the family went through?

16. What are your favorite moments from the Baxter Family Drama books?

17. Who were your favorite characters in this series? Talk about why they were your favorite.

18. Did you gain a better knowledge of God while reading the Baxter Family Drama books? In what way?

19. How have the stories in this series personally affected you? How have they touched or changed your life? How have they benefited the way you interact with the people you love?

20. What will you take away from your time with the Baxter family? In your opinion, what were the greatest lessons?

Other Life-Changing Fiction by

KAREN KINGSBURY

To see what readers are saying about Karen Kingsbury's fiction, go to www.KarenKingsbury.com and click the guest-book link.

REDEMPTION SERIES
Redemption
Remember
Return
Rejoice
Reunion

FIRSTBORN SERIES
Fame
Forgiven
Found
Family
Forever

SUNRISE SERIES
Sunrise
Summer
Someday
Sunset

RED GLOVE SERIES
Gideon's Gift
Maggie's Miracle
Sarah's Song
Hannah's Hope

SEPTEMBER 11 SERIES
One Tuesday Morning
Beyond Tuesday Morning

M ary Madison was a child of unspeakable horrors, a young woman society wanted to forget. Now a divine power has set Mary free to bring life-changing hope and love to battered and abused women living in the shadow of the nation's capital.

Divine

A NOVEL

BY BEST-SELLING AUTHOR

Karen KINGSBURY

A vailable now at bookstores near you!

www.KarenKingsbury.com